"A terrific read from a strong new voice."

—Barbara Gowdy

Author of *Falling Angels, The Romantic, Helpless*

"Dowhal's rich, evocative prose lets his hapless young hero leap off the page, an abused child whose brutal adolescence makes him candidate for either suicide or celebrity. *Flam Grub* is touching, startling, funny, romantic, and eminently hypnotic; once you pick it up you won't be able to put it down."

—George Anthony

Author of *Starring Brian Linehan: A Life Behind The Scenes*

"This is a funny novel with a dark underlay about a young man coping with the bedlam he was born into. A wonderful yarn of today's chaotic world."

—Maggie Siggins

Author of *Riel, Bitter Embrace, Revenge of the Land*

FLAM GRUB

Dan Dowhal

To Jason, with warmest regards, Dan Dowhal

Blue Butterfly Books

THINK FREE, BE FREE

Blue Butterfly Book Publishing Inc.
2583 Lakeshore Boulevard West, Toronto, Ontario, Canada, M8V 1G3
Tel 416-255-3930   Fax 416-252-8291   www.bluebutterflybooks.ca

Complete ordering information for Blue Butterfly titles can be found at:
www.bluebutterflybooks.ca

First edition, soft cover, 2011

Front cover artwork: Tania Boterman

LIBRARY AND ARCHIVES CANADA CATALOGUING IN PUBLICATION

Dowhal, Dan, 1954–
          Flam grub / Dan Dowhal.

ISBN 978-1-926577-41-8

          I. Title.

PS8607.O98744F53 2011   C813'.6   C2011-902873-5

Printed and bound in Canada by Transcontinental-Métrolitho

The text paper in this book, Enviro 100 from Cascades, contains 100 per cent post-consumer recycled fibre, is processed chlorine free, and is manufactured using energy from biogas recovered from a municipal landfill site.

To Anna and Oleksa
who gave me mine.

FLAM GRUB

CHAPTER 1

If Flam Grub had been able to regress beyond conscious memory and go back to the very beginning, it would not have surprised him to learn the pain caused by his name had started while he was still floating in the womb. There, the briny serenity had been disturbed by regular shouting and sporadic violence between his parents, with the words "Flam Grub" serving as a soundtrack to the upheavals, transmitted to the fetal Flam through his mother's belly.

Flam's parents had met at work. His mother, Mary Flam, was the office manager for the modest-sized trucking firm of Wheeler Cartage. Barely in her twenties, Mary was a tall, fair-skinned, red-headed beauty, with a nebula of freckles across the bridge of her nose, and green, otherworldly cat eyes that had a penetrating effect on anyone who fell into their orbit. Although she tried to hide it beneath a wardrobe of modest, almost dowdy dresses, her firm, lithe body would attract the attention of men wherever she went.

In the year and a half that she had been working for Wheeler, Mary had never given any of the truckers or dock workers a second glance, although she was fully aware of the lustful stares that tracked her like radar each time her heels were heard clicking on the stairs leading up to the office.

Mary had always been grateful her boss preferred to deal with the men directly, which allowed her to minimize her contact with the rough and greasy hirelings. That left her free to concentrate on the only man she was really interested in. Despite her relatively young age, Mary was expecting to become engaged shortly to Gerald Strait, a pharmacist she knew through her devotions at St. Ernest's Church, in whose flock Mary was one of the most pious of lambs.

A decade older than Mary, Gerald had an established business and a sober disposition on which a girl's future could be safely built. It had taken Mary months to orchestrate enough casual and seemingly chance encounters for Gerald to grow comfortable in her presence, and an even longer period of subtle encouragement to stoke his ardour to a potentially matrimonial temperature. As far as her own inner coolness went, Mary presumed that passion was something meant for the saints, and it was better to take care of her daily bread first.

Everything changed the day Mary's eyes fell on Steve Grub, newly hired by Wheeler to help with a large new delivery contract. Steve was dark-haired and handsome, with soft, seductive brown eyes and a square-jawed, flawless face. He had a mouthful of straight, glimmering white teeth, which he flashed often, for he was a glib, smooth talker, with a seemingly endless repertoire of *bon mots* and amusing stories. But it was Steve's body that cemented Mary's downfall. The sinewy splendour that rippled from beneath a permanently unbuttoned shirt was a living incarnation of Jesus' own lean physique, which Mary had guiltily contemplated over the years on crucifixes, statues, and icons with a fervour that sometimes strayed beyond religious.

She simply couldn't keep her eyes off Steve. Even without admitting it to herself, Mary started fabricating excuses to interact with him. The first time their fingers touched across a rush delivery order, she felt like a high-voltage jolt had passed through her entire body, before finally settling as a permanent electrical charge in her loins. They flirted over paycheques, courted over waybills, snatched their first kiss in the bathroom, and first groped each other in the rear of Steve's truck. Finally, on the Friday night of a Labour Day weekend, when everyone else had rushed off to start their holiday and Wheeler had left her to lock up, they consummated their lust in a secluded corner of the warehouse.

And so Flam was conceived, on a pallet of flattened cardboard, quickly stained by semen and virginal blood, with Mary profaning the names of her beloved saints as her long legs repeatedly pulled Steve's dimpled buttocks down onto herself.

The fighting started soon thereafter. They fought about the news of Mary's pregnancy, and whose fault it was. They fought about Steve's suggestion that they abort the fetus. They fought about Mary's demand that they should be married. They fought about the abysmal state of Steve's finances, and the gambling, drinking, and womanizing that had dragged him into indebtedness. They fought about the tiny, grimy flat, located above an old bookstore in the seedier part of town, which was all they could afford.

The biggest fight of all, as it turned out, was over Mary changing her surname. An only child, she was determined to keep the family name alive. Throughout Mary's whole life, she had been steeped in the family history and mythology of the Flams, a small clan of poor but stubbornly proud Irish peasants. For centuries, Mary's ancestors had steadfastly clung to the Flam name, despite being mocked for it, along with a tiny impoverished parcel of County Sligo soil.

Eventually, like so many others, the family was forced to emigrate by the Great Potato Famine. However, the displaced Flams never fully tore themselves free from their ancient roots, like ghosts unable to accept the fact of their own deaths. A century and a half later, they had failed to prosper in the New World, as some calamity after another managed to keep them pegged down in working-class purgatory. Still, no matter what other failures sucked their spirit or amputated their meagre fortune, the ancestral pride and family lore were fiercely instilled in each subsequent generation of New World Flams. So they had found their way to Mary, the sole offspring of a luckless cab driver and his bankrupt widow, and the last vestige of the Flam name. She could live with her latest misfortune, no matter what dreams she may have harboured, for it somehow seemed the familial fate, but she was horrified at the thought of being the final extinguisher of the Flam name. She prayed for guidance on the matter, interpreting God's silence as assent of her desire, and was grateful that Steve, who was not big on details or discussion anyway, never brought up the subject of names.

A few days after their hastily arranged wedding, which was attended mostly by Steve's cronies in hopes of a free drunk-up afterwards, and conducted out of shame in a parish where no one knew her, Mary dropped the dinner dishes in the sink and turned to face her husband.

"I'm keeping my name," she announced.

Steve, who had quietly been working on his fifth beer, almost fell off his chair.

"Like hell you are!" he shouted as he leapt to his feet. "You're my wife now, and you'll damned well take my name!"

Mary went on like she hadn't heard him. "What's more, my child will be christened a Flam too," she told him, her emerald gaze piercing his own dark-eyed disbelief.

"You goddamned ball-cutting bitch! You're the one who wanted to get married," he screamed. "Now you won't even take my name! Do you want people to think the kid's not mine? Are you trying to make a fool of me in front of my friends?"

"Ha! Like I care one bit about those drunken losers you call friends. The Flam name's a good name . . . a proud name . . . and that's what I'm keeping for me and my children." Here she played a trump by picking on Steve, who had been abandoned at birth and raised in institutional foster homes: "I can trace my family back a dozen generations. You . . . you don't even know who your father is."

Steve erupted in a barrage of curses and threats, but Mary stood firm. The argument went on for days. Sheer lungpower and verbal venom would not shake Mary's resolve, however, just as they had not in the previous battles, so Steve finally resorted to escalating force, shaking, and then striking her. Still, Mary resisted gamely, fighting him off with any blunt object she could grab, usually giving as good as she got.

Inside Mary's womb, the violence rocked the fetus' world along with its fragile psyche, while the phonemes of its future name, screamed regularly by both combatants at the top of their lungs, assaulted its sensitive ears.

Finally, during one exchange, Steve ducked beneath the swing of a skillet and tackled Mary forcefully, sending her flying backwards onto the faded, mismatched tiles of the kitchen floor. As he pounced on her like some predator bringing its prey down for the kill, hands reaching for her throat, Mary glimpsed for the first time the true depths of his dangerous, violent nature. Instinctively fearing for both her own life and that of the fetus within, she finally capitulated, and agreed to take the Grub name.

The next day Mary took the afternoon off work and, like a martyr, dutifully performed the legal rites to exorcise her family's surname. With her new documents stuffed into her purse, she sat empty and silent in the park across from City Hall as she contemplated her betrayal of the Flam heritage. There, on a bench in the Indian Summer sun, a plan worked its way into Mary's brooding thoughts, as bright and warming as the dappled autumnal light beams piercing their way through the red and orange leaves of the overhead maples and oaks.

Flam was born just before midnight on a Saturday, and christened the following Wednesday. It was during the blessed event, which was attended mostly by Steve's cronies in hopes of a free drunk-up afterwards, that Steve first learned Mary had surreptitiously reassigned the lost Flam surname as the newborn child's first name. He said nothing to his pals, but when the couple returned home afterwards with tiny Flam, Steve immediately questioned his wife's choice.

"Flam? *Flam!* What kind of name is that for a kid? It's totally stupid."

Mary put the baby down in its cradle, and then picked up a steam iron, waving it in front of Steve's face to show she meant business.

"Don't you dare say that. It's better than *Grub.*" She spat out the last syllable, tightened her grip on the iron, and waited for the combat to begin. Steve, however, knew full well the strength of Mary's resistance, and did not have the stomach for another prolonged fight.

"Whatever. I don't really give a shit. Have it your way," he conceded, and headed to the refrigerator for a beer.

Flam's parents, having irrevocably lost any glimmer of affection as a result of their continuous combat, fell back and dug into a sort of long-term psychological trench warfare, with Flam an innocent victim caught in the middle of No Man's Land.

Despite her son's first name, Mary found she was wary of the dark-haired, brown-eyed boy child, believing its gender and genetics gave it a natural affinity to her husband. She returned with fervour to her former religious devotions, regarding Flam as evidence in the flesh of her fall from grace, and lavished her love on the baby Jesus instead. Nevertheless, like the dutiful Christian she was, she faithfully exercised the responsibilities of motherhood. As Flam grew, she seldom struck him, though she found herself constantly criticizing and rebuking him, despite the boy's quiet, bright, and undemanding nature.

Steve, for his part, could not bring himself to show love for the child who bore his wife's hated name, and who had cost him his freedom, casting him down into the pit of a loveless marriage to a Bible-brandishing harpy. The angry, resentful father soon took to long-haul trucking in order to be away from the fun-killing fetters of home as much as possible. On those occasions when he was at home, Steve found he could barely stand to look at the boy. He could see that his pathetic son tried his best to stay out of view, but when the child wandered into his sight, Steve couldn't resist punishing the boy—even if it was only for the crime of being himself. And although Steve's disciplinary encounters with his son were far fewer than were Mary's, they were much more vicious, especially when Steve had been drinking, with any petty excuse sufficing for violence to suddenly be unleashed upon the boy.

Lashings with a leather belt were routine, as were whacks to the head, punches to the stomach, and twisting of the arm. Steve never showed any sign of remorse following these beatings, for inwardly he considered it proof of his parental devotion that the blows he delivered onto the child lacked the expert viciousness or intent to maim Steve would habitually employ when brawling in speakeasies or truck stops.

Still, there were times when Steve's brutality bottomed out into sheer evil. On one occasion, Flam, barely seven years old, accidentally dropped his dinner plate to the ground while licking up the last of his gravy.

Steve leapt from his chair and whipped off his belt. To show he meant business, he turned it around, and lashed Flam across the shoulders with the buckle end.

"You little piece of shit! I'm going to teach you a lesson once and for all," Steve bellowed. His second blow caught Flam across the back of the head, opening up a cut. The boy whelped and dove under the dining room table, leaving a trail of blood droplets on the parquet floor.

Steve, enraged by the escape, bent over and began flailing away in an attempt to reach Flam in the hiding spot. "Get back out here! I'm not done with you," he screamed, but Flam's small size and the proximity of the table legs allowed him to stay out of range of the belt.

Steve went to overturn the table, but Mary pressed her palms down on the tabletop and bared her teeth. "Don't you dare break my table or smash any more of my dishes," she screamed. "I paid for all of these, not you." So, Steve yanked away the chairs and crawled under the table to chase the boy. Flam, however, nimbly scurried out back into the open, then immediately dove back under cover when his father staggered out and stood up to try to renew the assault.

This dance repeated itself a couple of times, and the entire time Mary stood leaning on the table with her eyes squeezed shut, praying fervently, although exactly on whose behalf she was petitioning the Lord was unclear. Finally it became obvious the situation had become a stalemate. Out of frustration, Steve resorted to mercilessly flailing a doorjamb for a while, until he ultimately stormed out of the flat in search of a liquid tonic for his anger.

Mary bent down to pick up the pieces of the plate Flam had broken. "It's okay, Flam, he's gone. You can come out now," she urged her son, but Flam refused to leave his hiding place. He sat with his knees up to his chin, whining softly through clenched teeth and rocking back and forth. Mary tried several more times to coax the boy out, but he stayed put.

"Fine, then. Have it your way," she finally shouted, more exasperated than angry. "Sleep there on the floor if you want. I don't care," And so Flam did, curled up on the faded, scratched hardwood.

Within the cramped one-bedroom flat that constituted the Grub family home, Flam had never had an anointed space of his own, other than a small camp cot shoved permanently in a corner, and unfolded at bedtime for him to sleep on. Thereafter, the space under the dining room table became the boy's private refuge, and neither parent chose to forbid it. Steve actually preferred that Flam stay out of sight, and Mary secretly considered it a better use of the table than serving meals to her brutish husband. It soon became a moot point, as sit-down family dinners grew progressively rarer. Before long, the sight of Flam ensconced cross-legged and out of the way under the table became so common no one gave it a second thought.

CHAPTER 2

Just as at home he hid beneath the table from the constant acrimony between his parents, or Steve's periodic assaults on him, so at school Flam chose to fade into the background. He had learnt at an early age that to try to make friends meant having to introduce himself, and so bring his accursed name out into the open. He could never quite figure out what there was about those two syllables that so titillated and inflamed his peers, but he was acutely aware of the probabilistic outcome. At best he would have to endure name calling—taunts of Flam Chop and Grubby were common even from the younger children. Sometimes, however, it meant physical violence.

So Flam learned it was best not to attract attention—never stand out, never speak up, never challenge. This introversion led him naturally into the world of books, and from an early age he read constantly and voraciously, gleaning from the literature a heroism and adventure his own life lacked, and a personal morality beyond anything his parents or teachers chose to offer. At the same time, hiding behind a book seemed to magically render him invisible, providing some protection from parental rebukes, and to a lesser degree, from schoolyard savagery.

Flam's fear of attention translated into a doggedly undistinguished academic record. In reality, having sucked his books dry of, not only their factual content, but also their artistic soul and spiritual essence, he was capable of excelling far beyond the rudimentary level of his peers. Yet he purposely avoided the spotlight of scholastic stardom, having learned the hard way it would not provide him redemption at home, and would simply serve to further fuel the antipathy of the schoolyard terrorists.

With each passing year of her lamentable marriage to Steve, Mary too retreated, becoming progressively more devoted to her church and religion, finding there the inner nourishment that could not be provided by her husband and the strange, quiet child who was the fruit of their sinful union. She eventually returned, full of atonement and remorse, to her old parish of St. Ernest's, even though she no longer resided within its geographical boundaries.

Not only did she renew her worship with an almighty fervour, often attending several church services a day, but she also threw herself, body and refurbished soul, into every volunteer activity the parish promoted, plus any other good work she was able to conceive by herself. So invaluable did Mary become to the priests and parish officials, they ultimately made her a paid employee, albeit with a mere stipend of a salary, in order to permanently secure the rights to her zealous labours.

It was Mary who started Flam's addiction to books, supplying him with children's Bible stories and illustrated histories of the Holy Land that she brought home whenever she was filled with a guilty need to extend her missionary fervour to her own family. Eventually, Flam exhausted all the available Sunday school books, and Mary began to feed his literary cravings with assorted offerings culled from the parish's second-hand thrift store, mostly books with their covers torn off, or otherwise dog-eared to death.

Beyond selflessly choosing only merchandise too worn or damaged for the parish to resell, Mary never screened the content of the volumes she brought home, other than avoiding anything with clearly trashy or sinful subject matter, using steamy titles and cover illustrations of scantily-clad women as her barometer.

As a consequence, Flam's randomized readings proved quite varied and sophisticated—even for an adult, let alone a child. They ranged from ancient classics to modern masterpieces, but also included a regular diet of pulp fiction (whose titles were sufficiently obscure or cover art abstract enough for their violent or risqué nature to escape Mary's censorship). The only criterion was that the books had to have been abused or reread often enough to be in unsalable condition.

Flam's hiding place under the dining room table soon became a walled fortress of books, just large enough for him to lie in, buttressed by stacks of yellowed paperbacks and half-destroyed hardcovers. He would crawl into the refuge to escape from the cruelties of his life, pulling an old table lamp in after him to read by, its cord trailing behind like some electrical rodent's tail.

The problem evolved of what to do with Flam after school. Mary's schedule was being crammed progressively fuller with myriad errands and administrative responsibilities, to the point where there was now no predicting at what point precisely she would return home. Steve was of no help in taking up the slack. Although he was sometimes known to lie around the house for days in between his cross-country trucking runs, his absences were far more acute, his schedule wholly unpredictable, and even when he was at home, his contributions, both financial and parental, were nothing upon which Mary could depend.

Flam had been issued a key to the flat at a very early age, something originally intended for use in emergencies only, but it now became typical practice for Flam to find his way home and to occupy himself until his mother's return. Mary was fairly confident Flam would immediately stick his nose into his latest literary adventure and keep himself safely occupied, but she was constantly fearful some disaster would befall her son or their flat in her absence. It was not just concern for Flam's welfare that troubled Mary; it was also the thought of what damage might be done to the lily-white reputation she enjoyed among the clergy and parishioners if she were found to have allowed harm to come to her son through neglect.

A solution presented itself naturally when Mary arrived later than promised one evening only to find the flat dark and empty. She went rushing back outside to begin retracing the path to the school in search of Flam, panic rapidly mounting that the darkest of her inner fears had been realized. No sooner had she careened down the steep stairs out onto the street, than she spotted her son in the front window of the bookstore that lay directly below their flat. The youngster was perched calmly on a stool and totally lost among the pages of an illustrated history of ancient Greece.

Mary burst into the shop and lunged over the counter to grab her son by the front of his jacket, startling him from his book-induced trance.

"Flam, what in heaven's name are you doing here? You know damned well you were supposed to come straight home," Mary railed, a crimson sunrise of anger spilling over the snowy paleness of her face. "You stupid boy, how dare you worry me like that? When I found the flat empty, my heart almost stopped!"

The familiar sharpness of her tone left little doubt in Flam's mind about the extent and imminent consequences of his mother's anger. He instinctively recoiled and tried to squirm his way out of her grasp, suddenly wishing he was laid out safely among his books under the dining room table.

Flam's silent attempt at escape only served to fuel Mary's anger, and she tightened her grip. "Well, you little brat, what do you have to say for yourself?"

"It's my fault, Mrs. Grub," a basso voice countered from behind her, "I told him he could wait here."

Mary turned to confront the speaker, whom she recognized as Page Turner, the proprietor of the bookstore. He was a middle-aged roly-poly man who sported a chest-length beard and long hair, now faded grey and pulled tightly back over a substantive bald spot into a ponytail that flopped halfway down his back.

Turner was attired in a garishly patched blue jean vest worn over a colourful and wildly emblazoned T-shirt, and sported sandals over mismatched socks, a style he adhered to even in winter. Despite the fact she and her family had been living above the bookshop for a decade, Mary had never actually been inside the store before, disliking the dishevelled, unorthodox look of its proprietor. Although she'd passed by the store window on countless occasions, and had noted Turner's washed-out grey eyes staring at her curiously over top of half-moon bifocals, she had never returned that gaze, let alone exchanged a single word with the man.

Now she had plenty of words for anyone in her field of fire. "And just what business is it of yours, mister?" she demanded. "I wouldn't be surprised if you lured the boy in here. I've heard of men like you."

Turner laughed, which was not the reaction Mary had been aiming for.

"I can assure you there was no luring involved . . . I doubt if anything could have kept the boy from coming in and wallowing in the wares. As I'm sure you've noticed, Flam has a penchant for books."

The statement was so blatantly obvious it served to instantly disarm Mary. She took in the array of books crammed onto the shelves and heaped into stacks in every spare corner, and saw a macrocosm of the jumble under her own dining table.

Turner's manner was also proving reassuring—he had an articulate politeness, and the almost theatrical quality of his voice reminded her of a priest and belied his somewhat unkempt appearance. "I can promise you he's perfectly safe here, Mrs. Grub. I have him sit right up front behind the counter, and suggest books that will help him with his schoolwork. I wish I could say I was also teaching him how to use my computer, but the truth is he's such a quick study that he's long ago eclipsed me in that area, and has become quite a young wizard all on his own. You must be extremely proud of him."

Pride was not, in fact, an emotion Mary associated with Flam, but an intense, prolonged inquisition of both man and boy satisfied Mary nothing sinful or scandalous was afoot. Apparently, Flam, the compulsive bookworm, had gravitated to the store like a drunkard to a tavern, and had come to know the bookseller quite well, now treating his establishment like a second home. Mary accepted the situation as the divine intervention to which the saintly were entitled from time to time, and thereafter, it became not only acceptable, but common

practice, for Flam to wait in the store after school for his mother to
come home.

Turner and his delighted regulars soon made an unofficial store
mascot out of the surprising boy, whose ravenous appetite for books
and steel-trap memory made him somewhat of a *wunderkind*. For many
of the regular patrons, the store was not only a place to slake their
craving for reading material, but also a communal clearinghouse of
literary minutiae and esoterica. They congregated whenever the shop
was open to swap stories and share their passion for books. And Flam,
who felt an outcast elsewhere, now found himself part of this eccentric
little community.

If the group that gathered daily in the bookshop helped to make
Flam feel welcome, it was Turner who made Flam feel at home. Mr.
Page Turner was no simple monger of books. He had attended several
universities, and had earned undergraduate and post-grad degrees in
English Literature, Classical Studies, and Philosophy before profound
disillusionment with academic politics, and some tragic event oft
hinted at, but never related, ended his quest to become a tenured
professor. The discussions over which Turner presided still retained
an academic timbre, even if they were at times somewhat chaotic
and rambling.

In the beginning, Flam proved merely a source of entertainment,
but before long the eccentric inner circle of book worshippers, without
it having been agreed upon or even discussed, was collectively working
to polish and refine the boy's knowledge and appreciation of the
written word. Whenever Flam finished a book, they would quiz him
on his understanding of its message or theme, and point out the
intricacies of the wordsmithing or brilliance of the dialogue.

Poetry had previously constituted only a small portion of Flam's
reading, but in the bookstore he was systematically exposed to the
classics of verse. Turner, who had written a Master's thesis on the poetry
of Blake, was the prime instigator, laying out an ambitious roadmap
from Ovid to Ginsberg, but disguising its sophistic nature. Whenever
they found themselves alone, Turner would habitually pluck a book

from the stacks, and have Flam proceed to read poems aloud as the older man went about his chores.

"Flam, I have a yen for some Yeats," he might say. "Please read this to me while I alphabetize these paperbacks." And Flam, thinking he was doing the bookseller a favour, would wade into the words proffered to him.

> O sages standing in God's holy fire
> As in the gold mosaic of a wall,
> Come from the holy fire, perne in a gyre,
> And be the singing-masters of my soul.

Turner would interrupt to correct any mispronunciation, to explain a word, or to coach him on how best to recite a passage. And then the bookmonger would have the boy repeat key passages over and over again, unveiling their imagery and poetic poignancy.

"That's incredibly beautiful," Turner would sigh from the perch of his stepladder as he tried to find room on the shelves for his latest arrivals. "Don't you agree, Flam? Do you know what was meant by 'Perne in a gyre?' No? Your Irish ancestors would. Did you know Yeats came from County Sligo, just as your mother's people did? He's referring to the blur of a spinning wheel, just as each successive human life melds into the one before it. Read it again, my young recitalist. Stand up on the stool and enunciate it loudly so I can hear it over here, and while you do, see if you can glean the jewel of wisdom that lies nestled amongst those exquisite words."

In this way Flam came to know the giants of literature the way his peers knew the names of pop stars. And while many other boys his age might be able to enumerate the batting averages and recount exploits of their favourite baseball players, Flam could recite excerpts from classic poems with insight, fervour, and theatrical flair.

CHAPTER 3

The precious hours spent in Turner's Bookstore became Flam's only respite from the misery that permeated the rest of his gloomy life. When he moved on to attend the large and crowded local high school, he still made no friends, not even among the other outcasts and social misfits. Flam did once try to join the school's computer club, hoping to find camaraderie among those who shared his virtuosity with the digital devices, but there also he could not penetrate the tightly-knit clique, and was ridiculed and ostracized until he quit.

The bullying that Flam continued to encounter was subtler, but no less pervasive or cruel, although the name-calling was perhaps a bit more creative. The Grubby and Flam Chop of grade school was supplemented by Rack of Flam, Flamingo, Grub-a-Dub-Dub, and Flim Flam Man, among others.

In contrast to the cruel attention of his peers, Flam found his teachers lazy and uninterested, and although he soaked up as much as he could from them, he gave nothing back. He wrapped himself in his introversion, like some semi-perfect cloak of invisibility, minimized the contact with his peers, endured their taunts and assaults when they came, and counted the minutes until he could go running back to the bookstore.

At home, Mary's missionary sternness continued—a thing that Flam, in moments of black humour, thought of as his particular cross to bear. He was unable, however, to find any humour in Steve's dreaded irregular appearances, which often precipitated beatings and hateful verbal tirades. Steve's disdain for his son had now evolved to focus on the freshly-teenaged Flam's seeming lack of manhood, as puberty lagged in delivering its overt signs of masculinity.

Only once did Flam try to fight back against his father's abuse, and it ended up costing him dearly. On that occasion, Mary had taken advantage of Steve's unplanned, drunken appearance at home to rush off to a special night church service honouring a visiting bishop.

Mary had barely closed the door behind her when Flam, alerted by the crazed look in his father's face, tried to crawl into his book-walled refuge beneath the dining room table. Steve had anticipated this, and grabbed Flam from behind, spinning him around and back into the open.

"Oh no, you don't, twirp. You stay out here. You and me are going to have a little talk," Steve commanded, reaching menacingly for the boy. That was when Flam made the mistake of trying to resist, forcefully shoving away his father's arm and kicking out at his shin. Steve bellowed in outrage, and flung Flam up against a wall with a force that sent Mary's religious icons swaying on the wall. While a rake of yellow-stained fingers grabbed both skin and fabric in the front of Flam's shirt, rendering him immobile, Steve's other hand balled into a fist that wavered menacingly in front of the boy's fear-stricken face.

"You puny piece of shit!" Steve screamed at his terrified son, the reek of alcohol wafting from the man's breath in concert with his mounting anger. "Look at you! How did I ever end up stuck with a girly-boy like you?"

"Leave me alone! I didn't do anything to you," Flam protested, desperately squirming to try to pull himself free of Steve's grasp before the onset of the inevitable blows. The boy's struggles tore and stretched his T-shirt, but this only served to entangle him further as his father wound up the slack into a tighter knot, which lifted Flam up onto his toes and began cutting into his flesh.

"What do you want from me?" Flam began to scream, tears erupting. "Stop it . . . you're hurting me!"

His entreaty was met with a slap across his ear.

"Shut up, you little cry baby . . . you make me sick. I hate everything about you."

"Please, Dad, let me go, don't hit me, leave me alone." The words were barely intelligible through the heaving sobs now coming from Flam.

"I said shut up. Don't call me Dad . . . you're no son of mine. That goddamned bitch has turned you into some kind of a faggot freak, starting with that fucking stupid name of yours."

Now the blows began to rain down on Flam's head, a percussive accompaniment to Steve's taunting chant. "Flam!" Slap. "Flam!" Slap. "Flam!" Slap.

Flam was screaming hysterically now, so Steve reached down and grabbed his son's testicles, squeezing hard, forcing the breath and the resistance out of the boy.

"Flam . . . it sounds like some kind of fruit cake. Is that what you are, a fruit cake?" Steve growled, squeezing even harder. "Do you like this? Do you like a man grabbing your balls? Is that what turns you on, you fucking Fruit Flam? Is that what you do down there in that bookstore with those old men?"

It was doubtful Steve really expected any reply, for nothing more than rodent-like whimpers was coming from Flam at this point as he fought for air and consciousness. Finally, when the colour palette of the boy's face had played through hues of red and shifted towards a more malignant blue, Steve released his grip, in alarm that he might actually kill his son. Flam collapsed into a heap on the floor, his heavy breathing giving some reassurance he was still alive.

Steve bent over the boy and moved his face closer, until it was mere inches away from the boy's own. The father bared his teeth, and as he hissed his final statement every foul molecule of drunkard's breath was clearly detectable.

"I don't ever want to see you in that bookstore again. Do you hear me? If I ever find out you've been hanging around with those men again, I swear I'll cut your balls off and feed them to you. And I'll do the same to that old faggot friend of yours downstairs."

Steve straightened up, looked down at the whimpering heap at his feet, and delivered it a half-hearted kick. But the rage was now spent, and Steve shuffled off to the bathroom, enabling Flam to crawl to the table and drag himself into his sanctuary. As bad as his physical injuries were, the thought that he would be losing the one place that mattered to him, and the only friends he had in the world, was far more painful to Flam, and fueled his tears well into the night.

Mary returned home late and heard her son's muffled sobs emanating from within the walls of books under the dining table. Puzzled and concerned, she went to him to seek out the source of her son's sadness. Soon, however, she had problems of her own, as Steve awoke from a drunken languor, and attempted to cajole sex from his unwilling wife. Mary spent the night fending off her husband's stumbling advances, leaving Flam alone to cry in his refuge.

Despite an unshakeable terror that his father would catch him and make good on his threat, Flam could not bring it upon himself to simply disappear from the bookshop without an explanation or farewell. The next day, he stuck his head in the door, quickly dropped a couple of books that Turner had lent him onto the front counter, and stood there silently, not making eye contact. Turner looked up, confused as to why Flam was hovering apprehensively in the doorway.

"Hail, young squire. *Quid agis?*"

"My . . . my father says I can't come here any more," the boy blurted out, trying hard not to cry. "I just wanted to give you those books back . . . and to say thanks for letting me come here." With that the dam of despair burst and tears arrived in full force. Flam turned, as much to hide his crying as to depart.

"Flam! Wait! What's wrong? Why won't your father let you come to the shop? Let me go and talk with him."

Flam had no desire to converse about his father's abuse or threats. "He's crazy, that's all," he wailed through the narrowing crack, "just stay away from him . . . just leave us alone." And then the door closed, shutting out the friendship and sense of belonging the bookstore had provided to Flam, and the inner nourishment that had sustained him through his youth. He had never felt more alone.

Flam returned upstairs to the flat and crawled into his refuge beneath the dining room table, leaving the light outside. The pain within him now felt so intense he didn't think he could stand it any longer. And tomorrow, he knew, would bring another day of torment—neglect and abuse at home, ridicule and beatings at school, punctuated only by loneliness, self-loathing, and now the loss of his friends. Surely death was preferable to such a miserable half-life, especially if it put an end to the unbearable suffering once and for all.

Although he had grown too tall for the space, and one wall of books had been removed so his legs could protrude out, in the darkness, the remaining stacks of books around him gave the snug space the feel of a coffin. He stretched out on his back and oriented his hands appropriately across his chest, and took slow, deep breaths, exhaling each as if it were his last, only reaching up occasionally to wipe away the tears trickling down his face. Eventually he stopped sniffling and fell asleep.

CHAPTER 4

Despite Steve's attack on his masculinity, Flam had long been suffering the full heterosexual rampages of puberty, a suffering made only worse by his gluttonous diet of classical literary romanticism. At school, his debilitating shyness and pariah's status among his peers made it impossible to approach female classmates in any attempt to slake his burgeoning libido.

This new dimension to his loneliness, and the even deeper depression it precipitated, induced Flam to momentarily shed his disguise of mediocrity. He seized on an end-of-term poetry-writing exercise assigned by his English Literature teacher, Mrs. Boyle. Flashing the razor sharp blade of his hidden intellect, he poured his aching soul into the assignment.

In the midst of the other juvenile pap that floated in on a sea of depressingly bad grammar, Flam's submission shone like a beacon. Mrs. Boyle read it three times, and was so startled and moved by the verse submitted by the anonymous non-entity who haunted the rear of her classroom, she arrived at the only plausible conclusion—the work must have been plagiarized. So certain was she of this, even though a search of every anthology and literary journal in three libraries provided no substantiating proof, she summarily rendered judgment to that effect in front of the entire class.

"Did you really think I would believe you wrote this, Mr. Grub?" she growled, waving the double-spaced evidence around to emphasize her words, and accenting Flam's surname to maximize the mockery. "Plagiarism will not be tolerated. It cheapens the whole educational process, and is a despicable affront to the author whose work you have so callously stolen! Consider yourself lucky I don't have you suspended."

Flam fought back tears. "No, Mrs. Boyle, it's not true. It's mine! I wrote it. I swear to God I wrote it . . . all by myself. I didn't steal it."

His appeal was ignored. Mrs. Boyle brought the entire affair to a climax by ripping the paper into shreds and loudly awarding him an "F." His classmates, relishing the rare excitement in Mrs. Boyle's otherwise utterly boring class, tittered and guffawed around him.

Flam had found a rare joy and purpose when writing that poem. He had felt connected on a whole new level to the stories and characters and beautiful words that had sustained him since boyhood—so much so that for the first time in his life he had actually been lifted from his gloom and self-pity. He had felt motivated. He had been inspired. His life suddenly had a purpose. Now, thanks to Mrs. Boyle, the warmth from that fleeting artistic spark dissipated. Flam was plunged back into the darkness of his miserable life.

Not only was Flam's present filled with despair, but his future seemed to offer no hope either. With graduation from high school looming, the decision about his future as an adult had been weighing on Flam's mind. Until the humiliation in Mrs. Boyle's class, Flam had been summoning up the courage to approach his parents with the idea of going on to university, perhaps to study writing and literature. Now his ambitions felt empty and pointless, and the prospect of more years in school, suffering a whole new universe of degradation and scorn from classmates left him empty and utterly depressed.

Thoughts of ending his worthless life in an act of defiant heroism started to creep persistently into Flam's mind. One day, they finally drove him onto the railing of an overpass high above a local freeway, and there he wavered, picturing himself hurling down onto the traffic that was speeding by below, oblivious to his misery. It was not fear, or some tiny vestige of hope for a better future, or concern for the anguish he might cause others that ultimately pulled Flam back from self-obliteration. It was a novel he had been reading, and which lay in the knapsack on the sidewalk. He was suddenly struck with a strong desire to know the outcome of the story.

He sat down on the rough concrete railing that was to have been his springboard to the next life, and proceeded to finish the book. By the time he had tremblingly turned the last page and wallowed in the story's stirring ending, he was reading by the streetlight, and some semblance of peace had re-entered his soul. He took a final glance at the rushing stream of opposing red and white lights below, and turned to return home.

Two weeks later, and a hundred-or-so miles along the very same highway, Flam's life did change. His father, just heading out for a cross-country haul after having waited out the rush hour between the ample thighs of a bleached blonde truckstop waitress named Amber, was fishing around in his jacket for a pack of matches when he was cut off by a minivan. Steve lost control of his rig, jack-knifed, went sliding off down a steep embankment, and was killed instantly when the nineteen tons of galvanized steel rod he was hauling crushed his cab like a pop can.

Flam was reading in his lair beneath the dining room table, while Mary darned a priest's cassock, when the policeman rang the doorbell with the news. Flam was astounded by the ensuing display of his mother's grief. In the nineteen years of his life, he had never once known his parents to exchange a tender word or an intimate embrace. On those rare occasions when Steve had been at home, he and Mary had fought constantly, usually over Steve's drinking, and the meagre wages finding their way home.

Now Mary grasped her son to her bosom like a life preserver and wailed uncontrollably. At first Flam just stood there in shock, arms dangling limply by his side, but then the warmth of this mother's embrace spread through him. A lifetime of deprived closeness washed over him like a tsunami, and he put his arms around Mary, and squeezed her tight.

Eventually she looked up, like she was seeing her son for the first time. He had grown to be tall, and had his father's dark hair and eyes, along with her fair complexion, although unfortunately, he had neither parent's striking looks. "Oh, Flam, Flam. We're all alone now. We only have each other," she sobbed.

He soothed her, stroking her hair, supporting her as she leaned against him. "It's okay, Mother, it'll be alright . . . we'll survive." She looked at him again, and nodded bravely.

"Of course we will, son. We're Flams, after all. Misfortune is nothing new."

Flam spent the next three days almost entirely at the funeral home, acting as a silent sentry to his father's remains, and witness to his mother's periodic wailings of grief to her Lord and saints. It was there, in that place and time, that Flam Grub found a calling in life.

He absorbed the immaculate surroundings, revelling in the polished wood and plush velvet, all of it looking like it had manifested itself straight out of one of his Victorian novels. Flam watched the staff perform their solemn duties with quiet reverence, and he thought, *I can belong here*. This was a world where adolescent horseplay and sadistic pranks didn't exist. Here, a serious, sombre soul was not out of place. Dignity and a sensitive nature were in fact valued.

The funeral was attended mostly by Steve's cronies in hopes of a free piss-up afterwards, and once his father's corpse had been delivered to the earth, Flam approached Mary with the idea of joining the funerary profession.

"Mother, I've been thinking. I really want to become a funeral director," he announced, and tensed up to await the fireworks. Based on a lifetime of disapproval and criticism, he fully expected her vehement opposition.

Mary blinked hard, and her surprise was blatant. Before Flam had a chance to even flinch, she grabbed her son and wrapped him up in her arms. A whole new generation of tears sprung to her swollen eyes. "Oh, Flam! Praise God! I'm so happy to hear you say that. It's a good profession . . . a revered profession. I was so afraid you'd end up like all the other Flams . . . working for pennies at some menial backbreaking job that'll put you in an early grave. The parish has sent me to a lot of viewings and funeral services, believe you me, and I can tell you those from the home get *respect*. Why, I'd say they're almost above the priests themselves when it comes to the dead, yes I would. Oh my son, you'll be a proper holy worker." For the first time in his life that Flam could recall, his mother actually smiled at him.

Buoyed by his mother's blessing, Flam enrolled in the Funeral Services course at Prentice College, a vocational school on the outskirts of the city. He was helped in the matter by some insurance money, a posthumous windfall from his father, who had otherwise failed miserably to provide for his son.

With the teen purgatory of high school behind him, and a shiny destiny looming ahead, Flam felt like he was reborn. The newfound closeness with his mother was like rain coming to the desert, and his heart bloomed in the belated love and acceptance. Still, Flam was eager to plunge wholeheartedly into his new adult life, so he decided he would move away from home, and take a small apartment near the campus.

Mary voiced some displeasure, but largely took the news like a seasoned martyr. "First my husband, now my son. I don't know why the Good Lord is punishing me like this," she sighed, after Flam had meekly declared his intention to leave.

"I'm not a child anymore, Mother. Didn't you tell me once that Grandpa Flam already had a child and a fulltime job driving a cab when he was my age?"

"It seems like a waste of money, when this apartment is just sitting here empty most of the day anyway, what with my work and all."

"There's enough money to get me through school alright . . . and then, after that, I'll have a good job. Don't worry, Mother, I'll come and visit you every week. And, if you need me, I'm only a phone call away."

Flam also inherited his father's old but functional Ford Fairlane, and spent the summer acquiring his driving license. His mother, reasoning he would be called upon in his chosen profession to drive a hearse, made him gain extra practice by chauffeuring her to and from church and related social functions. In payment, the parish's thrift store supplied the sparse second-hand furnishings for Flam's new student apartment.

CHAPTER 5

Flam anxiously appeared for his first day of classes in September, his ingrained timidity heightened by the roomful of strangers around him. As he waited for the lecture to begin, out of reflex he stuck his nose into a textbook, and tried to shut out the people shuffling in to take their seats around him.

"I was expecting a roomful of weirdos," a female voice commented from beside him.

Flam reddened, thinking perhaps the statement had been some kind of barb directed at him. He pretended not to hear, and resumed concentrating on his book.

"Mind you, they're probably saying the same thing about us: 'Those two look normal enough,'" the voice added, and Flam realized the tone was self-deprecating, not derisive.

He turned to reply, and his mouth practically plopped open as he took in the young woman who had addressed him. She was a ravishing blonde with sparkling aquamarine eyes and a halogen-intensity smile. Even though she was seated, he could see she was tall and extremely shapely. To Flam, the girl looked like she would be better suited to strolling fashion runways than rolling away caskets. The thought of speaking to any woman, let alone one so beautiful, petrified him. Still, she had addressed him first, and her look was casual and inviting, so he swallowed hard and replied.

"Yeah . . . I was kind of curious myself as to what kind of student body would show up to study bodies," he quipped, and was rewarded with an appreciative chuckle.

"Hi, I'm Lucy, by the way. Lucy Giles," she introduced herself.

"Hi . . . um . . . I'm Flam . . . Flam Grub," he replied, and could instantly feel a flush of embarrassment come over his face.

"Ha! Great name!" someone exclaimed from the row behind them, then laughed—a loud staccato cackle that sounded like an air horn had been mated with a jackhammer. Flam spun in anger, but the speaker, a well-tanned young man with stylishly spiked brown hair and an expensive-looking sweater knotted around broad shoulders, seemed unfazed by Flam's ire; instead, he leaned forward with a menacing squint in his eyes.

"Something on your mind?" he snarled.

"Just ignore him . . . he's a jerk," Lucy whispered.

"You should be nice to me, gorgeous, I'm stinking rich," the bully replied. "The name's Nolan Paine—as in Paine's Funeral Services. Heard of us? We've got a hundred homes from coast to coast, and pretty soon yours truly is going to be running the whole show. I'm only here to get the token certification and make Daddy happy." He leaned closer until his mouth was only inches away from Lucy's ear. "You really should get to know me. You might like it." He brayed in laughter again, but was cut off by the professor calling the class to attention.

"Okay, people. Quiet everyone. Let's get started." Flam turned and directed his attention to the teacher. He was a tall, dour-looking old man, whose anatomical lines seemed to be out of alignment by a few degrees, making him look like a skeletal old barn about to collapse.

"My name is Mr. Basillie and the class is Microbiology. Together we will spend the next fourteen weeks learning about the many different organisms that spring up to feed on the dead."

Without even realizing he was doing it out loud, Flam joked, more to himself than to any audience, "Ahhh . . . so there *is* life after death." To his shock, it broke up the classmates around him. Flam reddened as laughing faces swivelled to stare at him in appreciation, but felt a sweet aftertaste of satisfaction to know he had amused his fellows. Warm memories of himself as a boy, standing on the counter of Page Turner's bookstore, and entertaining the inner circle of regulars with his dramatic recitations, flashed back to him.

The micromoment of satisfaction was abruptly interrupted by Nolan Paine's loud voice. "Yeah, you oughta know," he sneered, "you're dead from the neck up!" The heckler's guffawing at his own joke drowned out the rest of the class.

"Okay, okay, settle down!" Mr. Basillie admonished his students. "We'll begin today with an in-depth look at the different classes of bacteria . . .."

Flam slunk down into his seat. What little self-confidence he had brought to the classroom had suddenly decomposed, and as always, his accursed name, so easy a target, was at the core of it. It was grade school and high school all over again. Why had he thought this was going to be any different? *As soon as this class is over,* Flam told himself, *I'm going over to the registrar and I'm dropping out.* However, in the midst of the dark emotions seething within him, another voice spoke up. *No. You can do this. The past is dead. This is your destiny and no one's going to take it away from you. Ignore them. Ignore them all.* He straightened, took a calming breath, and focussed his attention on the lecture. Soon he was lost in the unfolding world of *cocci* and *spirilli.*

After class, Flam practically ran for the door, tripping over Lucy's long legs in the process. This became his pattern—first into the next classroom, first out, keeping largely to himself. It proved impossible, however, not to bond to some degree with his classmates, if only because of the atypical career choice they all shared. Despite his flagrant introversion, day by day, class by class, one snippet of painfully extracted conversation at a time, he grew friendly with most of his fellows, who were quick to note Flam's intelligence and wit.

One exception was the self-obsessed Nolan Paine, who assumed dominion over his fellow students, and made Flam his favourite target. Flam tried persistently to avoid Paine and the humiliation the bully habitually dispensed, but the geography of the Funeral Services classrooms made it difficult. Although Flam steadily accumulated enough of a store of self-esteem to make forays out of the island fortress of his timidity, his newfound confidence was constantly tested by the intolerable Paine. The bully took every opportunity to berate Flam, with cruel jabs that threatened to send the introvert's raped ego cowering back to its hole.

For once, though, Flam allowed the full extent of his intelligence to surface. He quickly rose to the top of the class, easily excelling in every subject they encountered. Above all, Flam remained a rapacious bookworm, becoming a familiar fixture in the college's library, and a regular scrounger through the book bins in the local Salvation Army and Goodwill stores, often voluntarily skipping meals to save money to buy more volumes in volume. Unplugged from the social network of his schoolmates, Flam contentedly spent his evenings and weekends alone in his tiny apartment reading, or in front of the computer. The pieces of furniture his mother's parish had supplied were soon overrun by mound upon stack of book upon book, in several corners literally running up to the ceiling.

The Funeral Services curriculum was an eclectic mixture of general courses and technical instruction related to the profession. The vocational subjects, on embalming and restorative techniques, were supplemented by college-level science courses on anatomy and pathology, and Flam's compulsive extracurricular reading kept him at a level far above the mediocre standard expected by the college.

Much of the study had to do with the basic operation of a funeral services business, including management practices, accounting, computer systems, law, and funeral merchandising. Flam meticulously soaked up this content as well, by now also serving as informal tutor to a few of the weaker students, including the lovely Lucy Giles. He noticed that Paine, who was otherwise an arrogantly apathetic student, seemed to wake up for these management subjects, evidently seeing them as valuable to his future anointed role as mortuary tycoon.

But there was another side to the business, the one that stressed the role of the funerary profession as caregivers, bereavement counsellors, and dignitaries in the ageless ritual of death. These sociology, psychology, and history courses were the ones that truly appealed to Flam, awakening a bottomless fascination. Entranced by the subject, he plunged beyond the stock readings and assignments prescribed in the syllabus, absorbing everything he could find in the libraries and bookstores and on the Internet.

At the end of his first year, after sizing up the state of his finances, Flam chose to stay in school during the summer. He took extra day and night courses from other faculties that were related to his newfound obsession, and devoted all his spare time to further reading and research. He immersed himself, body and soul, in the customs and mythologies of death, discovering the field even had its own name— thanatology. The more Flam read, the more he wanted to know, glimpsing among the mosaic of traditions and beliefs some higher order and pattern.

His sophistic paths led him from the mummification practices of ancient Egypt to the funeral pyres of India, via Heaven, Hell, Limbo, and Purgatory, among ghosts and zombies, into the inner workings of life-support hardware and medical maps of the mind, through accounts of near-death experiences and past-life remembrances, via a maze of mausoleums and monuments, past Boot Hill cowboys and New Testament miracles, all wrapped in white linen and cold as the clay.

His prodigious readings gave Flam a new perspective. While he had always felt a personal connection to death, which he could constantly feel hovering nearby, offering a potential escape from life's torments, now he saw it as a universal constant and the great equalizer that united him with all of humankind, past and present.

CHAPTER 6

In their final semester, as part of the college's ongoing struggle to raise its academic credentials, graduating students were required to take supplementary general arts courses. Flam, after vacillating over its complete lack of practical value to his profession and personal research, enrolled in a poetry appreciation course, succumbing to the phantom feelings that still throbbed in the amputated love of literature that had sustained him in his adolescence.

The course was taught by a wrinkled old relic of a woman named Ms. Dichter, who quickly surprised her students by springing to life during lectures with an energy, passion, and wit that was as unexpected as a polka party in a morgue. Ms. Dichter turned out to be a bona fide published poet of minor note. Her outrageous past spanned six decades and an equal number of continents, and included a Parisian studio, a lunatic asylum in Montevideo, a gilded Manhattan penthouse, a log cabin in Finland shared with twin brothers, and a sailboat, *The Ancient Mariner*, she had skippered solo throughout Micronesia. How these dots had connected to bring her to the backwater of Prentice College was a mystery she never expounded on, other than once to exclaim exuberantly, "Ah! Can you not smell the poetry in the air here?"

Ms. Dichter's class was attended by a mixture of students from various vocational programs, including would-be audio engineers, cosmeticians, mould makers, interior designers, and bookkeepers. To Flam's delight, the only other Funeral Services student in the poetry class was Lucy Giles. Having shared virtually every class over the past three semesters, the pair was reasonably well acquainted, but Flam also had helped Lucy with her schoolwork on a number of occasions. Once, after unfolding the mystery of spreadsheets in their business computing class, Lucy had rewarded him with a touch of thanks on his knee. Despite its obvious casualness, the physical contact had sent instant tremors through Flam's flesh, and had lodged in his memory.

Late at night, as he spread his legs under the sheets and reached for himself, Flam's unfulfilled sexual fantasies regularly featured Lucy as a headliner. Now, despite his shyness, he was able to grow progressively friendlier with the real-world Lucy, as they naturally banded together in the poetry class against the unfamiliar students from other programs.

Lucy had harboured no previous interest in poetry, and confessed to taking the course because she saw it as an easy credit, requiring minimal work. Nonetheless, she quickly fell under Ms. Dichter's spell. The poetess-professor's accounts of her uninhibited escapades, made all the more remarkable by the repressive era in which they had occurred, captivated Lucy, and made her that much more receptive to the gospel of poetry appreciation Ms. Dichter passionately preached. It was as if, for the first time in her life, Lucy had found something alive and soul-inspiring. When Flam proved to be, by far, the most gifted student in the class, and the only one who truly fathomed the verse Ms. Dichter proffered her students, Lucy began to look at Flam in a whole new light.

Impatient with his introverted nature, she dragged Flam out of his shell of shyness. Soon the pair was spending the entire school days together, sitting beside each other in all their regular Funeral Services classes as well. They also shared their spare periods in the library or cafeteria studying, or once Flam had opened up, just talking. Flam, despite retaining a preponderance of literary knowledge from his boyhood days in the bookstore, now pre-empted his private reading about death, and began refreshing and expanding his knowledge of poetry, just to be able to sagely satisfy Lucy's insatiable curiosity.

During the months of this new camaraderie, Lucy never once hinted she wanted their friendship to evolve into anything more intimate. Still, the thought was constantly on Flam's mind. It wasn't just that she was a spectacularly attractive woman who turned heads wherever she went—her regular closeness, the lingering melody of her laugh when he amused her, the sweet familiar scent of her combined perfumes and lotions, and the casual, friendly touches she regularly bestowed upon him all combined to create an unbearable and unfamiliar longing within Flam. He battled with himself, petrified by a fear of ridicule and rejection if it turned out he had misconstrued Lucy's warmth and attention. His books were full of such comedies— and tragedies—of errors. Yet, try as he might, he was unable to deny her clear admiration of him, especially her overt adoration of his intellect.

Finally, one Friday, as they sat together in a corner of the cafeteria, Flam summoned up the courage to ask her out.

"Hey, Luce, there's a poetry reading at The Gilded Lily tonight," he tossed out nonchalantly. "I thought maybe we should check it out." Lucy did not reply, so swallowing hard, Flam tried to act casual. "It would, you know, like be totally educational. I mean, I think it was Ms. Dichter who mentioned it."

Flam waited for what seemed an eternity for Lucy's response, trying to interpret her thoughts as she stared quizzically at him, her blue-green eyes locking him in a luminescent beam.

Finally she gave a nervous little laugh and jumped up from her chair to give him a quick hug. Basking in the afterglow of that electric contact, and shifting his legs to conceal his reaction to the intoxicating press of her body, it took Flam a few seconds to realize she was turning him down.

"Oh, I'd love to," Lucy exclaimed, "but I can't. But you should totally go, Flam, really . . . it'll be perfect for you. Omigod, you'll have so much fun. You'll have to, like, tell me everything." She immediately guided the subject back to their schoolwork, recounting her ecstasy over the latest literary epiphany Ms. Dichter had bestowed upon the class.

Flam sat mutely as the old familiar feelings of dejection welled up and washed over him. He tried vainly to muster the courage to challenge Lucy's motives for turning him down, or to garner an answer to the question that now overwhelmed him—whether her rejection was absolute, or only pertained to that one night. A few minutes later, Lucy glanced at her watch, quickly jumped up, swept her books into her knapsack, and excused herself with a half-smile.

"Don't forget, Flam," she called over her shoulder as she strode away, "I want a full report on Monday about the reading. I just know you'll have the best time ever."

Flam had never actually attended a formal poetry reading before, and did not have the least desire to go alone to this one. He mulled over excuses he might fabricate for missing the event, but felt honour-bound by his deep feelings for Lucy. He simply could not lie to her, and wanted more than anything to please her, so he convinced himself that, by going, he might be paving the way for future outings they might yet share.

That night he entered the small, dilapidated lounge where the poets would be performing. He found an out-of-the-way seat, and sat waiting for the presentations to begin—a pale, silent figure, slumped alone at the back, staring blankly down at his feet, fantasizing the whole time about what it would have been like with Lucy beside him to share the moment.

The audience barely filled a third of the seats, and congregated mostly around the front, where a crudely constructed plywood riser formed the stage, with only an uneven wooden stool and an ancient 1950s-era microphone on top. The house lights eventually went down, and a succession of poets took their turn at the microphone.

Flam had not known what to expect, and was utterly disappointed by the quality of the works being presented. *Good Lord, even I can do better than that,* he thought, for the poems he heard struck him as amateurish, mediocre ramblings, lacking structure, craftsmanship in their language, and any discernible profundity. He found it hard to believe anyone who had the least knowledge of or appreciation for poetry would enjoy the drivel these dilettantes were hissing or barking from the stage.

Yet the audience appeared to be enthralled. As Flam studied the interplay between the listeners and the recitalists, he began to realize the greatest enthusiasm came from a cadre of women in the front seats, who appeared totally mesmerized by the poets, hanging on their every syllable. When the performances had concluded, Flam observed that several of the poets reappeared to intermingle with the circle of waiting admirers, who swallowed up the bards in a crush of adoration. A collective chorus of chatter and laughter swirled around the room, like the wind at play with autumn leaves.

As Flam stood, transfixed by the scene, one beret-clad woman standing at the fringe of the assembly noticed the lone, motionless figure hovering in the shadows and studying them. She returned her interest to the milling group, but her head kept swivelling back in Flam's direction. Finally, she detached herself from the others and walked over, evoking a rush of panic in Flam when he realized his anonymity had been pierced, and the stranger was approaching him.

The woman was carefully made up, with just the right amounts of blush, lipstick, and eye shadow to accent her best features and make it impossible to guess her age. Her hair was dark, and cut short in a bold style that poured straight out from beneath the beret before crashing to an end just below the cheekbones.

"Excuse me," the woman began, but with an eye-to-eye confidence that belied any sense of apology, "aren't you Mark Young?" Flam was momentarily dumbstruck before he could half-stammer a weak, "No . . . no, I'm not." The woman's demanding stare made it obvious to Flam this wouldn't be enough, so he reluctantly added, "My name is Flam Grub." She blinked a few times, and smiled sardonically before turning and walking back to her clique. Flam quickly effected his escape. Just as he was exiting, a burst of laughter erupted from behind him, and he blushed, convinced he'd heard his accursed name at the epicentre of the group's guffaws.

Despite the pain caused by the laughter, not to mention the poor quality of the poetry, the evening hadn't been a completely negative experience. Flam had left the recital with an idea—to write a poem and dedicate it to Lucy.

Deciding what style to adopt proved extraordinarily difficult. *Should it be a classical love sonnet à la Shakespeare or perhaps Browning,* he wondered, *or would that be too old-fashioned, too corny? Or should I go for something a little more abstract, something a little more hip? And what should I say? Should I tell her outright how I really feel? Should I be subtle? Should I be mysterious? Should I be funny?*

Flam spent the entire weekend composing his opus, agonizing over every line, and polishing every word. Shortly before midnight on Sunday, Flam had finally finished. He was exhausted but elated, and pronounced himself satisfied with the five stanzas he'd managed to wrestle from his muse. They lay there, neatly printed out, ready to be unveiled—a deadly dart aimed straight for the heart. By now, he had the verses embossed in his memory, and he drifted off to sleep, reciting the poem again and again to the enthusiastic sighs of a dream-world Lucy.

CHAPTER 7

On Monday morning Lucy failed to show up in the cafeteria to share a coffee before class. This was not unprecedented, but it still torpedoed Flam's buoyant little fantasy of how the day was meant to unfold. He'd envisioned winning her over with the poem first thing in the morning, paving the way for a day spent at school together sighing over one another, and culminating in an evening of intimate discovery. Instead, he found himself waiting anxiously, and then rushing off to class alone.

Their first subject of the day was Psychology of Grief, normally one of Flam's favourites, but he found himself growing progressively more apprehensive as the classroom clock's minute hand reached the 9 o'clock zenith without any sign of Lucy. At two minutes after the hour, as the teacher, Mr. Wales, was outlining the day's lesson on the board, Lucy slunk into the classroom, looking befuddled and dishevelled. Instead of seeking out her usual seat, which Flam had saved in the front row, she chose to slip quickly into a spot at the back while Mr. Wales wasn't looking. Flam swivelled around and craned his neck, trying to offer her a sympathetic, inquiring look, but Lucy's head was hunched over her knapsack while she busied herself in its contents.

When class ended, Flam rocketed out of his seat to chase after Lucy, whose long-legged strides were already carrying her quickly down the hallway.

"Lucy!" Flam called after her, starting to wonder if she was purposely avoiding him. She turned, her azure eyes and luminescent smile instantly melting away any doubts Flam had been harbouring. His heart, which had been beating frantically out of control, slowed down to a more sustainable disco beat.

"Oh, hey, Flam," she greeted him casually, turning to walk beside him. She gave a little snigger. "I really slept in this morning. I'm like totally lucky Wales didn't centre me out for coming in late."

Now that he was beside her and able to talk, Flam didn't know where to begin. He felt like dropping to his knees and simply blurting out adoration for her, but even a guileless romantic like Flam understood that, in rock-hard reality, such things simply weren't done.

Their next lecture was only minutes away, and although he deliberately slowed down his pace to preserve their time together, Flam knew the poem needed a more appropriate moment for its debut. Still, he needed to break the silence, to set the stage for what he wanted to tell her.

"I went to that poetry recital on Friday night," Flam finally offered by way of a lead-in. Lucy turned, looking surprised and delighted, the old intimacy suddenly restored. The questions flooded out of her: "Oh, my gosh, I'd forgotten all about it! How was it? Did you enjoy it? What kinds of poetry did they do? Were there a lot of people? Did you meet anyone?"

They had reached their next class, a double dose of Funerary Law, and Flam, bolstered by Lucy's apparent gush of curiosity, opted to play it coy. "It was quite the experience . . . you really missed out on something," he said somewhat evasively, not wanting Lucy to feel she'd made the right decision by not having gone with Flam. They were in their seats now, and the opportunity for intimacy was passing as their classmates filled in around them.

"Tell you what," Flam offered, pretending to turn his attention to his texts and notebooks, "meet me in the cafeteria, and I'll give you all the juicy details over lunch." He held his breath until Lucy finally responded with a reticent "alright." Flam exhaled, and began to mentally prepare for their noon rendezvous.

The rest of the morning dragged by for Flam, and when the bell finally rang, he had only the fuzziest recollection of what had been taught for the past couple of hours. All he could think about was Lucy, and how the moment had finally arrived when he could win her heart. How would she be able to resist him, once he was revealed to her as a newfound poetical light, and she the apex of his inspiration?

Flam stood up, ready to shepherd Lucy to the cafeteria, but before he could utter a word, she turned and placed her hand on his shoulder. "Go ahead and save us a seat, will you? I have something I need to do." Flam felt the blood rushing to his face, as much from the warm sensation of her physical touch as from the frustration of having once again been sidetracked in his plans.

He managed a brave smile, and acted like it was no big deal. "Sure . . . I'll grab a table by the windows. You want anything to eat?"

She shook her head. "I'll see you in a few minutes," she told him, and took off in the opposite direction. He paused to watch her sway around the corner, and then dashed to the cafeteria.

Most of the eatery's seating consisted of aisle upon aisle of long, barracks-style tables, but along one side, where a wall of opaque glass blocks ran floor to ceiling, was a row of tables for two. These choice seats went fast at lunchtime, and Flam wanted to ensure he got one, thereby guaranteeing some intimacy and eliminating the possibility some passing classmates could join them.

He was in luck. There was just one table left, and with relief he dropped his knapsack on the spare chair and plopped himself down. His heart was pounding and his mouth was dry, making him briefly contemplate buying a drink—he was too nervous to eat—but the checkout line was already growing long, and he didn't want to chance wasting any of their precious time together standing in the queue.

Flam realized his back was to the door, and he hurriedly switched seats so he would be able to wave Lucy down the instant she came into the cafeteria. The minutes crept by, each one noted on Flam's wristwatch, and corroborated by the clock on the cafeteria wall, but there was still no sign of Lucy. By a quarter past, Flam was getting a sick feeling in his stomach, feeling his dreams being slowly crushed to death under the weight of Lucy's cruel indifference. By twelve thirty, Flam's despair had begun to morph into anger, directed as much at himself as at the latecomer herself.

He was getting ready to stomp out of the cafeteria, and was debating whether to tear up the poem first, when Lucy materialized in the entrance to the cafeteria. She spotted Flam and hurried across the crowded hall towards him, leaving behind a wake of admiring male heads, which swung around in rapid synchronized succession like cadets on parade.

"Hi, Flam," she offered, smiling innocently as he stood up to grab his knapsack and allow her to slide into the vacant seat. "So, tell me about Friday night!" she began immediately without any preamble or a word of explanation. She sounded genuinely excited, and although Flam had thought of challenging her for being late, he quickly dismissed the notion and instead launched into his well-rehearsed, somewhat embellished version of the Friday night poetry recital. He finished up by relating how he himself had been mistaken for a poet, although he purposely didn't mention it had been a woman who'd approached him, not wanting even a hint of possible infidelity to enter Lucy's mind.

Flam concluded with the *coup de grace*, a carefully planned segue to the poem he had written for Lucy. "One or two of them weren't bad, in a raw, shoot-from-the-hip kind of way, but frankly I think my own stuff is better."

Lucy blinked as she absorbed the statement. Then she took the bait, her eyes widening with unabashed delight, so alluring it caused an instant tingle in Flam's groin.

"Flam . . . you write poetry?" she squealed. "How come you never told me? All those times we were talking and learning about it, I didn't realize you did more than just read it!"

Flam acted properly bashful, but his pulse quickened as he realized the moment had arrived. "Oh, I haven't been into it long, and I've never shared it with anyone else. But, I've written a poem just for you, Lucy. Do you want to hear it?"

He didn't allow Lucy the chance to refuse, and quickly slid a copy of the poem out from beneath his binder, and rotated the printout into place in front of her. As she glanced down, he began reciting the lines from memory. All the inner aching and pent-up emotion that had been tormenting him now poured out into each stanza's reading. Even though the presence of students at the neighbouring tables made him keep his voice low, this only added to the poem's sensual and intimate nature.

Lucy sat motionless throughout the recitation, her reaction impossible to read. When Flam finished, an uncomfortable silence spread between them, accentuated by the hub of the cafeteria crowd and the clanking of dishes, which now seemed surreally louder. The seconds dragged, and still Lucy sat deadpan, staring down at the sheet of paper. This was not how Flam had envisioned the climax. Perhaps he had been too subtle. She must have missed the crux of the verse, and didn't realize the depth of his feelings. She clearly hadn't understood how profoundly he longed for her.

He was about to blurt out, "Lucy, don't you see . . . I love you!" when she finally spoke up, as if anticipating the words to come, and needing to intercept them, to prevent them from taking wing.

"Oh, Flam, it's lovely. I'm really, really flattered," Lucy sighed, her voice low, barely above a whisper. There was a sort of regret, almost a weariness, in her words, and Flam got the sudden impression she was speaking lines very familiar to her.

"Listen, Flam, I really like you a lot . . . ."

Please, God, no, Flam pleaded inwardly, anticipating the shoe that was about to drop, *please . . . not the 'F' word.*

". . . as a friend."

Thud. There was more about what a nice guy he was, and how smart he was, and how he deserved to find the perfect girl some day. It barely registered, as Flam stared down at the dull, institutional terrazzo of the cafeteria floor, which seemed to be spinning as he struggled to keep his mental equilibrium. He felt as insignificant as one of the stone ovals that made up the floor's mottled pattern.

Flam had the urge to get up and flee back to his apartment, where he could hide behind his wall of books, cry, and lick his wounds. He realized he had been a fool all along to delude himself into thinking a woman so beautiful, so desirable, could possibly be attracted to a loser like him. And yet he clung to Lucy's presence, even though everything was now a blur, and he felt like his insides had been torn out of him. Although she had rejected him, shredding his hopes and hurting him beyond words, he felt that as long as she was still there, across the table, he had not really lost her.

Lucy's words dissolved into a meaningless drone, or rather, their overall meaning became so painfully evident to Flam that there was no need to dissect the individual phrases and phonemes. But then the tone shifted; the substance of what she was saying now began to register, and jolted him back from his mental haze.

"I wasn't really looking to get involved with anyone," Lucy was saying. "It just sort of happened. I've only been seeing him for a little while, but I think it might be serious."

A boyfriend? Flam thought. *Lucy never mentioned a boyfriend.* Not that she had in fact told him anything at all about her personal life. Flam had never wanted to risk spoiling the magic of their precious moments together with nosy questions. Like a hiker who has a rare and beautiful butterfly light upon him and is afraid to move for fear of startling the creature, Flam had always avoided doing anything he thought might threaten his relationship with Lucy.

His continued silence, and the wretched look that had materialized on his face, evidently disturbed Lucy, and she reached over and placed her hand on his. Flam gazed up into her beguiling eyes, which seemed to be sparkling and shifting in colour as they caught the outside light through the glass blocks.

"Are you okay?" she asked, smiling encouragingly. The sheen of perfect teeth peeked out from behind glossy lips. "We're still friends, aren't we?"

"Yeah. Sure," Flam mumbled, barely able to speak. The bell sounded and immediately the local din increased as students gathered their belongings and shuffled towards the exit.

Flam and Lucy stood up together and she hesitated a minute, as if seeing for the first time, in his slumped shoulders and tightly pressed lips, the full extent of the carnage her words had wreaked. She stepped forward and threw her arms around him in a hug. Flam was caught totally off guard, and holding his knapsack in one hand, had to fight hard just to keep his balance, let alone return the embrace. The closeness of her body pressed against his emanated a warmth that enveloped him like a layer of melting toffee, a feeling that lingered even after Lucy had swiftly pushed away.

"Are you coming?" she asked. He nodded, forcing a weak smile. Together they walked slowly to their next class.

CHAPTER 8

For the rest of the week, Flam sleepwalked through his classes, avoiding contact with his classmates, rarely speaking, barely paying attention to the lectures. Despite their vow of friendship, Lucy now seemed to keep their contact outside class to a minimum, but Flam doubted it was because of guilt over his morbidly depressed state. He hypothesized she was either expressing distaste for his unmanly moodiness, or thought he might be trying to exploit her conscience. She would still come to him for homework help, and engaged him in perfunctory small talk during classes, but now always seemed to have something else to do during their spare periods.

Each night, Flam dragged himself back to his tiny apartment, where he would scrape together some half-hearted attempt at a meal, only to leave it largely uneaten. He would sit placidly in the dark, brooding, until his self-pity built up to saturation. Then he would erupt into tears. He tried unsuccessfully to study, and instead was compulsively drawn to one of the thanatological texts he had collected, which dealt extensively with suicide. Flam regularly found himself turning its pages and weighing which form of self-destruction would be easiest and least painful. During this time he slept little, as his mind wrestled with the overwhelming feelings of hopelessness that seemed worst during the smallest hours. By the end of the week, the insomnia had made itself clearly visible in his gaunt appearance, especially the dark circles that were painting themselves ever darker and deeper beneath his blood-shot eyes.

Their last class of the week was Ms. Dichter's, just after lunch on Friday. Lucy was absent, however, having already made an early start on her weekend. *She's probably rushing off to the arms of her lover,* Flam supposed, and the thought dragged him even lower into his gloominess.

On this occasion the poetry professor was in rare form, for the topic of the day was T.S. Eliot's *"The Love Song of J. Alfred Prufrock,"* and she had no reservations in raving exuberantly to the class about the sheer brilliance of its language, the profundity of its imagery, and its significance in literature's pantheon.

A short week ago, Flam, who adored the poem, would undoubtedly have been swept up in Ms. Dichter's enthusiasm. In an attempt to impress Lucy, he would have spearheaded some participation from the students. Now, as he had done all week, he sat as mute and motionless as a cadaver through the entire lecture.

Afterwards, as he shuffled out, Ms. Dichter called after him, "Mr. Grub, I'd like a word with you if I may." His name, especially the clearly enunciated delivery given it by the professor's flagrantly dramatic voice, generated, as usual, a couple of titters and snickers from some of the exiting students. A blush swept across the white barrens of Flam's cheeks as he turned to face Ms. Dichter, wondering what she could possibly want to talk to him about.

"Flam, I don't like to poke my nose where it may not be welcome," she began, her voice soft and intimate, "but I've got a lot of admiration for you and . . . and . . . ." She faltered trying to find the right words. "Oh, hell, I'll just come right out and say it. You look *dreadful.* Frankly, you look like you're about to become one of your own charges. Let me know if I'm being a big butt-insky but is everything all *right* with you?"

Flam was caught totally off guard. He coloured brightly and, stammering, began a couple of denials before stopping dead and blurting out, "No, actually, I'm not okay, Ms. Dichter."

"I notice you and Miss Giles seem to have had a falling out," Ms. Dichter offered, probing gently around the emotional wound like an experienced surgeon. Flam wondered how on earth she could have known something had changed between Lucy and him, but then realized there would obviously have been signs that any astute observer could pick up on. "Have you two broken up?" she pursued further.

"No . . . I mean, we were never together, at least not like that." It was an unexpected comfort to be able to talk to someone about the thing that had been weighing so heavily on him, practically tearing his tortured soul apart. Still somewhat embarrassed, but feeling relieved to have landed a friendly ear, he recounted the entire tragic tale.

Ms. Dichter listened attentively, saying nothing, her only visible reaction an occasional sucking of her upper lip. When he had finished, she sighed heavily.

"Flam . . . I don't want to belittle in any way what you're feeling because, Lord knows, I've had my heart broken enough times, and in my day, destroyed at least one life in the name of love, and I'll carry that guilt to the grave. But I survived it, and you can too, you're so *young*. You'll get over it. How cliché is that? But trust me, it's true."

She studied him to see if her words were having any sort of impact before continuing. "You want another truism? Here's a little poem you've probably heard: 'If you want to be happy for the rest of your life, never make a pretty woman your wife.' Believe me, wiser words were never spoken. I may be a traitor to my gender for saying this, but beware beautiful women. They are like great cats—powerful, striking, an exquisite joy to behold, be it stationary or in motion—but even the tame and well-trained variety can suddenly turn on a man and devour him whole. Unless you know what you're doing, and are properly equipped, they are best appreciated from a distance."

Flam sat motionless and crestfallen in his seat, a bent-over mirage of a man trying to digest Ms. Dichter's meanderings. She seemed to realize she was being somewhat patronizing, or at least abstract, and smiled apologetically. "I'm sorry . . . I'm probably not being much help." A long pause told her Flam was not going to join the conversation, so she leaned over and asked, "May I see it?"

Flam blinked once, twice, confused, until he realized she was asking to see the poem he had written for Lucy. He wondered why she

believed he was still carrying a copy of it a week later. Why didn't she
think he'd followed through on the urge, which he had entertained
every night, to rend the rhyme into pieces, as well as purge the stored
bits from his computer, thereby removing forever from his tortured life
all trace of his rhyming folly?

He knew he could simply tell Ms. Dichter he didn't have a printout
of the poem with him. He certainly hadn't intended anyone other
than Lucy to ever read it—except perhaps for their future children, to
whom the poem would have become the mainstay of a family legend.

In fact, Flam had been carrying the poem with him ever since
Black Monday. Suddenly, he very much wanted Ms. Dichter to read it,
if only to reassure him that in writing it he had done nothing wrong.
Or, he hardly wanted to admit to himself, perhaps to bestow on him
some magical poetic incantation that might yet bewitch Lucy's heart.

Flam unzipped his knapsack, fished through his notes, and
handed Ms. Dichter the dog-eared copy of Lucy's love poem. The
teacher took the page and, deadpan, scanned through its contents.
Then, Flam noted with interest, she read it again, this time mouthing
the words and tapping a cadence on the floor with her penny loafer. It
was as if, on some imaginary stage, she was reciting the poem out loud.

He waited, pale-faced, lips pressed together tighter than a miser's
fist, eyes afire within the sunken shadows of their sockets, acutely aware
that a literature professor and respected poet was actually reading his
painstakingly crafted words. Suddenly, he wanted desperately to know
her honest, critical opinion, not as love's labour lost, but as a piece
of deliberately crafted art. He felt humbled, and a little bit scared, yet
hopeful. More importantly, for the first time in days, he was motivated
by an emotion other than self-pity.

Ms. Dichter looked up at him and smiled. "Oh, Flam, I've known
a lot of girls who would have been putty in your hands if this were
written for them. Mind you, it's a little syrupy for my taste, and honestly,
dear, no one writes in iambic pentameter anymore, but considering,
from what you've told me, you've hardly put pen to paper at all, this is
really quite a remarkable effort. Some of your symbolism is first rate,
and you have an amazing gift for language."

She shook her head sadly. "I can see you're a real romantic of the old school, which is too bad, because I guess there's no chance in convincing you to go out tonight and find another girl to wax poetic all over. Frankly, if I were forty years younger and hadn't permanently locked my loins out of self-defense—not to mention it being frowned upon by the college—I'd drag you back to my place to get all Flamorous with you myself, just to get your chin off the floor and your head back into the game."

Flam recoiled at the disturbing mental image of grappling in the throes of passion with a woman old enough to be his grandmother. He wanted to protest, but all he could manage was a weak "Lucy . . .."

"I know, dear. Lucy's special. It's not like that with her. There's no one but Lucy. She's the real deal. Yada, yada, yada." She stood up. "Flam, I don't normally meddle in the personal affairs of my students, especially given the vast majority are a bunch of hormone-crazed, sex-obsessed ignorami. But in the ten years I've been teaching here in this vocational wasteland, I've never had a student with your breadth and depth of understanding for poetry, even as a critic, let alone—be still, my beating old heart—as a creator. You're an absolute rarity and a very, very sensitive individual, Flam, although believe me, that's more a curse than a blessing if you don't have what it takes to deal with the fallout. I'm sorry love and life have dragged you down, but hang tough, dear."

She returned the poem and got up to go, but then turned to face him again. "I've probably meddled quite enough for one day, but please do me a favour. I know a few words from a cynical, one-foot-in-the-grave lunatic like me won't change the pain you're experiencing, but go home and try to put down in words exactly what you're feeling. Turn that concentration of emotion that's eating you up inside into a poetic plus, instead of a melancholy minus that will destroy you if you let it." She gave him one last encouraging smile, and left him to his thoughts.

Back in the solitary gloom of his apartment that night, and reasoning it was far better than lying around and waiting to be overtaken again by another bout of despair, which was already descending upon him like some mental storm front, Flam did indeed take Ms. Dichter's advice. For the second weekend in a row, he wrote a poem dedicated to Lucy. This time, the words seemed to come much more easily, as if he were lancing an inner boil and letting the pus of emotion come spewing out onto the page. The real effort came afterwards, as he wrestled with the intricacies of wordsmithing, and struggled to lay a conscious stylistic framework and form over the substance of his thoughts.

The task had a therapeutic effect, as undoubtedly Ms. Dichter had foreseen. *I guess poetry has the power to move the poet as well as the audience*, Flam observed, and filed that knowledge away for future use. By Saturday afternoon, Flam had turned the page on his opus and started cleaning his apartment, tackling his homework backlog, and was contemplating sending something substantive down into his gurgling stomach. He fell asleep that evening in his armchair, fully clothed, with an unopened book on his stomach, and slept for fourteen hours straight, interrupted only by a change of venue to the bedroom, via the bathroom, circa 3 a.m.

On Sunday evening, as was his custom, Flam drove downtown to visit his mother and fulfill his weekly quota of filial obligation, having to wait first for Mary to deplete herself of the host of holy activities the day always bestowed upon her. On this occasion, he shook her somewhat, for instead of offering the monosyllabic reticence Mary normally encountered from her son's side of the dinner table (forcing her therefore to hold up both ends of the conversation by recounting in excruciating detail every bit of church news and parish gossip), Flam was uncharacteristically vocal. He showed particular interest in the details of how she and his father had met and courted. It was Mary's turn to become uncommunicative, having long forsaken the painful memories of those sinful days and her fall from grace. She was much more eager to talk instead about her progress on the interpersonal front with Gerald Strait, her long-lost pharmacist, now widowed like herself, and back in the picture.

Flam returned to his studies on Monday morning with all of his previous sense of purpose and indefatigable thirst for knowledge. Although his in-class contacts with Lucy were, at first, still painful, he fought hard not to let himself be sent into tailspins of despondency and self-loathing at the very sight of her. Lucy made this easier by acting noticeably cooler towards Flam. Initially, he thought this had to do with him declaring his feelings for her. He soon realized she had become lackadaisical about her schoolwork in general, and was often visibly distracted with some weighty thoughts of her own during lectures. While she had never been stellar in her scholastic efforts, Lucy's combination of raw practicality, strong will, and intuitive intelligence had previously allowed her to hold her own academically. She often needed help getting the gist of a topic, but she seized upon it like a pit bull once she understood, and never had to be shown twice. Now it seemed like she was sleepwalking through to the conclusion of the course.

Spring arrived, and the end of the school year was rapidly approaching. A spell of fair weather gave Flam an opportunity to take his books and join the migration of students outside into the fresh air. One day, he stumbled across a choice private spot at the back of the campus, right beside the student parking lot, where a square of hedges had been planted around a memorial to Prentice College's World War I dead.

There was a small triangular strip between the original line of shrubbery and a new fence that had been built around the student parking lot. The grounds crew, at first unsure how to deal with the spatial oddity, had opted to cut a passage through the hedge at one end, just large enough for them to maintain a strip of grass inside the tiny secluded clearing. Flam found it hard to believe he was the only student who knew about the spot—certainly it was ideal for make-out sessions and dope smoking—but as he continued to frequent his secret enclave daily, he never once stumbled across another occupant, and was grateful for it. At that time of year, the sun penetrated into the little strip during most of the afternoon hours, and the now-venerable hedge was attended by a number of small birds who regularly serenaded Flam with their natural selection of songs.

So well-concealed was anyone sitting or lying down in the secret spot, that on many occasions Flam had been able to eavesdrop on private conversations emanating either from the lawn in front of him or from the parking lot behind the fence.

Most of the time, he made a concentrated effort to ignore the voices. He would roll over and focus doggedly on his studies or his newly resumed explorations into the history and philosophy of death. On one day, during the first week of exams, however, with the spring sunshine trying hard to persuade him to nap, and an exquisitely dull accounting textbook acting as co-conspirator, Flam was stirred from his semi-somnolent state by a loud, familiar voice coming from the parking lot.

"I don't give a shit what he thinks," the speaker protested loudly. Flam recognized him immediately as Nolan Paine . . . but the real shocker came a second later.

"I don't want to start a fight between you and your father," came a response, and Flam's jaw dropped when he realized the voice was Lucy's. He rolled over and stuck his eye to a seam in the fence boards to see if he could discern anything. There was just enough separation to allow him to make out a red BMW Boxster convertible with its top down. His two classmates were seated in the front with their foreheads almost touching. Lucy's immaculate hair was backlit by the sun, and to Flam's eyes she had never looked more stunning. They must have just parked here, he surmised, and his heart started to pound wildly when the pieces clicked into place, and he realized Nolan Paine must be the very boyfriend Lucy had talked about.

Flam was staggered. In his imagination, the man who had been able to steal away the heart of his precious Lucy would have to be, by definition, someone extraordinary—tall, muscular, a veritable demigod, but with charm, wit, intelligence, and sensitivity. Not that Paine was necessarily unattractive, and he was further blessed with all the benefits of the best grooming money could buy, but he was mean spirited, self-centred, not to mention a bully and a braggart. Surely

Lucy, who could have practically any man she wanted, and like all the members of the class, had been subjected to daily doses of Paine, could not possibly be attracted to someone like *that*.

"The hell with my father," Paine was saying. "I'm of age now, and if I want to get married, I'll damned well get married. I say we do it right after exams."

Lucy reached over and embraced Paine, pressing her lips against his in a prolonged kiss, then pulling his head down to allow him to explore the splendours of her neckline. As he did so, she looked right past her paramour and off into space. For a second, Flam was convinced she was staring right at him through the crack in the fence. He held his breath and contemplated bolting, but after a second or two, it became evident she was in fact lost somewhere in her own private thoughts.

"I love you so much, Lucy," Paine was whimpering, "I don't care if he cuts me off without a penny. You're all I want."

Lucy pulled up his chin and gazed into his eyes. "You know I love you too, Nolan. I'd marry you today, but let's not be impulsive. Your father hasn't even met me . . . I'm sure once he gets to know me he'll see I'm perfect for you. Besides, we'll have all summer to work on him."

"Okay, but I'm going to buy you the biggest engagement ring Prentice College has ever seen," Nolan asserted. "That way he'll know we're serious."

That earned another passionate kiss from Lucy. "Oh, sweetheart," she cooed, "how did I ever get so lucky?"

"Are you sure I'm the one you really want?" Nolan quipped, "I bet you Grub would walk on hot coals for you . . . and write your exam for you too."

She feigned anger and punched him on the bicep. "Stop it," she scolded. "I've told you we were just friends."

"Are you kidding? You had him totally Flambéed. The poor guy couldn't take his eyes off you. Of course, who can blame him?"

Her mood darkened. "I think I really hurt him, but I didn't expect him to fall for me that hard." She seemed to be pondering recent events for a bit, and then exclaimed, "My God! Can you imagine being called Mrs. Flam Grub?"

Paine exploded in a huge hyena laugh and Lucy, unable to resist, joined him with her own birdlike titters.

In his hidden spot, Flam was turning red with anger as their laughter seared him. He fantasized about leaping over the fence and pummelling the pair of them, but as always, he stayed meekly and mutely in hiding. He was still sitting there, shaking, after they'd raised the convertible's top and headed off, hand in hand, into the college. It was the same old story, the same ridicule he'd always encountered, Flam fumed, and his reviled name, as always, at the core of it.

For a brief minute the old dark thoughts came flooding back: *quit . . . run away . . . kill yourself!* He closed his eyes and fought hard for control, and then a thought crossed his mind—a bittersweet musing with the weightless grace of a bird, and yet the crushing mass of inexorable truth.

Opening his eyes, he glanced at his watch to gauge the time left before his exam, then reached into his binder. Instead of pulling out his school notes, however, Flam tore out a blank sheet of paper. Angrily he jotted down a short, dark poem, which railed against the cruelty of the world to the misfortunate everyman. While not completely satisfying, the exercise had a sufficiently therapeutic effect to enable Flam to pick himself up and get on with life's business.

CHAPTER 9

The optimism and bright certainty that had led Flam to Prentice College slowly began to dim as he wrote the last of his exams and faced graduation. Only a handful of funeral home positions found their way onto the college's Placement Office job board, and competition for those proved fierce, especially for the outclassed Flam.

Despite his peerless book smarts, the introverted Flam was a veritable dunce when it came to dealings in the real world, from which he had spent so much of his life hiding. He certainly possessed no practical experience or skills when it came to landing a job. He naïvely assumed his top grades would be enough to clinch a choice of offers, and did not realize getting hired hinged on making a strong impression during the interview process.

After a half-dozen failed interviews, it began to seem to Flam as if the prospective employers were all engaged in a conspiracy. The interviewers inevitably began the sessions by commenting on Flam's unusual name, thereby instantly putting him hopelessly on the defensive. Utterly lacking in confidence, he slumped, or squirmed in his chair, stammered, barely spoke above a whisper, and refused to look his inquisitors in the eye. Without exception, his few on-campus interviews proved unadulterated failures.

Lacking a network of personal contacts to draw upon, or the pluck and hustle to go cold-calling the local mortuaries, Flam soon exhausted all obvious prospects of employment within his chosen profession. Increasingly desperate as his last school days slid away, he widened his scope, applying for any job that remained on the bulletin board, no matter how unqualified he might be for it. Now failure seemed to spread like a cancer, for he was unable to land even the most menial of jobs.

Flam began to feel outright panic. The insurance money that had paid for his college education was all spent—in fact, he had not had enough left to buy a proper suit for his interviews, and the rumpled shirt and hand-me-down polyester tie in which he appeared for interviews had done nothing to help his prospects. The shining path of mortuary manifest destiny, on which he had been treading, was now turning out to be the slippery back of some treacherous cosmic serpent, threatening to send him tumbling back to the coal-black despair of earlier days . . . starting with the loss of his precious apartment.

Despite his domicile's miniscule size and shabby condition, he hated to give it up. After all those years without a room of his own, the apartment was a *sanctum sanctorum*, albeit a cluttered one filled completely with books, whose precariously balanced stacks ran the periphery of available wall space. Flam cherished the seclusion his apartment provided. It was a private, utterly safe world where no one could abuse or insult him. In fact, he hadn't had a single visitor since moving in—beyond his mother's initial requisite inspection. That visit had resulted in a nightmarish day spent together cleaning and scrubbing, with his teary-eyed parent alternating between fervid prayer and entreaties to her son not to leave her, and to commute to school instead. Now it appeared Mary's prayers had finally been answered, and Flam was damned to move back home.

It's not that he wasn't profoundly grateful to have reconciled with his mother. He knew—he felt—how that rekindled connection had rescued him from despair and allowed him, at the most root level, to deal with and move on from the miserable memories of childhood.

Perhaps that was the very reason he dreaded now having to move back in with her again.

Nevertheless, the first of May, with a new rent payment due, was only days away. Utterly dejected, yet resigned to his fate, Flam began busying himself to vacate his apartment. He first notified his mother he was moving back in with her, and although she was suitably mournful about his failure to find a funeral services job, her unbridled delight at Flam's pending return under her wing was all too evident.

"Don't worry, dear," Mary consoled him, "perhaps I can find you work at the parish. God willing, we may be able to spend our whole days together. Won't that be grand?" Flam swallowed a planetoid-sized lump that had sprung up in his throat, and although he would not have thought it possible, grew more disheartened.

He glumly inaugurated the moving process with a purging of his unwanted possessions. He packed up two boxfuls of assorted books that were no longer of interest to him, figuring he could give them to his old friend Page Turner, before heading upstairs to his mother's to drop off the first load of possessions.

Turner almost fell off his stool when Flam walked into the shop. Although it had been several years since the two had spoken, not counting a brief exchange of condolences at Steve Grub's funeral, the older man seized upon Flam like a long-lost son. The bookmonger locked him in a huge, rib-crunching bear hug, and then pinched his cheeks, as if greeting some precocious toddler. A spare chair was dug out from under its load of bookstore flotsam to allow the prodigal to sit and bring Turner up to date on the latest chapters in the Flam Grub story.

Turner had heard second-hand of Flam's career choice, and it was quite clear he had some misgivings. "I guess it's like lawyers," Turner groused, "the crooked ones give the whole profession a bad name . . . bloody vultures, preying on the distraught."

"It is a business, I can't deny that, but I really think we perform a valuable service. Or 'they' perform a valuable service, I should say . . . it seems the profession doesn't want me in it." And Flam went on to describe his futile attempts at securing employment, his forthcoming loss of the apartment, and his return to the flat upstairs.

"I guess you'll be seeing a little more of me. I don't suppose you know of any jobs that might be available in the neighbourhood . . . you know, just to make ends meet and maybe help me save up for first and last months' rent so I can get my own apartment again?"

Turner's face, at least as much as was visible beyond the forest of whiskers, lit up with delight. "Talk about coincidence . . . why, you can come and work for *me*. I was just going to draft up a classified ad when you so serendipitously walked through the door."

"But I've never known you to have a helper . . . you've always run the store yourself."

"Precisely the point. Of late, I've been focussing more on the trade in rare and antiquarian books, but that requires regularly closing the shop in order to keep appointments and go on book-buying expeditions. I've had many complaints from my regular customers. It would be extremely helpful to have someone behind the counter I could trust. And the summer season is upon us, after all, when I normally like to keep the store open well into the evenings."

"So, business is good?" Flam asked.

Turner's whiskers sagged downwards into a frown. "Frankly, the second-hand book trade is no longer what it used to be. It's too premature to pronounce the printed word as facing extinction, but as the poet said, 'The times they are a'changing.' A lot of the other shops in the area have already closed. Which is why I wouldn't be able to pay you a fortune, I'm afraid, but I can give you a plethora of hours." Turner turned to Flam with an impish grin. "Mind you, it's extremely boring much of the time—all there is to do is sit around amongst all these thousands of books . . . and read." He winked when he delivered that last piece, and it cemented the deal.

"Okay, well I do need a job . . . at least until I can land something in the funeral business . . . and this certainly is ideal. Thanks, Page, I appreciate it."

Turner leaned over to punch open the cash register, lifted the money tray, and from underneath fished out a wad of bills. "Clearly, you're fond of your tiny domicile, so why not retain it? Here's an advance against your wages so you can remit your rent." Flam hesitated, and Turner thrust the money closer, not budging.

Finally, Flam reddened, and reached out to accept the loan. For the first time in days, he felt resurrected and hopeful again. However, just as he was wondering whether his mother was home so he could break the news, a potential problem surfaced, temporarily deflating his good spirits. Although Flam would be able now to manage the rent on his apartment, how was he supposed to rationalize commuting all that distance daily, when his mother could offer free accommodation right above the workplace?

It was Turner who devised a solution. "Surely that vocational academy of yours must offer a veritable cornucopia of night courses, even during the summer," he counselled. "Why not simply sign up for one or two, and then explain to your mother that you're still taking classes for extra credit. It won't technically be a prevarication."

There were, as it turned out, hundreds of courses offered through Prentice College's School of Continuing Education, so many so that Flam had difficulty figuring out what to choose. There were even some additional Funeral Services courses available he could take, like Advanced Restoration Techniques, which he had previously bypassed in favour of a progressive course on grief counselling.

Flam ultimately dismissed this option, rationalizing that an extra credit or two would not necessarily guarantee improved job prospects, given how poorly he had already fared despite his stellar grades. There were instead scores of general interest courses available that he found much more appealing. He could learn to do computer graphics, speak another language, study automotive repair, or take introductory offerings in one of the Humanities.

A course in Comparative Religion kept leaping off the page at Flam each time he passed it in the college calendar, and this was the one he finally opted to take. He rationalized it to Turner as a vocational choice, saying that if he ever managed to land a job in his field, the course would be helpful in understanding the different belief systems of the bereaved clients he might be called upon to minister to in a future role.

In fact, the truth lay much deeper. He had never been satisfied with his own Catholic experience, which his mother had practically force-fed him from an early age. Only once, as a boy, had he briefly tasted religious rapture, and that had been on the day of his First Communion.

He vividly remembered standing there in a brand new suit, bought specially for the occasion, and sporting a glossy white silk bow, so exquisitely smooth to the touch, wrapped around his sleeve. His hands had been sheathed in spotless white gloves, and in them, he'd held his very own Bible and rosary. On either side of him had stood a beautiful young girl, angelic in her immaculate white dress of satin and lace.

As Flam had tilted back his head to receive the communion wafer, he had been enveloped by the sun pouring in through the multicoloured mantles of the stained-glass saints, and had felt himself truly filled with the spirit of the Holy Ghost. For a rare moment, he had believed that, to God, Flam's soul was indeed special—something pure and unique to be prized.

But Flam's new suit, the last he would own until he acquired the black uniforms of his funerary profession, had for months been the catalyst for some especially vicious sparring at home. Mary had wrung the extra dollars for its purchase from the beer budget of a reluctant Steve. So, not surprisingly, it caused an uproar when Flam appeared a few short hours after the communion service, bleeding, dishevelled, and with his new suit hopelessly torn and soiled after an attack by two of the other boys receiving the sacrament. Flam had been vehemently reprimanded and severely spanked by both his mother and his father in a rare display of parental solidarity.

Amidst the tears, Flam had tried desperately to explain to his parents that he was guiltless, that he had been clinging to the ecstasy of a spotless soul and had tried to avoid the confrontation— had literally turned the other cheek when smote—but this had only served to provoke the other boys further. They had fallen upon him shouting, "God don't allow grubs into Heaven," and had taken it upon themselves—dutiful, newly anointed junior lieutenants of Jesus that they were—to enforce His will with their fists.

Later, during his voracious readings, Flam had grown even more disillusioned with Catholicism. He had read, with disgust, albeit also with rapt fascination, about the schisms and wars and hypocrisy and political infighting that had dogged Christian dogma since its inception. He'd also learned with horror of the violence and cruelty that had been his religion's trademark—the massacres of the Crusades, the brutal torture technology of the Inquisition, the roasting alive on spits of Jews during Church-led medieval pogroms—all in the name of Christ.

And once books had also explained the birds and the bees to Flam (for neither parent had troubled to do so), and then further catalogued all of sexuality's perversions and diversions, Flam had come to view with quite a different perspective those times in Sunday school when Father Dickinson had so lovingly anointed with salve the bare boy bottoms he had enthusiastically caned only minutes earlier.

Yet, despite the disillusionment and cynicism Flam had come to feel over his own particular brand of religion, he still clung to enough fundamental faith not to throw the baby out with the baptismal bathwater. That moment of divine ecstasy he'd encountered on his Confirmation Sunday, even if it had been the precursor to a particularly painful episode of abuse and humiliation, was not something to be denied. God was lurking out there somewhere, waiting to be discovered, of that Flam was convinced. Perhaps the course in Comparative Religion might help to find Him.

CHAPTER 10

Working behind the counter of the bookstore made it easier for Flam to see his mother on a regular basis. Now, instead of trying to find a mutually convenient time when she wasn't at a service, or a church function, or performing one of the myriad duties for which she indefatigably volunteered, Flam had only to sit quietly on his stool, reading a book, and wait for Mary to appear to him.

Typically, she would go upstairs and make a pot of tea, and bring it down for them to share, along with some pastry left over from one church function or another. Mother and son would sit together and make small talk, mostly low-key gossip about the goings on in the neighbourhood, or the latest happenings at the church.

Increasingly, Gerald Strait's name would surface, always in some incidental, oh-by-the-way role in Mary's rambling chatter. Flam began to suspect his mother, having been through her prerequisite period of mourning, was pursuing a relationship with the good pharmacist.

The suspicion bore fruit when Gerald himself turned up escorting Mary on one of her visits to the bookstore. As he shook hands with Flam, the pharmacist appeared as ill at ease as a teenager meeting his date's parents for the first time. Later, as Mary launched into a prolific and detailed testimonial of Gerald's assets and accomplishments, he stood shifting his weight nervously from leg to leg, then, bored with that, he leaned on the glass display case and scrutinized the books there with fierce concentration.

He was a tall, unhappy-looking man, a head higher and several years older than Mary, with grey thinning hair that had been shepherded carefully towards the baldest patches, and sagging jowls that jiggled when he talked. One ear seemed to be lower than the other, and the round, gold-rimmed glasses he wore tilted as a consequence, requiring him to constantly push them back into proper position with his index finger.

One thing was patently clear, however. Gerald was totally enamoured of Mary, who, even though she was now in her forties, was still quite an attractive woman. She had maintained her slim figure through constant worry, and her red hair through the help of Miss Clairol's Autumn Auburn (bought discreetly at a drugstore other than Gerald's). On several occasions, Flam caught Gerald staring at Mary with a look of utter delight, his eyes flitting over the features of her face with unabashed adoration.

It was a busy afternoon in the bookstore, and Flam was alone minding the shop, so he had to regularly excuse himself from entertaining his guests in order to ring up a sale or show a customer where a particular section was located. For some reason, this seemed to visibly annoy Gerald. Flam found that surprising, given that the pharmacist, of all people, should be empathetic to the demands of customer service.

Flam began to get the feeling there was something else in the air, that Mary and Gerald wanted to broach a subject with him. Finally, when a lull overtook the shop, the pharmacist cleared his throat and attempted to get to the crux of the matter.

"Even though I was married for twelve years before my dear wife, God bless her soul, passed on, the good Lord never saw fit to bless us with children of our own." Gerald paused briefly at this point, as if wrestling with some great inner pain, and Mary touched his arm in encouragement. Flam just stared blankly, wondering where this was going.

Gerald continued, "You're not a child anymore, you're an adult now . . . why you even have your own apartment, and very soon I imagine, a bright future in a solid, respectable profession. But I want you to know I'll think of you as if you're my own flesh and blood . . . ."

Mary interjected, clearly exasperated by Gerald's rambling tack. "Oh, Gerald, you're putting the cart before the horse." She turned to her son and explained, "Mr. Strait has asked me to marry him, Flam. We thought perhaps next spring."

"I wouldn't expect you to call me Dad . . . well, that is, not unless you want to," Gerald resumed, "and of course the name change would be entirely up to you."

"Name change!" Flam exclaimed, blinking hard, trying to process all the information inundating him.

Mary pressed her body closer to Gerald's, as if to show that in this matter they stood united. "We thought, dear, since I was going to change my name, that you might want to take Mr. Strait's surname too."

They paused and waited for a reaction, but Flam stood silent, his mental gears slipping as they tried to mesh. Slowly his wits returned. He leaned over the counter to embrace his mother, then took Gerald's hand and shook it enthusiastically.

"Well, congratulations . . . I mean, I'm really happy for you two. That's great. Really fantastic." He was working so hard to paint a smile on his face, he could feel his cheeks start to ache. But although outwardly he was managing to preserve a veneer of sincerity and buoyancy, in reality, Flam was awash in a whirlpool of confusion, and was not at all sure what he was really feeling.

True, he had harboured no love for his dead father. Steve, even at his absolute best, had been a callous, neglectful reprobate, and during his blackest moments had been an outright terror and tormentor to his family. Moreover, since the enmity between mother and son had thawed after Steve's death, Flam had come to project most of the blame for the misery of his childhood onto his father, choosing to suppress the reality that Mary had often been equally guilty of verbal abuse, and had, in general, been cold to her son.

Mary had, nevertheless, performed the perfunctory requirements of nurturing Flam—had been the one who'd fed and bathed and clothed the child, and had provided some degree of cursory comfort. Steve, brutish and violent by nature, had been the more overt and painfully memorable in his physical and psychological assaults.

Flam was grateful to now have a mother to whom he could feel close, the first step perhaps in some sort of cosmic reparations he felt fate owed him for the misery and deprivation of his life. He knew in his heart he should feel pleased his mother had a second chance at happiness with someone else, and that she would know companionship and intimacy in her middle years instead of loneliness.

But other feelings also washed over Flam now, jostling for command of his emotional state. He felt resentful of the man threatening to spirit away the only affection Flam possessed. He was also experiencing jealousy of his mother, who was feeling the splendour of requited love and the soul-lifting joy of planning a new life with someone—a joy Flam had once longed to share with Lucy. He also felt instinctively threatened on some subliminal primate level by Gerald, this outsider who had appeared to challenge Flam for dominance of their tiny tribe.

All these conflicting emotions tugged at Flam as he congratulated his mother and stepfather-to-be, but the feelings that were hardest to reconcile and truly fathom for Flam were the ones conjured up by the suggestion he might change his name. So ingrained, so primal was the hatred of his name, that just evoking it as a topic of discussion had unleashed a torrent of latent memories and emotions, throwing him off his equilibrium.

A lifetime of self-preserving reflexes instantly kicked in, and made him want to close his ears, to run away—or at least to change the subject, as he had, in fact, instantly done by launching into his congratulatory performance. But, having been exposed to the light of day, the unexpected prospect of salvation from the lifelong curse of "Flam Grub" could not now be ignored. Even without fully admitting it to himself, inside his mind he was trying on the new name, turning it over, and feeling its nature.

Flam Strait . . . Flam Strait, he thought. *Is that a better name?* But no revelation, no great relief or gratitude overtook him. *Why am I not overjoyed*, he wondered, *what am I really feeling?* But he already knew the answer. It had not been the Grub surname alone that had haunted him. Despite his mother's oft-voiced love for her legendary ancestors, "Flam" had always led the way in his suffering. That oddity of a first name had instantly centred him out, and because it was so easy to rhyme and pun with, had been an equal partner in the abuse conjured up by the world around him. Would merely changing surnames be enough? A long-suffering veteran like Flam knew better, and he automatically foresaw new fodder for his future tormentors. "Flam Damn Straight" and "Straitjacket" came instantly to mind. No, Flam was utterly unconvinced there would be any salvation for him in this name change.

Perhaps he would have been more open to the idea were it not for the underlying offence he intrinsically felt from the whole proposal. This had not been conceived purely to alleviate Flam's personal pain. On the few occasions in boyhood when Flam had sought solace from Mary over the name calling by the other children, her reaction had been brusque and unsympathetic. She had instructed him to turn the other cheek, and to take pride in his name—specifically the Flam half. He had eventually given up trying to confide his pain and humiliation to his mother, and doubted whether she truly understood how much he'd suffered over the years.

In Flam's mind, Mary and Gerald were simply treating him like a child, whose care represented another administrative detail in their relationship that needed to be resolved to fit the new scheme of things. In the process, the pair was refusing to acknowledge the fact that he was now an adult, entitled to manage his own affairs and make his own decisions. True, they had not demanded outright that Flam change his name, but the very fact they had taken it upon themselves to propose it showed how little they acknowledged his right to self-determination. It proved that Gerald believed he was entitled to some degree of control over Flam, simply by marrying his mother.

Flam soon exhausted his repertoire of contrived congratulations, and, striving hard to conceal his mounting annoyance at the affront the happy couple had committed with their offer, fell into an awkward silence as a blush bloomed on his pale face. The enthusiasm he had just feigned ended up working against him. Gerald seemed to sense some advantage in the pause, and having received no noticeable opposition to his proposal, pressed the matter further.

"There will be some legal details that would need to be tended to, of course. Petitions to the court for the name change, of course. Your mother tells me you've reached the age of majority so I'm not sure whether we can legally file for adoption. But I have an excellent lawyer. Anyway, she can handle all the details, so you wouldn't have to worry about a thing. And, of course, I would pay for everything."

Even the habitually passive Flam could not suffer the perceived insult any longer.

"I don't want to change my name . . . you can't make me," he blurted out with more of a whine than a shout. He turned to square off face to face with Gerald, but his eyes refused to cooperate fully and the eyeballs, traitors to the rebellion, skulked at the edges, studying the rows of books instead of bravely taking on the enemy, giving Flam a wild, animal look.

Gerald looked bewildered, then angry, and exchanged a what-did-I-tell-you look with Mary. "Well nobody's making you," the prospective stepfather offered, "your mother . . .."

Mary quickly interceded, closing ranks and taking Gerald by the arm. "It was my idea, dear. I just wanted us to be a family, that's all. You understand, I'm sure. But take all the time you need to decide. It would mean so much to me . . . to us." This was clearly not the way she had wanted things to go, and now she evidently felt caught in the middle.

Flam sensed her discomfort and instantly regretted his outburst. "Well, I'll think it over," he offered, although inwardly he had made up his mind, and the matter was permanently closed as far as he was concerned. A change of subject was in order. "So . . . when's the wedding?" Flam asked, trying his best not to betray the tumult playing out inside of him.

The couple exchanged a pair of goofy grins and pressed closer together. "We haven't really set a date yet," Gerald said. "I mean, yesterday wouldn't be soon enough for me, but your mother, calm head that she always is, has a much better sense of things, and feels a proper engagement is in order." He took Mary's hand and showed it to Flam, flipping the palm over to reveal a modest-sized but tasteful engagement ring, proof that all proper protocols and steps were being followed.

"We have the rest of our lives together, Gerald, darling," Mary giggled, suddenly looking years younger in Flam's eyes. "There's no need to rush into anything. Besides, no need to give the rumourmongers in the parish any extra fuel for their fire . . . they'll have plenty to say as it is."

She retrieved her hand and stood up on tiptoes to offer Gerald a kiss on the lips as a reward for his consideration. Flam was shocked to see their lips stay pressed firmly together for several seconds, and their hands begin to gravitate towards each other's body.

Flam had a sudden disturbing image of the two of them, naked and entwined together, executing one of the more exotic positions from the *Kama Sutra*, several copies of which resided in the bookstore. He was immensely relieved when the pair broke off their embrace and restored an aura of propriety.

"We should have dinner to celebrate, and get to know each other better, um, Flam," Gerald proposed. "Are you doing anything tonight?"

"Oh, not tonight, it's Flam's school night," Mary responded before Flam could even open his mouth. "How about Saturday night, dear?"

Flam was grateful for the reprieve his night class offered, yet realized that dinner—and another discussion about his name—had only been postponed. He was greatly tempted to invent an excuse for Saturday night as well, but knew a celebratory dinner could not be avoided indefinitely. As unappealing as the prospect of spending an evening facing off against his mother and her overbearing new paramour seemed, he saw no escape. Ultimately, he told himself, the matter will have to be dealt with, and they will have to see things my way. But he felt far from valiant, dreading the encounter.

"Saturday night's fine," Flam relented, generating a pair of radiant synchronized smiles from Mary and Gerald. "The shop closes around seven." He was going to suggest a nearby bistro that Page Turner recommended highly, but Gerald instantly took charge.

"Great," the future stepfather beamed. "I'll make reservations at Eddie Spaghetti's. We'll be like one cozy, happy family, just the three of us. That is, unless you want to bring someone . . . a date. She'd be more than welcome."

Flam reddened, instantly embarrassed by the fact there was absolutely no one, not even a causal friend, he could call on to be an escort for the occasion. The bleak mantle of his loneliness wrapped itself around him once again, its familiar dark weight smothering his composure. But he could feel himself being watched, and forced a half-hearted smile, trying hard to make his reply sound casual.

"That's okay . . . why don't we just keep it a family affair?" Whether it was the exclusion of any strangers, or Flam's reference to him as family, the reply had Gerald beaming from ear to lopsided ear.

The next day, when a lull appeared in their shopkeepers' duties, Flam broached the subject of a possible name change with Page Turner. He supplemented the topic with a tirade about how much he hated his own name, and confessed the anguish and humiliation he felt it had caused him throughout his life.

"As long as I can remember, it's caused me nothing but suffering, especially at school. You have no idea how much real pain can come from something as intangible as a name," Flam complained, relieved to finally be unburdening his longstanding suffering. If he had expected unconditional sympathy from his boss, though, he was quickly disappointed.

"Oh, grow up! Do you really think you're the only child who ever suffered in the schoolyard? With a name like Page Turner, don't you think I encountered some serious abuse in my day? I think mostly it was because Page was considered to be a girl's name, but I can't remember for sure, it was a long time ago. All I know is that it doesn't take much for a kid to become a target. There was a time when I would have given *anything* to have a so-called normal name . . . no matter what it was . . . just so long as I wouldn't stand out . . . so I would be more like everyone else."

Page stroked his beard as he digested the memories. "Now I've done a complete about-face on the subject. I may not have chosen my name, but I believe in a way it chose me. Certainly, I've come to accept that, in some not altogether insignificant way, it's had an influence on the areas of interest I chose, and on where I ended up in life."

"But Page Turner is such a *cool* name," Flam protested, "not like this abomination that I'm stuck with."

"That's just the point, Flam, you're not stuck with it. If you really hate it so much, then go ahead and change it," Turner countered.

Flam reddened, earlier anger at Gerald's presumptiveness and bossiness instantly flooding back. "Screw that . . . I'm not going to change my name to Flam Strait just because my mother's getting herself a new husband."

"No, that's not much of an improvement," Turner agreed, "and I certainly don't think you should be forced to accept a stepfather's name you don't want, as if you're a calf changing brands. But what I meant was that you can choose absolutely any name you want, and then adopt it legally. Well, *almost* any name. I know there are some oddities and obscenities even our enlightened legal system will not allow, but beyond that, the sky's the limit, from Aaron to Zachary."

The idea of acquiring a different name was not altogether new to Flam, but in the past, it had been only an abstraction contemplated during some of his saddest moments. That fantasy had provided an occasional escape from a sadistic universe. It was usually accompanied by imaginary rich and loving parents who turned up, like avenging angels, to take home the long lost son who'd been switched at birth with the real Flam Grub. Now, the reality struck him that there was, in fact, absolutely nothing preventing him from taking on any name he chose.

Flam spun on his stool and faced the lines of books, all categorized, alphabetized, and arrayed on their shelves. He thought of the thousands of characters he had encountered in his literary excursions, and about the authors who had created them. Perhaps from among this collection of names he might find or forge one for himself—give birth to a bold new label that reflected his beliefs and sensitive nature, and would serve as the harbinger of a new phase in Flam's thus-far pitiful life.

Turner was apparently doing some contemplating of his own. "Good heavens," he finally offered, "where would you begin? Think of all the possibilities . . . of all the names out there to choose from."

"Mind you," Turner continued, "you can probably eliminate 95 per cent of humanity's names right off the bat . . . that is unless you're planning to adopt another culture at the same time. I used to have a grandmother who loved to watch the closing credits of television shows just so she could show off her knowledge of the world by calling out the ethnicity of the names. 'O'Brien—Irish. Goldstein—Jewish. Bertucci—Italian. Ramashandram—East Indian. LaFleur—French. VanVeer—Dutch.'" Turner chuckled as he remembered. "She was always a little hesitant with Lee, though—never knew whether it was someone Chinese or the descendant of a Confederate general."

Turner swivelled to face his assistant. "What nationality are you, Flam?" he inquired. "I know your mother's Irish, but what about your dad? What kind of name is Grub?"

Flam coloured at the mere mention of his despised surname. "I don't think my father even knew for sure," he replied. "He was raised in an orphanage, and that surname was all that was left behind when he was dumped there. There was some talk it was anglicized from Grubbini or Grubov or Gruber when his family first came over, but all that's just speculation."

"Well, half a family tree's better than none. If you want to pay homage to your Irish roots, perhaps you can be an O'Something or a McSomething . . . hey, how about McCool, as in Finn McCool, the great folk hero of Irish mythology?"

"Hmm . . . sounds like an ice cream bar you'd find under the golden arches. Besides, doesn't the 'Mc' actually mean 'son of' or something like that? I don't know, I just wouldn't feel right taking a name that overtly claims I belong by lineage to another Irish clan . . . it would be, well, a lie."

Turner frowned. "You're being too hard on yourself, I think. Any new name you adopt would in some sense be a lie . . . well, except 'Stevenson' I guess, since your father was called Steve, although I suspect you'd rather not pay that kind of tribute to him. But I doubt if you should take *any* name literally. After all, how many Fishers have ever cast a net, or how many Coopers have actually built a barrel? Funny, isn't it, how so many of those basic Anglo-Saxon names are derived from old professions . . . Smith, Miller, Archer, Mason, Potter, Wright, Bailey."

This last statement sent the pair back into contemplation, and they sat there silently, sipping their coffees and watching the parade of passersby on the street, who were framed by the bookstore's large arched window like the figures in some animated, shifting painting. All of a sudden, Flam was acutely aware that every individual who moved for a moment through his view carried a name with its own associated history, each one not only a chain intertwined with the past, but also staking a unique presence in the here and now.

I doubt if any of these people hate their name as much as I do, Flam thought. *Maybe some are immigrants, or the children of immigrants, who have opted to change their names, or adopt another for everyday use . . . but they probably hate the prejudiced society that forces them to do so, not the name itself. Most people probably don't even give their names a second thought, even if they have to publicly reveal them many times a day. Oh, why was I so accursed?*

As Flam lamented his fate, Turner had come up with another idea. "How about choosing a name that ties you in with that natural world so often lauded by poets, say like Hill, or Woods, or Waters, Stone, Forest, Lake . . . or, for that matter, Night or Day. They're all simple and common, but I think they're also very strong—one might almost say primal."

Flam mentally explored these new possibilities, and then abruptly laughed. "Well, technically speaking, Grub ties me to the natural world too . . . the world of insects."

"Okay then," Turner persisted, "what's your favourite colour? There are several popular surnames based on colours—Brown, Green, Grey, Black, White."

Despite Turner's sincerity, again the options ended up making Flam laugh. "Actually, my favourite colour is purple . . . but I don't think I'd pick it for a surname, although it wouldn't surprise me one bit if there were hundreds of people out there bearing that name. Still, I suppose I'd gladly take *any* one of those other colours for a name instead."

Turner seemed pleased they had made a modicum of progress, and took another slurp of his coffee before moving on to address the other part of the equation. "Then, of course, there's the matter of the first name. Again, there are so many to choose from. Is there any one, perhaps, you have long harboured a preference for?"

"Anything's better than Flam . . . but I can't say I've ever favoured one in particular."

"Historically speaking, many of our most popular names come from the Bible, although some of the Old Testament prophets that were all the rage a couple of centuries ago, like Ezekiel and Jebediah, have fallen out of favour. No, I think you'll perhaps want to turn to the Apostles and the writers of the Gospels for the most popular choices—Thomas, John, Peter, Paul, Mark, Matthew, Simon, Luke, James—all solid, familiar, no-nonsense names. Well, except for Judas, of course . . . not a name you would voluntarily take on, even if his role was perhaps the most important, in many ways, of the whole entourage."

Flam shook his head. "No, I'd almost prefer Flam, although I suppose you could go by Jude for short. Hmmm, I guess even a James has to decide whether he'll go by Jim, or Jimmy, or Jamie . . . or Jimbo, for that matter."

"Depends on the environment they're from, or even the profession they choose, I guess," Turner offered, "although I suppose it's often just what you get used to, or whatever becomes habitual to those around you. Still, it's somehow hard now to think of Jimi Hendrix as James Hendrix . . . or James Joyce as Jim Joyce."

"Just one more factor for me to consider," Flam sighed, "and technically, it only increases the number of options I'd have to consider, since my name wouldn't have a lifetime to naturally evolve from, say, a Richard to a Dick."

Outside, the sun had shifted during their conversation, so that the rays were now reflecting brightly off a second-storey windowpane somewhere across the street, and spilling in unabashedly through the north-facing store window, bathing the conversationalists in a rare solar splendour.

"Ah, and we haven't even touched upon middle names," Turner pointed out, closing his eyes to bask in the surprising gift of sunlight. "Some people have several . . . I seem to recall reading about a man who fully had a dozen middle names, each one with some special significance to family history."

"I don't know. Maybe it's because I never had one, but middle names have always struck me as a way to appease relatives, or as a consolation prize to the runners-up in the name-choosing game."

"You are wise beyond your years, my young friend," Turner chuckled, raising his coffee mug in a toast, "although middle names shouldn't be so easily dismissed. In Russia, for example, the middle name is often patronymic . . . meaning it's based on the father's name, so a boy whose father was called Ivan might have Ivanovich as a middle name, or the daughter Ivanova. At the same time, the middle name forms part of the most familiar form of address. The mother might then call her daughter fully Natalia Ivanova at those times when she's being most loving and intimate. But, if nothing else, a middle name can certainly provide an instant substitute to those who dislike their first name. Like you, my folks never gave me one . . . maybe they thought it would spoil the Page Turner gag . . . but I might be standing before you as a Tom or Frank if I'd had a second choice beyond Page."

"Of course, there's also the tradition of providing an alternative form of a name by just using the initials, like T.S. Eliot, or e.e.

cummings," Flam added. "But, damn, that just makes a choice that much more complicated!"

He returned to silently scrutinizing the volumes that ran in rows before his eyes. "Maybe you're right. The answer for me might very well lie somewhere in those books. Perhaps I could combine a couple of my favourite writers to create a new name that pays tribute to them. Hmmm . . . let me see. How about Marlowe Shelley? Or Blake Chaucer?" His lips tightened as he mentally journeyed through the legions of authors and poets he had encountered over the years.

Some of the names that surfaced seemed to stir Flam's thoughts in a new direction. "Mind you, some of those names still deserve to be avoided, no matter how famous their owners may have become. Why do you suppose parents do what they do, I mean giving kids a name that's obviously going to be problematic? Like giving a boy a girl's name . . . Joyce Cary, or Evelyn Waugh, for example. Can't the parents see they're going to cause embarrassment and suffering to their child? Don't they actually sound the name out loud and picture the reaction it's going to have with the other children?"

"It's hard to say whether they're simply oblivious, or perhaps they're actually trying to bestow some deeper lesson upon their children about the nature of individuality," Turner offered. "After all, both of the writers you mentioned managed to succeed despite their names. Some might even suggest *because* of them. And perhaps there's the moral. When we're young, we strive for conformity . . . we'll give anything to fit in with the others. But for a lot of those who aspire to excellence in some field of human endeavour, say become a renowned artist or a famous athlete, they'll ultimately bear any unusual name like it's some special badge or title—the final crowning touch distinguishing them from the pack of mediocrity."

Flam sighed, and pressed his palms against his forehead as if to stem a tide of thoughts that was threatening to overwhelm him. "Sorry, but I can't see my name ever being something I'd be proud of. It's caused me nothing but grief and suffering. I'm going to think seriously about changing it . . . if I can ever come up with a new one."

Outside, the sun had moved on, and the bookstore returned to its habitual gloomier state. But the far side of the street was still bathed brightly in the waning sunrays, and Flam noticed the riot of names that seemed to be spotlit everywhere, on storefronts and the sides of trucks, on street signs and billboards, as if mocking him.

Out on the street, an older, dapperly dressed couple stopped and examined the books on display in the front window—a haphazard collection of literary jewels Turner had selected and arranged to entice upscale customers into the shop. After some contemplation and a quietly exchanged conversation, the pair entered the shop. Turner rose in anticipation of being of service. As he did so, he turned to Flam with a mischievous smile.

"I've got one for you, given your choice of profession," Turner chuckled, "although I doubt I'm the first to think of it. How about Phil Graves?"

CHAPTER 11

The class that night started punctually at 6:30 p.m., making Flam glad the insider knowledge of the building's geography from his fulltime student days had allowed him to find the room without trouble, and arrive in time to grab a good seat. He looked around the room, evaluating the dozen-or-so fellow students who had chosen to give up their summer's Wednesday nights in order to take a Comparative Religion class.

There was one other student around his own age, but overall it was a much older group. It included one shriveled-up and hunched-over, white-bearded gnome of a man in the back. *Maybe religion is something most people don't start paying serious attention to until they're nearing the end*, Flam thought, causing him to reflect on why he then had ended up there.

The instructor, a gangly and grim-looking man in his fifties, introduced himself as Professor Abbott. His gaze seemed permanently fixed on a spot high on the back wall, and he stood virtually motionless as he talked, with his hands pressed in front as if he were praying. Flam thought at first this was a contrived theatrical device, given the course's subject matter, but eventually came to the conclusion this was an unconscious habit of the teacher's.

"The objective of this course is to assist you in developing an informed appreciation for the spiritual traditions of humankind as manifested in the most influential and widely recognized religions of the world," Professor Abbott began, giving Flam the distinct impression his new teacher was reciting well-worn words from rote, as if talking in his sleep. This impression was strengthened by the professor's naturally uninterested and droopy-eyed look.

As Flam looked around for something else in the class that might be worthy of his attention, his gaze was captured by a woman a few seats over. She was furiously making notes, even though the professor was simply regurgitating the course syllabus, a copy of which he had already handed out to the class.

The woman had a high-cheeked, angular face, and a close-cut crop of snow-white hair sticking off the top of her head in a riot of pronounced spikes. Despite the white hair colour, however, she appeared to be only in her thirties. She wore mauve lip-gloss, which highlighted full, pouty lips, but her large, hazel-coloured eyes, liberally accented with eyeliner and mascara, were the most noticeable feature.

Her appearance was made even more striking by the fact she was also dressed completely in white, including the pantyhose under her flowing floor-length skirt. They were visible only because she had hoisted her legs up onto the seat, and was sitting cross-legged, while she continued to rapidly jot things down in a large, ornate, hard-covered notebook, also white.

Despite her unorthodox appearance, Flam decided the woman was quite attractive. As he studied her, she suddenly looked up, as if she knew she was being watched, catching Flam in the act. Before he had a chance to look away, she suddenly smiled at him with the sort of sweet, familiar grin lovers might share upon seeing one another across a crowded room. The woman added a little wink before resuming her enthusiastic notetaking.

Flam realized he was blushing and forced his attention back to the deadpan Professor Abbott. The teacher was still standing in the same stiff pose, staring off into space with hands pressed in front of his chest like a carved graveyard angel, droning on in an emotionless monotone.

"I must emphasize," Abbott was saying, without any emphasis whatsoever, "this course is not intended to try to convert you to any one religion. Nor will I endeavour in any way to convince you to reject any particular religion, or for that matter to discard all religion in general. Now, I will hand out the reading list, which includes the required course texts plus a number of optional books I strongly urge you to read." Despite the admonition, there was nothing strong or urging in Abbott's oratory.

Flam chanced another glance at the woman, but as soon as he started his observation she again caught his gaze and smiled, as if some secret sense had alerted her to Flam's attentions. Her smile was so friendly, and her look so inviting, that this time, despite his natural bashfulness and the frenzied drumbeat of his heart, Flam offered a slight smile of his own and maintained eye contact for several seconds until the circulating handouts reached him and demanded his attention. When he looked back, the woman had returned to her fervid scribbling, even though Professor Abbott was standing silently, waiting for the papers' distribution to be completed.

Flam found the rest of the introductory lecture disappointing. Whether it was because of Professor Abbott's expressionless demeanour and uninspired presentation, or the distraction of the woman in white, at whom Flam kept peeking in hopes of once again exchanging even a fleeting glance, the class totally lacked the spiritual stimulation and revelatory quality he had hoped to find.

Give it a chance, give it a chance, he kept telling himself, *it's only the first lecture.* But within a half-hour, after establishing the woman was not going to smile or even look at him again, Flam found himself all but tuning out the lacklustre teacher, and instead toying with a limerick, which started: "A glum-faced professor called Abbott." After an hour had painfully dragged out, Flam was contemplating dropping the course and getting a refund, and wondering how he'd conceal that fact from his mother without lying.

When Professor Abbott mercifully announced their mid-lecture break, the woman in white sprung from her seat and made a beeline straight for Flam. Her long white skirt billowed around her and made her resemble some Christmas pageant angel, lacking only cardboard wings and an aluminum foil halo to complete the effect.

"Hi, I'm Angel," she announced, the synchronicity of her name with his thoughts making him smile. She casually reached out to squeeze his arm, and then plunged onward before Flam could utter a word in response. "I saw you looking over earlier and I'm convinced we're connected on the spiritual plane . . . it really feels like our souls are drawn to each other. I have to be honest—and I bet you hear this all the time—but I am *totally* blown away by the size of your . . .."

She stopped abruptly at this point, and held up her finger in a just-a-minute gesture, leaving Flam hanging in suspense and completely confused. Angel suddenly squeezed her eyes tight and let go a girlish sneeze. Still keeping her eyes closed, she raised her hands up to shoulder height, rotated the palms outward, and chanted a handful of strange words under her breath that were totally foreign to Flam. Finally, she reopened her eyes, smiled innocently, and resumed talking, her words flowing and tumbling from her non-stop, like spring water down a brook.

". . . the size of your aura, omigosh it's *huge* and, wow, it has such really cool colours too. I've never seen one like it. I can just tell that you're the most amazing guy. So, what do you think of the course so far? Abbott is so interesting, don't you think?"

Angel kept right on talking incessantly while Flam just stood, mouth agape, unable to respond or slip in a word, even though every second sentence was posed to him as a question. In fact, he was relieved that her unending stream of words allowed him to avoid having to reveal his name.

As she continued to merrily babble, Flam studied Angel more intensely. She was shorter than she'd appeared in her seat, barely coming up to his chin, and had an ample bosom, which sloped down to an enticingly slim waist. He saw from her eyebrows, despite the fact they'd seemingly been dyed at one point as well, that she was naturally a brunette, making him wonder why she had opted for pure white as a hair colour.

All of her fingers and both thumbs were covered in an eclectic collection of hand-crafted rings, some quite large, all of fine silver and worked intricately into exotic flowing shapes and runes. A few of the symbols Flam recognized from his readings, but most were totally unfamiliar. Each wrist was likewise adorned with several silver bracelets. When she lifted her hand and sent the jewellery sliding down her arm with a soft, musical tinkling, it revealed, coiled completely around her right wrist, a tattooed *ouroboros*, with the juncture where the artfully inked serpent's mouth swallowed its own tail appearing on the soft inside of her wrist.

She had a constant, childlike smile, and a persistent habit of familiarly stroking his arm as she spoke. This, plus an intoxicating scent—not really a perfume but some unusual yet pleasant organic soap or lotion—all combined to create an instant aphrodisiacal effect on Flam. This effect was made stronger still since, as Flam had quickly noticed, the buxom Angel was not wearing a bra. He had to work hard to keep from gawking at the protuberance of her nipples that was easily visible through the taut fabric of her satiny white blouse.

He was standing there mesmerized by her charms when she grabbed his arm and shook him from his reverie. "Hey, look at the time! We should grab a coffee or something before class starts again," she suddenly suggested, abruptly changing the course of her monologue yet again. But now she began to look around, as if searching for someone, and Flam's heart dropped instantly when he heard her say, "Where's Joe? We should ask him along too . . . he's *such* a sweetie. Oh, there he is."

Flam was unexpectedly stabbed by jealousy and glanced over to see who she was looking at. He naturally expected the worst, and immediately hated himself for naively believing again that an attractive female's attentions were anything more than casual friendliness. His fears seemed to be confirmed when he saw a tall, good-looking, fair-haired man in his thirties presiding over a clique of their classmates, and looking over with obvious interest when Angel floated towards that group. To Flam's delight, Angel did not so much as glance in the blond man's direction. Joe proved instead to be the wizened, hunched-over old-timer Flam had noticed earlier. Angel quickly wrapped her arm around the little fellow's shoulders, and guided him back to where Flam was standing.

As he loomed over the small old man, Flam noticed for the first time that Joe, in addition to his beard, wore a *yarmulke* nestled onto the back of his head, and found it commendable that a devout Jew of the old school had the curiosity to take a Comparative Religion class. But there was no time for Flam to comment on this as Angel neither offered nor allowed introductions, and instead, casually slipped in between the pair of oddly-matched males and, taking her newly acquired escorts arm in arm, proceeded to guide them without resistance towards the coffee kiosk. She babbled merrily the whole way about how she'd once been an Elizabethan midwife and nurse in a past life, and felt certain the three of them had known each other intimately in that period.

There was something alluring and stimulating, yet at the same time relaxing, about Angel's presence. Flam was content to be passively carried along by the spirit and energy of her inexorable mile-a-minute personality. So it also seemed was Joe, because a wide, amused smile never left his extraordinarily wrinkled face. As he shuffled along at a surprisingly lively pace, he continued to beam up at the girl, for despite her short stature, no more than 5-foot-2, Flam reckoned, Angel was still an inch or so taller than the elfin Joe.

Flam tried on a couple of occasions to answer one of Angel's constant rhetorical questions, or make a contribution to one of her trains of thought. So did Joe, but both soon found it was pointless and gave up trying. Instead, the two men found themselves making eye contact and smiling knowingly at one another over Angel's amusing oral meanderings.

By the time they returned to the classroom, the pointedly punctual Professor Abbott had already resumed the lecture, and the trio quietly slunk back into their respective seats. By now, Flam had decided against dropping the course, and began taking some half-hearted notes. He had to force himself to focus on the course content, which was now dealing with the widespread influences of Zoroastrianism. Although

Flam would have been loath to admit it to himself, this resurrected academic interest had little to do with the lecture's content, and could be attributed directly to the influence of the exotic Angel.

Meanwhile, the newfound object of his desire had no sooner settled into her seat than she started again busily writing in her large white notebook with a fervour and concentration that bunched up her pretty brow. Something in the professor's pedantry must have hit home for her, for when Joe and Flam instinctively gravitated back to her side after the class had ended, she seemed deep in thought, almost troubled. As she gathered up her belongings, she was now apparently in no mood for chit chat.

An awkward silence fell on the trio. Flam was about to seize the opportunity to impress his newfound acquaintances with an erudite comment on some of the more obvious omissions in the lecture about the evolution of Heaven and Hell, for the book-loving Flam had encountered Zarathustra often during his earlier, single-minded research into funerary rites. Angel suddenly broke the quiet with a soft, "Sorry, boys, I have to go," and promptly dashed off. As she hurried away in her oddly agitated state, instantly causing Flam's heart to sink in her wake, she turned and flashed a sparkling smile back at the bemused pair. "We should all go out for coffee together after class next week," she offered. Then, like some ghostly white apparition, she disappeared out the classroom door.

CHAPTER 12

As the Saturday dinner with his future stepfather loomed, Flam grew more anxious about the pressure he would face to take the Strait name. Reasoning he should be prepared to counter with a name selection of his own, he spent the next few days poring over literary encyclopaedias, authors' indexes, and Internet name sites, before finally plodding page by page through the telephone book in an attempt to invent a new alternative.

The exercise proved far more tedious and difficult than Flam had possibly imagined, not from a shortage of potential new names, but rather from an overabundance of them. The clever and studious Flam had quickly devised scores of possibilities, but then had formulated hundreds of additional permutations and combinations by mixing and matching first names with surnames, so that he could not now decide among the rather daunting list of candidates. Instead of forcing himself to reach a verdict, he ploughed forward in search of more possibilities. This only exacerbated his dilemma, as the catalogue of prospective names grew steadily longer.

Flam would sit for hours studying his burgeoning list, sometimes sounding the names out loud to try to feel their verbal weight and impact. He also went through reams of paper, signing possible name choices on the pages in an attempt to intuit their suitability by the looks of the signature alone. Sometimes he tried to imagine the reaction others might have upon hearing each of the names for the first time. He acted out imaginary introductions in front of his mirror, which sat propped up to head height on a stack of books leaning against one of the walls of his apartment. "Hi, I'm Dale Valley. Hi, I'm Aldous Yeats. Hi, I'm Pierce Hart. I'm Othello Lear. I'm Gawain Scrivener. I'm Plato Copperfield. I'm Emerson Moriarty."

Despite these efforts, he only grew more confused and overwhelmed by the sheer volume of possibilities. Whenever he thought perhaps he'd made a final decision, or had at least narrowed the choices down to a short list, more prospective candidates would materialize, and quickly drive him back to the frustration of uncertainty.

Somehow, Flam had always assumed his glorious new identity would prove to be self-evident, appearing from out of the pack of possibilities like some shining fairytale champion to soundly defeat all other contestants, and finally rescue him from the oppression and ignominy of "Flam Grub" once and for all. Alas, no such clear salvation manifested itself. Although any one of the names on the list would, in Flam's view, be a more suitable and desirable alternative, there were simply too many of them. Each passing hour, instead of bringing a revelation, simply brought yet more choices to further fuel the dilemma.

Saturday night arrived, and even as he stood combing his black hair, which had grown long under Page Turner and Prentice College's combined bohemian influences, Flam continued to unsuccessfully audition candidate names. Nor did he know precisely what he would say to his mother and her fiancé when they again raised the issue of the name, as he was convinced they surely would.

Flam solemnly drove across town to the designated rendezvous at Eddie Spaghetti's, a gaudy franchised Italian restaurant known more for its décor and carnival atmosphere than the quality of its food, feeling the whole way like he was driving to his own funeral.

His mother and Gerald Strait were late, and as he stood waiting for them in the restaurant's foyer, hoping they might not show up at all, Flam's thoughts ascended towards the mercurial Angel. Despite being probably a decade older than Flam, and having only recently flitted into his life, she had now supplanted the treacherous Lucy Giles as leading lady of Flam's bedtime fantasies.

When Gerald and Mary did show up, Flam thought he detected some sort of strain between the couple. They were certainly not the same giddy, touchy-feely couple they'd been when they had happily told him about their engagement, but he quickly dismissed any further thoughts on the subject. He was still far more concerned with his own personal dilemma.

Gerald grew loudly agitated when they were forced to wait at the bar for fifteen minutes, despite having a reservation, and refused to allow them to order any drinks. "It's all a ploy by the restaurant to force us to spend extra money," he complained, deliberately making his words loud enough for the bartender to hear, although she gave no indication of being in any way interested. "I'll bet our table's just sitting there waiting for us. I have a good mind to go and complain to the manager, not that it would do any good. But you're not to order anything but water, do you hear? Two can play this game!"

By the time the trio had been seated, the atmosphere at the table was palpably tense. Even Flam, who was a lifelong habitué of solitude and quiet (and was profoundly grateful they weren't yet discussing him taking on the Strait surname), ultimately found the awkward silence disconcerting, and tried to initiate some small talk. He eventually had success when he steered Gerald onto the subject of work. The pharmacist loved to talk about himself, and was soon bragging about his store's prosperity, despite fierce competition from the large drugstore chains.

"Their volumes mean they're always able to undercut my prices on the everyday over-the-counter stuff," Gerald groused. "But I bring something to the table they'll never be able to give their customers, and that's old-fashioned service and experience. My regulars love me, and they wouldn't think of going anywhere else for their drugs."

Unpredictably, this last comment brought a strange gush of air from Mary, something between a sob and a snort, catching both men off guard. Mary dropped her fork onto her plate of lasagna, which she had barely touched, quickly excused herself, and headed off to the ladies' room. Confused, Flam was sure he had detected the beginnings of tears in her eyes.

Now alone with Gerald, he felt certain the dreaded name-changing lobbying would begin in earnest, but after blushing slightly and issuing the singular exclamation, "Women!" which was obviously meant to sum up the entire situation, Gerald grew strangely reticent once again. By the time Mary returned, sporting freshly applied make-up, which nevertheless could not conceal a telltale redness in her eyes, the conversation had again ground to a complete halt. This time Flam was content to let it rest in peace.

All parties declined dessert and coffee, as if they had all silently agreed that they wanted to get the uncomfortable dinner over with as quickly as possible. To Flam's surprise, and Gerald's obvious consternation, Mary, instead of going off with her beau, asked Flam to drive her home, even though she obviously realized it meant him going significantly out of his way.

Flam extended a sheepish farewell to Gerald, but noticed that Mary, in turn, whipped her face to the side, almost in recoil, when Gerald proffered a goodnight kiss. Now Flam was positive something was seriously amiss between the lovers, and was determined to pry it out of his mother when they were alone in the car.

There was no need to initiate an interrogation. They had barely cleared Eddie Spaghetti's parking lot when Mary started to bawl uncontrollably. "Oh, Flam! Flam! Why is God punishing me so?" she sobbed, burying her face into her son's shoulder and causing the car to momentarily swerve.

"Mother . . . what's wrong?" he demanded, shaken by the outburst of tears.

"It's Gerald . . . I can't . . . I *won't* marry him! Saints preserve us, my good name, my good name!"

At first Flam thought they were back on the subject of adopting the Strait surname, but in between crying fits, the story emerged, albeit in a somewhat rambling and hysterical fashion. The straight-laced and oh-so-respectable Gerald, as it turned out, was under investigation for illegal distribution of narcotics and other prescription drugs. The beleaguered druggist was vehemently pleading his innocence, claiming he had had no knowledge or suspicion that thousands of prescriptions he had filled, all paid for via untraceable cash transactions, had in fact been forgeries.

There had also been several break-ins in at the pharmacy, during which drugs in demand on the street had been stolen, but again Gerald had denied any involvement. And, in fact, despite their substantial suspicions, it seemed the police could not make a strong enough case against him, and the druggist had thus far avoided arrest.

Flam wasn't certain whether his mother, always so concerned about propriety and her reputation amongst the parishioners, would have stood by her man under those circumstances, but there was more. Gerald had used their moments of intimacy to pry into Mary's financial affairs, apparently convinced she had received a huge insurance payment after Steve's death.

Flam knew this was not the case. Traces of alcohol in Steve's blood, and accounts from witnesses who had seen him cavorting about a truck stop prior to his accident, had given the insurance company enough ammunition to significantly dilute the amount of the final settlement. To the beleaguered widow and her son, so used to living on a pittance as Steve drank, gambled, and whored away his money, the settlement, such as it was, had been a godsend. Although it had been enough to boost them a few rungs above their poverty—and to help Flam attend college—they were by no means wealthy. Gerald, however, did not know this. He apparently believed the rumours of wealth that Mary herself had, if not fostered, nonetheless allowed to flourish in order to raise her status. As a result, the suitor had been constantly pressing Mary for details about the extent of her holdings.

The ultimate deal breaker, Flam learned from his wailing mother, had come in the form of a certain Detective Cuff, who had visited Mary that very afternoon. The detective had revealed his suspicions that the former Mrs. Strait's death might not have been of natural causes, and Mary's own life might be in danger if she married Gerald.

"To think we were going to take that bastard's name," Mary spit out angrily as she slowly regained her composure. It confirmed Flam's certainty that the couple had taken as a *fait accompli* his adoption of the Strait family name.

"If you knew all this and you feel the way you do, Mother, why did you go ahead and see him tonight anyway?" Flam asked, although he was really thinking, *Why the hell did you have to drag me through that dinner too?*

"Oh, Flam, my sweet child," Mary exclaimed, fresh tears erupting, "no one in the parish knows yet . . . can you imagine what they'll all say when they find out? Oh, my good name! My good name!"

And so the bedrock truth was revealed. Mary was simply putting off an inevitable break up, deceiving Gerald in the process, in the hopes she might still somehow be able to perform some preemptive miracle that would salvage her all-important reputation. Yet the longer they spoke, the more evident it was to Flam his mother was losing all hope. She was slowly becoming all but resigned to the fact that, for the second time in her life, she would have to abandon her blessed St. Ernest's church and flee from the disgrace and humiliation brought upon her by a sinful entanglement with an evil man.

"Would you really have to leave St. Ernest, Mother?" he asked, as much out of worries for the ramifications such a disruption would have on his own life as any concern for his mother. He knew the salary Mary drew from the church was a small one, especially factored against all the hours she ungrudgingly devoted weekly in her service to the parish. Nevertheless, it was an income on which she depended, and losing it would probably bring his own cherished independence to an abrupt end, given his limited means.

Another equally disturbing thought occurred to Flam—what would Mary do with herself if she did not have the needy souls and social life of her parish work to focus her energies on? As glad as he was at having reconciled with his mother, Flam had no desire to become the singular missionary focus of her daily life. He needed his freedom. He cherished his solitude. He lusted after his sweet and alluring night school Angel. How would he be able to pursue her and become intimate with her if he were suddenly sucked into the irresistible crushing gravity of his mother's collapsed life?

Unfortunately, Mary was all too aware of how the sanctimonious parishioners loved to spread gossip, and mercilessly tear down the reputations of others behind their backs. In her advanced standing amongst her peers, she had long been one of the most prolific harbingers of hearsay and a relentless purveyor of scandal, even when it had the thinnest of substance. Flam knew the thought of Mary carrying on her duties while tongues wagged wildly in her wake horrified her, and her pride would not allow her to endure such a fall from grace.

So he found himself digging into his repertoire of literary clichés for any sort of private inspiration, finally settling on 'Heroes are made, not born.' Certainly, more than once in his readings, he had come across references to the unpredictability of personality, and how it took a crisis to establish the true measure of a man. And if ever there was a crisis for him, this was it.

Although the introverted Flam could not recall even once having presumed to tell another person how to live his life, he now laid mercilessly into Mary. "Mother, I'm shocked that you would think of giving up!" he exclaimed, causing Mary's tear-swelled eyes to open in surprise. "Don't you remember all the stories of the blessed saints you used to read me as a boy?" This was an exaggeration, for Mary had seldom done little more than bring home stacks of religious books and feed them to her book-crazed son, but Flam deliberately stroked her ego and pressed on.

"Just think about all the trials and tribulations those sacred martyrs endured for their faith. How can a little embarrassment compare to the suffering of St. Felicity or St. Agatha? Why, men and women have been burned, crucified, and mutilated through the ages for their Christian faith . . . surely, Mother, you can stand the scorn of a few old women who don't even deserve to be in the same room with a good soul like you."

His stage performance of a Bible-thumping evangelist was completely cliché, Flam knew, but he was desperate. His conscience did tweak him a little over the hypocrisy of his words, however. Hadn't he himself been driven to near self-destruction by the scorn of his peers, and didn't it still weigh mightily on him daily? Nevertheless, whether it was the appeal to Mary's religious convictions, or the fact that the sermon was shockingly emanating from her normally meek son, the words seemed to be hitting home.

"Don't you know how vital you are to St. Ernest's, Mother?" Flam preached. "Why, outside of the priests, you're the most important person in the parish. Just think of what will happen if you're not there to take care of things . . . oh, dear Lord, think of all the *souls* that will be lost if you're not there to save them!"

It was time to close the sale and, although he worried he might be laying it on a little thick, Flam pulled the car over to the side of the road so he could fully face his mother, and pressed on with his sermon.

"Mother, isn't it possible God put you in St. Ernest's for a reason . . . that He has brought this moment of tribulation upon you to test your faith . . . to test *our* faith?" The last admonishment was meant to imply to Mary she would not be alone in her ordeal—that her son would stand by her—and Flam was relieved to see his mother now close her eyes and start to mouth a prayer.

"Forgive me, my Lord, for my moment of doubt. Grant me the strength to do Thy bidding, and to be a faithful servant in this time of torment," Mary prayed, one hand fondling a crucifix that had been miraculously conjured out of some pocket.

Now Flam's conscience was practically throbbing, for despite an open mind and active curiosity about the subject of spirituality in general, he did not really believe some Judeo-Christian Jehovah had reached down from Heaven to single out his Mother and test her faith. But he easily rationalized his lies with the sincere belief he was ultimately helping Mary—practically saving her from herself—and no matter how self-serving his motives might be, he was urging her onto the correct path. Clearly, the right thing for her to do was find inner strength in the face of adversity, and to resolutely stand up and not let her life be destroyed by the scorn of her peers.

He put the car back into gear and drove on, as his mother was now semi-silently working her way through a succession of *Hail Marys* as some self-inflicted penance, and before long they were parked on the street in front of her flat.

"You know what you're going to do, Mother?" Flam said, still forcing an authoritative tone into his voice. "You're going to go upstairs, get on the phone, and break off your engagement to Gerald. And tomorrow, you're going to march into St. Ernest's, with your head held high, and make a point of telling everyone up front what you've done, before the rumour mill can grab hold of it and twist it out of shape. Remember, gossip only truly hurts when it spreads unchecked behind your back . . . the best way to diffuse it is to face up to it like the brave woman I know you are, and show everyone it doesn't bother you."

Mary had never known her son, who had almost always been some soft-spoken spectator, to talk with such power and conviction. Little did she realize he was evoking the dramatic flair and rhetorical skills he had acquired during her frequent absences in boyhood, when he was persuaded to parade across the countertop of the bookstore, reciting poems and plays to Turner and his literary brigade.

She started to get out, but Flam gently took her shoulder. "I wouldn't have done it, you know," he told her softly. Mary blinked, confused as to what he was talking about. "I mean, I wouldn't have taken Gerald's name," Flam explained. "Lord knows, I hate my own name, and I'm seriously working on changing it, but I wasn't going to simply let you and Gerald Strait tag me with his."

"I know, dear," Mary smiled, stroking his cheek, "I've always hated being a Grub myself." An idea suddenly percolated upward into her thoughts. "Why, I think I'll change it back to Mary Flam . . . ha, that will certainly give the old biddies something else to flap their gums about."

Now the idea was crystallizing fully, and she earnestly took Flam's hand. "Listen, dear," she said excitedly, "why don't you change your surname to Flam as well? It's such a proud name, a grand name . . . it would mean so much to me if you and I could keep the Flam family name alive."

Flam certainly hadn't seen that one coming. Evidently it hadn't dawned on his mother that he'd been talking with equal enmity about *both* halves of the name that had afflicted him since first memory. He sat there stunned for a moment, his mouth opening and closing. "Flam Flam?" was finally all he could muster.

She laughed, a rare occurrence for Mary, which sent freckles dancing on the snowfields of her face. "No, of course not, silly. You would have to choose a new first name. Now let me think. Your great-grandfather was called Samuel, and I've always been partial to that name. What do you think—Samuel Flam?"

Sam Flam? Like that's much better, Flam thought, but kept it to himself, even as he bristled at the thought of someone trying to run his life, and dictate what he should be named.

However, now was not the time to be starting new feuds with his mother, Flam reasoned, especially given her fragile state of mind, so he delicately deferred the Sam Flam can of worms. "Oh there's plenty of time to think about all that later," he offered diplomatically. "Right now you have a job to do, don't you? Now, I want you to go up there and deal with that no-good Gerald Strait. You have to be strong, Mother . . . remember the saints!"

Mary was jolted back to the crisis at hand, but Flam was relieved to see a look of resolve take hold of her. "You're absolutely right, son. A stitch in time saves nine, and there's no time like the present. I'm going to tell that snake-in-the-grass exactly what I think of him."

But then she wavered, and slowly brought up her left hand to where the light from the streetlamps would catch it, and wistfully contemplated the diamond ring Gerald had given her. Steve had never provided her with an engagement ring, and, in fact, she had paid for both their wedding bands. Flam saw that even a brooding, bitter, middle-aged widow with a heart of stone could still reconnect with the bright fantasies of her girlhood.

"I suppose I'll have to give it back," she sighed, seemingly mesmerized by the sparkle of the jewel in the lamplight. Flam could tell his war of independence had not been won in a single battle. "Who knows what wages of sin might have paid for that ring," Flam reminded her. "Come on, Mother," he urged gently, "I'm opening up the bookstore tomorrow anyway, so why don't I spend the night here?

I'll make you a nice cup of tea, and I'll be standing right beside you when you telephone that rat. We'll get through this together."

Later that night, with the engagement broken off, and the logistics of love's annihilation all neatly worked out, Flam surveyed his old home, while an emotionally drained Mary slept soundly in her bedroom. It had barely been two years since he had moved out, but it felt like an eternity ago to Flam. Eventually, he unfolded his squeaky old cot and flopped down on its lumpy surface, the smell of mothballs tickling his nostrils. Hours later, sleep still eluded him, as he lay haunted by resurrected memories of his father's abuses and a lifetime of misery.

Flam got up and sat on the edge of the cot. Although he had taken most of his books with him when he had moved out, beneath the dining room table a sizeable haphazard stack of tattered, coverless texts and paperbacks remained, looking like the ruins of an ancient citadel.

He got up, and crawled under the table, dragging some pillows and blankets in with him. Slowly, he rearranged the books until some semblance of a protective wall had been restored around him. With the smell of decaying old paper reassuringly enveloping him, Flam curled up into a fetal ball, let out a long, heartfelt sigh, and finally slept.

CHAPTER 13

As the next Comparative Religion class grew nearer, Flam found himself growing progressively more excited, and yet apprehensive about seeing his Angel again. There was one part of him, still emotionally scarred from the bitter experience with Lucy Giles, that screamed caution. It insisted vehemently that he should avoid the inevitable disappointment and simply start treating and thinking of Angel as some casual night school acquaintance and nothing more.

Certainly, if Flam had deliberately wanted to find excuses for distancing himself from Angel, there were plenty available—the difference in their ages, her somewhat bizarre appearance, her flaky beliefs, her self-absorbed behaviour. But there were other parts of him, further south, which were wholly enchanted and enamoured by the exotic and erotic creature, and yearned to pursue her glorious possibilities. Inevitably, it was these parts that won out.

Not content to simply wait and see what the future would bring, Flam had been preparing in his own unique way for their next encounter. First and foremost, he had been reading voluminously about the Jewish faith, which, as Professor Abbott's course took the predictable chronological route from Zoroastrianism to Judaism to Christianity to Islam, was to be the next religion covered in their upcoming lecture. Although Flam was already far more learned than most people on a variety of religious subjects, he wanted to make absolutely sure, if the opportunity arose, he could take command of any scholarly conversation, and awe Angel with the impressive size of his intellect.

At the same time, Flam was boning up on the act of making love to a woman. Since he had no practical experience in this matter, he wanted to make sure he did not disappoint the obviously more worldly (and yet strangely other-worldly) Angel in the event (something that had already happened in Flam's bedtime fantasies) the nature of their relationship became more intimate and physical.

And, finally, after vacillating wildly about it, Flam had decided to write a poem for Angel. Although memories of the disaster with Lucy still haunted him, he also remembered how he had been bolstered by the favourable post mortem from Ms. Dichter. In the end, he reasoned the fault had not been with the intent or quality of his verse, but rather, failure had come from Lucy's callous and unappreciative nature.

This time, though, Flam would not write a syrupy love poem in which he poured out his adoration like a locked-out dog howling in the night. No, that much of a lesson he *had* learned. Besides, he wasn't altogether sure how he would term his feelings for Angel. He certainly was not inflicted with the same uncontrollable, all-consuming, spend-eternity-with-you love he had felt for the oh-so-juicy Lucy. So, he decided to write something much subtler—a light, lyrical tribute that praised his Angel's spirit and beauty, without making any serious emotional commitment, or potentially embarrassing confessions of love.

Even the typically scatterbrained Turner soon noticed something was amiss with Flam's behaviour. On several occasions, he caught Flam staring out the window into the sky with a wistful, blank look. While it was not unusual for Flam to lose himself in a book, it had hitherto been unheard of for him to abandon the planet altogether. Then Turner (who, despite the perpetually cluttered state of his shop, had an uncannily precise mental inventory of his books and their locations) noticed *The Joy of Sex* and *Size Does Matter: Big Brains Make Better Lovers* were missing from the shelves. After a brief hunt, he found the books hidden under a newspaper beside the cash register.

The most compelling evidence regarding his young assistant's mental state was ultimately retrieved from the wastebasket under the front counter. Thinking the discarded balls of papers were more attempts by Flam to contrive a new name, Turner had uncrumpled one out of curiosity, and had stumbled upon drafts of the poem Flam was writing to Angel.

Turner was by no means a busybody by nature, and although he found his friend's new obsession deliciously humorous, he reasoned that the painfully introverted Flam, whom Turner loved like his own son, would not welcome an invasion of privacy. But when the normally punctilious assistant started to make uncharacteristic, albeit minor, clerical errors, Turner could hold back no longer.

"Listen here, my lost little Flam," he joked, "in what layer of *cumulonimbus* clouds should I go looking for your head these days, for in its absence, it seems your heart has been let loose to run rampant over sense and sensibility?"

Flam, who had just absentmindedly dumped a pile of outgoing mail in the accounting in-basket, before hastily returning to the penning of his poetry, lifted his head and blushed when he realized what Turner was intimating. The older man retrieved the mislaid envelopes and waved them in front of Flam's face.

"Far be it for me to begrudge a young man his hormone-fueled fancies," Turner chuckled, "but the last time I checked our little social compact, you were here to ease my burden, not to cause me extra work."

Flam shifted uneasily in his chair, mumbled a quick "Sorry about that," then flashed a sheepish grin at Turner, meanwhile trying nonchalantly to slide the poem he was writing out of sight under a literary bulletin.

"Oh, spare me the prestidigitation, Flam. I know full well Eros has given you the shaft and, fear not, I won't pry. I remember all too well what it feels like for someone to have your gonads in gear and your heart tripping the *tête à tête* tango. My, my, writing poetry no less. I knew you dabbled . . . I've seen you jotting down scraps in that little notebook of yours and, frankly, I've always been curious about the rhyme and reason of your verse, but figured you would have shared it with me if you truly desired an audience. But I always thought you just pot-shot poetry as a sort of literary target practice. I had no idea you were actually a hunter of game."

Even though Turner was his closest friend, in fact his only true friend, and the tone of their conversation was generally lighthearted, Flam still felt self-conscious about discussing his dreamed-for love life. He declined to get into the subject in any depth. "I just met her in Comp Religion class last week. We'll have to wait and see what happens," was all he'd say on the subject, his terse reply and standoffish body language making it abundantly clear he wasn't comfortable pursuing the matter.

Turner could read Flam's unease, but the seal on the subject having been broken, elected to pass comment. "If you'll let me offer you some unsolicited advice, falling in love is like jumping into a lake. If the water's too cold, it'll leave you gasping for air with your genitals shrivelled up, and you'll eventually die of exposure. If the water's too hot, you might very well find yourself scalded to death, although there are worse ways to go. Naturally, it's hard to find a temperature that's just right, which is why the swimming is seldom really comfortable. Now, some people like to just dive right in. Me? I believe in testing the waters thoroughly for temperature and acidity before *I* take the plunge."

He chuckled heartily, although whether it was from enjoyment of the supposed cleverness of his analogy or amusement over Flam's predicament was unclear, and then Turner ambled off to go poke around in the stacks at the rear of the store. He returned shortly, however, and addressed his colleague again.

"Well, I wish you luck, my young Lothario. Lord knows there were times when I could have used some in my love life. But, Flam, *please*, even if the girl is Aphrodite herself, she's not worth losing your head over. *Do* try to keep at least one foot firmly in the world around you." He then dropped a large book in front of Flam, its dust jacket showing an artful soft-focus photograph of a naked man and woman asleep with their backs to one another. The title read *The Complete Anatomy of Lovemaking*. Flam had not spotted it earlier when he went looking for instructional guides to sex on the bookshelves. "That's an especially good one. It has pictures and everything," Turner said, a huge smile beaming from one hairy cheek to the other. He gave Flam a big wink. "I swear by it."

Since last week's class, Flam had puzzled over how Angel had already known what Joe's name was on just the first night of classes. He concluded she had probably met the little old fellow before class had started—making her one of those conscientious new night school students who, whether out of eagerness or some quirk of their personal schedules, always showed up excessively early for their classes (something unheard of for a veteran day student). Acting on this hunch, Flam pleaded with Turner to let him leave work extra early on Wednesday night, although it meant enduring the embarrassment of a raucous, ribald, I-know-what-you're-up-to guffaw in the process.

Prentice College lay towards the outskirts of the city, and as Flam guided his car in the direction of the school, he was instantly swallowed up by the worst of the rush-hour crush. He sat in his vehicle, practically shaking with frustration, as the traffic crawled car-length by car-length out of the downtown core. He was, however, rewarded for his efforts when, upon entering the school a half-hour before the start of the class, he spotted a beatific Angel, sitting cross-legged as usual, in one of the oversized, quasi-modern, eggplant-coloured lounge chairs that adorned the building's main lobby. She was furiously scribbling away in her notebook, just as she had been in class the previous week.

Angel was again dressed completely in white from head to toe, although even the fashion-comatose Flam could see it was an entirely different outfit. Embroidered skintight denim pants were tucked into high-heeled, shiny vinyl boots, and an expensive-looking, loose-fitting sweater, which hung low off her shoulders, was worn over top of a white, men's tank top, which had been artfully torn in various places. It was, as before, a completely original and rather dramatic ensemble—the admiring Flam would not allow the word "bizarre" to manifest itself in his mind.

He supposed that her obsessive predilection for white was some idiosyncratic fashion statement, and under different circumstances he might perhaps have paused to consider its peculiarity. Within seconds, though, it was the farthest thing from his mind as Angel spotted him. She leapt up with a squeal of excitement to wrap her arms around him in a passionate hug, as if they were the most intimate of acquaintances.

"Hey, you" was all she said, and then practically dragged him down into the lounge chair on top of her.

Angel's enchanting scent overcame him, and the bushwhacked Flam quickly found his lust was beginning to raise its all-too-noticeable head as she rubbed against him in the confined space of the chair. As much as he relished the feel of her hard-yet-soft body so close to him, he shifted uneasily because he didn't want her to feel his burgeoning erection. Suddenly his body stiffened, and he let out a little cry as something stabbed him in the back.

Angel gave a little titter of a laugh, and reached behind him to pull out, with some effort, the large notebook in which she had been so busily writing. Flam noticed it had elaborate embroidered designs on its white leather cover, rendered in beautifully ornate old-fashioned motifs.

"I was just working on a poem," Angel explained, "but it's not going very well."

"Really? Do you need any help? I'm a bit of a poet myself." Flam could not have contrived a better lead-in to the verse he'd composed for Angel, but before he could pull out a copy for her to read, he was, as per Angel's habit, interrupted as she squealed with delight and rubbed her cheek against his.

"I just knew it! I could tell from the second I saw your aura that you were a totally creative soul!" She leaned back, practically hanging off the edge of the chair, as if getting a better look, and seemed to study him very carefully. Flam felt self-conscious, and found himself wishing he'd gone to the washroom first to preen a bit before approaching her.

"Hmmm," Angel pondered, "something's going on with you today. Your aura's bigger . . . like three times its usual size, and the tip of it's some weird colour . . . kind of purplish."

Flam had no idea how to respond to Angel's remark, but was spared having to do so when, suddenly, she squealed, "There's Joe!" and was out of the chair so quickly Flam collapsed into her vacated space, bounced his head off the far armrest, and tumbled to the floor.

As he picked himself up, hoping no one had witnessed his clumsiness, Flam could see Angel hugging the little man intimately. Although Joe was probably old enough to be her great-grandfather, Flam felt a sudden stab of jealousy. He tried to dismiss it by reasoning that there was no way a young woman like Angel could have any interest in the wizened ancient. *She's just being friendly*, Flam told himself. But then his heart stepped off the ledge and plunged down into familiar dark depths, as the logic swiftly followed that Angel was therefore, in all probability, just being friendly with Flam as well.

She led Joe over, her arm still wrapped around him, and Flam, now feeling guilty over the pang of jealousy he'd just experienced, greeted Joe warmly and forced himself to adopt a plucky nothing-wrong-here smile.

"I guess you could probably teach tonight's class as well as anyone," Flam offered in the way of an icebreaker. He was met by a blank stare from both his companions, and realized neither one was aware of the day's lecture topic. "We're doing Judaism," he explained.

Joe chuckled as he got the joke. "I doubt if that Professor Abbott has ever been inside a synagogue, or heard the Talmud recited," he said, his English spoken with a heavy accent, which sounded German. "Just my luck. I've been a Jew for ninety years, and when I take a course to learn about other religions, they want to teach me about being a Jew." He laughed again.

Amazingly, Angel had remained silent through their short exchange; it was the longest they'd ever known Angel to allow anyone else to monopolize the conversation, but now she burst back in, evidently having clued in at last to the situation.

"You're Jewish!" she exclaimed. "Why didn't you tell me?" And instantly she had both men laughing, and utterly awestruck and amused by her naïveté, for Joe's skullcap and its significance should have been impossible to miss. But Angel seemed very serious and now quite determined. "Well, then, tonight's class should be extra special. I'm going to pay close attention in case I ever decide to become Jewish. Let's go see if we can find three seats together." And, handing Flam her notebook to carry, she merrily hooked up to her bemused men's arms, and led the peculiar threesome towards their classroom.

Flam found the class as totally boring as its predecessor. At one point, he propped his head up on one arm, let the bangs of his hair hide his eyes from observation, and succumbed to sleep, very much doubting he was alone in his somnolent sojourn. Although Flam had become a dedicated and conscientious student during his time at Prentice College, he felt no guilt in taking his nap. Professor Abbott's droning lectures were incredibly monotonous, and Flam doubted if the teacher actually paid attention to his students while he stood virtually motionless in his peculiar praying stance, staring blankly at the far wall as if he were in a hypnotic trance.

As Flam drifted off into a delicious dream state, he amused himself by coining a couple of epithets for the boring lecturer—Professor Robott, and The Abbott and the Snore. Flam had no qualms about amusing himself in this manner while he nodded off, since he had already researched the evening's topic in encyclopaedic detail, and was in no danger of missing anything.

He awoke with a start. He'd been having an extraordinary dream in which he'd arrived in Heaven only to find his way barred by Professor Abbott. Flam had felt panic because he needed urgently to find his Angel, then God had appeared, in the guise of Joe, trying to reassure him that everything would be okay. It was when Flam had suddenly thought it peculiar that God should be wearing a *yarmulke* that the entire dream had evaporated.

For a second, he thought he might have attracted attention, but the classroom around him was a silent tomb, except for Professor Abbott's plodding pedantry, and no one appeared to have taken any notice of Flam. Across the aisle from him, Angel was scribbling madly in her notebook again, and Flam, now recognizing the symmetry and structure of the lines she was writing, knew she was not taking notes.

He wondered why she paid good money just to come to class and write poetry.

That thought got him thinking of his latest poem, lying in his notebook, needing only the opportunity to be unveiled—a paper Cupid's arrow just waiting to wing its way straight to Angel's heart. Yet the unpredictable and self-absorbed Angel was proving to be a difficult quarry to bring to ground. Flam again found himself worrying that he was totally misinterpreting her behaviour—that she in fact had no romantic interest in him whatsoever.

It'll be Lucy all over again, he chided himself, *and if you pursue her, you'll just end up rejected and heartbroken.* But then the lady in question, with that uncanny sense she seemed to possess that Flam was looking at her, glanced up. She fixed him with her seductive hazel eyes and unleashed the full thousand-watt radiance of her smile upon him, and his pounding heart decided she was worth the risk.

"It's not that anything our esteemed professor said was wrong," Joe was saying, "it's just that he omitted so much."

As forewarned by Angel the previous week, they had been rounded up after class and shepherded to Java Gardner's, a coffee shop and Internet café close to the campus. Angel had then excused herself to go to the ladies' room, leaving Flam and Joe alone to conduct a post mortem of Professor Abbott's class on Judaism.

"I know what you mean," Flam agreed, excited to be able to share his thoughts on the subject with someone. "I had the same feeling last week. I know he can only cover so much of one religion in a three-hour lecture, but it's like he leaves out so many important concepts and fills in the space with trivialities. For example, this week I noticed he totally excluded the whole topic of Jewish mysticism."

"You are, I think, my young friend, a scholar and a seeker of wisdom, yes?" Joe observed.

"Scholar? I'm not sure about that . . . I'm a day student here at Prentice. We're just a vocational college. But I've always loved to read, and if something interests me I like to find out everything I can about it. I've filled my head with a few facts, I suppose, but wisdom? I'm afraid it eludes me'"

A wry smile rippled the beard on Joe's ancient, wrinkled face, as if Flam had just proved the old man's point.

"And what vocation, if I may ask, have you chosen for yourself?"

"I'm, uh, taking Funeral Services," Flam answered reluctantly, wondering when he'd suddenly become self-conscious about it.

Joe, however, just nodded as if it was the most common response in the world. "I myself was for seventy years a tailor."

"Seventy years? Wow, that's *two* careers!" Flam exclaimed.

"I was still a little boy when I began cutting fabric in my father's shop in Berlin. It was in the 1920s." He could see Flam doing the arithmetic, and smiled. "Yes, I am ancient. I celebrated my ninety-fourth birthday only a few months ago." But then a profoundly sad expression came over Joe's face.

Flam instinctively felt the old man was carrying some secret burden, which weighed heavily on his spirit, and wondered if that was what had brought Joe to learn more about other religions. Or was he perhaps questioning his own faith, and its probabilities of a hereafter, now that the next world loomed so closely?

"Now what are you two going on about?" a sweet soprano voice chimed from behind them. Joe and Flam had been so engrossed in their discussion they hadn't seen Angel reappear. She gave them both a hug, as if she'd been gone for years instead of minutes, and worked a chair in between the two kibitzing males. "Did you boys miss me?" she asked, patronizingly. And then she proceeded to take over the conversation again with a detailed inventory of all the faults with the women's washroom.

Afterwards, Joe insisted on taking the bus home by himself. Since he had driven to campus that night just to meet up with Angel as early as possible, Flam felt the decent thing to do was chauffeur the old fellow home now that he knew Joe's true age. But Joe would not hear of it, nor would he accept Angel's invitation to accompany him on the bus.

"Someday, God willing, if you are my age, you will understand the need to cling to the little everyday things that younger people take for granted. These days, my personal triumphs are such modest ones, but I seek my victories over death and age wherever I can find them. Thank you, my friends, but no, I shall be fine. Good night. *Mazel tov.*" With a final wave, he laboured up the steps of the crosstown bus and departed, leaving Angel and Flam alone.

"How about you?" Flam asked. "Do you need a ride?"

Angel put her arms around Flam's neck, and for a second he was convinced she was going to kiss him. Instead, she whispered in his ear, so softly he was unsure he had heard her correctly, "I'd love to have a ride with you sometime." Then she laughed and pushed him gently away, threw her arms out wide, and started spinning down the sidewalk, an ethereal white whirl giggling with glee.

Flam stood there, not knowing what to do next. He wanted to run over and grab her and pull her curvaceous body against his and flood her with kisses. *But what if she doesn't want that?* he thought. *What if she says no and pushes me away, or maybe even screams and hits me?* And so he remained, frozen with the paralysis of self-doubt and uncertainty, until she had started to get too far away from him, and now he finally took a step, intending to catch up to her.

"No, stop!" she yelled, ceasing her spinning. She pointed a finger at him, as if brandishing some invisible magic wand, although she was still smiling exultantly the whole time. The moon, one dark sliver shy of being full, sailed out from behind the clouds to shower her in its light, and with her white clothes and hair and pale skin she seemed to take on an otherworldly, ghostlike appearance. Then abruptly she started spinning again, although now her spirals were counterclockwise, and brought her back in Flam's direction. She dizzily collapsed into his arms, making him struggle to hold them both up, and all the while she kept on laughing like some maniac.

"The moon's in bloom and I'm in tune," she giggled, but stood back up on her own feet, and looked him sternly in the face. "You go home now," she commanded him, "and write me a poem."

He started to say he'd already written one, practically panting at the chance to whip it out and show it to her, but before he could do or say anything she pressed a finger against his lips, like she was silencing a child. "Shhhh," she whispered. "Not tonight. Go on now, like a good boy. I need to be alone." She must have read something in Flam's expression then—disappointment, rejection, perhaps even fear—and so now she did kiss him, lightly, on the cheek. "I'll see you next week," she whispered, and then laughed again. "The orb's alight and I'm in flight so off I go into the night," were Angel's last words, and then she went skipping like a little girl down the moonlit boulevard.

CHAPTER 14

In his past readings, Flam had stumbled across references to human auras numerous times, but had never given the idea much credence or attention. Now, Angel's constant references to the alleged size and splendour of Flam's own aura spawned a selfish new interest in the topic. It was, he knew, a hugely popular idea among New Age devotees as well, and as a consequence, the bookstore had a number of volumes that dealt with the subject to varying degrees.

It didn't take long for Flam's latest fixation to attract Page Turner's notice, and the older man turned out to be a counterpoint to Flam's own skepticism on the topic. "Don't get me wrong," Turner harrumphed, pushing aside a number of the books with obvious contempt, "a lot of this is unadulterated rubbish, but I wouldn't be so quick to dismiss the idea altogether."

"Oh come on, you don't really believe any of it, do you?" Flam asked, surprised by this side of Turner he'd never seen before. Although some people misinterpreted his throwback hippie attire and idiosyncratic behaviour as signs of flakiness, Turner was nevertheless one of the most intelligent, level-headed, and, also, patently cynical individuals Flam had ever encountered.

"'If the doors of perception were cleansed, everything would appear to man as it is, infinite,'" Turner quoted in the way of a retort. The merchant waded into the stacks, and returned with a nondescript hardcover book. "I had this under biography . . . it just didn't seem right to put it with all that other syncretic neo-mystical stuff," he sighed deeply, as if the discussion had reopened some past organizational aggravation. "It's a book about Kirlian Photography . . . not the cameras and gimmicks you'll see them flogging today at any New Age get-together, but the original scientific research old Semyon Davidovich did in the Soviet Union during the 1930s. In a lot of ways, the old evil empire was way ahead of the West in studying paranormal phenomena."

Flam skimmed through the book, still unconvinced. "So why can't I see any auras, while someone else can allegedly see mine?"

"Ah, because my fine young skeptic, you do not have the *gift*. It's reportedly a talent, like so many other unexplained extrasensory perceptions, that a small number of people are born with, although it's also claimed to be an ability that can be developed over time . . . and I can assure you there is no shortage of practitioners out there who will gladly take your money to purport to teach you how."

Flam lapsed into silence, except for the faint squeak of his stool as he slowly spun from side to side, wondering if Angel really was some exceptional human being who possessed special powers, allowing her to perceive things others could not. He badly wanted to believe, not through any innate faith in some paranormal world to which he was not privy, but because it might really mean that Angel truly saw something exceptional—and therefore attractive—in Flam. And that would mean, her elusiveness and flighty nature notwithstanding, his desire for her might yet be fulfilled.

Turner meanwhile had embarked on an altogether different train of thought as he leafed through the book he had just offered Flam. "I wonder if Kirlian had any clue his peculiar accidental discovery would guarantee his name would live on after his death, albeit out on the fringe, with the mainstream hurling insults at him."

"I imagine any fame is better than none," Flam replied.

"Do you really think so? What does it matter if we're dead and in no position to appreciate it?"

"I guess it helps to alleviate the fear of death," Flam suggested, "or of the meaninglessness of life . . . as if by leaving behind some name droppings we're marking a place in posterity, proving our brief existence had significance. Or perhaps it's plain vanity, like those rich men who used to sponsor polar expeditions, just so they'd have some obscure inlet or peninsula named after them in a frozen and desolate corner of the world."

"Maybe, but few who went seeking fame ever found it, while many others have had their greatness thrust upon them." Turner chuckled as another thought occurred to him. "My favourite case is Amerigo Vespucci. He was already a middle-aged man when he went chasing the New World gold rush that Columbus had opened up. By the time the dust had settled, Vespucci had two continents and an A-list country named after him. That's pretty amazing, when you consider only a handful of people have ever merited country-level branding, let alone an entire hemisphere. Poor old Cristofo, first on the scene, and don't get me wrong, he's certainly a historical superstar in his own right . . . every school kid can name his three ships . . . but it seems to me he deserved more credit."

"It's not like he's forgotten."

"True, but what did he end up with? His biggest namesakes are Columbia, a South American banana republic best known for its cocaine cartels, British Columbia, a Canadian province that prefers to use its initials, Columbus, Ohio, a minor city in the rust belt, and the District of Columbia, a geo-political oddity created to hold the U.S. capital. I suppose the real moral of the story is that Vespucci ultimately had the heavy-hitting Florentine PR connections back home to ensure his exploits got wider circulation, even if some of his claims of discovery are in dispute. So, a German mapmaker hears the stories and sticks Amerigo's name on his newest creation, which ends up becoming the next de facto standard for world maps. And *voilà*, 500 years later, that Johnny-Come-Lately is still on a first-name basis with posterity."

"Hmm," Flam pondered out loud, "I wonder what kind of an aura Vespucci had?"

Although he already had one completed poem for Angel in reserve—tucked in between photocopied handouts from Professor Abbott's class, just waiting for the right moment to be unveiled—Flam opted to craft a fresh ode to his heart's desire.

The task was not an easy one, for splendiferous summer weather had arrived. In its wake, sun-worshipping urban dwellers had come spilling out onto the sidewalks, and into the now-trendy shops of Flam's reborn old neighbourhood. Page Turner's Bookstore was therefore doing a comparatively brisk business. Turner himself was out of the shop much of the time, tending to various vague errands, leaving Flam alone and scrambling to keep up with the demands of the customers. As a consequence, Flam had little time for waxing poetic during the shop hours themselves.

At one point on Saturday afternoon, as Flam dispensed with one customer and looked down the line to tend to the next, he was surprised to see his mother standing there with a small abstract smile, and a stack of paperbacks in her hand. He recalled having seen a woman come into the store, and even recollected having flashed her a cursory be-with-you-in-a-minute acknowledgement; now he was embarrassed to realize he had failed to recognize his own mother. He was even more ashamed to think she felt the need to buy some books just to be able to converse with him.

"Hello, dear," Mary greeted her son. "You look terribly busy, so I won't bother you. I just want to buy these."

Flam had kept a watchful eye on his mother since her break-up with Gerald Strait, and had been relieved to see she was bearing up well; indeed, it seemed as if she were perhaps even flourishing despite the burden of her latest disgrace. Today she looked positively content, with a relaxed posture and an uncharacteristic smile, which, although modest, appeared sincere and completely at home on her face. There was something else Flam couldn't quite put his finger on—changes to her hair or grooming that, although subtle, made her look younger and more vibrant.

"Oh, Mother, you don't have to buy books just for my sake. Why don't you come here behind the counter and maybe things will quiet down in a bit and we can talk."

Mary laughed, the sight striking Flam as a merry antithesis to the frowning and fretting woman who had nagged and bullied him throughout boyhood.

"Silly, boy. I really *do* want to buy these. This *is* a bookstore, isn't it? And we can talk some other time . . . I'm in a bit of a hurry today."

Flam blushed and took the books to ring them up. As he flipped open the front covers to where Page had penciled in the new resale price on each of the title pages, Flam noted the books were all classic mystery novels—a couple of Agatha Christies, a Lawrence Block, and an Ellery Queen. He looked up at Mary, somewhat puzzled by this newfound interest in the detective genre, and wondering how on earth it might be tied to her parochial duties.

"Why don't you let me treat you to these," he offered, still finding it awkward to be conducting business with his mother.

She laughed again, now officially registering more mirth per minute than Flam had witnessed in an entire lifetime. "Save your money, dear." She handed Flam a bill and watched as her son fished through the till for the proper change.

"Your hair's getting long," she commented, as he handed her the bagful of books. She impulsively reached up and tucked a runaway strand behind his ear, its jet-black colour a sharp contrast to Flam's chalky-white skin. "I'm not sure I like it this way, although I suppose it's considered stylish . . . but oh my goodness, you're so pale. You should really try to get some sun, son," then giggled at her little pun and leaned over and pecked him on the cheek.

"I'll see you later, dear," she called over her shoulder. "Don't work too hard."

"Bye, Mother. Have a nice day," Flam replied as the shop bell tinkled her departure. He turned to take care of the next customer, a regular with a fetish for French existentialism. The man was looking at him oddly, then reached in his pocket and offered Flam a Kleenex. Flam stood puzzled by the gesture, until the man pointed up at Flam's

face. "You have lipstick on your cheek," the customer explained. Flam
blushed as he accepted the tissue and wiped off the stain, wondering
meanwhile when precisely his mother had started wearing lipstick.

With such a hectic pace to the business days, poetry had to wait until
the evenings, when the shop had been locked up, night deposits
made at the bank, and miscellaneous errands disposed of on the way
home. Flam's ancient apartment building did not have centralized
air conditioning, so after concocting some half-hearted dinner out of
a can or a frozen foil packet, he would take his notebook and head
outside in search of cooler air and inspiration.

      After the busy days spent in the shop, catering to the whims of
the public, the quiet nights afforded the reclusive Flam the anonymity
and inner calm he craved. He especially liked to wander the residential
streets of his neighbourhood, revelling in the stimulating scents wafting
from the myriad flower gardens, their perfume as varied and exotic
as the ethnicity and tastes of the different working-class homeowners
who had planted them.

      Flam would do the rough composition of the poem in his head
as he strolled the side streets, letting the "aha" of imagination strike
him with all the force his muse could muster. Later, he would find a
park bench or outdoor café where he could sit and perform the more
involved process of refining the thoughts, selecting the right rhymes
and words, then rewriting and editing in his pocket notebook.

      After a few nights of this process, Flam had finally completed
Angel's second poem, and was ready to transfer it to his computer for
printing. Now he was wrestling with two additional problems—what to
call his new opus, and which of the two works to offer Angel first. Titles
were not something on which Flam normally expended much effort
during his poetic endeavours. Most of his previous writing output
had been little more than miscellaneous stanzas or incomplete verses,
sparked by some incident or momentary inspiration. They had tended
to focus on stylistic gymnastics done more for their own inherent sake
than for packaging and delivery to the world at large. But now that he

again had poems destined for a very special audience, pregnant with all the unspoken aspirations and secret longings in Flam's soul, they needed to be perfect. That meant investing some thought and effort into what they should be called.

The first poem he simply called "Angel," and to Flam's mind, that minimalist title, with its double meaning and innate imagery, perfectly captured the essence and spiritual nature of both the poem and the person to whom it was dedicated. This newest creation, however, fueled by the mounting physical frustration and fervent longing Angel continued to foster within Flam, was rawer, and far more sensual, although its overtly sexual nature had been purposely veiled behind metaphors and symbolism he had laboured hard to achieve.

Flam did not know the true extent of Angel's education or grammatical skill. He suspected she was not some erudite literary scholar, despite being an alleged fellow poet. Flam therefore wanted a title that was not so cryptic or obscure as to obfuscate his passion, yet was still subtle and witty enough to be seductive in its own right.

Delivering this last crowning touch on his new creation preoccupied and vexed Flam to the very last minute. Wednesday arrived, and the next encounter with his Angel loomed, and still her poem lay unchristened. It was certainly not any lack of inspiration that stalled Flam. He had conceived, and discarded, dozens of possible titles, from the sickly sweet to the hopelessly corny, before settling on "Seraph Hymn," more out of eleventh-hour desperation than its natural perfection.

He beamed down at his handiwork, full of pride and relief, and decided he would let mood and circumstance dictate which poem he'd show to Angel first. It dawned on him, however, that his two compositions were unsigned. As inevitably happened whenever the familiar name shame re-entered conscious thought, his stomach began to churn, and a darkness instantly eclipsed his mood. It rattled his soul that he was mentally incapable of appending a Flam Grub byline . . . or even a simple "To Angel from Flam" dedication to these pages, on which he had laboriously obsessed, and which now represented so much desperate hope.

The matter of a byline also brought up the whole submerged issue that thus far his relationship with Angel, despite their instant bond and his physical attraction for her, was virtually anonymous. He knew her first name only, while she didn't know his name at all. This didn't seem to bother Angel, and was perhaps fully indicative of her deliciously quirky nature, but it was inevitable that sooner or later the Flam Grub curse would resurface, as it had throughout his life, and unavoidably lead to suffering.

All of his futile efforts of the past weeks to select a new name for himself now weighed even more heavily on Flam, for he could have used it to sign the poem. Running late, he fled the downtown with the rest of the commuters, and hastened towards Prentice College and his waiting Angel. In the car, he again leafed through his ever-burgeoning list of candidate names, actually relieved when an accident on the causeway brought the commuter traffic to a virtual standstill, for it bought him precious moments to try to reach a decision.

Now the names had a new barometer. As he read each one out, Flam was evaluating it in the context of a byline on Angel's poem. *By Dante Freeman? No. By Milton Creed? No. By Woodsworth Wolfe? No. By Apollo Sage? No, no, no!*

It did not matter that any name he might spuriously select would not legally be his. That was a mere technical detail he could easily rectify at a later date, and it was not as if Angel were going to ask him for identification. In the unlikely event his new name was ever challenged, Flam figured he could just say nonchalantly it was his *nom de plume*.

The fact he could still change his mind at any time should have worked to Flam's tactical advantage. After all, was the name he was attempting to select any different than a costume he might choose for a masked ball or Halloween party? Despite its importance for making the right impression for a specific occasion, it had no long-term significance and could be discarded after it had served its use. *Just pick any name, for heaven's sake, and put all the agonizing indecision behind you,* he chided himself.

But even as he pulled into the college parking lot, having already lost some of the precious time he'd hoped to spend with his Angel before class, Flam still hadn't been able to reach a decision. Each name he'd methodically evaluated had some fundamental flaw that caused him to veto it. It was either too pretentious, or too harsh-sounding, or too contrived, or potentially lent itself far too easily to ridicule, or reminded him of someone he had disliked in the past. So, for the time being, his poems were left unsigned, and he was still Flam Grub, although he was inwardly praying the anonymity of the past weeks would be preserved, and further names would remain unspoken, no matter where the night led.

CHAPTER 15

Angel was sitting in the very same armchair as the previous week, scribbling away again in her giant white leather notebook. She looked so beautiful and desirable Flam instantly decided to go with his newer poem, the one with the erotic undertones. She was (no surprise) dressed again all in white, this time sporting a simple, sleeveless cotton dress, which was cut well above the knees to reveal trim, bare legs that ended in a pair of white sandals. Her toenails were also painted white.

The front of Angel's dress was unbuttoned at the top, exposing a tangle of silver necklaces, which hung down into just enough of a show of cleavage to set Flam's heart instantly racing. When she spotted him and wiggled out of the armchair to hug him, the untangling of shapely calves and thighs provided a brief, delicious glimpse of the mysterious nether regions beneath her dress, and left him speculating what kind of sheer undergarment, if any, she was wearing. But then the intoxicating Angel smell totally enveloped him and made all further thought impossible.

"Hi," she cooed into his ear. "I was just thinking about you."

"Good thoughts, I hope?" Flam asked as he led her back to the armchair and collapsed into its foam-cushion paradise with her, wallowing in the instant honey-warmth as her body pressed against his.

"Funny kind of thoughts, anyway," she replied. It was not the sort of answer Flam had hoped for, but at least he had merited a place in her musings. The smile that accompanied her response, along with an enticing sparkle in Angel's eyes, provided ample compensation, and seized him by the heartstrings, sending him soaring up towards Heaven.

There he would gladly have stayed indefinitely, content to revel in the sheer delight of physical contact, all his dark days of longing and uncertainty now evaporating in the sunshine of Angel's feast of the senses, but his anxious mind would not allow him to relax. He weighed the ripeness of the moment, contemplated the time left until class would start, pondered the probability of Joe interrupting them, and tried to judge whether this was indeed the right moment to show Angel his poem.

As it turned out, Flam could have spared himself the mental effort, for he had neglected to take into account the Angel factor. Once again, she sent the scheme of things pattering off into an unpredictable direction.

"Oh my God!" she exclaimed. "You should see our auras. They're joining together . . . like, blending into a single big one. Wow, I've heard of this, but I've never seen it before." Then she began to giggle uncontrollably. "Aural sex. Get it?"

Flam did get the pun. *Here we go with auras again,* he thought, and then, pondering her jest more fully, wondered if she was simply making a harmless joke, or if some genuine sexual innuendo was hidden in her humour.

"Hey, Joe! Want to make it a threesome?" Angel called out laughingly, and Flam looked up to see their little old friend grinning down at them through his beard as they nestled in the armchair.

"You are very kind to offer, young lady," Joe chuckled, "but I'm afraid that if I were to join you, my poor stiff old body would not be able to extricate itself from that chair." He shook his head, still clearly amused, then pulled an ancient timepiece from his jacket pocket. "Besides, are we not late for class? I believe we are doing the Old Testament today. Hurry along. The Prophets await."

After enduring another excruciatingly monotonous lecture from Professor Abbott, the three went out to Java Gardner's again after class, Angel chirping non-stop the whole way to the coffee shop about Noah's Ark and the Great Flood—the only part of the three-hour lecture that seemed to have sunk in—and what it must have smelt like with the animals puking and pooping. When she excused herself to visit the ladies' room, Flam took advantage of her absence to query Joe on his opinion of the latest lecture.

"I guess it was all old news for you, tonight?" Flam asked.

"And you too, no? This is, after all, the common ground we Jews share with you Christians, at least in terms of scripture . . . the same God, the same Devil, the same angels. Abraham, Noah, Moses, the Ten Commandments, the psalms of David . . .. they are sacred to us both. With so much common ground, it's hard for me to understand why your people have been so quick to persecute and vilify us over the centuries. If you truly adhere to your Christian religion then we should be pitied, do you not think? Your messiah has already arrived, and you have had him for two thousand years. Alas, we poor Jews, infinitely patient, eternally suffering, still await ours."

"I guess I am a Christian, in the strictest sense, because I was baptized as one, when I was a baby—long before I was able to voice an opinion, or think for myself—but I don't really practise anymore, and can't say I really think of myself as one. I guess I'm taking this class because I'm searching for answers . . . hoping to see a bigger picture, even though Christianity purports to offer me one that's infinite."

Joe frowned, seemingly disturbed by Flam's confession of a spiritual crisis. "Then I am wrong. It is you who should be pitied, my young friend, not me. I lack many things, but faith is not one of them, for I have been blessed to feel His hand, and I believe."

"Then, if you don't mind me asking, why are you taking this course? I thought you were perhaps . . . well, questioning your beliefs after a lifetime of unthinking devotion."

Joe laughed, and it brought forth even more wrinkles and creases in his crinkled, time-worn face. "You thought I was making sure I knew which name to call out when my time came? True, I wasn't always so devoted, and my beliefs have been tested and found wanting at times, but that's a story for another time. Let us just say that I am taking this class in order to do penance . . .."

Angel, just then returning to their table, caught the last phrase and playfully pounced on it like a catnip-crazed kitten. "Penance? What in heaven's name for? What have you been up to, Joe, you naughty boy? And here I thought it was this young hot-blooded one I had to watch out for."

Her joke managed to democratically elicit blushes from both men, although for his part, the red-faced Flam was quick to forgive Angel as she sat down beside him and slipped her arm into his, pressing her bountiful breasts up against him in the process.

Joe laboured to his feet. "And now, my fellow scholars, I must bid you good night. I'm checking into the hospital tomorrow morning and still need to pack."

"Hospital? Oh, no, Joe! Are you okay?" Angel exclaimed, concern painting her face.

"Okay? Surely you know, child, that living to old age is a capital crime. For me, there is never a shortage of ailments . . . but fear not, my sweet young Angel," Joe assured her, "it is just for one day and night for some testing and treatment that my doctor regularly insists upon."

Flam and Angel made to get up, but Joe waved them back into their seats. "No, please, you two, stay and finish your coffees," he chided, a sly smile on his lips as he studied their expressions, "I know you will again offer to assist me getting home, and I thank you, but I assure you I will be fine on my own. It is a beautiful night and my cane and I will enjoy the walk, even if it may be a slow and laborious one." With that he bowed politely, and left.

Flam was practically bursting with excitement as he watched Joe shuffle out the door. As much as he had come to like and respect the little old man immensely, and although he had to admit that Joe had as much right to share Angel's company as he did, Flam had been feeling progressively more frustrated by their little *ménage a trois*. He had half-convinced himself he would never have the opportunity to be alone with his elusive Angel, and to attempt to seduce her with his verse. Now it was just the two of them at last, and it seemed like some amazing dream as she slipped her arm back into his, and placed her chin on his shoulder.

"There goes our chaperone," Angel said in a husky voice.

"What's the matter? Are you afraid to be alone with me?"

"Dream on, Boy Wonder. You're the one who should be scared."

"Gosh. Never took you for the vengeful Angel type. I always had you pegged as more of a cherub."

"A what? Are you saying I'm fat?"

"No, no. Cherubim . . . it's a class of angel that attends God. Trust me, it's a compliment."

"Hmm," she mused, hugging Flam's arm more tightly, but then she abruptly straightened up in her seat. "Hey, I almost forgot. Did you write me a poem?"

Flam's gargantuan grin provided her with an instant answer. *At last*, he thought, and started to reach into his knapsack to retrieve his opus, but Angel stopped him with a squeeze of his thigh, which sent tremors to his loins. "No, no, I want to show you mine first," she insisted, and swung around to dig through her bag.

Flam sighed, but kept smiling like a hopeless idiot. By now Angel's caprices were becoming practically predictable, and almost endearing. They certainly could not spoil the perfect anticipation of the dreamlike moment, which went beyond anything Flam had ever experienced in his small, book-lined life, and wrapped him in a melted-toffee warmth of fantasy realized.

Angel opened her ornate, monogrammed notebook, spent a few seconds further building the suspense as she leafed through the pages, seeming to have difficulty finding the right one, then cleared her throat, preparing to read aloud.

Flam had always been extremely curious about the nature of the poetry he had seen Angel constantly scribbling in her white leather notebook. His own recent poetic efforts had demonstrated how difficult the craft could be, but although nothing in her continuous verbal outpourings had given any indication Angel was capable of writing anything beyond rudimentary love/dove cat/hat rhyming couplets, he resolved to be as open-minded and receptive as possible. After all, he was evidently the subject of this particular recitation, and this Angel might very well be providing him with revelations of the inner depths of her feelings, and how she might be prepared to let those feelings manifest themselves.

Even given his earlier apprehensions about the quality of her verse, Flam was caught totally off guard by what sprang from Angel's lips, and he was hard pressed not to let his surprise show. The poetry was wildly disconnected—a careening oral ramble in free verse, devoid of pattern or rhythm, and sprinkled with unfamiliar words, which appeared to have been made up.

> . . .Chulurining is time blightblack on the white forever duneside up,
> After the nonflection all wane tapped how to feel mightness of crystal emprisoms,
> Counter workingstacks at the biology to the deflection of reternity. . .

Flam found it utterly inaccessible and incomprehensible. He had no idea what Angel's theme or message was, and felt somewhat betrayed, and again left in emotional limbo, no closer to understanding this mercurial enigma of a woman.

Maybe if I had a chance to analyze it . . . to study it, I could figure out what it means, Flam thought in a bit of a panic, but before he could pick up the notebook and reread the poem, Angel had thumped the book shut and spirited it away.

Flam smiled nervously, his previous inner exultation now evaporated. "Wow . . . that was something else," he finally offered diplomatically, forcing a big smile. Then he fell silent, praying the chatterbox Angel would now kidnap the conversation and spare him any further painful commentary.

His companion, however, seemed spent by the effort of her recital, and became uncharacteristically quiet as she picked up her cup and finished off the last of her herbal tea. The expression she bore was impossible to read, all facial markers of mood sitting in an inscrutably neutral position beneath her crown of spiked, white hair.

Flam mentally struggled in search of some noncommittal phraseology that would disguise his disdain and befuddlement over Angel's poem. He looked for inspiration in her lovely face, revelling in the exquisite valleys her cheekbones made in the smooth, milky skin, and admiring her full, luscious lips, their plateaus ripe with promises of pleasure.

As she glanced up and met his stare, her hazel eyes lit him up like an LCD, and he longed for her so deeply and profoundly, yet still could not bring himself to counterfeit compliments only to curry favour. Having endured a lifetime of hurtful insults and mockery, Flam valued the crystalline power of words far too much to mutate them into lies, and remained true to the chivalrous credo books had taught him as a neglected and abused child. *My God, why has she got me so . . . terrified,* he thought, and the nanosecond of introspection over the feeling and the true meaning of that word brought him a solution to his crisis of conscience. He leaned closer.

"That was so *terrific,*" he said, and smiled at his private joke.

The childlike look of unfettered joy he got in return instantly sent Flam's heart pulsing wildly. Unexpectedly, Angel turned away and started to gather up her things.

"Come on, let's go," she insisted. Flam was again thrown into mental confusion. He couldn't decide whether this latest turn of events was a godsend or a disaster. Was she now initiating a new, more intimate stage in their relationship . . . perhaps implicitly inviting him back to her place? Or was their evening finished, and with it all of his hopes and fantasies, once again shot down in a fireball of sexual frustration and interpersonal confusion?

"What about *my* poem?" he finally asked.

Her mischievous, you'll-just-have-to-wait-and-see expression showed she was definitely the old Angel again, and to prove it, she threw back her head and laughed, then grabbed him forcefully by the arm, talking up a storm in the process.

"You can read it to me under the night sky. Come on . . . we'll use your beautiful aura for a light to read by, and the stars above will be your audience." She suddenly dropped his arm, as if she couldn't wait a second longer, and practically ran out the door, leaving Flam in a hasty muddle as he furiously fumbled through his wallet to leave money for the bill, and hurriedly collected his schoolbooks.

CHAPTER 16

When Flam rushed outside the café in pursuit of his fugitive Angel, she was lying in ambush, and with a shout of glee pounced on his back.

"Carry me!" she commanded, letting loose the same wild uninhibited laugh he'd heard from her in the moonlight the week before. "Take me off someplace and read me your poem." Flam could distinctly feel her breasts pressed against his back, and her bare, lissome legs were wrapped around him, squeezing hard as he struggled to hold her up while hanging onto his knapsack.

Angel babbled non-stop in his ear about the secret songs of the night, and the dappled beauty of the stars, and how she'd once had an out-of-body experience where she flew so high there were stars below her as well as above. Flam struggled and huffed a bit as he carried her piggyback. Despite her wasp-waisted figure and short stature, his Angel was surprisingly heavy, or perhaps he was simply too scrawny for this kind of physical activity.

He had thought to take her back to his car, reasoning its back seat might serve as an impromptu venue for some passionate play if the opportunity arose. They were, in fact, two-thirds of the way across the still surprisingly busy parking lot when he spotted the car, and from a distance and in the harsh glare of the overhead halogen lights, the old Fairlane's rusting shell looked cheap and decrepit. Unexpectedly embarrassed, he racked his brain for some alternative spot where the two of them could be alone, under the stars—hopefully someplace nearby where he could unload the Angel on his back, for the initial scrumptious sensation of her body pressed closely against his was quickly giving way to fatigue and straining muscles.

Then Flam remembered his secret spot, between the hedges and the parking lot fence, where he used to hide and study, and where, what now seemed like ages ago, he'd overheard Lucy and Nolan Paine talking about marriage. *It's the perfect location,* he happily told himself, *it's outdoors and secluded, and as long as we're quiet no one will even know we're there.*

Flam cut across the parking lot, and staggered along the lawn in front of the Prentice War Memorial, its raised obelisk a phallic silhouette in the dark. He found his way to the opening in the hedgerow, and upon entering the secluded patch, collapsed to the ground, sending Angel tumbling and giggling on top of him.

"So, is this your secret make-out spot?" she asked, rolling onto her back, and stretching out like a cat.

"No...I mean...you...I never..." Flam stuttered, taken aback by the suggestion he was some practised Don Juan in the midst of another tawdry seduction, and yet mesmerized by the possibility she might be trying to woo him. The moon, even with a crescent sliced off, combined with the neighbouring lights of the parking lot to provide adequate illumination so he could make out Angel clearly, even lying on the ground,. Her breasts were rising and falling with each breath, and her skin seemed to have some luminescent sheen. A glint within her hazel eyes showed Flam she was looking directly at him, and he so badly wanted to jump on her and inundate her with kisses, and run his hands across her body. He was held back, however, by the absence of any overtly spoken permission, paralyzed by the possibility he was imagining it all, as he had with Lucy, and that his physical advances might be greeted with rejection, even horror.

"This is kind of my private hiding place," Flam finally got a sentence together, "but you're the only one I've ever brought here."

She laughed, although he couldn't tell whether it was pleasure at the implied compliment, or because of some cynical womanly disbelief. She rolled towards him and propped herself up on an elbow, the flex bringing out pleasing definition in her well-muscled bicep. "So, mister, didn't you say something about a poem?" Angel asked accusingly.

Flam was in heaven. *At last!* Nervously he reached into his knapsack and retrieved his printout. The dim light made in difficult to read, but he had the stanzas practically memorized, and so was able to recite without pause. He half whispered the words, partially because the late hour and the hidden place seemed to require it, but also because a *sotto voce* delivery somehow seemed to suit the poem's sensual and intimate nature.

Flam kept glancing up at Angel as he recited, hoping to get some inkling of her reaction, but her eyes were closed and she seemed lost in some private trance. Flam chose to interpret this as a hopeful sign of his poem's deep emotional impact. Even after he had finished, however, she remained lying there, unmoving and apparently unmoved, and all the splendour of the moment began to disintegrate into the abyss of the night.

For a brief, disquieting moment, Flam even thought Angel might have fallen asleep, and sudden anger and resentment and frustration swept over him, sparking an urge to grab her, to shake her, to force himself upon her and punish her. So contrary was this impulse to Flam's true gentle nature, the thought alone of the carnal evil he had been contemplating lashed him with a fresh wave of emotion, all shock and shame. Unable to stand it, he flopped over onto the ground, and squeezed his own eyes shut in an attempt to stem the scrum of jostling emotions threatening to overwhelm him.

A kiss, light as a butterfly's sigh, brought him back to his senses. He opened his eyes and Angel was staring down at him, her beautiful face only inches away. Flam began to lean upwards to return the kiss, but Angel slid away and onto her back, pillowing her head on his chest, and taking the printout of the poem from his hand to study.

"You typed it," she said after a few moments, the slightest hint of accusation tinting her tone.

"It's a copy for you," he countered, "I have a notebook for composing, then I do my final version on a computer. It's easier to edit and print copies . . . in case I want to get published." The latter was an impulsive afterthought, submitted out of self-defense or an attempt to impress, for in fact Flam had never before entertained the notion of publishing his poetry.

"I have to write all my poems by hand in my sacred notebook," Angel replied, "just one virginal verse for me to sing to the universal mother."

Flam had no ready retort for that, mainly because he hadn't a clue what the hell Angel was talking about. In fact, he felt helplessly mystified by whatever was going on between them—excluding the sheer animal delight from the warm press of Angel's body against his, and her intoxicating womanly scent, which seemed to mix with the earthy smell of the grass.

He felt full beyond capacity with longing for her, and yet almost defeated by the effort it had taken to have gotten this far, and was clueless as to what he should do next. Off across the campus, the Prentice College clock tower tolled the hour, and Flam realized how late it was, and how tired he felt. He decided that he just wanted to go to sleep. No! He didn't want this moment, this magic to end, for it would mean returning to his empty, pitiful life.

Angel had released the paper, and her hand was instead playing with the bottom of his T-shirt, which had ridden up his torso, leaving his midriff exposed. Then the hand meandered down to his naked belly and the fingers spent some time lightly stroking the downy hair there before moving further down and exploring the geometry of Flam's belt buckle.

He was fully aroused now, and knew his suffocated erection must clearly be evident to her—that she *must* realize what effect she was having, and where this had to end. Mentally he willed with all his might for Angel's hand to keep going, and it did, sliding down to briefly test Flam's zipper before pressing down more firmly and making one circumnavigation around the bulge in his pants.

And then, predictably unpredictable, Angel stopped. She sat up, suddenly upset, her head in her hands. "I'm sorry . . . I didn't mean to . . . I can't . . . I promised," she whimpered, before breaking outright into tears

Up to that point, Flam had been the one who felt like crying. His fantasies had been so flagrantly and frustratingly close to fulfillment, his sexual urges on the verge of a virginal breakthrough—only to be dashed and crashed and burned—but Angel's unexpected anguish was real and troubling. Her tears made him forget his own woes, other than to guiltily wonder if he somehow was responsible for what was happening.

He sat up and wrapped his arm protectively around her. "Angel, what's the matter?" he pleaded. "What promise? Did I do something wrong?"

She leaned into him, still sniffling. "No, no, it's not you." She looked up at him and smiled through her tears. "You're perfect," she said, and kissed him, before resuming her sniffling. "I know you want to make love to me, and I want you so badly too it hurts," she told him, "but I can't. I made a promise. I shouldn't have let it go this far but you're so sweet, and so gentle, and so nice, and so smart, and your poem was so . . . so . . . *awesome.*"

"What's this about a promise?" Flam asked, desperate to get to the bottom of things, "I don't understand."

"I . . . I belong to this group of women. A lot of them used to be Wiccans, but they left and started their own sect . . . kind of a sisterhood you might say. Some of the girls call it a coven, but I don't like to use that name because it makes people think of crazy-assed witches and stuff. But it's very . . . well . . . *spiritual* anyway, and they've really helped me, so much, to get in touch with the natural and supernatural world that's all around us, and to feel, like, empowered. That's why I wear white—because the sisters who have made it into the inner circle all wear these white robes—even though I'm not supposed to yet, on account of I'm still only an ac . . . acol . . . .." She paused trying to think of the right word.

"Acolyte?" Flam suggested.

"Yeah, that's right, an acolyte, but I wear white all the time anyway when I'm away from the other sisters because I really want to be like them and I guess it's my way of telling myself that I *know* I can make it . . . I mean, they really helped me when I was in a bad way, and they've taught me so much about, well, about everything. They've opened up a whole universe I didn't even know existed. Anyway, so part of my training . . . they call it my initiation, and that's why my hair is so short, is to avoid men, especially like having sex and stuff with them. So, you understand, I'm sorry, I really like you . . . a lot, you have no idea, but . . . I just can't. I promised."

Jesus Murphy, I really know how to pick them, Flam thought, and gently let go of Angel and collapsed backwards onto the grass, feeling for a second maybe the earth would open up and swallow him up. Silent, immobile, he stared skyward, blinking rapidly to prevent any tears of self-pity from welling up.

"You're not pissed with me, are you?" Angel asked, lying down beside him and nuzzling into his armpit.

Flam sighed—a long, deep, soulful sigh of frustration and consternation and resignation from the lowest *chakras* of his befuddled being.

"No, I'm not angry with you," he replied. "Don't get me wrong, Angel, I want you more than you can possibly imagine, and any way I look at it, this still feels like rejection to me, and that really hurts." He sighed again, his self-imposed code of honour feeling like a weight beyond bearing. "Aw, hell . . . if you've really taken a sacred vow, or even just made a promise, then I'm certainly the last person in the world who'll blame you for it."

That seemed to brighten Angel's mood a little and, bathing in his apparent forgiveness, she nestled even closer, throwing one delectable bare leg over top of him, seemingly oblivious to any renewed physical hardship this might have on her sexually thwarted companion.

"Can I ask you something?" she said, studying his face in the darkness.

"Mm. What?"

"Do you think I'm nuts?"

Flam mulled that one over for a moment then shook his head. "No, I don't think you're crazy to go searching for answers to *the* biggest question. I mean, after all, that's why *I'm* taking our class, isn't it . . . I have the same sort of root questions as you do. Look, if you really feel passionately about what you're doing . . . if you truly think you've stumbled on some sacred truth that resonates right inside of yourself, or honestly think you feel a tangible cosmic energy that helps the universe make sense, or even just makes day-to-day existence seem a little saner and easier to deal with, then I say more power to you, and the hell with what people think.

"But do I think the Old Gods of the Wiccans, or whatever you gals worship, are the real deal . . . more believable than the single universal deity the other religions generally tend towards? No, absolutely not."

Flam pondered some more and plunged on. "Seems to me too many people join religions just because they want to belong to something shiny and glorious that's bigger than them . . . or maybe they think there's some kind of spiritual safety in numbers, like a metaphysical herd instinct. Personally, I'm starting to think the path to God is actually a pretty lonely one, not some liturgical group excursion where everyone has to kowtow to the tour guide along the way. "

Flam was surprising himself with his rhetoric. The earnest nature of the moment and the simple, sincere question had crystallized beliefs and feelings whose existence he had not yet fully admitted even to himself, despite all his past and present forays into religious investigation. He looked down at the utterly desirable woman who was clinging tightly to him, and judging from her furrowed brow and the way she was gnawing on her lower lip, Angel seemed to be finding more confusion than comfort in his answer.

"Just be sure you know what you really believe in, and are not just aping someone else's credo," Flam added, reaching down to tilt up her chin so he could look into her eyes.

Angel smiled drowsily, and nestled harder against him, as if she was trying to disappear completely inside of him. "You're really smart, aren't you?" she asked, making it more of a statement than a question.

"Somehow, right now I feel pretty stupid," he replied.

That erased the smile from Angel's face. "I'm sorry," she said, "but you shouldn't blame yourself. I'm the one that's all confused. You're really a pretty amazing guy."

She sat up and started to tug and smooth her attire back into place, and, watching her, Flam got the distinct impression she was trying to find the words for something else. Sure enough she suddenly plopped back on top of him, pressed his shoulders hard against the grass, and glowered down at him, the silhouettes of her spiked hair giving her a beastly quality in the half-light.

"Listen," she said, sounding deadly serious, "I have no idea what you're thinking and feeling . . . but don't get hung up on me, okay? I mean, I'll take the blame for what happened . . . for what *didn't* happen tonight . . . but even if I ever did jump your bones, it wouldn't mean a damned thing. I've got my own shit to deal with, understand? And I sure as hell don't need you or any other man!" Angel looked down at the bewildered Flam, runaway strands of his black hair forming a tangled mask over his pale youthful face, and she broke into tears again.

"Christ, look at you, you're just a kid!" she sobbed. "What am I doing? What's wrong with me?" A pair of her tears splashed down and trickled into Flam's mouth and he could taste their saltiness. He wanted to get up to try to comfort Angel, to feel her womanly softness in his arms again, but she showed remarkable strength despite her small stature, and kept him thoroughly pinned while she had herself a good cry.

After a while, her blubbering became fainter and the heaves more subdued, and she released him and rolled over onto her side, brought her knees up to her chest and tightened into a ball. Flam reached over to her and began stroking her cheek and making soothing sounds, as if pacifying a baby, but to no effect. Angel just lay there motionless.

It wasn't until the college clock tolled again that she stirred and sat up, awoken from her trance. She stood up, fished through the tangle of silver necklaces and chains around her neck and retrieved one, flipping open its pendant to reveal a small watch inside.

She squinted to make out the time in the darkness then moaned. "Shit. It's late. I've got to get going. I've got prayers with the sisters at first light."

"I can give you a lift . . . my car's right there in the parking lot," Flam offered.

"Thanks. You *are* sweet," Angel replied, rewarding his chivalry with a peck on the cheek. "I'm not far. Do you know the apartments over on Longview? It'll only take ten minutes this time of night."

CHAPTER 17

Flam's sleep was a fitful one. The abbreviated night was haunted by longings for the unobtainable Angel, plus a thousand belated questions about her life in the strange occult sisterhood, which swirled madly around his addled brain like swimmers in a Busby Berkeley aquacade. When the alarm clock signalled an official end to Flam's pitiful attempts at slumber, he barely had the will to move, feeling as if he'd died, physically and emotionally. He lay there, wishing the stacked columns of books surrounding his tiny bed would come collapsing down on top of him, like the temple of Dagon on Samson, and bury him and all his worldly woes once and for all.

Despite the muzzy mind and bodily fatigue, a desire not to let Page Turner down asserted itself. It offered sufficient motivation to drag Flam out onto the cracked terracotta tiles of his washroom floor, and under the restorative cold spray of the shower nozzle. It was his responsibility to get downtown that morning in time to open up the bookstore, part of his standing agreement with Page in exchange for leaving work early on school nights.

For Flam, the drive downtown barely registered, so preoccupied were his clouded wits with lingering thoughts of rejection and remorse from the night before. He parked and fetched a coffee to jumpstart his morning, and was fumbling with the key that opened the ancient brass locks of the bookstore's front door when he was startled and almost knocked over by a man exiting the adjacent door that led to the upstairs apartments.

There were two other flats upstairs in addition to his mother's, and Flam did not find it especially unusual to encounter a stranger here. The Grub family's long-term occupation of their apartment was quite atypical. The remaining low-rent spaces had, over the decades, housed a seemingly endless stream of itinerant tenants, from the working-class immigrants of his boyhood, who had only stayed as long as it took them to find better accommodation, to the more recent parade of wannabe artists and twenty-something nomads who never seemed to be able to successfully muster more than a few months' rent.

The particular man who emerged from the doorway on this occasion, however, seemed much more interested in Flam than vice versa. The stranger was a tall, broad-shouldered, rugged-looking fellow with slicked-back black hair and a goatee, which were just starting to concede the first frosts of middle age. He was wearing an elegant, black leather coat over top of extravagant-looking, matching black shirt and slacks, and although the morning sun had not yet cleared the neighbouring buildings, the man sported dark sunglasses, which he now tilted up onto his brow to study Flam more closely. Despite the stylish attire, there was a dangerous-looking quality about the stranger that was unnerving.

Flam pretended to be oblivious to the man's gaze, and instead focussed ostentatiously on urging the door lock's recalcitrant tumblers to end their resistance. His attention was suddenly drawn back to the man when the stranger placed a hand on his shoulder and addressed him by name.

"Flam Grub, right?"

Flam was caught totally off guard at being addressed directly by name and could only stare blankly, unable to verbalize a response.

The stranger laughed in a hard, sneering way and unexpectedly reached inside of his jacket. Something about the man's whole physical demeanour was so menacing that, for one brief moment, Flam was suddenly convinced the man was going to kill him, a belief that seemed to bear fruit when a large black pistol in a shoulder holster became visible. But it was a black leather wallet with an ID card and a gold shield, not a gun, that was deftly flipped open in Flam's face.

"My name's Sergeant Cuff, Mr. Grub. I'm a detective. I was just up talking to your mother. Do you mind if I ask you a few questions?"

The fact he was not going to be gunned down was enough of a relief for Flam to manage a reply. "Yes . . . I mean, no, I don't mind," he replied.

"Mr. Grub, I believe you knew a Gerald Strait," the cop said, his voice all of a sudden falling into a soft and calming tone that was at odds with his physical presence. By now, Flam's universe was starting to slowly resume its rightful rotation, and Flam had fully collected his wits enough so that Sergeant Cuff's use of the past tense was not lost on him.

"I've only met him a couple of times. He was engaged to my mother for a little while, but she broke it off," Flam responded, knowing full well this was all old news to the detective. "Why? What's this all about?"

"Mr. Strait was found dead last night," Sergeant Cuff replied, and with this his eyes narrowed into slits, and he seemed to study Flam closely, as if clinically gauging his reaction.

Although a thousand thoughts suddenly exploded into Flam's mind, his instincts told him to play things cautiously, at least until he had better assessed the policeman's intentions and understood any lurking threats to Flam or his mother.

"Dead? That's awful," Flam answered, trying to effect just the right tone of common decency and concern, although he had never liked Gerald, and frankly didn't care one bit about the man's demise. "How did he die?"

"The coroner hasn't released a cause of death yet, and we're still looking into what might have happened. Now, you say your mother broke off her engagement to Mr. Strait? When did this happen?"

"A couple of weeks ago," Flam told him. "The three of us went out for supper together, and she phoned him with her decision later that night."

"And why did your mother say she called it off?"

Flam was finding the line of questioning a little alarming. Wasn't Sergeant Cuff the very one who had broken the news to his mother about the criminal charges Gerald was facing? The cop had even gone so far as to add suspicions that Gerald might have murdered his first wife . . . even though, as far as Flam could tell, those allegations had been largely unsubstantiated. And didn't Cuff just tell him he had already been speaking to his mother? So if the policeman already had all the details, why was he asking Flam? It almost seemed like Cuff was seeking corroboration of Mary's story, which might mean she herself was under suspicion.

"You know all this already, don't you? You're the one who told her about Gerald," Flam protested, his note of resistance inspiring a ripple of tension to pass across the policeman's jawline.

"Listen, *Flam*, just answer the questions," the sergeant shot back, clearly irritated, and adding a mocking intonation to the name. "You're saying that your mother broke off the engagement because of what I told her that day . . . that she believed Strait was no good?"

"Yeah, that's right," Flam replied, and thought he saw a glimmer of a smirk appear on the cop's face.

"So, is Mary . . . is your mother seeing anyone else now?" Cuff asked.

"No!" Flam's indignant reply provided the obvious subtext that his mother was not that sort of woman. "Look, Gerald is the first man my mother's been involved with since my father's death, and that was almost three years ago. Just what the hell's going on here?"

"Take it easy, kid. They're just routine questions."

"Really? Well I don't like your questions," Flam replied angrily, surprising himself with his bravery.

"Well I've got news for you. I'll ask whatever fucking questions I want, understand?" Sergeant Cuff responded, jabbing a finger hard into Flam's breastbone. "Like, where were *you* last night?"

Flam swallowed hard, suddenly frightened. "I was at a night school class . . . I just graduated from Prentice College, and I'm picking up extra credits during the summer."

"Oh yeah? What time did you get home?"

Now Flam felt like he was the one under suspicion. "Um . . . around one o'clock."

Cuff cocked an eyebrow. "One o'clock? That's a helluva long class."

"I . . . I went out afterwards with some friends," Flam answered, feeling completely on the defensive. He was convinced his face had to be turning tomato red.

The detective, however, seemed to lighten up and suddenly changed his tack. "Prentice, eh? I'm a Prentice Law Enforcement grad myself you know. Class of '79. So what course are you in?"

"Funeral Services."

Cuff threw back his head and laughed aloud. "Flam Grub, the undertaker. Good one."

Inside the bookstore, the phone rang. Flam, unsure of his next move, glanced down at the key that was still in the front door's lock, before looking up expectantly at the policeman.

"You'd better get that, kid," Cuff snorted, and walked off.

The phone call turned out to be from Flam's mother, sounding half hysterical and blubbering uncontrollably. "Flam? Oh dear Lord, Flam, there you are. Where on earth have you been? I have the most terrible news. It's Gerald . . . Gerald Strait. He's killed himself! Oh why, Lord? Oh why?"

"Mother. Shhh. Calm down. It's okay, it's okay . . . I know," Flam said, trying to soothe her. Then it hit him. "What do you mean killed himself?" Sergeant Cuff had said the cause of death was still unknown.

"He shot himself, dear, last night. I tried to call you . . . where were you? Oh, it's just awful . . . I feel so guilty. It's all my fault! Oh, Gerald! Oh Gerald! Why? Why? What have I done to you?" Mary's torrent of words was almost as fast flowing as the current of alternating thoughts now electrifying Flam's mind, and ended in another aria of wails.

"Stop it, Mother! Now listen to me! This is *not* your fault. Do you hear me? You haven't done anything wrong," Flam insisted, wanting desperately to stop the bawling, which could be heard clearly at the other end of the phone.

"I know . . . I know . . . that's exactly what Lee told me last night, but I can't help it, I feel so guilty. Oh, Gerald! Why? Why?"

"Who's Lee?" Flam asked her, still trying to get a handle on the whole shape and spin of events.

His mother's sobbing seemed to abate somewhat. "That nice Sergeant Cuff, the policeman I told you about, dear . . . he was the one who found poor Gerald, you know, and, well, he was kind enough to come right over, and break the news to me." Her tone abruptly hardened, raising spectres of boyhood rebukes. "I tried to call you last night . . . where were you?"

Outside, one of the passersby stopped and pressed his face against the front window of the bookstore. Flam realized he hadn't even turned on the shop lights yet.

"Mother? Listen to me. Don't blame yourself for anything . . . you've done absolutely nothing wrong except stand up for yourself. That Gerald was just plain bad. That's all there is to it. Now, look, I've got to go right now . . . I have to finish opening the store. But why don't you make yourself a nice cup of tea and bring it downstairs and have a sit with me. We can talk about it some more."

"Oh, no, dear, I can't. I've already missed early mass, and I just *have* to get to mid-morning services. Poor Gerald . . . he's charged with a grave, grave sin, you know, taking his own life. Dear me, with all the other awful things they say he's done, I wouldn't be surprised if the bishop refuses to allow them to give Gerald a funeral mass. I just can't help feeling responsible . . . I've got to go and pray for him. Maybe the Lord will take pity on his poor soul after all. Oh, sweet saints in Heaven, what have I done? What have I done?"

With that, Mary abruptly hung up, leaving a bewildered Flam hanging on the other end of the line. The startling news of Gerald's death, his mother's guilty reaction, and the surprise encounter on the street with Sergeant Cuff were all adding up to a massive dose of distress. Flam had instantly disliked the cop's attitude, especially his sneering pronunciation of Flam's name, and was convinced there was something mysterious going on, which Cuff was involved in up to his bull neck.

The phone rang again, and this time the caller was Page Turner, checking in with his young assistant. Flam was in the process of relaying

an abridged, but heavily annotated version of the recent events, when
he saw a large black sedan with tinted windows pull up in front of
the bookstore, and moments later, his mother, wearing a short-sleeved,
knee-length chiffon black dress over matching pantyhose, come
quickly out onto the sidewalk and, without so much as glancing in
the bookstore's direction, get into the car. Flam stared at his mother,
amazed. The overwhelming thought in Flam's mind was that the
dress, which he had never seen his mother wear before, was very chic
and somehow seemed better suited for dining than praying.

Somewhere around noon, having mentally exhausted all the imaginary
scenarios in the puzzling circumstances surrounding Gerald's
apparent suicide, some of which read like the tawdry, yellow-leafed
detective fiction that crammed the bookstore's Mystery section, Flam's
thoughts migrated to the other woman—the woman in white—who
was troubling his life.

After weeks crafting verses of adoration to the elusive Angel, Flam
now sat idle and brooding, feeling his efforts at seduction through
poetry had once again been a colossal waste of time. And, yet, unlike
the bottomless despair he had felt after the tragedy of Lucy's rejection,
this heartache did not quite cut straight to the soul.

Despite her ultimately rejecting him, Flam had nonetheless
momentarily tasted Angel's interest, even her outright lust. Her
kisses and caresses had been real, and still burned brightly in his
memory. Although those reminiscences only served to further stoke
his unfulfilled craving for her flesh, he could take solace in the fact
rejection was not apparently because of Flam the man per se, but
rather Angel's vow of chastity to her coven of Wiccanesque sisters. No,
this failure had a much more, well, *poetic* timbre to it, a sort of storied,
star-crossed flavour, which made him feel more like a tragic hero than
a gangly, pasty-faced virginal loser.

This thought appealed to Flam, and he pulled out his pocket
notebook, fully intending to sketch out a new poem, chronicling how
selfless and noble he was to stand aside and allow the woman of his

desires to journey onward in pursuit of spiritual fulfillment. The words, however, just wouldn't come. No matter how hard Flam scrubbed and rationalized his thoughts, he simply could not brainwash himself to turn this latest personal setback into a triumph. Dark depression was again lapping at his feet, threatening to pull him under.

The truth, though, was that he hadn't stepped aside . . . he had again been pushed away. And he didn't really care one iota for Angel's neo-pagan beliefs, and would gladly have sex with her right on top of whatever holy altar she and her sorority of witches might use for their worship.

His creative efforts having been thwarted by the familiar feelings of failure and self-pity, Flam slumped back on his stool, and leafed through his well-worn notebook. As he flipped past pages containing unhatched poetic ideas and half-baked snatches of verse, a piece of folded paper tumbled out. Opening it up, he found a list with some of the potential new names he had recently been evaluating for himself. One name jumped out at him—he could barely remember having contrived it—and made him snort. *Lance Allcock? Geez Louise, What was I thinking? Sounds like a name for a porn star,* he told himself, vaguely recalling some nebulous Arthurian influence. *Porn star? Ha! I only wish. With the luck I have with women, I should call myself Dick Less.*

CHAPTER 18

Although he might have denied it, while on the job Flam would consciously find ways to avoid his mother. Since she lived right above the bookstore, Flam, of course, often saw her, at least in passing, several times during the course of a work day. But he had tried to ensure that these sightings didn't turn into extended meetings. Given the fact that he was now working seven days a week, Flam had felt that these passing moments of interaction served as entirely adequate examples of filial devotion for any twenty-one-year-old fighting a war of independence, let alone the obsessively reclusive Flam.

While contact with customers was an unavoidable part of working in the shop, Flam had nevertheless managed to create an environment that largely shielded him from the public. Page Turner, the incurably curious shopkeeper, had set up his station at the front counter so it was practically in the bookstore's window, affording an excellent view of all the happenings out on the street. The shy Flam, however, disliked this configuration, having always felt like he was the one on display, perched prominently on the tall stool to be gawked at by passersby.

When Page began spending more and more time away from the shop, Flam had subtly made adjustments to his working environment. First, he slid as far away from the front window as the dimensions of the counter allowed, even though this meant having to get off his stool to ring up transactions at the cash register. Eventually, he had also ensured a protective wall of books was always stacked up on the counter, so it obscured him from the world at large.

Whenever he was sitting up front, Flam would habitually lean forward onto the counter and purposefully hide behind these books, usually first laying down a newspaper to prevent his elbows from sticking to or smudging up the thick glass top of the massive oak display case, which served double duty as the counter. Hunkered down this way, he would be well hidden from view.

Following the encounter with Sergeant Cuff and the news of Gerald's death, however, Flam abruptly changed this practice. Now he practically hovered in the front window, trying unsuccessfully to catch sight of his mother, even taking down his wall of books to make her easier to spot. All of it was to no avail. He took to dropping by the apartment after work, once waiting for several hours, but she never materialized. In the evenings, he telephoned her, sometimes trying repeatedly into the late night, but was inevitably forced to leave messages on the answering machine.

By the time Sunday came around, Flam had not yet seen or connected with his mother. Only a short note, found slipped under the bookstore door the previous morning, testified to the fact she was still alive and inhabiting the planet. The hastily scrawled, mildly apologetic communiqué said simply that she was extraordinarily busy, had had several late nights, and would see him soon.

The affairs of the parish and demands of her constituency being what they were, it was not unheard of for Mary to become preoccupied with her duties virtually to the exclusion of everything else. Flam therefore struggled hard to dismiss any rising paranoia, but try as he might, he could not shake the nagging notion something unusual was afoot, and his mother was purposely avoiding him.

Flam had just gotten home and was picking away at the burnt offerings of a frozen dinner when his mother finally connected with him.

"Flam, dear, how are you? Is everything okay? You sounded so worried in your telephone messages," Mary began.

"I *have* been worried . . . about *you*," Flam chided her. "Are you alright? I haven't talked to you all week, ever since you told me that Gerald had been . . . well . . .." He stopped, unsure how to finish his sentence.

"That's why I'm calling you, dear. I want you to get time off on Tuesday morning for Gerald's funeral. You really have to go, dear . . . he was almost your stepfather."

"Um, I guess so, but I'll have to ask Page first," Flam squirmed, feeling ambushed and trapped. He also resented her imperative tone, and thought he would rather eat nails than attend that particular event. "What time is the service?" he asked glumly.

"There won't be a mass at the church, I'm afraid. There was no one but me to speak up on Gerald's behalf, and they just wouldn't listen, even though I practically got down on my knees. Those smug, self-righteous bastards! You would think after all my years of working like a slave for the church they would have some consideration for me, if not for poor Gerald. How dare they throw scriptures in *my* face! I know damn well the bishop has leeway in these matters, but he won't even see me, the fat old lecher." The whole matter evidently still angered Mary tremendously, and her flamethrower tone brought memories flooding back from Flam's boyhood, making him instinctively sink lower into his armchair for protection. All of a sudden, he felt very grateful they were only talking over the phone, although it was destined to be a very one-sided conversation.

"To hell with the lot of them, the ungrateful hypocrites!" she spat out. "They'll rue the day they crossed Mary Flam." Flam barely had time to register she had not called herself Mary Grub when his mother plunged onward with the details.

"At any rate, I've managed to get them to agree to have Father O'Meara come and say some words for Gerald at the funeral home. I'm afraid it will just have to do. He's being released by the coroner tomorrow during the day, and we'll have the vigil tomorrow night. I expect to see you there when you're finished work. Then the service will be at ten o'clock on Tuesday morning, and I want you to try very hard to get off work. Have you got that? Ten o'clock. They're going

to cremate him right after the service." Thus far, Mary had been all
business and brass, as if deftly dispensing with another routine parish
matter, but at the mention of the cremation she evidently had to stop
talking momentarily, and choke back a lump in her throat.

"Now, do you know the Morton Funeral Home on Station
Street?" she asked, pausing long enough to allow Flam to slide in a
grunt of acknowledgement. "I'd like you to get there early, let's say
nine thirty. Okay? Phone me right after you've talked to Mr. Turner
to confirm that you can make it. Leave a message if I'm not at home,
which is more than likely. I'm afraid I'm in a bit of a rush, dear, I have
to go out again, so we'll have to chat some other time. Bye, Flam. See
you tomorrow night."

Flam hung up the receiver, and turned to reflect on her call over
the detritus of his supper. Finally managing to talk to his mother had
not alleviated the questions and uneasy feelings fermenting in his mind
over the past several days. Now he was left bristling with resentment
over being forced to attend both the vigil and the funeral service.

He walked into the kitchen to toss the crumpled remnants of the
aluminum foil tray into the garbage, and ended up kicking a cabinet
door in anger, unleashing a small avalanche of books in the opposite
corner, and stubbing his toe in the process.

"Who the hell does she think she is?" he screamed to the empty
apartment. "Does she think I'm still the little kid she used to boss
around and treat like dirt? I'm an adult now! She can't tell me what
to do!" And yet the anger was hollow, for despite the vocal outburst
of bravado that continued for several more minutes, he had already
resigned himself to doing what she commanded.

Flam was still smouldering the next morning when he dutifully
asked Page Turner for the next day off. "I know it's short notice, and
I'll understand if you say no," Flam hinted, hoping Turner would
garner the resistance that Flam, the weakling, could not. He was
therefore caught off balance when the older man not only quickly
consented, but in fact seemed downright enthusiastic about Flam
attending the funeral. When Flam's body language made it clear he

dreaded the prospect, Turner slammed a palm into his own forehead in exasperation.

"Flam," he exclaimed, "for somebody who's so patently intelligent, you sure can be egregiously dim-witted." He chuckled and switched into a mockingly patronizing tone. "Okay. Try to follow my logic, young disciple. Where do funerals take place?"

"Um, a funeral home?" Flam replied hesitantly, trying to figure out the angle.

"Excellent, young wizard. Now, what do they have at funeral homes?"

"Um . . . funerals?" he replied, but Turner's expression dictated he should keep guessing. "Coffins? Dead bodies?"

"No, no, no. Is your skull really so crammed with words you can't see the world that gives them meaning? Think hard, Flam. What they have at funeral homes are . . . *jobs!*"

Understanding flooded over Flam's face like the sun rising on the ocean, and his mouth mimicked the orb's shape too. He realized sheepishly that he had been so preoccupied, resenting and resisting his mother's dictates, he had neglected to spot the golden opportunity hanging before him. *I am such an idiot*, he thought, *I can't see the cemetery for the tombstones.*

Meanwhile, Turner had punched open the cash register and, extracting a small bundle of bills, offered them to Flam. The short-lived sunshine of understanding disappeared from Flam's face, and the pall of ignorance returned.

"What's this for?" he asked.

"For a new suit, a black one of course. I'd suggest single-breasted with two buttons. Don't look at me like that . . . just because I choose to protest the tyranny of fashion doesn't mean I'm oblivious to it. If you hasten over to Suits Me on Second Street right now and insist on it, I'm quite sure they will be able to conjure up an affordable new suit off the rack, and have it ready by the end of the day."

Although he saw the logic in it, Flam was embarrassed by Turner's act of generosity. "I can't accept this. I already owe you for my rent . . . it'll take me forever to pay you back," he protested.

"On the pittance I pay you, that's probably true," Turner laughed, "but I'm sure even an entry-level job in a funeral home will get you back in the black, no pun intended, in no time."

"I thought you disapproved of the funeral business," Flam said. "Vultures, I seem to recall you calling them."

"Well, in your case I believe you honestly want to help people, Flam, so if you can stand the company of the dead then I suppose it's one profession that won't turn you into a nervous wreck the way some can. Besides, people are always dying, so at least you'll always have job security . . . once you secure a job, that is. Look, it's been wonderful having you back in the bookstore and working beside me, and I'm glad to be able to help you out, but while I've certainly never been one to believe in some Hollywood cardboard-cutout version of cosmic destiny, I just honestly don't think this is where you were meant to be, and it would be supremely selfish of me to try to keep you here."

Flam hesitated, almost unable to cope with the gratitude and affection he was experiencing for the bearded and ponytailed eccentric who had taught and helped him so much. Finally he reached over and took the money.

"Get some shoes too, while you're at it, a pair of black wing-tips I'd say . . . nice and conservative. Go on, now. I'll watch the store. Make sure you insist on having the suit ready today. If they complain, threaten to take your business elsewhere. Assert yourself, son."

Flam smiled and headed towards the door.

"And, Flam," a grinning Turner added, giving his ponytail an exaggerated flip as he turned away, "get a haircut, you longhaired bum."

CHAPTER 19

The Morton Funeral Home had been occupying its piece of Station Street since the mid 1800s, easily beating out the local tavern as the longest continuing enterprise in the neighbourhood. The original white limestone building, with its stained-glass gothic windows, had been haphazardly added to both vertically and horizontally at various times over the decades. A charcoal-grey paint was now applied to all the new sections to downplay their lack of architectural unanimity, and to foster a degree of sombre uniformity.

Flam studied the building critically, noting the rows of bricked-up windows on the upper stories. He then walked around the side to check out the part of the structure where the real business of the home would be conducted. The odd design of the loading area puzzled him for a moment, until he realized it had been built before the automobile age to accommodate horse-drawn hearses.

When he walked through the tall arched doorway of the funeral home's front entrance, Flam was greeted by a middle-aged man, perched behind an ornate oak lectern like a *maître d'* at an upscale restaurant. The man had a smooth, tanned face beneath a towering, immaculately arranged pompadour of wavy, salt-and-pepper hair, and as he studied Flam his small, beady, know-it-all eyes darted around frenetically like a guppy in a pool.

"Good evening," the man greeted him, a hint of an accent tinting his formal, reassuring tone. "Are you here for the Wormsley viewing?"

"Um, no, Gerald Strait," Flam replied, noticing the man seemed to visibly lose interest upon hearing this.

"The North Room, down this hall, last door on the left," he instructed curtly, and immediately returned his attention to a book on the lectern.

Flam paused for a second, wondering if he should broach the subject of possible employment now, but the man's bearing made it clear he considered their interchange concluded. Flam sighed softly and shuffled down the prescribed wainscotted hallway, wrinkling his nose slightly at the unusual sweet odour, and gazing down in admiration at the ornate pattern intricately woven into the plush navy blue carpet.

The North Room was unoccupied except for Mary, who was kneeling in prayer before the simple, closed maple casket that held Gerald's remains. Her forehead was pressed against the lustrously varnished lid, and she was uttering her intonations to God in a barely audible whisper. Flam hesitated at the doorway, surmising by the room's smallish size and its institutional drabness that it was reserved for the less noteworthy clientele. His mother was wearing the same black dress and pantyhose he had seen her in last, and it disturbed him when he saw the extent to which her legs were visible when she knelt, although the irritation was more at himself for dwelling on the exposed legs than at any perceived impropriety on his mother's part.

Flam came up to the front row of seats and softly cleared his throat to let his mother know he was there, but the only indication she had heard him was a slight increase in the pitch and pace of her prayers. He dismissed the notion of kneeling beside her, and instead lowered himself into the closest chair—it was of a cheap, folding variety, another indication, along with the dearth of flowers surrounding the coffin, that this was a low-budget funeral.

Eventually Mary concluded her communion, and made to rise from her supplication, but she appeared to stagger a bit, as if trying to rise from under a tremendous weight. Flam sprang up to offer her a hand, only to be taken aback by a sudden look of shock that came over her face. It took him a second to realize it was his made-over appearance that had caught his mother by surprise.

"Saints preserve me, dear, I didn't recognize you. For a second I thought Death himself had come to take me away!" Mary exclaimed, a look of delight now taking over her face. "Good heavens, just look at you. Oh my, you look so grown-up . . . so dignified." She reached up to stroke the lapels of Flam's new black suit, then ran her hand lovingly through his hair, now cut conservatively shorter. The smile disappeared, however, as she seemed to catch herself, and she quickly returned to a sombre demeanour. "Thank you for coming, dear," she sniffled through newly minted tears. "It would have meant so much to Gerald. He was very fond of you."

Flam recalled that she had practically commanded him to attend, even though he barely knew the man, but suppressed a sarcastic retort. He forced himself to look sympathetic instead. Lovingly putting an arm around his mother, he allowed her to slump onto his shoulder in a marriage of black on black, while he gently guided her into a chair.

"There, there, Mother. I'm here for you," he consoled her, mentally searching through his repertoire of poetic quotations for something profound to say, but coming up blank. "It's the Lord's will," was ultimately all he managed—an anodyne comment that was nonetheless rewarded with a brave half-smile of thanks.

They sat together in silence for a while, and Flam began to wonder if perhaps they were going to be the only ones in attendance that evening. Try as he might, he couldn't bring himself to feel sorry for Gerald, and chose to interpret the lack of mourners as proof in death of the pharmacist's unsavoury nature in life. Eventually, however, a pair of old women appeared at the door, each supporting the other as they shuffled in, and Flam rose to help them be seated, getting them to sign the guest book first.

Mary seemed to know the two women, and the trio quickly collapsed together into a huddle of fervent sobs and consoling endearments. Two more people soon arrived, this time a middle-aged couple wearing decades-old suits, and looking uncertain and uncomfortable. Flam went over to receive them as well.

"Good evening. I am Oleg Chebutnik," the man introduced himself with a thick Eastern European accent, "and this is wife, Natalka. We have store next door with Mr. Strait for twenty years."

"Such tragedy it is!" the woman chimed in. "Ach, so sad." Flam nodded supportively, and ushered them into the room. Another half-dozen people dribbled in over the course of the next hour. Flam, whether because of his tenuous pseudo-familial connection or his training in the funerary profession, found himself taking charge by default, and making sure all the new arrivals were suitably greeted and seated. Before long, Mary, having either conceived of additional entreaties to present to the Lord or having found fresh inspiration in the presence of an audience, dropped to her knees again and resumed her fervent prayers at the side of the casket, eliciting a counterpoint of supportive refrains from some of the other visitors seated nearby.

Standing at the back of the room, Flam took that opportunity to slip out and investigate the rest of the funeral home, starting with the other vigil that was taking place in the main chapel at the front of the building. Peeking into the high-vaulted chamber, Flam saw that in contrast to Gerald's low-key affair, the Wormsley family had evidently spared no expense for their dearly departed—a pointy-nosed woman in her sixties who lay serenely in a lavish oak coffin surrounded by a veritable forest of flowers. Dozens of people were milling around the room, which had a cocktail-party buzz to it, many clustered around a large TV screen, which displayed a slide show of photos of the deceased, dating back to childhood.

The pompadour-sporting man, who had originally met Flam at the door, was chatting up a prosperous-looking couple nearby. Although his verbal train never slowed, a suddenly raised eyebrow indicated he had spotted the interloper in the doorway. Eventually, the man finished recounting his vignette to appreciative smiles and murmurs from the couple, then excused himself and headed over towards the chapel's entrance. Knowing he had been spotted, Flam's first reflex was to turn and flee the scene, but a spark of determination made him fight the impulse and stand his ground.

"How are you, sir? Is everything alright?" he asked, and Flam noted with admiration there was not even a trace of disrespect or impatience in the man's level, calming tone, even as he expertly guided Flam out into the hall.

"Um, no, everything is fine, as far as Mr. Strait goes. Actually, well . . . I was wondering whom I might talk to about possible employment."

The man huffed himself up, and looked Flam over critically, literally from head to toe, and all the deference was gone in his voice when he replied.

"Do you have any experience?" he asked.

Flam was feeling uneasier by the second, and was positive his face was taking on a reddish hue, but he forced himself to hang in. "I'm afraid not, but I just graduated at the top of my class in Funeral Services at Prentice College." He reached into his inside pocket and handed the man a copy of his résumé, which he had brought along at Page Turner's insistence.

Pompadour Man stood staring for a moment at the neatly addressed envelope, as if contemplating some excruciatingly difficult plan of action, then returned the packet to Flam's hand. "I'm not the one you have to talk to," the man said, some of the pretentiousness gone from his voice. "Are you going to be here for the Strait service tomorrow morning?" Flam nodded assent, his heart beating faster with anticipation. "Then this is what you have to do," the man continued. "Before the service starts, go to the office and ask for Mrs. Clarke." He indicated a door labelled "*Private*" midway down the hall.

"Tell her you talked to Bruno Helman. She'll give you an application form to fill out, but Mr. Morton does all the hiring himself . . . if there are any positions available." Bruno gave Flam one last up-and-down look and then, without another word, spun gracefully on his heels and returned to the chapel.

Flam was feeling elated, as much at having survived his face-to-face solicitation of Bruno as at having inched closer to possible

employment. Excited, he turned to return to the North Room and
Gerald's vigil, but an imposing shape suddenly stepped out of the
shadows and blocked Flam's way. It was Sergeant Cuff.

"Hello, there, Flaaaam," the cop greeted him with a lopsided and
malignant smile on his face. "What's up?"

Flam's good spirits evaporated like a raindrop on a hot hood, to
be replaced by a mixture of annoyance and apprehension. "Nothing,"
was all he could muster in the way of a reply.

"Nothing?" Cuff echoed. "Oh, I don't think so. Is my little Grub
looking for a job? Here, let me see." And before Flam could even
flinch, the sergeant deftly whisked the résumé from out of Flam's
inside pocket, and then used one of his broad shoulders as a barrier
to prevent Flam from attempting to snatch the envelope back. With a
dramatic flourish, the cop opened up the page and skimmed through
its contents.

"Hmmm, pretty skimpy, if you ask me," Cuff snorted, "kind of
like you."

"Give me that back," Flam protested, yanking hard on the cop's
arm. Cuff's smile suddenly vanished. He bared his teeth in a vicious
grimace, and slammed his shoulder hard into Flam, forcing the
younger man to backpedal until he banged against the wall.

"Are you kidding me?" Cuff growled, taking Flam by the throat, "I
could drop you with one finger. Never ever touch me again. Shit, don't
you know I could have you arrested for assaulting an officer?"

But then, just as suddenly as he'd angered, his mood changed and
the cop released Flam, chuckling as if it was all a big joke, and handed
the résumé and its envelope back.

"Come on, kid," Cuff urged affably as if nothing had happened
and wrapped a friendly arm around Flam. "Let's go see what's
happening at the wakey wakey."

As he walked back down the hall under the policeman's escort,
Flam could not get up the nerve to ask any of the questions ricocheting
through his mind. Cuff unnerved Flam at a raw, visceral level, and
Flam was too terrified to try to interrogate him about his involvement

in Gerald's death, or the nature of his relationship with Mary. It was up to the cop to broach the silence.

"So, you'd really want to work in a place like this?" Cuff asked. Flam just shrugged. "Well, I guess hanging around with the dead is no worse than some of the deadbeats I have to put up with," Cuff chuckled. "At least they don't give you no lip. Come to think of it, I could name quite a few guys I came up against who were a hell of a lot easier to deal with once they turned up dead."

"You mean, like Gerald?"

Cuff shot him a dirty look. "Don't kid yourself, Flam, the biggest favour Gerald Fucking Strait did the world was leaving it. Everybody's better off with him dead, yourself included."

They reached the North Room and went in together. Despite the presence of a few more stragglers, who had arrived in the interim, the pitiful handful of mourners was a mean and meagre assembly compared to the upscale affair Flam had just witnessed. Mary was still hard at prayer, and her generous showing of black-nyloned legs captured both men's attention, one staring in obvious admiration, the other in concealed embarrassment.

"Hard to believe a hottie like your mama was going to marry that no-good crooked Strait," Cuff said, lowering his voice. "Good thing she's got a guardian angel looking after her."

He winked at Flam, and sauntered up to the front to stand reverently by the casket. Mary, spotting the cop's arrival, terminated her prayers and stood up to give him a polite but prolonged hug. Cuff leaned close to Mary, and engaged her in some private whispered conversation that, within seconds, had her eyes twinkling, and a childlike smile of delight on her face, although she hid it diplomatically behind a black glove.

Whatever personal revulsion Flam might have felt for the policeman was clearly not shared by his mother, nor for that matter by her female acquaintances, as Cuff soon found himself at the centre of a small gaggle of women who were all smiling and hanging off his every word. Annoyed, without fully knowing why, Flam made his way up to

the gathering and interrupted by asking his mother if she needed a lift
back to the apartment.

"Oh, no, Flam," Mary replied. "Thank you, but I'm going to stay
here for a while longer, then Sergeant Cuff has been generous enough
to offer to drive Charlotte, Pauline, and myself home. So you go ahead
without me, dear."

Flam wrestled inwardly with his annoyance, and was tempted
to announce that he had decided to spend the night at his mother's
place, just to see what kind of a monkey wrench that might throw
into the evening's agenda. But as morbidly curious as he was about
his mother's personal goings on, mostly he just felt tired. More than
anything, he simply wanted to escape back to his own apartment, take
off his constricting suit and throat-choking tie, and lie down among
his books in the serenity and peace of his little sanctuary. He forced a
smile, kissed his mother on the cheek, and hugged the churchwomen
one by one. Cuff was last in line, waiting with a big uneven grin on his
face and his hand already extended to wish Flam goodnight.

"Straight home now, Flam, my man," Cuff called after him.
"Don't do anything I wouldn't do."

CHAPTER 20

Waiting in his day-old black suit at the door of the Morton Funeral Home's office promptly at 9 a.m., Flam heard Mrs. Clarke's laboured breathing and grunts of discomfort from around the corner long before she came huffing and shuffling into view. Mrs. Clarke turned out to be a huge, ruddy-faced woman with a rust-coloured perm and a disposition like a constipated watchdog. She had huge, tree-trunk legs, which ran straight down from her body without any trace of curvature before being squeezed into a pair of impossibly small white shoes, whose tops were obscured by the overhanging folds of fat. Even through the knee-high, peach-coloured orthopedic stockings into which her legs were crammed like sausages in their casings, streaks of angry purple veins were clearly visible all over her calves and shins.

The rotund woman did not seem pleased to discover Flam lurking at the door of her office. She waved off any attempt at an introduction until she had wrestled open the lock to the office, and then waddled across the floor to collapse into her heavily padded executive tilter chair. Despite being made of steel, the seat appeared to sag under her weight. She turned on her computer, plugged in a kettle and a humidifier, and then punched a bunch of keys on a large phone console before turning in Flam's direction.

"I talked to Bruno Helman last night and he said I should see you about applying for a job," he began when it appeared Mrs. Clarke had finally settled in and caught her breath. She stared at him blankly for a few seconds, and Flam began to wonder if she had even heard him. Then, with surprising dexterity, she rolled her chair across to the filing cabinet, gracefully slid out a well-oiled drawer, daintily extracted some papers, then used the recoil from pushing the drawer shut to glide herself, with one and a half spins, back into perfect position across from Flam. There she grabbed an empty file folder and pen off her desktop with one hand, while offering him the papers with the other.

"Fill out this application form, attach your résumé, then place them in this file folder and write your name on the label, in capital letters, surname first," she instructed Flam in rapid-fire sequence. "You can sit over there," she added, indicating a black leather loveseat and glass-topped coffee table set up in the corner for visitors. Finally, she sighed deeply through her mouth, as if she had just completed some supremely physically grueling task.

Flam obediently followed her instructions, and while he laboured to fill in squares on the form so small they almost appeared to have been placed there to serve double duty as an eye test, he overheard her talking to someone on the phone about an interview, after which she grunted and dropped the phone back onto its cradle.

"Mr. Morton will be in to see you in about ten minutes," she advised Flam, sending him into a mild panic. His application was only partially completed, and although much of its requested data could be transcribed from his résumé, Flam had to pick up the pace of his punctilious printing in order to provide all the requested information. Moreover, he had not expected to have an interview on the spot. Gerald's funeral service was scheduled to start at ten o'clock, and his mother had been adamant about Flam's punctuality. His anxiety mounted at the risk of being late for the service.

Still, even if he had had the temerity to speak up and postpone the interview, Flam felt like he was being carried swiftly along on a current of rapidly unfolding events. He was suddenly hopeful that fate was smiling on him this morning, ushering him towards the start of his sought-after career in the funeral business.

He had just finished labelling the file folder GRUB, FLAM when a door at the other end of Mrs. Clarke's office flung open, and a frowning, heavy-set man with a half-dozen chins and huge dangling jowls leaned into the room. He had a significantly advanced receding hairline, which had left behind one prominent stranded forelock of grey hair, and sported large, black-rimmed glasses. "You Bruno's friend?" the man asked gruffly. Flam swallowed hard as he stood up, heart pounding faster at the realization a misunderstanding had occurred, but afraid of the repercussions of correcting it now.

"I'm . . . I'm," he began, but the man waved him impatiently into the next room.

"I'm Don Morton," the interviewer growled. "Come on, let's get to it. I got a funeral at ten."

Flam meekly followed Morton into his small, plain office, noticing with professional interest the catalogues and files on the man's desk. "Sit down," Morton told him, indicating a vacant chair, then plunked down behind his own desk and began skimming through Flam's file. It seemed the folder's contents did little to please Morton, and his frown lines seemed to etch themselves even deeper into the proliferation of jowls.

"Cripes. You're as green as a garden hose," Morton concluded quickly, and tossed the folder onto his desk. He glared at the applicant for what seemed an eternity, the only visible sign of activity being an impatient tapping on his chin with a forefinger.

"Where did you say you know Bruno from?" Morton finally asked, stopping his tapping and picking up the folder again half-heartedly.

"I think Mrs. Clarke, well . . . she . . . she . . . must have misunderstood me," Flam stammered, turning red. "I don't actually know Mr. Helman personally. I just asked him last night how to apply for a job, and he directed me here."

That elicited a harrumph from Morton, and seemed to make up his mind. "Well, I'll tell you, Mr. . . . Mr. Grub, however you pronounce that," he said, checking the documents again, "we need someone with a lot more experience, someone who can hit the ground running, know what I mean? We don't really have a training program here. Sorry . . . and good luck." He stood up and offered Flam his hand, then pointed at the door back to the outer office. "Leave your application with Mrs. Clarke on your way out. You never know, maybe something will come up."

Despite its hopeful tone, the distracted manner in which Morton delivered his last comment made it blatantly clear it was merely a perfunctory dismissal. Flam left feeling dejected, to the point that he was actually blinking back tears as he fled the administrative offices and hurried down the hall to where Gerald's funeral service was taking place.

Although Father O'Meara, the B-team priest Mary had managed to round up to deliver the unsanctioned benediction over Gerald's remains, had not yet arrived, Flam was nonetheless met with an icy stare of disapproval from Mary when he came through the door. There was twice the number of people in attendance as on the previous evening, although the small room was still far from crowded. Mary's usual posse of churchwomen was prominently seated at the front, as was Sergeant Cuff, dressed for the occasion in an impressive-looking blue pinstriped suit and an immaculate white shirt with conservative blue silk tie, which Cuff was absentmindedly caressing in a slow, almost erotic fashion as the women nattered around him.

Flam waved at his mother and went to seat himself at the rear, hoping to avoid any verbal rebukes from her by doing so, but Mary would have none of that. She came stomping emphatically to the back, yanked him to his feet, and practically dragged him to the front, where a seat was reserved for him. He tried to whisper an explanation for his lateness, but Mary shushed him angrily, and fixed him with a "we'll-talk-about-this-later-mister" stare, which sent a reflexive shiver of foreboding down the full length of Flam's lanky body.

Agitated, Flam puzzled over the deeply ingrained reaction his mother still managed to garner from him. *Why should a woman who no longer holds physical power over me still frighten me so much?* He wondered whether he would ever have the courage and inner strength to stand up to his mother. That thought inspired him to mentally begin composing a couplet of condemnation wherein he delivered a severe and highly lyrical tongue lashing to his domineering mother, until a murmur from the neighbours around him indicated the arrival of Father O'Meara.

Flam had assumed the priest would delicately dance around the subject of Gerald's suicide, and was surprised when Father O'Meara brought the matter up front and centre in a mini sermon before beginning the prayer service.

"It is the teaching of Holy Scripture and of Mother Church that the taking of one's own life is a most atrocious crime," he began, his tone more one of sorrow than condemnation. Father O'Meara's own hangdog appearance, reinforced by a heavily pockmarked face whose scars continued upward to mar the shining dome of his bald pate, helped one believe that here was someone who knew a thing or two about sorrow. "Life is God's most precious gift, and He has instilled in every living creature the most powerful and invincible tendency for the preservation of that life."

Flam shifted uneasily in his seat. True, the instinct for self-preservation was instilled in the most rudimentary of life forms—even a mangled cockroach will continue to struggle desperately to save its life. But he remembered how often he had wanted to die—in fact, at this very minute, with all the recent setbacks and disappointments, life hardly seemed worth living—and he recalled vividly how close he had actually come to bringing the curtain down on the comedy-drama that was the Flam Grub story.

Is killing oneself really an abomination to God and Nature? There are so many nebulous situations where the immorality of suicide is not so cut and dry, Flam pondered. *A soldier in the trench who throws himself on a grenade to save the lives of his comrades would be considered a hero, for the lives of the many would outweigh the life of the one in those circumstances. Never mind the fact soldiers are generally expected to be prepared to commit de facto suicide, charging into the face of certain death if so ordered. Balk in the face of the enemy . . . turn and proclaim the right to self-preservation, and you will be called a coward and probably put up against a wall and shot afterwards. So much for the sanctity of life.*

The crux of the paradox, Flam realized, *is the reality that all human life does not hold equal value. A mother who gives up her own life to save her child's would be revered, not reviled. And aren't bodyguards expected to protect their charges with their very lives? Willingly and knowingly take a bullet for the President and you'll be guaranteed full honours at your funeral, that's for sure, whether you're Catholic or not. But just because I was born to a mother who dragged me into her Mother Church, I'm expected to adhere to tenets I don't believe in, like condemning the terminally ill who take their own lives to end their excruciating suffering and the second-hand suffering of those around them.*

Flam recalled the other cultures he had read about where suicide was not only tolerated, but also in some cases expected or actually revered. Take the ancient samurai, who would perform *seppuku,* especially the excruciatingly painful and bloody stomach-slicing ritual of *hara-kiri,* for a variety of reasons demanded by their code of honour, or even in some cases just to make a point to their superiors.

"In hatred of this grievous sin, and to arouse the horror of its children, the Church denies the suicide the right to burial in hallowed ground," Father O'Meara continued, and this brought a huge sob from Mary and, seconds later, a supporting chorus of wails and sniffles from the other churchwomen.

Flam, however, got a private chuckle out of that one. *You can't blame the Church,* he thought. *After all, without some rule forbidding it, wouldn't the hordes of faithful who are poor, and oppressed, and downtrodden— the very mainstay of the Church—be tempted en masse to shorten their own miserable lives here on Earth in order, as Mother Church has promised them, to spend blissful eternity in Heaven? Jesus, if they allowed that, then pretty soon there wouldn't be anyone left to fill the coffers of the Church. Strategically, it would be suicide for a religion.*

Whether it was the influence of the women wailers, or had been his rhetorical intent all along, at this point the priest's tone softened, and became almost tearful. "But it is not for us to judge. It is not for us to call this act evil, or cowardice, or insanity. I knew Gerald Strait, and I knew him to be a man who loved God. Certainly he was a sinner, but let he who is free of sin cast the first stone, as Jesus admonished us. Therefore, I say to you, let God be his judge."

Amen, brother, Flam thought to himself, and something inside told him Father O'Meara had perhaps at some point lived through a similar bottomless despair, for somehow his insight and empathy seemed to be coming from experience. No wonder they got him to do this service, he thought, and wondered whether perhaps this wasn't some ecclesiastical specialty, like the exorcists that parishes purportedly still secretly kept on call for those special, unholy occasions that required them.

The priest concluded his prologue, and proceeded to lead the small gathering in prayer, giving them all a chance to stand and stretch their legs. Flam glanced down his row of chairs and was annoyed to see his mother propped up against Sergeant Cuff, who had his arm tightly around her waist as she simultaneously prayed, fingered her rosary, and dabbed her eyes with a handkerchief. Although she was ostensibly leaning on the cop for comfort, and this being a public occasion where she was the leading lady, naturally there was not even a hint of impropriety implied in Mary's demeanour, yet Flam still found it bothered him. Shouldn't he be the one consoling her? Was she punishing him for coming late to the service, or was she in fact revealing more evidence of some secret entanglement with the policeman?

Sergeant Cuff caught his stare, and the cop's eyes narrowed to scrutinize him, making Flam quickly look away and busy himself pretending to join the others in prayer. After a few minutes, he chanced a quick furtive glance back his mother's way, and was convinced the policeman's hand had deliberately slid down from his mother's waist.

Meanwhile, Father O'Meara continued with some intonations and blessings, sprinkling holy water over the casket as he did so; then he called upon the mini-congregation for another round of prayers. Finally, he turned to the assembled and asked, "Does anyone wish to deliver a few words of remembrance for the deceased?"

There was a quiet murmur through the gathering as people looked around to see if anyone would be providing the eulogy. Flam was not surprised that there seemed to be no takers, especially given the fact that Gerald had no immediate family in attendance. As the buzz grew more intense, he supposed this would be just one more layer of ignominy on the disgraced Gerald—one more bit of gossip to be spread around the parish.

But then Flam spotted his mother glaring at him, and trying to convey some signal with her head by jerking it in the direction of the casket. Flam couldn't believe his eyes. She clearly was indicating she wanted *him* to go to the front and speak. He felt his stomach churn with anxiety and fear at this prospective public humiliation. He looked at his mother then pointed at himself, to clarify her intentions, and she nodded emphatically. Flam just stood there, frozen and mortified, refusing to believe this could be happening.

"Well, then, if there's no one . . ." Father O'Meara began, but Mary interrupted.

"My son will say a few words," Mary announced, sealing Flam's fate. Knowing he couldn't now embarrass his mother in public by refusing, Flam dutifully got up and went to the front, his mind reeling. It was bad enough he had to speak to this roomful of strangers, but he didn't have a clue what he could possibly say about a man he scarcely knew, actually disliked, and who, furthermore, was reputedly a criminal.

But, as he stood there shaking, convinced he was about to faint dead away on his feet, he spotted a sneer on Sergeant Cuff's face. It was a look of such patronizing contempt that it angered Flam, and incited in him a sudden stubborn desire to perform well. Boyhood memories of his literary recitals in Page Turner's bookstore before the supportive clique of patrons flashed back to Flam, and he remembered how much he had enjoyed standing on the countertop, basking in the attention and warm regards, and how badly he had wanted to please Page's inner circle with his performances.

He had loved those precious moments of escape from the torrents of torment life otherwise dealt him. And suddenly, in the here and now, he felt the connection with that seemingly lost time and place, and an idea wriggled into his brain to replace the panic that had been festering there. When Flam spoke up, it was with a clear, well-enunciated voice that surprised everyone but himself.

"You often hear it said funerals are not for the dead, but for the living. Each of us is here today because in some way Gerald Strait touched our lives, be it as a friend, or a neighbour, or a pharmacist, or a church member, or a businessman. Or simply as a man. In this regard, as we, the living, congregate here in the name of the deceased, he touches us still. For, like ripples that spread on the surface of the pond long after the stone has sunk beneath the surface, his memory and his actions echo in our collective spirits." Here, Flam paused and spread his arms, as if embracing the gathering before him. "In this present, Gerald Strait's past is connected with our futures. As Father O'Meara has already admonished us, it is not for us to judge the departed. Let us instead use him as a mirror to judge ourselves, and to reflect on our own deeds, and to consider what ripples each one of us sends out into the universe."

Flam could tell from the rapt expressions staring back at him that he had succeeded, if not in moving the audience, at least in garnering their undivided attention for a period. He was going to finish up by citing Shakespeare's "Life is but a walking shadow" speech from *Macbeth*, when a more uplifting passage occurred to him.

Taking a deep breath, and stepping forward with one foot in the classic thespian's pose Page Turner had taught him, Flam proceeded to recite a trio of lovely, albeit cryptic, stanzas about the smallness of life in the shadow of angels' wings. The appreciative listeners had no way of knowing he was in fact quoting from "Angel," the first—and previously unread—love poem he had written for his would-be paramour. The frustration and helplessness he described in the verse worked beautifully as a metaphor for life in general.

When he finished and returned the podium to Father O'Meara, the old priest, clearly moved, stepped forward and grabbed Flam's hand with both of his own. "God bless you, my son," he whispered to Flam under a beatific smile. "You're certainly welcome to come and say a word over my poor old remains when the time comes."

Flam returned to his seat, relieved the unexpected ordeal was over. After thanking them for their attendance, Father O'Meara dismissed the gathering. Although everyone else around him stood up immediately, Flam remained for a moment, head down and eyes closed, regaining his composure.

"Flam, dear, that was such a wonderful eulogy. I'm so proud of you, and I'm sure Gerald would have been moved," his mother's happy voice roused him. He looked up to see her smiling proudly at him, with Sergeant Cuff rubbing up right behind her. Flam, however, was not in such a forgiving mood.

"What was the idea of centring me out like that in front of everybody, without any warning?" he groused.

His mother's good mood fizzled like soda on a hot griddle. "That's what you get for being late, mister. I *told* you to get here earlier . . . I was going to ask you then, and give you a chance to prepare something. Instead, you come waltzing in like the cock of the walk just when the service is about to start."

"It wasn't my fault!" Flam protested, instantly back on the defensive as always. "I went to drop off my résumé at the front office and Mr. Morton hauled me in for a job interview on the spot."

"A job? Flam, dear, that's wonderful," his mother squealed and gave him a quick hug, clearly not really wanting to stay angry with him.

"Old Man Morton himself, eh? I'm impressed," Cuff echoed, actually looking less than hostile for an instant. Flam, however, reddened and lowered his eyes.

"I didn't get the job. They . . . he said they wanted someone with more experience." He swallowed hard and struggled to hold back his tears, knowing the contempt they would doubtless elicit from the hardnosed, reproachful Cuff. Mary and her sergeant exchanged a poignant, coded glance, giving Flam the distinct impression that his news directly related somehow to a private discussion the two had shared recently. No one said anything for a few seconds, and the faint sound of solemn organ music could be heard from the direction of the main chapel.

Flam hung his head, and examined the shiny black surface of his new shoes, gleaming like night rain on asphalt. He felt himself a total failure who had let down everyone around him, especially Page Turner, who'd coaxed him into applying for the job, and had even advanced him the money for the very clothes he was wearing. Page would accept it with his usual affable stoicism, Flam knew, but that did not make him any less reluctant to have to break the news of his rejection.

He looked back up at his mother, who had a tight-lipped, pained look on her face. Cuff had reverted back to his habitual sneer.

"I've got to get back to work," Flam said softly, suddenly needing to get away and escape the humiliation of the moment. He endured a patronizing hug and a few biblical platitudes from his mother, then a bone-crushing handshake from Sergeant Cuff, before he muttered his goodbyes and left. On his way out the door, Flam cast one last glance at Gerald Strait's lonely-looking coffin, now waiting only for the room to empty so his last earthly remains could be delivered unto the final fires of cremation.

CHAPTER 21

It was after he had left the funeral home, and was sitting behind the wheel of his idling Fairlane, a ticket for expired parking now also clutched in his hand, that the need to cry finally caught up with Flam. This time he made no attempt to staunch the flow of his tears, letting the drops meander down his cheeks, one of them catching the corner of his mouth so that he tasted the bitter brininess, while the animal sounds of his despondency gurgled from his throat.

So wretched and empty of hope was Flam, he truly wanted to die, and when the faint odour of the car's exhaust fumes found their way through his open window, he contemplated ending his misery by gassing himself. At first, he thought he could simply roll up the window and let the carbon monoxide slowly overwhelm him, but then it occurred to him he had driven for hours on end without adverse effect, and just because he could smell something didn't mean the old car was dilapidated enough to allow a lethal quantity of exhaust fumes to leak into the interior.

Since he didn't have an enclosed garage he could park in, Flam thought the best solution would be to acquire a hose and run it from his exhaust pipe in through a window, then seal up the gap with some duct tape. He started to ponder where the closest hardware store was when he remembered he had no cash on him beyond a handful of loose change. As generous as Page Turner had been in funding the new suit and shoes, Flam had ended up supplementing the purchase with his own money in order to buy a shirt and new tie, then had spent the last of his cash putting twenty dollars into the gas tank and paying for parking. So, while he theoretically had enough fuel to asphyxiate himself, he didn't have the rest of the means to do so.

Yet, instead of this being one more failure that nudged Flam yet lower into unfettered misery, the irony of the situation amused him. It actually tickled his sense of humour enough to stem the tears, and ultimately make him contemplate life instead of death—specifically, he now turned his mind to returning to the bookstore, and despite being a bearer of bad tidings, allowing Turner to get out from behind the counter and tend to other business.

When Flam did shuffle dejectedly through the door of the bookstore, he found his old friend perched excitedly on the stool at the front of the store with a huge cat-that-ate-the-canary grin.

"Congratulations, Flam," Turner said elatedly, "I knew you had the right stuff, my boy!" Flam's confused expression made Turner raise one bushy eyebrow and explain further. "The job! You got the job, my young lion. It's true. You're about to undertake being an undertaker. A Mr. Morton just phoned here looking for you. He wants you to call him back the minute you arrive," Turner told him, offering a slip of paper with the telephone number.

Flam could still not understand what was going on, and dialled the number in a daze. Morton came on the phone with a curt and forceful "What?" but when Flam identified himself the gruff tone changed immediately.

"Yes, listen, kid. I'm terribly sorry about the bum's rush I gave you this morning. Now that I've really had a chance to, um, consider it properly, well, I'd like to offer you a position," Morton said, sounding somewhat uncomfortable.

He went on to talk about entry-level salary, probation, benefits, annual reviews, and how Flam should talk to Mrs. Clarke about the details and appropriate paperwork, but much of the minutiae slipped through Flam's head without absorption. He stood incredulous,

cynically waiting for the dark cloud that must surely overshadow this
silver lining—the cruel cosmic punch line that had to be lurking behind
this reversal of fortune.

"I don't know what kind of notice you need to give your present
employer," Morton continued, his words now coming out so fast they
were stumbling over one another, "but if the offer's to your satisfaction,
you can start whenever you like . . . hell, you can start tomorrow if
you want. Like I said, just talk to Mrs. Clarke; she'll take care of all
the administrivia."

Morton concluded his pitch and waited for some reaction, his
heavy breathing clearly audible over the line.

"Well, how about it?" he urged, after the dumbfounded Flam
was still unable to find words to fill the pregnant silence. "Now, don't
get me wrong, heh heh, I'm not trying to pressure you here . . . think
about it if that's what you'd prefer, but I just wanted you to know we're
keen to have you."

"No . . . I mean yes . . . that is, no, I don't have to think about it. I
accept," Flam finally stammered out his answer. "I'm not sure when I
can start, though . . . I'll have to work things out here."

"That's great. Once again, I'm sorry about this morning, but I'm
glad we got things squared away. Well, I've got to go now, but I'll see
you soon, Fran."

Morton's voice sounded so relieved as he hung up it puzzled Flam,
and it took him a second afterwards to realize his name had been
mispronounced. Still, he was grinning like a skull when he turned to
face an equally exuberant Turner.

"He says I can start right away," Flam explained, "but don't worry,
I'll stay until you can find a replacement and get things sorted out.
And I can still work weekends for you, if you like."

"Nonsense," Turner replied, his smile evaporating into the forest
of facial hair. "First of all, I was fully prepared for this very occurrence,
so trust me, my young apprentice, you're not leaving me in the lurch.
After all, I'm the one who instigated the vocational assault on Morton's
casa de los cadáveres, you may recall. No, I insist on you starting your
chosen career immediately, and there ends any debate.

"And, besides, where did you concoct the naïve notion you will have weekends off? I'm willing to wager that, as low man on the proverbial totem pole, your free weekends will be few and far between. For that matter, I bet your profession requires its mortuary minions to work with the mourning in the morning, and the dead in the dead of night all through the week."

Flam stood choked with emotion, unable to find the words to express the gratitude and affection that had welled up inside him like a spring flood. The hairy old hipster had been so kind and generous to him, and had practically single-handedly forged the firmament of Flam's inner intellectual being.

At the same time, he was feeling mounting anxiety over the uncertain new life that was now looming large before him. As that reality sunk in, he found himself also dealing with an unexpected and disturbing sense of loss, and trepidation over again leaving the familiar and safe haven of the bookstore after having just so recently recaptured it.

Flam walked out from behind the counter to stare nostalgically down the main aisle of the bookstore, which ran like a spine down the full length of the shop.

"I guess I'm kind of scared to leave. I mean, I really wanted that job at Morton's, and when he turned me down, well, I . . . I . . ." Flam paused as memories of his all-too-recent self-destructive urges resurfaced, and wondered for a minute whether he should confess them to Turner. But so much had changed in such a short time, and somehow it didn't seem right to soil the moment with the dark stains on his soul.

"I guess it didn't really dawn on me that I would actually have to leave you behind," Flam continued, feeling the emotion swelling inside him. "I can't begin to tell you how much this place . . . how much *you* have meant to me."

"No need . . . no need. But remember the words of my beloved Blake: '*He who binds himself to a joy, does the winged life destroy; but he who kisses the joy as it flies, lives in eternity's sunrise.*'"

Turner joined Flam in the aisle, and together they surveyed the rows of crammed bookshelves, which ran from the floor up sixteen feet to the ceiling.

"I have a confession to make," Turner went on. "That day you walked back into the bookstore, and back into my life . . . good Lord, was it only a month ago? Well, I was in fact teetering on the precipice of uncertainty over what to do with my own life. It was one of those watershed moments when the multifaceted future lies fractured and diffused before one's eyes, like the myriad shiny but distorted images one might get from looking through some great cut crystal."

He wrapped an arm across Flam's shoulders. "As you already know, young squire, last month marked the twenty-fifth anniversary of this shop's opening. And so, galvanized by that numerically significant occasion, I found myself pondering the future. Although the used book business has declined, and the rent on the shop has increased as the neighbourhood has gentrified, my needs are modest, and I daresay I could continue to operate here indefinitely. But your fortuitous return to the shop gave me the time necessary to honestly reflect on my situation—to fully explore and evaluate my possible options and arrive at a decision. I'm pleased to report I have searched deep within my soul, and like the temple bell calling me to prayer, a bright new future is now beckoning me."

Flam cocked an interrogative eyebrow, but remained silent, waiting for Turner to go on. The older man smiled and extended the pregnant pause, clearly relishing the anticipation he was building. He then reached inside his vest and extracted a folded piece of paper, which he passed to Flam. When Flam unfolded it, he was shocked to see it was a computer printout from a website for Asian mail order brides. The photos of smiling and preening young women were lined up like students in a high school yearbook, with eagerness, and to Flam, a hint of desperation clearly visible in their liquid black eyes.

Near the bottom of the page, one woman's photo had been circled with a magic marker. She had a pretty, inviting face, with a sweet, toothy smile, and looked to be in her thirties. There was a flower behind one ear, and she was wearing a strapless top, revealing slim, shapely shoulders. The caption beneath the photo read, "*Banglamung, Chonburi, Thailand.*"

"Her name's Tum . . . Hitapot Tum to be formal, but I'm planning to make her Mrs. Tum Turner," Page said, and then sighed fervently. "She's so beautiful." Flam's expression must have betrayed his shock and skepticism, because Turner chuckled and looked sheepish.

"I can only imagine what you must be thinking of me," Turner said, taking back the printout, and gazing at the photo as if to find reassurance for his words, "but believe me, while you and the rest of the world may look upon this as the crazy and desperate act of some lonely, middle-aged man, I am fully cognizant and confident of my actions."

"Are you bringing her over here to work with you in the bookstore?" Flam asked, trying to picture the exotic girl in the photo behind the counter, dealing with customers in broken English. Of course, based on some of the stories Flam had read, there was a good chance she would simply divorce the decades-older Turner as soon as her citizenship was established, and probably walk off with half the store in the process.

"Oh, no . . . I'm closing the shop," Turner said, clearly excited to be sharing his bold new plans. "Actually, I'll be relocating to Thailand. Starting September, I'm going to be a professor of English Literature at the American University at Hua-Hin in Petchaburi. It's a lovely spot on the coast, a couple of hours south of Bangkok. Tum has agreed to meet me there, and barring some last-minute change of heart, become my spouse."

Flam's mouth had popped open, but nothing was coming out as his mind worked hard to digest the news. Turner, however, seemed very pleased with the shockwave his bombshell had delivered. "In fact," Turner said, "now that we've rubbed out the last impediment to my closing the shop, and have you gainfully employed, I'll likely be departing even sooner than envisioned."

"You mean you were just waiting for me?"

"In the end, yes. If truth be told, I had at one point simply considered handing over the bookstore for you to manage, and becoming a long-distance, absentee owner. But as much as this cloister would certainly suit your patently introverted nature, I fear I would be guilty of an inexcusable disservice if I allowed you to congeal here."

"How do you mean?" Flam asked, suddenly seeing the bookstore in a whole new light, and bristling at the notion Turner had not seen fit to discuss any of these life-altering plans with him.

"Don't ask me from which intuitive plane this notion springs forth, Flam, but I don't honestly believe your destiny lies here as a shopkeeper. You need to continue on the path you've already embarked upon, even if it should prove to be some cosmic *cul de sac*. Now I personally don't regret having spent the past quarter-century here . . . I arrived as an arrogant, half-mad, burnt-out, disgraced, and disillusioned soul with a herd of inner demons to tame, and while I was in there, I needed to find myself as well. Well, I believe I've accomplished all that now, and it's time to move on to the final chapters of my life. Your return to the shop helped solidify matters in two ways," Turner explained, holding up a pair of fingers in the V-for-victory sign.

"First of all, you provided me with the time and freedom to fully immerse myself in the mercantile machinations of the book trade, allowing me to discover that I really, truly dislike the crass world of commerce—despite these decades spent drifting in its backwaters. Secondly, and most importantly, you allowed me to see the modest impact I'd had on your intellectual development, and this made me think that perhaps I'd made a mistake by leaving academia. As much as the dull students deaden the joy of teaching in a hurry, the rare and truly gifted ones—like you, Flam—make it all worthwhile."

Flam, unused to compliments, blushed at this, but inside felt a warming glimmer of pride. He looked up at Turner and smiled. "So, just like that, you decided to run off?"

"Actually, there was one last, major enabling factor. About two weeks ago, whom should I run into at an antiquarian book fair but Professor Ben Foster, an old thesis advisor of mine? By wildest coincidence, or perhaps it was fate of the truest sort, he was in town just for the day to interview teaching prospects for his Thai university. It turns out one of Ben's interviewees cancelled at the last minute, and finding himself with an hour to kill, the good professor went out for a walk, and just happened to stumble across the book fest . . . and me. He didn't care that I hadn't been inside a classroom in decades—he recruited me on the spot."

"And, what about Tum? Was she some kind of a signing bonus?" Flam asked. He had meant it as a joke, but saw Turner's eyes narrow in disapproval even as he chuckled.

"I suppose, on some level that's true, given that her interest is naturally purely pragmatic, but I mean to prove she's made a wise choice. Matrimony for personal gain and financial security is as old as humankind, Flam, and since I despise hypocrisy, the monetary nature of my marriage will be out in the open for all the world to see. Actually, I've been carrying around that printout of Tum for months, using it as a talisman against my late-night loneliness, too much of a pessimist and a coward to contact her. But after running into Ben, I finally clicked on her photo and she and I began chatting online. Would you believe she lives less than an hour from the university? In fact, as a girl, she had dreamed of going to school there. Even an old existentialist like me has to take serious notice of that sort of synchronicity."

Flam shook his head in amazement, realizing he had no choice but to wish Turner well and be happy for him, no matter how sudden and surprising the departure.

"So, will you hold a going-out-of-business sale?" Flam asked, thinking Turner might still need some part-time sales assistance before departing for his new career.

"Good heavens, no! I can't be bothered with all that aggravation for the sake of a few kilobucks," Turner snorted. "I've found a broker who has agreed to liquidate everything and send on the net proceeds. In fact, as my final gift and act of tutelage to you, why don't you go and fetch that venerable old jalopy of yours, and pull it up to the back door? We'll fill it with as much literature as it will hold."

"Oh, gee, thanks Page, but I don't want to deprive you of the money you'd get from selling them."

"Nonsense. I'll gain far more from the wisdom they put in your head than the pennies they put in my pocket." Turner gestured around the room. "Besides, as much as I love books, the vast majority of these are mere literary chaff. You see, Flam, while you've been here minding the store for the past month, I've been out discovering that I've been sitting on a modest treasure trove."

Turner could see Flam's mind trying to work out the puzzle, so he interceded to spare him the mental effort. "By my calculations, I've handled over a million books in my decades here, in this ramshackle old temple of tumbleweed tomes. During that time, I've shrewdly and meticulously fished out several rare first editions, and other antiquarian delights, from the passing paperback parade and hodgepodge of hand-me-down hardcovers. So, I can live quite comfortably in my little Shangri La for years to come, even without my academic's salary . . . although my lovely young bride-to-be need not know that."

"You're kidding?" Flam exclaimed.

"I'm quite serious. Books need not be hundreds of years old to be worth good money. Why, an original *Catcher In the Rye* from 1951 is worth thousands. It's like panning for gold . . . most of what washes by is of little value, but if you're patient and discerning, bit by bit, you can build up a tidy nest egg from what's left behind in your gold pan." A sly look came over Turner's face, and he pulled Flam back behind the counter, and reached down to pull out the fireproof strongbox that had sat there as long as Flam could remember. He had never seen inside, and knowing money never came in or out of it, had always assumed it held legal documents of some sort.

"Here, my fine young profferer of poetry," Turner said, unlocking the box, "you'll appreciate this." He pulled a book out from a plastic sleeve and gingerly held it for Flam to look at, but making it clear it was not to be touched. Flam saw it was a copy of *Prufrock and Other Observations* by T.S. Eliot, clearly quite old but still in excellent condition.

"You'll forgive me if this is one volume of poetry I don't allow you to cart off," Turner chuckled, fondling the book lovingly, "but I'm told it's worth over fifty thousand dollars."

CHAPTER 22

It was just before 9 a.m. and Flam stood on the grey sidewalk, looking across at the dark pall of Morton's Funeral Home. As he mentally prepared himself to enter and embark upon his first day of work in the mortuary profession, it dawned on him he was standing in the very same spot, at the very same time, in the very same clothes, as he had exactly twenty-four hours earlier. Despite the bright, sunny promise of that freshly minted, late-spring morning, and the equally shiny potential of a newborn career, Flam felt an inexplicable sadness and sense of foreboding.

He was also still feeling sleepy. Today's commute had required rising much earlier than he was used to. Working at the bookstore had enabled him to use a parking spot designated for tenants of the upstairs flats. There would be no such luxury in his new position. Despite the salary he was now garnering, Flam was still cash-poor, and was both unwilling and unable to pay what he considered exorbitant downtown parking rates every day.

So, instead, he'd travelled to work via a succession of buses—the silver lining to his groggy awakening after a sleepless night being the opportunity to read one of the new books Turner had given him the previous afternoon.

With anxiety spreading inside him like maggots on carrion, Flam walked around the side and looked for the way in. The old wooden coach house gates he had noted the day before appeared locked, although he noticed that water was running out from under them, and streaming down the blacktopped driveway into the sewer grates of the street. A little further along the venerable stone wall was an ornate, oversized black door cryptically labelled with a small, tarnished brass plate reading *Public At Front*. Heart thumping, Flam entered there.

He found himself standing in a cramped, dark garage area where a hearse and two limousines sat crowded together with barely enough room to squeeze by. Overhead ran a jumbled network of ducts and plumbing, and one of these pipes was leaking profusely, spraying water and causing a huge puddle on the garage floor. Past the vehicles was another entranceway, apparently leading to the funeral home proper, but there was no way for him to get into the building without getting soaked

"Watch it, Jack!" a voice sounded from overhead, and Flam looked up and spotted a workman perched on top of a tall stepladder, attempting to apply two large wrenches to the pipe works at a spot upstream of the downpour. "Just give me a minute," he added, and proceeded to grunt forcefully as he torqued and twisted with such effort the stepladder began to teeter precariously beneath him. Flam instinctively hurried over and grabbed the ladder to steady it, and after a few more groans from the worker the cascade of water abated and turned into a mild drip.

"Hey, thanks, DaddyO," the man said as he lowered the wrenches and made his way down the stepladder. "Damned handle on the cutoff valve sheared right off. These pipes are friggin' antiques . . . I keep telling Morton they need to be replaced, but that old cheapskate refuses to spend a penny more than he has to."

Now on ground level the man revealed himself to be a gigantic, barrel-chested, dark-skinned figure of indeterminate ethnicity. He was a head taller than Flam, and wore coveralls with an embroidered label that proclaimed his name to be Charlie.

Charlie looked down at the huge puddle covering the floor of the garage and whistled. "*Water, water, everywhere, and all the boards did shrink,*" he commented, pensively.

Flam added, without thinking, "*Water, water, everywhere, nor any drop to drink.*" That elicited a smile from Charlie, and he responded with, "*The very deep did rot, Oh Christ, that ever this should be,*" then stopped and waited, a hard-eyed squint of dubious anticipation on his face for Flam's dénouement of, "*Yea, slimy things did crawl, with legs, upon a slimy sea.*" Clearly delighted, Charlie threw his head back, and issued forth a deep resounding bass laugh that echoed surreally through the garage, then thrust a massive hand out at Flam.

"Charlie Duvuduvukulu. I'm the janitor and handyman here."

Flam accepted the handshake, and was surprised by the delicate way Charlie gripped him, even as the caretaker's huge hand practically swallowed up Flam's entirely.

"Er . . . my name's Flam Grub. I'm just starting today."

Charlie nodded knowingly, and his eyes wandered down and studied Flam's shiny new shoes for a minute. Then, with surprising grace for such a big man, he swiftly wheeled around and thrust his mammoth butt out. "Here," Charlie said, "hop aboard and I'll piggyback you to the door . . . no point waiting until I squeegee out this slimy sea." Flam gratefully obliged, and a few seconds later was standing high and dry at the doorway, while a retreating Charlie waved off his thanks.

Flam went into the building, and ended up in a long brick hallway lined with a half-dozen closed doorways, where he stood uncertainly, contemplating his next move. When he had phoned Morton back to confirm a next-day arrival, there had been only a terse, "Okay, see you tomorrow . . . use the side entrance," but no additional instructions. Some odd noises crept into the hallway, but they were too indistinct for Flam to discern their origins, sounding more like ghostly sounds from another realm. Unsure how else to proceed, Flam finally started trying the doors one by one.

The first one was locked, and the door immediately after it turned out to be an odiferous supply closet filled with cleaning supplies, stacks of linen, and a variety of unlabelled bottles of liquid, neatly organized in small cardboard boxes. Just as he was reaching for the handle of the third portal, the sounds behind it picked up, leading Flam to believe this was a good choice. However, when he opened the door and stepped inside, he found the tiled room seemingly empty, except for the body of an emaciated old man lying on a large, well-worn, stainless steel embalming table, a sheet strategically covering the private parts.

Flam gulped, and felt the short hairs standing up on the back of his neck. It wasn't that the sight of a corpse especially shocked him— this was a mortuary, after all. At Prentice College, Flam and his fellow Funeral Services students had even been exposed to real cadavers in their final semester's Advanced Embalming lab. Each had, in turn, been required to practise the correct method for inserting tubes for draining and replacing the bodily fluids, although in reality there were few fluids left in the bodies they were given. Working cadavers were a precious commodity, and Prentice's supply had often first passed through the anatomy class of a local university, arriving with the vital organs already removed and packaged in plastic bags, like the giblets of a Christmas turkey.

Flam had, however, mostly seen these dead volunteers from a few rows back, so his up-close-and-personal encounters had been limited. He now recalled, with a twinge of resurfaced melancholy, that his actual hands-on practice sessions had taken place during the zenith of his infatuation with Lucy Giles. He had suppressed any repulsion and queasiness in order to make a good impression on his would-be love interest, who herself had breezed through the sessions with remarkable coolness.

A faint rattle, as if chains were being shifted, came from the direction of the dead man, followed by a soft breathing sound, and Flam's inner resolve to be brave now abandoned him completely. He wasn't sure if he believed in ghosts or the supernatural realm— although there had certainly been enough eyewitness accounts in his rambling thanatological readings to give him pause—but this was not an occasion for rational thought.

Panicking, he turned to flee the room, only to find the door had swung shut behind him. As he fumbled clumsily with the unfamiliar latch, there was a light padding sound behind him, like a child's feet, and suddenly something pressed against his leg. He leapt backward with limbs flailing, and a pathetic whimper of terror emitted from deep in his throat.

Just as Flam was sure he was going to faint from terror, or lose control of his bowels, he saw that his imagined ghostly assailant was in fact only a dog, albeit a mean-looking bull terrier. The canine was now standing in front of the door, dripping droplets of drool as it sat panting and eyeing the interloper suspiciously. As great as his relief had been to discover he was not being assailed by some ghoul or otherworldly creature, Flam now stood facing the beast with uncertainty as to how to get past it and out the door.

Slowly he slid a foot forward, and cautiously made to extend his hand outward for the dog to sniff, having read somewhere this was the correct procedure. At the same time, he was preparing to whisk his hand back, and kick out in self-defense, if the animal made any threatening moves. His diplomatic overture was greeted by a slight cock of the head, so Flam stood his ground and gamely inched closer. Now the dog's tail flickered ever so slightly, then began to rhythmically sweep slowly across the floor. Flam knew he had survived the peril. Gingerly, now that the dog had registered and accepted the scent, he patted it on the head and began to scratch it around the neck and cheeks. Soon the beast's stubby tail was gyrating madly back and forth, and was banging loudly against the door.

"Sarah! What the hell's going on in there?" a voice called from the hallway, and the door opened as a head poked in to investigate. A grandmotherly sort with chubby cheeks, bifocals, and her hair pulled back in the prerequisite bun, blinked a few times as she took in the sight of Flam petting the dog, which had been shoved a few feet forward by the door's opening, but had refused to abandon its rubdown.

"Um . . . I'm a new employee," explained Flam, "I just wandered in here . . . wasn't sure where I was supposed to go."

The woman pushed her way into the room. Her plump figure seemed to complete the matronly appearance, but the benign impression soon evaporated, for Flam noticed that her apron was made of black rubber, instead of lace, and that she was wearing long, matching gloves, which went well past the elbow. A scowl had worked its way onto the woman's face. She smelt of cigarettes and formaldehyde.

Flam offered her his hand. "I'm Flam Grub. How do you do?" he said, his voice automatically lowering as it always did when he offered his name, almost as if apologizing. She looked surprised, and squinted fiercely at him as if unsure whether she was being kidded, then with a sort of impatience worked herself out of one of the gloves and shook Flam's hand.

"Sorry, what was that again . . . did you say *Flam?*"

"Uh, huh," he confirmed, now blushing outright over the undue attention, and wondering how many more times today he would have to suffer through this painful embarrassment he always felt during introductions.

"Well, *Flam,*" the woman said, stressing the newfound name, "I'm Leetch . . . Hannah Leetch." She fixed him with a cold look. "I do all the embalming and make-up here, and that's the way it's going to stay . . . so don't get any bright ideas about taking over my job, understand?" Flam gulped and nodded.

"Okay then, *Flam,* you should probably go find whoever it is you're supposed to see about starting work. I have to get this old stiff stuffed before his family shows up. Don't ask me to tell you where you're supposed to go . . . didn't even know they'd hired someone new, but then, nobody tells us anything around here, do they Sarah?" She bent over and ran a rubber glove across Sarah's spine, allowing the dog to lick her face in return.

Flam wondered at the propriety of keeping a pet in a mortuary, but didn't recall having heard any rules prohibiting it, and couldn't imagine there would necessarily be any health regulations against it. Hannah no doubt enjoyed having some live company while performing her duties, although he found it surprising somehow that crabby Old Man Morton would allow it, even if Hannah looked like a woman used to getting her way.

When Flam made to leave, the bull terrier detached itself from Hannah's hand and came scampering across the industrial terracotta tile floor, sliding up against the door with a loud thump, and again blocking it from opening.

"Don't mind her, she always does that. Just give her a shove," Hannah instructed him without looking up, preoccupied as she began to make some adjustments to the cadaver's position on the table, grunting with the effort of moving the dead weight. Flam obeyed, using his foot to slide the wildly panting dog off to one side, and seconds later emerged back in the confounding hallway.

A tiny *Exit* sign above the fifth doorway gave Flam hope he had finally found a way out of the hallway, and sure enough, upon opening it he found a set of concrete stairs. These led him up to yet another door, this one wooden with ornate moulding and stained panels, and through that out into what he recognized as the long main hallway of the funeral home.

Although relieved to be on somewhat familiar ground, Flam still had no idea where to go, or whom to talk to about beginning his duties. He stood indecisively in the hallway for a few minutes, pondering his next move, all the while absorbing the well-appointed surroundings with a new insider's perspective. He could hear the drone of a vacuum cleaner running somewhere in another room, then the sound abruptly ceased, only to be replaced by a periodic clanking, apparently emanating from the walls, and which he suspected might be the echoes of Charlie working on his pipes.

Just as Flam decided to head towards the front office and present himself to Mr. Morton, even though he found the prospect intrinsically intimidating, someone called out angrily from behind him, "Gruber, you're late!" Flam spun around to see Bruno, the pompadour-sporting employee he'd approached at Gerald Strait's vigil, standing there with an impatient look, and holding a vacuum cleaner. Rattled by this perceived grievance against him, Flam didn't know where to start defending himself—by correcting the erroneous use of his surname, or by explaining his alleged lateness.

"I'm . . . I . . . I was here on time," Flam finally stammered. "You can ask Charlie . . . or Hannah. It's just . . . well, Mr. Morton didn't tell me where I was supposed to go." Perhaps invoking the owner's name had a diffusing effect, for Bruno simply shrugged, dropped his offensive posture, as well as the vacuum, and just walked away.

"Go upstairs and do the rugs in the showroom and the consultation rooms. And make it snappy, before any customers show up," Bruno instructed without turning. "Then come find me in my office when you're done."

Flam obeyed, lugging the surprisingly heavy industrial-grade Hoover up the stairs to the rooms Bruno had mentioned, where he spent the next hour learning the machine's operation and idiosyncrasies as he pushed it over a seemingly endless expanse of plush carpets.

The sedately styled consultation rooms, where the home's funeral directors met with the families of the deceased, consisted of small boardroom tables around which were arranged a half-dozen executive-style leather chairs. Although the rooms were relatively small, vacuuming them required considerable effort, since all of the chairs had to be moved out of the way. The showroom, on the other hand, was huge, occupying most of the second floor, and had row upon row of different styles and models of caskets, from cheap plywood boxes that met the bare minimum in legality and propriety, to exquisitely crafted stainless steel containers that looked like they were meant to carry their inhabitants into space.

Bruno, having evidently grown impatient waiting in his office, came upstairs to check on the progress. He rebuked Flam for his inefficiency, claiming the cleaning was taking far too long, and pointed out a number of spots where the work had allegedly been sloppy. When Flam, taken aback by this criticism, made to go back over the deficient areas, Bruno forcibly snatched the Hoover away from him, growling that it was too late now for vacuuming, and demanding Flam come in a half-hour earlier the next morning to make up for it. Then Bruno chastised Flam's appearance, saying he was unfit to be seen by clients, and ordered him off to the bathroom to make himself presentable.

Flam, unaccustomed to working in a suit, had not had the presence of mind to remove his jacket while vacuuming, so his hair was now dishevelled, his face flushed, and his suit dusty in spots. He certainly felt out of sorts, and his superior's criticism only flustered him further. After he splashed some water on his face, wiped off his clothes, and patted his hair back into place, he felt somewhat restored, and now vowed to make a better impression on Bruno.

Alas, the tone set by his first failure was to reverberate the rest of the day. Flam was assigned a number of tasks to perform, and was inevitably criticized harshly by Bruno after each one. Next, he was sent downstairs to help Hannah dress her latest subject, and load him into a coffin. Hannah ended up pushing Flam aside, insisting she could do the job alone, thank you very much, even though the way she grunted and groaned as she awkwardly manhandled the corpse into the box made it clear she was being obstinate, and could have used Flam's assistance. But it was Flam who was chastised afterwards by Bruno for the way the body was lying in the casket.

"Didn't they teach you anything at that college, you useless idiot," Bruno cursed, then proceeded to perform some esoteric adjustments, which had Flam wondering whether he had indeed missed some aspect of his training, for he could not discern any visible difference in the presentation of the corpse afterwards. And so it went all day. Whether unloading supplies, carrying in flowers, or dusting a chapel, Flam could not seem to do anything to his boss's satisfaction. To make matters worse, Bruno kept calling him "Gruber" while Flam, already exasperated by the constant reprimands over the quality of his work, did not have the courage to correct him.

Things did not improve when Flam was sent to the front office that afternoon to complete the prerequisite paperwork Mrs. Clarke demanded of new hires. Flam was grateful just to be away from Bruno's abrasive supervision for a while, even if the sour Mrs. Clarke continued to treat him no better than a piece of the furniture. Flam found it difficult to have to listen to the gurgles and arduous breathing of the permanently pained secretary as she laboured over her administrative duties.

Although Flam was initially pleased to read that he had been awarded the promising title of Associate Funeral Services Manager, Mrs. Clarke quickly burst his bubble when he mentioned it to her.

"Ha!" Mrs. Clarke laughed gleefully, even though the effort sent her into a paroxysm of wheezing and made her fight for the next breath, "that's just Morton's way of making sure he doesn't have to pay you for overtime."

"I don't understand," said Flam, clearly a neophyte to the nuances of the labour market.

"Well, technically you're designated as salaried management, even if you're the low man on the totem pole and have to take orders from the janitor," Mrs. Clarke explained with an amused look, "so Morton doesn't have to worry about labour regulations for the length of the work week, or extra pay for extra hours . . . and, believe me, you'll see plenty of those."

Mrs. Clarke's prognostication seemingly bore fruit as soon as Flam returned to Bruno Helman's harsh dominion. The pompadoured taskmaster was waiting in his office, mulling over a laminated calendar page, and gestured impatiently for Flam to come in.

"Gruber, the home is going to be pretty busy tonight—we've got a viewing in Room Two, and another in the North Room, and there's an evening service in the Chapel—so I'm going to need you to work until nine o'clock tonight."

Flam's stomach sank at the gloomy prospect of spending another four hours on the job after such a frustrating day, and then it occurred to him it was Wednesday night.

"I'm sorry, I didn't realize you might need me tonight. I know I've just started . . . but I can't . . . I . . . I have a night school class tonight," Flam replied, feeling like he was yet again failing to live up to Bruno's expectation and knowing full well he could easily skip the class. Yet he was beginning to feel exploited and abused, so he was also more than a little pleased to have an opportunity for token resistance, and to escape from the man who had made his first day on the job such a misery.

Bruno accepted the news silently and stared pensively back down at the schedule in front of him. "Night school, eh?" he finally said, creases forming in the brow beneath his hairdo. "So, I guess you'll be wanting every Wednesday off."

Flam said nothing, waiting on tenterhooks for Bruno's inevitable next rebuke, but it never came. Instead, a sly smile manifested itself and Bruno nodded.

"No problem, Gruber. You can make it up Saturdays and Sundays," he pronounced, and made the appropriate entries on the laminated sheet.

"Grub," Flam interjected.

Bruno blinked, not comprehending. "Pardon?"

"Grub. My name's Grub, not Gruber."

Bruno burst out into a huge guffaw, which shocked Flam, who up to that moment would not have thought the man was capable of laughing. Bruno plucked a tissue out of its box and erased the new entries on the schedule, then proceeded to ostentatiously reprint them in large block letters.

"*Grub* . . . oh, that's perfect. Well, *Grub*, you've got enough time to polish the caskets before leaving for the day. Don't forget to get here early tomorrow so you can get the vacuuming done . . . and try to do a better job of it when you do, okay, *Grub*?"

CHAPTER 23

Angel did not show up for class that night. Flam had not thought very much about her over the past week—or more accurately, with all that had been going on in his life, he hadn't had time to obsess over her with the same all-consuming ferocity he had in the previous weeks. Still, as he had boarded the bus, trying unsuccessfully to read his book while being jostled and squeezed among the evening commuters, troubled visions of Angel and the previous week's frustrating episode on the night grass had manifested themselves, only adding to his day's quota of anxiety.

Flam had originally planned to first go home and change before class, but he was already running late by the time his bus reached the suburbs, finally achieving some velocity now that most of the downtown tangle had been left behind. So, instead, he rode straight to the campus, and jogged the last distance to the classroom. Professor Abbott had already started his lecture, droning on about the schisms in Christianity, and didn't stir from his pedagogical trance when Flam entered the classroom and looked around for an empty seat.

It was then, after checking twice, that a disappointed Flam noted Angel's absence, although he was pleased to see old Joe turn around to nod his head and smile in greeting. By break time, Flam had abandoned all hope that Angel would perhaps show up late, and he was fighting hard to stay awake as Abbott inventoried all the current flavours of Christianity, including Catholics, Eastern Orthodox, Protestants, Anglicans, Baptists, Presbyterians, Adventists, Lutherans, Unitarians, Episcopalians, Pentecostals, Mormons, Christian Scientists, and Jehovah's Witnesses.

Flam was starting to notice by now that Professor Abbott had a very taxonomical approach to his religious teachings. The instructor preferred to clinically inventory and summarize religious beliefs, as if each one was wholly unique and should stand alone on its own properties, rather than explore the spiritual underpinnings of religion in general—the universal psychosocial commonality shared by all creeds.

Flam suspected Abbott simply wanted to put in his hours and get paid, and in the process stayed away from any hint of controversy or unorthodoxy. His lecture, for example, had treated the Bible as a *de facto* Christian standard, without any mention of the other gospels from the Gnostics and other early Christians that had not made the final edit. And there had not even been a hint of the holy hullabaloo surrounding the Book of Revelation, that troublesome appendix that had been tacked onto the end of the Bible by the Paulist Christians.

At the break, as the students stood up to stretch their legs or groggily stumble out in search of a cup of coffee, Joe shuffled over to say hello.

"Nice to see you again, Joe. I hope your hospital visit went okay," Flam inquired.

"It was the usual poking and prodding and drugs dispensed, thank you for asking. Healthy or not, any man approaching one hundred can be said to be a dying man."

As Joe spoke, Flam noticed the old man was eyeing him with a critical, discerning look.

"You have a new suit, I see. Tsk, tsk, and already it needs a good pressing."

Flam blushed, as uneasy memories of his first day came flooding back to him. "Yeah, I started a new job today at Morton's Funeral Home, as a matter of fact. Mind you, I didn't realize my profession required so much physical labour. They didn't mention that at school."

"Congratulations on your new position, my young friend! No doubt your employer and your colleagues are merely ensuring you earn your money . . . it is the natural order of things," Joe chuckled. "May I?" he asked, gesturing at the jacket, and Flam shrugged and took it off, allowing Joe to finger the fabric and examine the inside seams.

Joe sighed. "Please do not be offended, but in my day I would have been ashamed to produce a garment such as this. Still, I am sure it was a most cost-effective purchase. Now, when you are working, you should always remove your jacket. If you cannot hang it on a chair, then you must fold it from the back, like so. And, your pants should be hung up every night, from the cuffs, and kept in the bathroom where the steam will help keep out the wrinkles."

Flam grinned sheepishly as he took the jacket back and put it on. "Thanks. I guess I'd better learn to take care of what I've got . . . although I suppose I should probably make some extra suits a financial priority."

Joe nodded thoughtfully. "Come," the old man said, "we should get some refreshment before the good professor resumes his litany."

After class had mercifully ended, Joe approached Flam again, and suggested they go for their now traditional after-class refreshment. When Flam seemed reluctant, Joe assumed it was due to the absence of Angel's company, and shrugged philosophically. "Yes, I understand I cannot provide the same incentive as the beautiful and vibrant young lady. I think perhaps you are quite fond of her, no?"

It was a question that merited pondering, but when Flam blushed, it was not because of the reference to Angel, but rather due to the fact he was currently living on pocket change until his first paycheque materialized. He could barely afford the bus fare to and from work, so even a modest night out to the campus coffee shop was embarrassingly difficult.

"No, it's not because Angel's not here tonight. I really would like to join you for a coffee, Joe, but, I'm ashamed to say, it's not in my budget until payday. I am so-o-o broke. Hell, I even had to borrow the money for this cut-rate suit you were commenting on earlier."

"Come, come, young Flam," Joe retorted gaily, "surely you will let me stand you for a coffee, and I think also a snack would be in order, no? Oy yoy yoy, I can hear your stomach growling like an angry dog."

It was true. Flam had eaten only an apple and a muffin all day long, and his deprived stomach was gurgling with resentment. Still, he hated the thought of bumming a meal, but Joe's inviting, elfin smile won over Flam's pride, and he consented. They strolled over to Java Gardner's, and along the way Flam worked himself into a lather over Professor Abbott's approach to the course. Joe, however, was a little more forgiving.

"For me, this is the part of the course I was most interested in," Joe confessed, "and I found today's class quite fascinating. I did not realize there were so many different types of Christianity. Here I thought you goys were all alike."

Flam remembered a comment Joe had made on a previous night. "You mentioned you were taking this class as a kind of penance," Flam prodded Joe. "What did you mean by that?"

The good humour evaporated from Joe's face, and Flam instantly regretted having brought up the subject.

"I'm sorry," said Flam. "I didn't mean to pry."

"No, not at all," Joe reassured him, "and you have a good memory. Yes, I did say that, and it's true. As you can tell, I am . . . or, perhaps I should say, I *have* been for many years, a devoted Jew. But I also have a granddaughter, Ester, my only living relative, and the most precious thing to me on this earth. In my religious zeal, I forbade her to marry outside the faith, and in so doing, I drove her away from me. She has married an Anglican and renounced her religion . . . and me . . . and I have not exchanged a word with her now for many years. And so, I am taking this class to better understand her point of view, and to try to make myself more tolerant . . . in case I get a second, or should I say a third chance."

The latter statement confused Flam, and his knotted brow must have relayed this consternation to Joe, who chuckled at the reaction.

"It's a long story, but no matter, we'll order some soup and perhaps a couple of bagels, and I'll tell it to you as you eat." And so they did, while Joe related his life's story to Flam.

"You will recall me saying, perhaps, that I was a tailor in Berlin before the war. I, in fact, come from a long line of tailors, and my father . . . and three uncles . . . were all tailors. Ironically, my family came to Berlin from our old village in Poland, because it was a more tolerant society towards Jews . . . and also a place of greater opportunity."

Flam had wolfed down his light supper as he listened attentively, and Joe stopped and smiled at the young man's appetite, pushing another bagel Flam's way before continuing.

"Did you know it was we Jews of Berlin who practically invented the department store clothing trade, what we called *konfection*? It's true. During our acme between the wars, we were exporting *prête à porter* clothes around the world . . . as far away as India and South America. My family was reasonably prosperous, although we were not by any means wealthy the way some of the others were, those who built up great fashion houses, for we were humble and pious Jews who followed the old ways. I can still remember my grandfather reciting the Psalms, and singing the songs of the High Holy Days as we all sat together and worked by the light of a tallow candle."

Joe noticed Flam staring down at the general area of the old man's wrist and chuckled. "You are perhaps wondering if I have a concentration camp tattoo on my arm. Patience my young friend, for there is an important chapter to my story, even before the bombs start falling and my fellows stop screaming." He took another sip of his coffee, and stared intently off into space, as if seeing suspended there an album of the ancient memories he was recounting.

"My father loved me, and wanted the best for me, and so committed the grave sin of providing me with the finest of educations. You must understand, Berlin was at that time the greatest city on the continent, and one of the world's intellectual and cultural centres. In the exclusive schools my father paid dearly for, then later at the university, I met so many new ideas and new friends, at times I felt my head and my heart would burst. There was so much I hadn't conceived, and I ate it up like a hungry beggar at a banquet.

"At night, my friends and I would frequent the cafés and jazz clubs, and debate the works of Klee and Picasso and Gershwin and Brecht and Lang and Marx . . . ach, there was so much happening that the rise to power of the little man with the Charlie Chaplin moustache just seemed like another farce at the local cabaret."

Joe was growing more animated, as he recounted those amazing years, and for the first time, Flam could see the young man trapped within the ancient, wrinkled body. But despite the energy and enthusiasm Joe brought to the telling of his story, Flam knew this tale would not have a happy ending.

"As you might suspect," Joe continued, then hesitated as he contemplated the awkward Flam for a second, "or in your case, perhaps not, I began to dress and talk and act like my friends. I had long ago discarded my *yarmulke*, and elected to shave and groom like all the young dandies. I forsook my people and my religion, became an atheist, a modernist, a socialist. Over time, I became a user of various stimulants, then later, when my poor father, in exasperation and desperation disowned and disinherited me, I became a user of people. I dabbled in a half-dozen different crafts and trades—I wanted to make films, erect buildings, fly airplanes—and in the end discovered I was suited only for one.

"I also fell in love, and that proved to be both my salvation and my downfall. Her name was Lili . . . perhaps you have heard of 'Lili Marlene' from the song 'The Girl Under the Lantern,' which first appeared at the time? It became very popular with both sides during the war. I remember the two of us sharing a laugh the first time we heard it played on the radio. Lili was the most beautiful and desirable woman I have ever known. She was also very mysterious, never talking about herself, but keeping herself with such a bearing and elegance that the rumours she fostered all hinted at some fine, probably aristocratic, upbringing.

"When I met her, I was still outwardly living the life of the prosperous *bon vivant*, but secretly, I was beginning to despair over

my poverty and indebtedness, and was scared to my very soul that I
would lose Lili as a result. She had many suitors, and all I had to my
name were the elegant suits that made everyone certain I was affluent.
In fact, I sewed them myself in a progression of hotel rooms I rented
under assumed names, and then abandoned when the manager came
knocking on the door for the payment."

The waitress came to bus their table and offer a refill, which Joe
accepted. Flam glanced at his watch, and asked for a glass of water
instead, not wanting more caffeine to potentially keep him awake
when he had to be at work early the next day. He knew he would
regret it in the morning, yet he keenly wanted to stay and hear the rest
of Joe's story.

"Then came *Kristallnacht*, and all the hatred and anger that had
been simmering under the surface for years boiled over, and Germany
became an outright madhouse. Now, of course, Jews had been leaving
Germany for years, since Hitler and his Nazis came to power and
started passing law after law to strip Jews of their rights and livelihood.
But after those two nights in November of 1938, all Jewish businesses
were closed . . . many in fact were burned to the ground. Among those
closed down was one of the biggest *konfections* in Berlin, owned by a
certain Abraham Goldstein."

Joe stopped as a thought occurred to him. "Do you know the
origin of the name 'Goldstein'?" he asked. Flam shook his head.

"It was one of many similar names—Goldstein, Silverstein,
Rubenstein—forced upon the Jews of Europe by Napoleon Bonaparte
so they would sound more agreeable to the rest of the population. It
means 'gold stone' and refers to the precious jewels it was assumed
every Jew secretly hoarded. At any rate, in Goldstein I saw a golden
opportunity. You should know that, by this time, none of my friends,
not even those closest to me . . . not even my darling Lili, suspected
that I was a Jew. I had made no contact with my family for many years
and my surname, Schneider—which is German for tailor and had
been adopted several generations earlier—did not betray my origins.
So, with the help of some well-connected acquaintances, I managed
to seize possession of Herr Goldstein's business. Through bribes

and administrative tricks and other shrewd manoeuvres, we had it proclaimed *judenrein*, which means free of Jews, using false papers that showed me to possess four generations of pure Aryan blood.

"Our biggest customer was Hitler himself, as we produced uniforms for his burgeoning regime, and seemingly overnight, I became wealthy . . . so much so, in fact, that my darling Lili fell hopelessly in love with me. She soon became pregnant with our child, and we were married immediately thereafter. It was a modest civil ceremony, although the celebration afterwards was quite lavish, as befitted my new station."

Flam was doing some mental arithmetic. "This would have been very close to the start of the war," he mused out loud.

"Exactly so . . . in fact, my son, Herman, was born on the very day Warsaw fell," Joe said, his face softening at the memory. "It was at this point that I discreetly tried to make contact with my parents, for I felt it only right they should know of their grandson, and despite what I had considered to be their unfair treatment of me, I thought, rather magnanimously in my mind, that, with my newfound connections, I might be able to help them leave the country, if they hadn't done so already."

"Did you find them?" Flam asked, hoping for a reprieve from the depressing way he saw the tale heading.

Joe sighed forlornly, that one pitiful exhalation in essence giving Flam his answer. "No, I found no trace of them, although at the time, I naïvely chose to assume the best. Only years later would I discover they had been shipped off to the death camps. Both of them perished there, as did my baby sister, Miriam. I do not understand why they would have stayed . . . they had many opportunities and enough resources to flee, as two of my uncles in fact did. Surely, like King Belshazzar, they could see the writing on the wall . . . surely they could tell where it was all heading in a society that burned their synagogues, and smashed their shops, and forced them to wear the yellow badges, and publicly forced all male Jews to take the name Israel, and all the women Sarah. No, I have lived my whole life with the dreadful suspicion Mama and Papa stayed because of me, hoping the prodigal would return."

Joe stopped and squeezed his face tight, clearly fighting off deep emotions and the tears they elicited. After a moment, he reopened his eyes, took a reestablishing breath, looked sadly at Flam, and resumed his narrative.

"While the world marched towards Hell, I was in Heaven. I had achieved everything I had sought . . . prosperity, acceptance in the best of circles, a beautiful wife, a newborn son. Naturally, as you doubtless are now thinking, it was a fool's paradise. It all ended with one telephone call in the middle of the night from an acquaintance in the police, for whom I had once arranged some free custom-tailored uniforms, warning us that they were coming."

Now Joe shook his head, although there was a wry smile on his face. "But, and here you must surely share this irony with me, the police were not coming for me, but for one Lilith Hildesheimer, my own darling Lili, who had disguised her Jewishness from me as completely as I had hidden my roots from her. We fled like thieves in the night, to Vichy France, then Spain, then Portugal, where Lili took our son, and almost all our money, and disappeared, leaving me to go on by myself to England. And it was there, alone, again impoverished, deliberately wandering the streets of London during air raids and hoping a bomb would fall on me, that I was recruited to fight against my native country, not with a gun, but with, of all things, my needle."

The last statement caught Flam by surprise, and it was evident Joe had expected this, and relished the reaction. "You are astonished? Yes, as was I, but my skill as a tailor, and my intimate knowledge of German uniforms and fashion made me invaluable to Britain's spymasters. I would be responsible for properly dressing their agents operating on the continent, where a single overlooked detail could cost a life. I joined a covert group of Jewish tailors who spent the war working in a secret workshop near Oxford Circus, sometimes visiting the synagogues to buy authentic labels from refugees. And so it was, one night during a blackout, as we worked by the light of a tallow candle, when one of the older men began singing the same holy songs my grandfather used to sing, that my faith and my God returned to me, and I have been a devout Jew ever since."

"You mentioned a granddaughter," said Flam, remembering how the story had been initiated. "Did you get back together with Lilith?"

"No, I never set eyes on her exquisite face again, but like the complete fool I was, I never stopped loving her, and so never took another wife. After the war, I joined a highly regarded tailor's shop on Savile Row, and spent the next three years helping to clothe the elite of the British Commonwealth. Then, one day, I received a telegram from a hotel in New York saying Lili had skipped out without paying her bill, and wanting to know if I was willing to come collect my son. He had been left in the care of a hotel maid, with a packed lunch, some pocket money, plus instructions and my address, which was mysteriously pinned to his sweater. I left everything behind, and was on an airplane for America as soon as I could manage it.

"It must have been quite a shock to little Yankee Herman to meet me, this strange little German Jew from London, but in time, after we moved here to this city, at my strong urging, he accepted both me and our faith. His *bar mitzvah* was one of the happiest days of my life, and equally so his marriage to Rachel, a lovely rosy-cheeked girl from a good, pious Jewish family. So strong were the faith and traditions I had force-fed Herman, he insisted on moving with his pregnant Rachel to Israel to work on a *kibbutz*. I was invited along, and part of me was, of course, strongly attracted to that Promised Land of the Jews. But by this time, I had established a successful shop of my own, and was an elder of the temple, and active in many Jewish organizations, and felt I had finally found peace and a permanent home. I had no inclination to start wandering again."

"So your granddaughter was born in Israel?" Flam asked.

Joe smiled sadly, apparently gratified to know Flam was paying attention to his story, but then the old man's expression sank into something profoundly painful. "Yes. Her name is, as I mentioned, Ester, and she was just five years old when her parents were destroyed by a bomb, a crude but deadly homemade device planted in the road, I'm told, by a teenager. The bomb was meant for an army vehicle, but it found Herman and Rachel's car instead. The other families of the kibbutz wanted to adopt Ester, but I brought her back here to live with me. And, as I had with Herman, I patiently and determinedly raised her as a devout Jew.

"Alas, there was more of me in that sweet willful child than I realized, for when I sent her off to be educated at the best schools, she discovered a bigger, more complex world than the narrow one I had been painting her, and rebelled against me, and renounced the traditional ways I represented, calling them archaic, fascistic, and misogynistic."

". . . And married an Anglican," Flam filled in.

"Yes, and married an Anglican, Mr. Colby Sharp, a computer engineer who works for some international software company, and she has willingly converted to his faith, although with what sincerity I cannot say. We had such an ugly exchange of words the last time I saw her, with both of us resolving never to talk to the other again. I called her a traitor and an ingrate . . . she called me a hypocrite and a zealot, and accused me of driving her parents to their death in Israel through my fanaticism.

"Now ten years have passed, and I do not even know where she is living, or how to get in touch with her, or if she is well and happy, or if I have become a great-grandfather. I yearn for my Ester beyond description, and have come to regret my harsh words and immutable position, and would tell her so to her face if I were granted the chance. I have come to question my beliefs. It is not that I reject them so much as I am trying to understand whether they are compatible with, or perhaps even part of, some larger scheme of global faiths that my God . . . that *our* God has created."

"And that's why you took Professor Abbott's class," Flam commented, wondering if anything their lifeless professor had taught so far had impacted Joe's perspective of faith. "Well, Joseph Schneider, I wish you luck in your search, despite our teacher's shortcomings."

"Joash," Joe corrected, "my name is Joash, not Joseph, although of course I simply went by Joe back in Berlin, and it has stuck. It means 'fire of Yahweh.'"

The old man burst out laughing after saying this, leaving Flam bewildered until Joe explained. "I have a rabbi friend who would have cringed at me even casually mentioning the name Yahweh out loud, but now I think he is overly superstitious. Ah . . . perhaps I *have* mellowed a bit in my ways."

"Hmm. I've come across that in my readings," Flam mused, "the Ineffable Name of God, but I've never really understood it."

"Quite so, for even amongst we Jews there is disagreement, and some say there has been much additional secret knowledge lost over the millennia. But, simply put, the Name of God is believed to hold great power, and should not be spoken out loud except in an acceptable context, such as on the holiest of days, by one who has been purified and properly prepared. Many, many representations of God's name have evolved, usually categorized by the number of their letters, and these too are deemed to have miraculous properties. The old Kabbalists are said to have meditated on these names in their spiritual quests, and used them to perform their magical rites. Some claim the famous magical incantation 'Abracadabra' is one of these. "

"I remember now," Flam said excitedly, forgotten facts from the books he had read now surfacing as dormant synapses fired again, "doesn't the Torah mention the Tetragrammaton, the four letters YHVH?"

"Yes, yes, that's correct, and 'Yahweh' and 'Jehovah' are derived from that, although the original unutterable pronunciation, the one that holds such power, is said to have been lost, or hidden from us. But there are also many other supposed versions of God's name that run from one letter to 'The Holy and Awesome Seventy-two-Part Name,' made up of seventy-two triads of numbers. That name is said to have been revealed to Moses by the burning bush, and used by him to part the Red Sea. Jewish tradition also says Lilith, the first woman according to Haggadic legend, and my own dear wife's mythical namesake, used God's name to rise into the air and escape her husband Adam's demands she be under him. I have always found that story especially poignant."

"'*Our Father, Who art in Heaven, Hallowed be Thy name.*'" Flam quoted, seeing now some of what he had missed at Sunday school.

"We Jews are not unique in holding to these metaphysical beliefs. Many cultures around the world think there is power in names. There are some who guard their true names, giving their children a pseudonym to use instead when out in the world, for they believe any sorcerer who knows someone's true name can gain power over them."

What had been an engrossing story and an interesting discussion to this point now suddenly lost its appeal as Flam was led to ponder his own name. He instantly slipped into the shame and regret this topic inexorably elicited.

"I don't know about the power of sorcerers, but my name has cast a dark spell over me my whole life," Flam told him, feeling he could be completely honest with this sad little old man who had opened up and bared his soul to him that night.

"It is an unusual name, although in this so-called New World, there are many names I find utterly strange, even after having resided here so many years. You are, I take it, unhappy with this name?"

Flam nodded, self-pity practically dripping from his pores. "I'm thinking of changing it," he confessed.

"You'll forgive me if I have no patience with your dissatisfaction," Joe said sternly, surprising Flam with his lack of sympathy. "That name was given to you by your parents. It is your birthright. You should hold to it, not cast it aside like an unwanted garment." But then Joe seemed to catch himself, and slumped down into his chair. "Forgive me, my young friend," he said, reaching over to touch Flam on the forearm. "I have no right to tell you what to feel or how to lead your life."

"It's okay, don't worry about it," Flam said, feeling sorry for the old man, although anger had in fact been starting to reflexively rise when Joe had begun his chastising over Flam's name.

"Everyone's story is different, and their path is their own. You must do what your heart tells you to do. Old men do love to preach . . . especially when they have already made a mess of their own lives. We profess to possess wisdom, for after all, we have little else to offer the universe."

"Please, don't feel that way. I really enjoy talking to you," Flam said consolingly.

"You are a good listener, and a kind soul. I will pretend I was able to provide at least a modicum of the enjoyable company our lady friend might have offered." Joe's smile showed he had regained some part of his good spirits. "But come, it is late. Let us gather our bill, and perhaps you can accompany me to my bus."

As they stood silently waiting at the bus stop, relishing the clean evening air, which was mildly mixed with the smell of roses and gladioli, Joe reached into his pocket and produced a business card. On it he wrote a few indecipherable words in what appeared to be Hebrew, before handing it to Flam.

"Please go see this man . . . he inherited my shop after I grew too old to thread a needle, although the tailor's business is not what it once was. He will make for you a lovely suit at a very special price that even a young apprentice like yourself can afford."

Flam accepted the card, although he was inwardly embarrassed by Joe's continuing generosity. "I don't know what to say . . . I mean, other than thank you."

Joe shrugged then gave a polite little bow. "*Shalom*," he replied. "Perhaps there will come a day when you will be in a position to return the favour."

Later, lying in bed, Flam found himself reflecting on Joe's sad history and their discussion about names. When he considered all the adversity the little man had overcome in his life, Flam felt a twinge of guilt about the melancholy he was allowing to rule his own existence. And yet, his depression was real—as deep and pervasive as the darkness surrounding him in his bedroom. He could find none of Joe's faith in himself, as badly as he wanted to. If only his name was not such a curse, and possessed some of those magical properties they'd talked about.

"Flam Grub," he said out loud, and waited, but there was no discernible shift in the fabric of the universe. Sighing, he rolled over onto his side and waited for sleep to find him.

CHAPTER 24

Flam's second day on the job proved as disheartening as the first. Arriving a half-hour earlier, as dictated, he spent the day vacuuming, dusting, polishing, stacking, and fetching under Bruno Helman's watchful eye. However, despite his efforts, he earned nothing but constant rebukes and insults from Bruno, who seemingly considered Flam incapable of performing even the most menial of chores correctly. Bruno did now pronounce Flam's name correctly, but the disdainful manner in which he addressed Flam, constantly referring to his young charge as "you Grub," had Flam wishing he was Gruber again.

Each time he suffered Bruno's admonishments and reprimands, Flam told himself to be patient, fighting to find the inner strength to carry on. He wanted to believe this was all part of some probationary rite—an initiation every new employee was expected to tolerate. Once he had proven his worth, Flam assured himself, he would be able to take on other more meaningful tasks around the funeral home, for so far, he had not been asked to do anything befitting his vocational training.

With each new castigation, however, Flam grew more depressed and unsure of himself. He stopped assuming this was some passing test of his mettle, and began to believe he was being purposely and unfairly discriminated against. The only respite in the day came in the afternoon, when he was led to the garage area, commanded to wash the cars, and then turned over to Charlie's custody. "Keep an eye on this lazy screw-up," Bruno commanded the handyman before leaving.

Charlie nodded obligingly, but once Bruno was out of sight, began washing the first vehicle himself. This left Flam wondering whether the big man felt his territory was being encroached upon, and if he too resented Flam's presence. But Charlie's gargantuan grin quickly made it clear he was only demonstrating the proper washing technique, before showing Flam where all the equipment was located, including a protective smock to wear over his clothes.

The giant handyman had an infectiously affable and pleasant manner about him, and after he pulled out a small radio and tuned in the local jazz station, Flam found himself relaxing for the first time since arriving at Morton's. Soon the pair was soaping and rinsing merrily together under the sway of Duke Ellington and Dizzy Gillespie. Flam eventually felt confident enough to engage Charlie in conversation.

"You been working here long?" Flam asked.

"Ten years . . . ever since I arrived from Fiji."

"Fiji! Wow, you're a long way from home. I've read it's beautiful there. You know, I was sort of trying to guess where you were from."

"I would have thought my name gave me away," Charlie retorted with a deadpan delivery. "Duvuduvukulu is a classic Fijian name. Your name's Flam, right?"

Flam nodded, but fell silent at the mention of his name. Charlie, sensing the younger man's reticence, changed the subject.

"You like poetry, Flam?" he asked. "That was a real gas the way you laid that Coleridge on me yesterday. Back home, our English teacher used to make us memorize a different poem every week. Not as useful as the Bible, I suppose, but I never minded. I think the teacher was a heathen."

Flam brightened. "Yeah, I love poetry . . . I read a lot of it as a boy, and I just finished a course at my college. In fact . . ..." He paused, his habitual shyness holding him back, but seeing nothing threatening in Charlie's affable grin and soft brown eyes, decided to open up. "In fact, I write a little poetry myself."

Charlie bellowed out a huge laugh, which echoed eerily around the old stone and concrete of the garage like something from a bad horror movie. Flam blushed, instantly regretting having been so forthcoming. The big Fijian, however, was not ridiculing him. Instead, he grabbed Flam's hand and pumped it wildly, childish delight spreading his big toothy smile even further.

"Too much! If that doesn't beat all. A poet! I'm kind of artistically inclined myself. Me and a couple of buddies from back home have put together a jazz band and we're pretty tight . . . call ourselves the Cannibals, and I play sax . . . and we've even written a few of our own songs. Hey, maybe you can help me with some lyrics sometime. Man, that's tricky work."

"Well, I've never written song lyrics before, but sure, if I can help, I'd love too," said Flam, instantly warming to the notion.

"Never thought I'd meet a poet here of all places," Charlie chuckled. "Man, they're all a bunch of stiffs." He started to laugh at his own joke, then, all of a sudden, he stiffened himself, as frozen in place and attentive as a dog on the point, his eyebrows taut as he listened intently. Then, with surprising deftness for such a big man, he pounced on the radio, turned it off, slid it out of sight under the hearse, then pulled out a pressure gauge and proceeded to busily fiddle with one of the tires.

Flam had heard nothing, but then across the garage a door creaked, and footsteps could be heard approaching. Seconds later, Bruno arrived on the scene and looked around suspiciously. He seemed disappointed to find Flam busily working away and evidently making good progress.

"Charlie, there's a light burnt out in the North Room," Bruno finally addressed the handyman, who nodded and shuffled off towards his storage closet. Bruno then turned to Flam, who was hosing off the last of the suds. "Try not to make such a mess, you Grub, and don't leave any spots. Man, you're some piece of work. Don't you know a hearse has to be immaculate? And when you're done, go up to where we store the caskets, get a Royal Oak off the racks and take it down to Leetch. Make sure it's got the Imperial brass fixtures. Don't go banging it up . . . that box is worth five K." He gave Flam and the hearse one last flint-eyed look, and went back out the way he had come.

Charlie emerged from his closet, carrying a stepladder, and whistled ominously. "Man, that Bruno has a hard-on for you," he commented, shaking his head sympathetically. "What did you do to make him flip his lid like that?"

"Nothing, I swear," Flam protested. "He's been on my case ever since I got here."

"He's no prince, I'll grant you, but I've never seem him razz *anyone* the way he does you."

"It's not just him . . . so far, everyone around here I've met treats me like dirt . . . well, except for you, Charlie. You're alright, but everyone else is being horrible to me, and I don't think it's just because I'm the new kid on the block. It's like . . . like . . .." But he couldn't find a phrase that properly explained the injustice to which he felt he was being subjected.

"Like you've got an albatross around your neck?" Charlie prompted.

Flam couldn't help but smile. "Well, yeah, in a way," he agreed.

"I wish I could help you, but Charlie's a bit of an outcast himself around here. Oh, it's not like they're going to fire me or anything . . . they'd be hard pressed to find someone else who can do everything I do around here for the chicken scratch they pay me. No, I figure they're just scared of me, and I don't much care for those jive-ass mothers anyway." Charlie switched the stepladder to his other arm so he could offer Flam his hand again. "Not you, Flam. You're fly in Charlie's book."

That evening, Bruno left work around 6 p.m. Although he had heaped an extra helping of insults and criticisms on his young charge before departing, Flam was hopeful the end of his day would now be easier to endure, even if he was feeling somewhat spent as he entered the home stretch of his long shift.

On his way out, Bruno informed his underling there were two remaining staff members of the home working that night, workers whom Flam had not yet met. They were evidently junior employees like himself, and he was eager—although with his habitual shyness also filled with apprehension—to meet these new colleagues. He hoped they would be friendlier and more accepting than the domineering and curmudgeonly crew, Charlie excepted, he had encountered thus far.

Flam's introduction to his unmet funerary fellows came as he was washing and disinfecting the refrigerated, four-rack, stainless-steel body storage cabinet in the embalming room, having first endured a rambling and caustic caution from a departing Hannah Leetch. While a drooling Sarah strained at her leash to get out of the room, Leetch sternly advised Flam which fixtures he was and wasn't allowed to touch, any contradictory instructions from Bruno notwithstanding.

As Flam worked, the noxious fumes from the cleaning solution built up inside the enclosed cabinet, causing his sinuses to burn and his eyes to water. He had paused to catch his breath when he heard boisterous voices out in the hall drawing nearer. Curious to meet his co-workers, he quickly stood up, banging his head on one of the upper racks, and causing him to break out in a coughing fit as a lingering cloud of cleaning solution wafted into his nostrils. He was hacking, tears streaming down his cheeks, when the door opened and two men entered, escorting a bagged body on a gurney. One was a squat bulldog of a man in his early thirties, with close cropped blond hair, beady, close-set eyes, and no visible neck. The other was an older man, with thinning brown hair, a walrus moustache, and thick eyeglasses in huge black frames. He had a protruding pot-belly, made more prominent by the shortness of his necktie, which ended well above the navel.

"Whoa, you hear that?" the moustached man commented as Flam fought to bring his coughing under control, "I think the place is haunted, 'cause I hear a ghost. Shit, I *see* a ghost . . . this guy is whiter than the one we got in the body bag."

"Naw," the bulldog sneered, "it's only Bug Boy."

"Bug Boy?" his partner asked, a snicker forming under his moustache in anticipation of an explanation.

"Yeah, Bruno calls him The Grub, but I like Bug Boy better."

Flam had recovered enough to address the tandem, although he had now taken an instant dislike to them, seeing in their cruel insults a reincarnation of all the debasing tormentors he had regularly faced in high school. His hope of finding other empathetic co-workers who would afford him some support or sympathy on the job was now evaporating.

"Um, I'm Flam," he introduced himself with a raspy voice.

"Get that? We got us a *flamer*," the pot-bellied man snorted, ignoring the hand Flam had offered.

"We know who you are, Bug Boy," his squat sidekick snarled, waving a finger in Flam's face. "Bruno the Hell Man told us *all* about you. And, just so you know, we don't care what kind of a big shot you think you are, or who's got your back. This is our turf . . . just remember that. Now I'm George Pugsley, and my four-eyed friend here is Josh Steptoe, and you take orders from us, got it?"

Flam was feeling flustered now, totally confused by this instant animosity, and wondering what Bruno could possibly have been saying about him. He wanted to challenge the pair, to stand up against their bullying, and dispel any misunderstandings they were harbouring. But instead, he lapsed into his habitual meekness. A weak "Whatever you say" was all he could manage as he stared at the floor, not even able to look them in the eye.

With the act of submission having been performed, Pugsley and Steptoe broke out into laughs, and jauntily went about their business, as if Flam was no longer of any importance.

"Hey, Bug Boy," Pugsley called out as he unzipped the Naugahyde bag containing the cadaver they had brought in. "Get a load of the honey we picked up tonight."

"Oh, yeah," Steptoe joined in, brimming with excitement, "this is one sweet piece of meat. Here. Let's get her onto the table." Together they pulled the body out and laid it down onto the stainless steel tabletop. The woman had indeed been beautiful, with long, flowing, ash-blonde hair, high cheekbones, full lips, and a petite patrician nose. She was dressed in a lacy white nightgown, which revealed shapely calves and slim ankles. Flam was aghast to see Steptoe pull the garment all the way up until the breasts and pubic area were fully exposed.

"Hey, check it out," Steptoe interjected, fluffing the dead woman's silky pubic hair, then violating her with his finger. "She shaved her bush in the shape of a heart. How many studs do you suppose tapped this?" His other hand had gravitated to his own groin, where he began to rub himself.

"Wow, and look at the shape of those tits," Pugsley exclaimed, reaching out to tweak a nipple. "They're like something out of *Playboy*. Hey, Bug Boy, you wanna feel her hooters?"

Pugsley might honestly have intended the offer as a genuine courtesy, but Flam was suddenly feeling sick. He backed up hard against the wall, as if he were hoping it would swallow him up and take him away from the disturbing scene. He started to head for the exit, but Pugsley sprang forward and put an arm against the door to keep it closed.

"Whoa . . . not so fast, Bug Boy," said Pugsley, giving Flam a menacing look. "You're not thinking of squealing on us to Morton, are you?" Flam had not, in fact, had any thoughts at the moment beyond getting outside and away from his two wicked co-workers, and their criminally perverted entertainment. He opened his mouth to protest, but had trouble forming any words.

"You breathe a word of this to anyone," Pugsley growled menacingly, "and we'll tell them we came in here and caught you humping the dead chick."

"I . . . I won't say anything, I swear," Flam finally said weakly. "Let me out. I just have to go to the bathroom."

"Damned right you won't say anything," Steptoe added, coming up to sandwich Flam, "because if you cross us, we'll teach you a lesson you'll never forget, and even your cop friend won't be able to help you then."

"I tell you I won't say anything," Flam said, his voice and temper rising. "Let me go. I don't feel well. Or do you want me to puke all over you?"

Pugsley evidently believed him and took a step backward, although his beady eyes continued to burn a hole in Flam. "Okay, get out, but think good and hard about what we said, and don't get any ideas, Bug Boy. Trust me, you don't want to fuck with us. When you get back, wash off the table and the body bag. Me and my man, Josh, are gonna go upstairs and keep Morton company in the chapel."

Flam went to the bathroom and leaned over the sink, but mercifully didn't vomit. He splashed some cold water on his face and pulled it back through his black hair. Looking at himself in the mirror, he had to turn away, ashamed of the reproach he saw staring back.

His thanatological books had made mention of necrophilia more than once, and even back in college there had been crude jokes whispered among the students. ("What does an undertaker do after a hard day at the funeral home? He cracks open a cold one.") Nevertheless, to his mind it was an aberration beyond reason. What he had witnessed Pugsley and Steptoe doing violated every sense of morality—not to mention the sacred trust undertaken by his profession—but Flam had once again played the cowardly weakling. Try as he might to rationalize his backing down as a tactical retreat in the face of a superior enemy, the overwhelming sense of guilt would not leave him.

He replayed the encounter with his co-workers, and it only now occurred to him to wonder what Steptoe had meant by "his cop friend." He could only have been talking about Cuff, but how on earth did this relative stranger know about Flam's involvement with the detective? Did Cuff have some sort of association with Morton and the funeral home? A new apprehension seized Flam, causing his stomach to churn again, and sending him back to the sink for another attempt to regain his composure.

When he finally returned to the embalming room, it was empty, and the cadaver had been put away. As instructed, he wiped off the table, then cleaned and disinfected the bag in which the corpse had been transported, and stowed it and the gurney away.

The room was quiet—*as quiet as a morgue*, Flam thought, and smiled ruefully—except for the faint buzz of a terminally ill fluorescent light

bulb. He opened the door to the body storage cabinet, and pulled out
the top tray where the woman had been stowed. It slid out smoothly
on its heavy-duty rollers to reveal the occupant. Her gown was back in
place, and a sheet now modestly covered her up to the chin as well.
Her pretty pale face bore the passive, patient look of the dead. Flam
read the woman's name—Cindy Sexton—off a card left behind on top
of the sheet. He reached over and lightly stroked her cheek.

"I'm sorry that had to happen to you, Cindy," he whispered, "but
soon the last of life's indignities will be over and you can rest in peace."
A sad, poignantly poetic notion worked its way into Flam's thoughts,
and he smiled sadly to himself. He pushed the woman back into her
steel cradle, closed the cabinet door with a thud, and sat down on the
stool Hannah used when she worked. Pulling out his notepad, Flam
committed his latest poetic thoughts to paper.

CHAPTER 25

The next few days were a blur of double shifts for Flam, spent in mind-numbing drudgery, performing every menial task the disapproving Bruno Helman could muster, punctuated only by bouts of terror when he was turned over to the supervision of the seemingly inseparable Pugsley and Steptoe. The duo was now making Flam the butt of interminable practical jokes, in addition to dumping off their chores onto him whenever possible. They seemed to take especial delight in startling him by leaping out of doorways or closets. By now, the jittery Flam was moving around the funeral home as if he were trapped in a haunted house full of malevolent spirits that might attack him at any moment.

Saturday, at least, brought a large, elaborate funeral, and a chance to escape outside alone for a while. He was tasked with posting *No Parking* signs along the street in front of the funeral home. This was to assure spots for the hearse and limousines that would be accompanying Cindy Sexton, the earlier object of Pugsley and Steptoe's attentions, to the Anglican cathedral for a funeral mass, before leading a final procession to the cemetery.

It was surprisingly cool for June, and a steady drizzle had been falling all morning, although Flam didn't mind in the least. Charlie, who remained his sole ally and comforter, had lent him an umbrella, and the damp dreary day somehow suited Flam's own sad, sodden perspective on the state of his life. As he patrolled the block to shoo off any cars that tried to encroach on the funeral's turf, he mentally worked on a dark, woeful, and lyrical lament that he was hoping to turn into a possible blues song for Charlie's jazz ensemble.

Flam's mental respite was further bolstered by the pending opportunity to participate in the public side of his vocation at last. Other than the corpses he had helped usher in through the back of the building, he had not as yet come into contact with a single one of the funeral home's clients. The Hell Man (Flam had privately adopted Pugsley's nickname for their supervisor) had predicted a large turnout for the mass and the procession to the cemetery afterwards, and all the staff were being pressed into service. Even Hannah had surfaced from her basement embalming room, appropriately uniformed for the occasion, and poised to contribute.

A quartet of surly motorcycle cops arrived—rented to shepherd the funeral procession. They seemed to Flam to be in foul humour, evidently because the steady drizzle had forced them to don raincoats and attach sidecars to their vehicles, so their usual dashing look and macho manoeuvres were now compromised.

Flam attempted to start up a conversation with the policemen, but other than acknowledging his presence with some nods and grunts, they seemed content to band together and drink the take-out coffees a junior officer produced from under the buttoned-down leather cover of a sidecar. Soon Bruno showed up driving the hearse, with a grim-faced Mr. Morton himself occupying the passenger seat, and shortly thereafter the limousines slid up, chauffeured by the other staffers. Hannah brought up the rear, barely visible over the top of the steering wheel.

Flam hovered expectantly, ready for instructions and eager to know what his role would be in the proceedings, but both Morton and Bruno left the lead car and went back into the home without uttering a word to him. Staring after his bosses in disappointment, like a spurned wallflower at the prom, Flam was unaware Pugsley had left his limo and snuck up to the entrance. Suddenly the loud pop of an air-filled paper bag caused Flam to jump, soliciting raucous laughter from all the witnesses, especially the cops, one of whom feinted going for his gun in mock panic.

Flam, maddened by these persistent jokes at his expense, spun on his heels, ready to confront his tormenter. Before he could utter a single word of retort, Pugsley gave back a wry look and gestured smugly with his head towards where Bruno was coming out of the home ahead of a small crowd of black-clad people. These were the deceased's immediate family and closest friends, who would be escorting the casket to the funeral service, where they would meet up with the rest of the mourners.

Everyone scrambled to open up the doors and shepherd the guests into the waiting vehicles, and Flam was once again left standing idly by with no part to play. He noticed an old woman without an overcoat, standing neglected on wobbly legs at the fringe of the group, and looking dazed and distraught. Flam hurried over and offered her his umbrella and an arm for support, and the woman looked up at him gratefully and managed a brave smile.

"Thank you, young man," she whispered. "I'm afraid I forgot my cane. Oh my, I've become so absent-minded in my old age."

"Days like today are a heavy burden, even on the young," Flam said reassuringly. "Please let me help you to the car."

She nodded, and leaning on him heavily, allowed Flam to escort her to the lead limousine, where Morton was holding the door open and watching Flam appraisingly. When they reached the vehicle, the woman turned and studied Flam's face.

"Do I know you?" she asked. "You look familiar."

"Perhaps you've seen me around the funeral home," Flam suggested, although he knew full well he had been kept busy in the rear over the past few days, and had not encountered any of the Sexton party—with the exception of Cindy herself down in the embalming room the evening she'd arrived.

The woman shook her head, rejecting his answer. "No, that's not it. I feel I know you from somewhere. Never mind. Perhaps it's just a glimpse into the future—I've been told I possess the gift, and you do have a light about you. Would you be so kind as to help me into the automobile, dearie?"

Flam obliged, handing off the umbrella to Morton in order to support the woman with both hands as she laboured in through the car door. She seemed reluctant to let go of Flam's hand, even after she was deposited safely in her place, until one of the other mourners in the limousine slid over and took charge of the old woman, who slumped back against the huge black leather seat like some limp, overdressed rag doll.

As Flam swung the door of the limousine shut, he caught Morton's eye. The look was hard to read, and for a second Flam thought he was about to suffer yet another undeserved rebuke until the old man gave him a nod—ever so slight, almost imperceptible, but as clear to Flam as a pat on the back—and returned the umbrella.

"You ride with Bruno in the hearse," Morton instructed. "I'm going to stay here and mind the store. Saturdays can get pretty crazy."

Flam did as told, but when he opened the door to the hearse Bruno turned and growled at him, "What do you think you're doing?"

"Mr. Morton's staying here . . . he said to ride with you," Flam explained. That shut Bruno up, and he turned with a scowl and started up the ignition. Within seconds, the cops were also revving up their motorcycles.

"Well, what are you waiting for, you Grub, Christmas? Get in," Bruno commanded, "and for Chrissake, do up your seatbelt."

Bruno drove in silence, and Flam passed the time studying the way the motorcycle cops peeled off, each in turn, to halt traffic at the intersections, then sped up expertly to fall back in formation with their fellows.

"They're pretty good," Flam offered in the way of conversation at one point, but that only earned a snort from Bruno.

"Yeah," The Hell Man said sarcastically, "it would be pretty tough to have a funeral without them, wouldn't it?" Something in the way he said it bothered Flam, but he shut up rather than pursue it.

At the cathedral, Flam was left in charge of the hearse, as Bruno went out to marshal the pallbearers while the drivers of the limousines started ushering the passengers into the building. There was some confusion at one point as Bruno spoke with the men who had apparently been designated to carry the casket, and Flam was puzzled to see all their heads swivel his way during the conversation. He assumed they were talking about the hearse, although he couldn't imagine how there could possibly be any logistical difficulties in something as straightforward as discharging the coffin. Bruno and one of the others, a tall, athletic-looking man in his twenties, separated from the group and came his way.

Bruno did not look his usual cocky self. "Mr. Grub, the family is requesting you be one of the pallbearers," he said with exquisite politeness.

"Grammy Sexton insists," the other man explained. "She says Cindy wants you to take care of her. Yeah, yeah, I know . . . the old bat's totally loopy, but no one dares cross her. What Grammy wants, Grammy gets."

Flam shrugged, as surprised by Bruno's uncharacteristic courtesy as the request itself. "Naturally," he replied, "it would be my pleasure." The other man, whose body language practically screamed of strength and vitality, was clearly sizing up Flam's spindly frame, but if he had any reservations, he kept them to himself.

Bruno opened the back of the hearse and slid out the casket. Flam and five other pallbearers assumed their grips, and carried the coffin solemnly into the cathedral, its pews full of mourners. Flam recalled a professor's anecdote from school, telling how once an especially obese dead man in an oversized custom oak casket had been too heavy for those doing the carrying, and had been dropped on the church steps. No such calamity befell the slender Cindy Sexton and her expensive rosewood box, and Flam reckoned the other men could easily have managed the trip without him.

Standing beside Bruno against the inside wall of the cathedral directly beneath its huge stained glass windows, his hands folded before him in an appropriately officious fig-leaf position, Flam had an opportunity to ponder the dearly departed Cindy in more depth. Given the venue and size of the turnout, it was clear that her family carried some stature, which made Flam wonder why his downscale funeral home had been chosen for the final arrangements. The probable answer came during the eulogy, when it was revealed the Sexton family fortune had been made in the warehousing business, and Flam surmised, given the Morton Home's long-established location near the old railyards, many other members of the clan had likely passed through its doors in the past.

Flam also learned the deceased's full name was Lucinda Athena Serena Sexton, she had died of a brain aneurysm, and the old woman he had helped into the car was her great-grandmother, who seemed to go by no other name than Grammy Sexton. Flam also learned that Cindy's death had ended an aspiring career in the theatre, and broken the hearts of several suitors.

On hearing this mention of her suitors, an image of Cindy's heart-shaped pubic haircut, which had so fascinated Steptoe, came immediately to Flam's mind. Although he knew he would have hardly warranted a glance from a girl like that while she was alive, it seemed in death she still had the power of attraction to reach out and pull him to her. And the power to remind him of his own loneliness.

The front of the cathedral was so crowded with flowers, it was almost impossible to make out the altar. Their bouquet filled the air, and a choir in the balcony of the cathedral sang several sacred selections from Bach and Mozart. Flam tilted his head back to wallow in the smells and sounds wafting about him, and his itinerant gaze was captured by the frescoes painted on the inner dome of the nave.

One of the scenes depicted angels attending the birth of Christ. Flam's aimless musings found themselves grounding onto the subject of his own lost Angel, and he wondered whether he would ever see her again. Despite the frustration and subsequent spasms of self-pity spawned by that night wrestling together on the lawn at Prentice College, Flam had clung to the fantasy he might yet become her lover—if only because abandoning that lingering hope now would open the door to the onslaught of despair and hopelessness, threatening to overrun his otherwise barren life.

Flam was moved by the time and place towards some rare religiosity. He began a half-hearted entreaty for divine salvation from his loneliness when he was struck by the impropriety of praying for a lustful (and technically sinful) encounter—although he knew full well no pious reservations would stop him if the opportunity arose in all its engorged passion. *Would the Virgin Mary entertain a prayer on the subject from the Virgin Flam,* he joked to himself. *Hmm, better make that* Saint *Mary,* for he was in an Anglican church, and he recalled the Immaculate Conception remained the source of some thorny theological dispute to this day. *Ah, but I'm an anointed Catholic,* he told himself. *Don't I qualify for an exemption despite the venue? Or, when not in Rome, do I do what the non-Romans do?*

Flam's thoughts returned to earth, and he glanced over to find Bruno staring at him disapprovingly. "Pay attention, for Chrissake," The Hell Man scolded under his breath. "At least *try* to pretend like Morton's employees are interested in their own funerals."

Flam reddened, angry at this freshest rebuke, but he nonetheless straightened, and attempted to look appropriately solemn.

The choir finished its recital, and after some final benedictions from the attending bishop, it was time to take Cindy on her final journey. Flam followed Bruno to the front and joined the other pallbearers in carrying the casket back out to the hearse. Behind him, a subdued din arose as the mourners filed out of their pews in anticipation of the final funerary act, and headed for their cars.

The motorcade was a long one—looking back during the drive Flam noted the line extended for several blocks—and the motorcycle cops now really earned their overtime pay, shepherding the procession to the cemetery through the late Saturday morning traffic. Flam was surprised when the route took them to Ash Grove, a small, venerable cemetery in the heart of the city, for he had heard that ancient burial ground had long ceased to have space for any new plots.

The mystery was solved when he saw Cindy would not be interred into a common grave, but was to join other Sextons in the family mausoleum, a neo-Classical stone edifice still looking properly majestic despite the fallout from years of inner-city grit and exhaust fumes.

As the final on-site benediction reached its zenith, Flam could see the majority of attendees growing noticeably restless. They were doubtless anxious to complete their ceremonial obligation to the dead and get on with the more social part of the program, presumably a lavish reception at the Sexton home. Finally, the proprieties had been dispensed with, and the family and friends quickly dispersed, except for Grammy Sexton and a couple of the immediate family members, who insisted on staying and bearing witness to the very end.

The cemetery's workers, who now had charge of the final steps of entombing Cindy's remains into the designated crypt, appeared to be in no great hurry to complete their solemn duty, and a visibly annoyed Bruno huddled his staff together to work out a plan of action for the remains of the day. The Hell Man had snuck out earlier to check in with Morton, and reported that things were getting lively back at the funeral home—including a couple of bodies urgently needing to be picked up and prepared for viewing.

After some of the waiting limousine passengers were parcelled out to ride with other mourners, the rest were packed into two of the sedans, and Flam was ordered to stay behind with the remaining limo, and transport the last of the hangers-on when they had completed their final farewells.

"Try not to bang up the car," Bruno growled as he handed Flam the keys, "and get back as soon as you can. I've got shitloads of work saved up for you." Flam was half-tempted to snap his heels together and deliver a mock Nazi salute, but managed to look properly servile and complacent, at least until Bruno and the others had driven off.

When Flam re-entered the mausoleum, the workers were just finishing the entombment, hefting a large carved pink marble panel into place, complete with built-in vases. For the first time that day, Grammy Sexton had visible tears in her eyes, and went up to lovingly finger the surface of the stone monument. Behind her, two other remaining mourners—the athletic young man who'd asked Flam to be a pallbearer, and a gaunt forty-something blonde woman who looked like a worn-out older copy of Cindy herself—were exchanging looks and shifting impatiently on their feet. Finally, the blonde woman seemed to get up enough nerve to approach the sniffling old lady still fondling the stonework.

"Grammy . . . the wake . . . they're all waiting. We should get going," she suggested in a little girl's voice.

The old woman reeled like a snake about to bite. "Take a cab then if you're in such a hurry to go get soused and start screwing the help," she hissed. "Go on, get out of here . . . both of you, and leave me alone." Grammy spotted Flam standing across the mausoleum. "*He'll* take care of me," she announced, and turned back to her contemplation of the crypt with a contemptuous look of finality.

Flam wasn't sure what to say or do next, but was spared any need to decide when the blonde woman spun on her stiletto heels and stormed angrily out the door. The younger man stood indecisively for a moment or two, then exhaled irritably through his nose, and went after her. Thinking they might be waiting outside, Flam stuck his head out the door, but the two of them had not stopped, and were marching determinedly towards the cemetery's exit, so he returned to his post and waited patiently.

Either from the weight of her sorrow, or the emotional aftershock of her angry exchange with the other woman, Grammy suddenly slumped and wavered on her feet. Flam rushed over to support the old woman, just as she seemed ready to collapse. She looked up at him, pale as chalk, her face a mask of misery.

"She was my last hope," she whispered to Flam, as she clawed at his arm in an attempt to regain her balance. Flam put one arm around her waist and steadied her.

"I thought, maybe, after all the failures, after all the spineless, self-indulgent, back-stabbing brats I spawned, that finally Cindy might be a true heir, a protégé . . . someone actually worthy of the Sexton name." Grammy started to cry in gulping spasms, burying her face in Flam's chest. "Oh, Cindy. Cindy. Why did you have to die? Why is God punishing me?"

Flam let her cry, reasoning this was as therapeutic as anything he could offer in the way of platitudes or truisms, and to his mind better than those who denied their grief, suppressing or sublimating it with

coldly compulsive behaviours. He tried to recall the practical lessons
he had absorbed concerning grief, and how, despite its recognizable
universal patterns, everyone's sorrow is in its own way unique.

What is Grammy feeling at this moment? he wondered. *Is it survivor's
guilt for having outlived her grandchild, and violated the natural order of things?
Is she perhaps feeling hopelessness—an inability to contemplate resuming a life
that is now empty and devoid of meaning? Perhaps she's deliberately clinging
to her bereavement, even after the ceremonial catharsis of the funeral, as her
last earthly connection to Cindy, feeling that to stop grieving now would be a
betrayal, an insult to the memory of her beloved one?*

All these clinical concepts, once faithfully copied down in lectures
and gleaned from textbooks, their key points dutifully highlighted with
a neon-yellow marker, somehow seemed of little help now. Real grief
was manifesting itself in the form of a frail old woman, hanging onto a
perfect stranger for sheer contact comfort, her ancient timeworn body
wracked by uncontrollable sobs that poured forth from the darkest,
most guarded places of her being.

"What would Cindy want you to do now?" he finally asked tenderly,
pulling up Grammy's chin like a lover so she would meet his eyes. He
hardly realized he'd said it out loud, but the simple question seemed
to have a healing effect, as if on some level she had been depending
on him for an answer, for salvation from her overwhelming emotion.

Grammy laughed then, Flam's query apparently having tickled
some cherished reminiscence. "Cindy? She would have said, 'Life's
a bitch, Grammy, so be a bigger one.' Oh, she could be as sweet as
caramel, that one, but she was hard too . . . a diamond, beautiful
and unbreakable."

The last thought seemed to sap Grammy's resolve, and she sagged
back into Flam's arms. "I can't even give Cindy her final wish," she
told him, her voice sounding tiny and distant as she pressed her face
further into his sleeve.

"What do you mean?"

"We were here once, visiting my husband," Grammy said, and
raised her head to indicate the tomb in question. "Cindy told me what
she wanted inscribed on her own crypt for posterity—something about

death and a key—but she never put it down anywhere . . . no one knew she'd go so soon."

"*Death is the golden key that opens the palace of eternity,*" Flam suggested quietly, and Grammy's eyes widened as if he'd just performed a miracle. She nodded vigorously. "It's Milton," Flam added. "Here, I'll write it out for you." Still supporting the old woman's weight, he reached into an inside pocket for his omnipresent pen and notebook, tore a blank page out, and wrote out the verse.

Grammy stared at the paper for a moment then looked up at Flam. "What's your name, young man?"

Flam reddened, as always, but could see no way to avoid answering. "It's Flam . . . Flam Grub."

"Flam Grub," she repeated, as if testing the name for some secret property. "Well, Flam, Cindy would also have said, 'Life is short, Grammy dearest, so let's have a tall drink.' Ah, she knew how to make the most of life, my beautiful little Cinderella did. So, I suppose you're right, Cindy certainly would not have wanted me to give that pack of vultures that pass for my family the satisfaction of seeing the Boss Bitch fall apart. Come now, let's go and I'll drink a toast to her memory."

She halted abruptly, an acrid grin coming over her creased face, and confused Flam by clucking a disapproving sound as she reached into a pocket to pull out an embroidered black lace handkerchief. Grammy moistened the fabric with her saliva and brought it up towards Flam's shoulder and began rubbing. He turned his head and watched her removing a white splat where a bird dropping had fallen on him.

"That's supposed to be lucky," Grammy told him as she wiped away the offending stain. When she had finished the job to her satisfaction, she put away the handkerchief and commanded, "Take me to the car."

Flam escorted her out to the limousine, and after receiving directions, cautiously guided the large, unfamiliar vehicle out into the noonday traffic. He kept an eye on Grammy in the rear-view mirror as he drove, but she seemed to have totally collected herself. She now had a purposeful, almost angry look, as she contemplated the passing cityscape through the window, interrupting her meditation only to issue Flam instructions on where to proceed.

The downtown buildings gave way to houses, which then grew progressively larger and more opulent as he neared their destination. This was, Flam knew by reputation, the most affluent part of the city, but he had never actually seen massive mansions like these before, all sitting behind wrought-iron gates on enormous plots of land with lush, immaculately kept lawns.

The Sexton home was at the end of a heavily treed street that wound lazily along the edge of a ravine. While perhaps not the largest building in the neighbourhood, it was clearly the oldest, with high, ivy-covered stone walls and a huge steeply sloped black slate roof. The long cobblestone driveway was lined with dozens of expensive automobiles. As Flam pulled up to the front door, he could see through the row of tall leaded-glass windows that the main floor of the house was teeming with people.

There was a rustle behind him and something brushed his ear. Flam turned around to see Grammy Sexton holding out a folded bundle of hundred-dollar bills in front of his face.

"Here, Flam," she commanded, "take this."

He shook his head. "That's really not necessary. It's all part of our service." Her lips tightened into a hard, disapproving line, and an angry glare sparked up in the middle of her puffy, wrinkled eyes, as again she thrust the wad at him.

"Don't be an idiot. Take it . . . I know you can use it, and you can be damned-well sure I won't take no for an answer." Flam could see now why the other members of her family found Grammy Sexton so formidable. Gone was the fragile old woman who had been on the verge of collapse in the crypt. The person now staring him down with an indomitable, steely-eyed look was clearly someone used to getting her way. But then she softened a little and seemed to permit herself the faintest hint of a grin. "Besides," she added, "Cindy would want you to have it."

Touché. He smiled at that and accepted the money. "Thank you . . . both."

She returned the smile. "No, thank *you* . . . for everything. I don't know what it is about you, but you're clearly an exceptional young man. Oh, on the outside you carry yourself like the world has ground you down to dog food, but inside . . . well, it's almost like your soul is two sizes too large for your body. I wish you well, Flam Grub. Now, if you'll excuse me, I have to go and tend to my guests."

Outside, their arrival had been noted, and a pretty young brunette in a maid's uniform came rushing from the house with an umbrella to help Grammy exit the vehicle. Once out, however, the old woman shook off the helping arm. Holding herself erect, she walked towards the house with majesty and determination.

Driving back to Morton's, Flam found himself in rare good spirits. The long hours of menial tasks and on-the-job abuses of the past week receded into memory. Although he doubted he'd brought out anything that wasn't already in Grammy Sexton's character, he nevertheless felt like he'd helped her manage her grief. In so doing, he had achieved his first real professional contribution.

Add to that the roll of hundred-dollar bills in his pocket, which he had to admit he needed badly, plus the feeling of driving a large expensive vehicle, and Flam felt like life was perhaps worth living after all.

It took less than five minutes for the mood to evaporate, though, once he returned to Morton's. Bruno immediately castigated him for being late, and accused Flam of having deliberately dawdled on his way back from the cemetery just to avoid working. When Flam tried to explain he had waited around to drive Grammy Sexton home, this only served to further fuel The Hell Man's ire.

"I don't care how many big shot friends you think you have, you Grub. Do you think you're going to get a free ride around here? You may be able to scare Old Man Morton, but you sure as hell don't scare me. If it was up to me, I'd fire your ass right now . . . but you can bet I'm going to be keeping my eye on you to make sure you pull your weight. Now, we have two viewings tonight, so you can start by cleaning the place from top to bottom. If I see so much as one piece of lint on the carpet or one spot on the bathroom sink, you're toast. So get cracking."

Bruno turned and stomped off. Flam opened his mouth to let some of the violent thoughts teeming inside him pour forth. He wanted nothing more than to unleash a tirade at this petty tyrant in defense of his innocence—to launch a poetic salvo of stinging curses that would put the pompadoured persecutor in his place. But although some choice, sharply barbed phrases easily formed in Flam's forebrain, nothing but silence issued forth, and this inability to speak up for himself just made his pathetic state more depressing. He felt defeated, ashamed, and utterly damned. *Cindy Sexton's the lucky one,* Flam thought, and turned to meekly obey his instructions.

CHAPTER 26

Sunday evening loomed, finally promising Flam the opportunity for some time off, and a chance to see his mother. He had tried repeatedly, every day, to get in touch with Mary, placing the calls late at night—first from work after he had finished his shift, and then again from his apartment, following the bus ride home—but she never seemed to be in. She also did not return his calls, despite recorded entreaties to phone back no matter how late she might get in.

Finally, Mary managed to reach him, late on Saturday evening, as he was scrubbing down the embalming table, and happened to answer the outside line from Hannah's desk.

"Flam? For heaven's sake, dear, there you are. I've been trying to reach you all week, but they keep saying you're busy. Didn't you get my messages? The nice man who kept answering promised he'd pass them on."

"Messages? No, I never got any messages." Flam instantly suspected Bruno's involvement, and bristled with anger. Yet, at the same time, he was petrified The Hell Man might walk in that very instant and catch him talking on the phone . . . or might even be listening in on another line.

"Listen, Mother," Flam said, wanting to be brief, "I can't really talk now, but I'm off at five tomorrow. I wanted to drop by and see you . . . are you going to be home?"

There was a brief pause on the other end of the line, and Flam got the impression Mary had placed her hand over the receiver to talk with someone. "Why, yes dear, of course I'd love to see you," she finally answered. "There are some things I want to talk about . . . why don't I cook us a nice dinner, and we can chat."

"Yeah, great. I'll see you then. Look, I'm really sorry, but I have to go." Flam hung up, disturbed by the various shades of suspicion tinting his mood. Under a cloud, and grinding his teeth with anxiety, he went about finishing his chores.

On Sunday evening, after a mere single shift, but one that was spent nonetheless largely on his knees, cleaning every obscure storage space and corner of the funeral home Bruno could think of, Flam headed over to meet—and, in his mind, to confront—his mother. It was the first time in days he had left work while the sun was still out, despite the fact the summer solstice, and with it the longest day of the year, were fast approaching. Even the warm, scented summer eve did little to improve his murky mood, though, and the sight of the darkened, derelict bookstore downstairs certainly did not help.

As he climbed up the stairs to her flat, Flam was determined to get some answers from his mother. The continuous references by Flam's co-workers to "his friend, the cop" had spawned various suspicions about how he had obtained his position at Morton's, and he was hoping his mother would have some information for him on the subject.

As it turned out, Flam would be able to go straight to the source for his intelligence. Not altogether surprisingly, Sergeant Cuff was there too, helping a giggling and giddy Mary in the kitchen, moving about the place and pressing against her with a casual familiarity, as if he'd lived there forever.

"Aye, there's the Grub," Cuff called out in jovial greeting when Flam entered the apartment. "How was your week on the kick-the-bucket brigade?" It irritated Flam that neither the cop nor Mary made any effort to pull apart from one another or disguise their obvious intimacy. "Care for a glass of vino?" Cuff offered.

"No thanks," Flam said, flopping in a chair and studying the pair. "So . . . you live here now?"

"Flam, mind your manners," his mother scolded him, but her face reddened, betraying her guilt. Cuff, however, merely grinned, and wrapped his arms around Mary's waist.

"What's it to you . . . you a cop?" Cuff quipped back.

"No, but I guess I have one looking out for me." That earned a huge guffaw from the sergeant, who disentangled himself from Mary, and crossed the room to loom over Flam.

"Is that what's got a bee in your bonnet? So what if I leaned on Morton a little to hire you. So I told him I'd have the police brotherhood boycott his stinking funerals if he didn't take you on. You should thank me."

"*Thank* you?" Flam was livid. "I didn't ask for your help . . . now everyone at work's treating me like a pariah because of what you did!"

"So what? You got the job, didn't you? You should get your damned nose out of those books and learn how the world really works. Connections are what count, kid. Be grateful you at least had *one* . . . it's not like you could have kept working in that shitty little bookstore downstairs. Hell, even that sorry-assed gig dried up, didn't it? And where's your pal, the old hippie, now? He dumped the place . . . and you . . . and is halfway around the world. Christ, if it wasn't for me, you'd probably be back here, living with your mother and crying under the table."

The rage in Flam reached its incendiary point and he made to leap up at Cuff, but the cop saw it coming and shoved him effortlessly back into the chair. Cuff made no other move, other than swivelling subtly on his feet and shifting his weight. Flam saw instinctively he was no match for a man trained in the use of physical force, and accustomed to violence. Suddenly Flam recalled the time he had tried to combat Steve, and memories of the pain suffered, and the price ultimately paid for that futile insurrection, came flooding back, leaving him limp.

Mary, who had been standing silently by with her mouth agape, came over and knelt before her son. She was wearing make-up and the flowery scent of an unfamiliar perfume came wafting up from her. "I asked Lee to help you, Flam," Mary said softly. "He did it for me. He did it because . . . because we're in love."

Flam snorted. The declaration came as no real surprise, and part of him was almost relieved to know his suspicions had been spot on. Wrapped in his own misery and feelings of worthlessness, however, he was in no mood to be magnanimous. "Wow, you really know how to pick them," he said sarcastically.

Mary pressed her cheek up against his thigh and said nothing. For a moment Flam thought she was going to cry, but when she raised her head to stare at him, he saw only anger, and the same familiar look of uncaring contempt that had dogged him throughout his boyhood.

"I love him, and I don't care what you or anyone else thinks. I love him like I never dreamed I'd *ever* love anybody. We're going to be together, and if you don't like it, you can go to hell."

"What about Gerald Strait?" Flam asked, taking an emotional shot in the dark, searching for anything that might unnerve or hurt Mary, wanting suddenly to punish her for the way she had neglected him throughout his life, and for the way she was abandoning him now.

"What about him?" Cuff interjected, moving closer. His eyes had narrowed into slits, and he looked alert, even dangerous. Flam didn't care one iota. At this point, he would have welcomed a bullet to his brain —a point-blank, hollow-point, 9mm cure for his miserable, pitiful life.

"It wouldn't surprise me a bit if Lover Boy here framed Gerald to get him out of the way. Maybe he even helped him find the door out of this world. Funny how you were the one to find him."

"Flam! What are you saying?" Mary exclaimed, getting up to embrace the detective. "Lee *saved* me. Why, if it wasn't for him, who knows what would have happened to me."

"Look, kid, you don't know what you're talking about. The guy was a total sleazeball. If you must know, I found him because I'd gone over to have a talk with him. We finally got one of his drug-pushing partners to roll over on him—we were just haggling with the lawyer over the terms of the plea bargain. It was only a matter of time before Strait was finally arrested, and I was going to warn him so he could get out of town."

"Warn him? Why would you do that if he was such a crook?" asked Flam.

Lee looked sheepishly down at the ground, then glanced at Mary, who was chewing her bottom lip nervously. "Because I didn't want your mother to suffer anymore, that's why. The gossip was bad enough for her with just the accusations against Strait floating around. I figured I'd spare her the further humiliation of an arrest and trial, even if she had already dumped him by then. Didn't matter, though. When I showed up he was already dead."

Flam shrugged. Somehow it made no sense—not that he purported to be any kind of authority on the abnormal mind, despite his voracious readings. "So, why do you figure he'd kill himself? Why wouldn't he just run for it?"

"Because of me," Mary answered the question. She looked up at Cuff, who shook his head, as if pleading with her, but Mary brushed his face gently with her fingertips, and turned back towards her son.

"I was there when he died," Mary said quietly.

"What?" Flam exclaimed. He was petrified now of what might be unfolding, of what he had started with his jealous petulance against his mother. "You don't mean . . . ."

"Yes. I killed him," Mary said, suddenly looking very pale, and very much older.

"Sweetheart . . . don't," Cuff implored her, but she ignored him.

"He called me up, said he had to talk with me, said it was important. I tried calling Lee, but there was no answer, so I left a message and went over. Gerald was half out of his mind. He was drunk, and was talking utter nonsense about the two of us being together again. When I tried to leave, he . . . he grabbed me, tried to force me onto the bed. I got away from him and ran into the kitchen. That's when I saw the gun, beside a bottle of vodka on the table. Funny how you recall some things so clearly, like they're burned in your memory. I remember seeing the label of the vodka bottle—it was called Silent Sam, and I recollect thinking it was an odd name for a brand of liquor. But I didn't mean to shoot him, so help me God . . . I just wanted him to leave me alone, but he came at me, like the devil himself . . . said he was going to kill me . . . tried to take the gun away from me . . .."

"Jesus H. Christ," Flam exclaimed, and sat back down heavily on the chair he had just vacated. His mind was trying desperately to adjust to the Pandora's Box he had unwittingly opened, with all its ramifications. Cuff was giving him a now-see-what-you've-done look, and trying clumsily to comfort Mary. She, however, was not visibly in need of any support, but was instead standing stiffly, with an almost triumphant look, her fists balled by her side.

"So I sent him to hell," she spat angrily. "Lee arrived just after it happened and took care of everything, even though I tried to talk him into letting me stay and tell them what happened."

"Jesus H. Christ," Flam repeated, unable to find any other words to express the firestorm sweeping through his brain. It actually surprised him that, when his thoughts finally crystallized, the first reaction was a profound, horrible, gut-wrenching fear for his mother's welfare.

"And she's completely in the clear? The cops bought the story?" The question was directed at Cuff.

The policeman nodded. "I was worried the forensics guys might find a hole in our cover story somehow, but we lucked out. At first they thought maybe I had gotten trigger-happy and killed Strait myself, mainly because the hole was in his chest . . . not your typical suicide. But he must have had his hands on the gun when it went off, 'cause there was gunpowder residue all over them . . . and, of course, none on mine. They wanted to know what I was doing there, but I said Mary had phoned to say Gerald had called her and was threatening suicide . . . which matched the phone records. Good thing I erased her message. They talked to Mary the next day, but she was a real trooper . . . and I guess by then they'd kinda lost interest. I think in the end they liked the nice neat package it all wrapped itself up into."

Flam came over and jostled a little with Cuff for a share of his mother's body space. "Oh, Mother. Thank God nothing happened to you." She smiled and hugged him with one arm, still clinging to Cuff with the other.

"I killed him," she repeated, her voice barely above a whisper, "and because of my lie to save my own skin, because the police ruled it a suicide, Gerald couldn't be buried in hallowed ground." A tear worked its way out of the corner of her eye, and hesitated on the crest of her cheek before gravity took over, and nudged the droplet lazily down Mary's cheek. Flam reached up and rubbed it away with his finger. "Oh, sweet Lord, what have I done? I've sinned and I haven't the strength to confess," she murmured.

Cuff rolled his eyes up at the ceiling, his look of impatience making it clear this was a topic he had not wanted reopened. He sighed, but said nothing. Flam supposed that the cop, clearly a street-smart pragmatist, untroubled by spirituality, had counselled Mary to let the matter drop, and was not pleased with her lingering doubts and crises of conscience.

Flam's own conscience was also bothering him at that moment. He had come into his mother's house full of spite and indignation, his tongue dripping venom and spoiling for a fight with Cuff, who, in fact, had done nothing more than try to help. And why? Was it because Flam was jealous of their happiness, that he envied the passion these two had found when he had none? As much as he had set out to hate Cuff, and no matter how much Flam might have wanted to continue resenting the man who was taking away the only semblance of affection in Flam's life—who had stood there minutes ago, and insulted him, and lied to his face—now something, call it respect, or gratitude, had flipped his emotions completely on their head in some cosmic act of interpersonal jujitsu.

Flam spun his mother around and stared her down. "Mother, stop it this instant! You and your damned literal-minded Bible thumping. Do you think God is some cosmic locker-room lawyer sitting on high, and waiting to damn people on some Catholic technicality? God knows what was in your heart, knows you had no intention to kill Gerald . . . that it was an accident. And God, and God alone, will dole out any divine retribution Gerald's got coming to him, hallowed ground or not. Throwing two lives down the toilet for the sake of a dead criminal will not serve some higher purpose. That's right . ... *two* lives. 'Cause if you go blabbing now, you'll take your man here down with you. I think he's proven his love, and deserves better than that."

Mary was just standing there with her eyes and mouth wide open, and Flam had no idea whether his message had hit home, or whether he had simply succeeded in annoying her with his irreverence. Eventually she blinked a few times, and her lips tightened into an inscrutable line, but still she said nothing. Suddenly Cuff broke out into a huge laugh, and went to lean on the kitchen counter.

"I'll be damned," he chuckled. Mary smiled too, and wrapped her arms around Flam in a big hug.

"Okay," she said, "since everybody's so adamant about it, I'll keep my mouth shut. But I'm so glad you know now . . . I hated having to keep it from you." She pushed back and gave her son a tender look. "So, dear, are you hungry?"

Flam was indeed famished. For days now he had been surviving on little more than potato chips and chocolate bars. That had partially been because he had little money for meals. Mainly, though, he was so stressed and oppressed at work that he had had the stomach neither for food nor for the minor rebellion it would have been necessary to stage in order to obtain decent meal breaks.

"I could eat," he replied coyly, allowing himself to then be guided to the dinner table while Cuff merrily went about hauling supper out of the oven and loading up plates.

Mary seemed content to let her lover have command of the kitchen, and instead sat down next to Flam, her expression revealing that the night's revelations were not over.

"There was something else we wanted to tell you, dear."

"What's that?" Flam asked, apprehension suddenly rising up again, and jostling for a spot in his gurgling stomach.

"Lee and I are going away next week . . . to the Bahamas."

"Aw, Mary," Cuff chided from the kitchen, "don't toy with the kid. Spill it."

"On our honeymoon. We're going to be married as soon as possible." For a moment Flam's bitterness returned in full force, although he wasn't sure whom he resented more—Cuff, the brash cop outsider, for breaking into his life and stealing his mother away, or the fickle, unfeeling Mary for abandoning him, as she often had, and leaving him alone to struggle with a meagre, meaningless life.

"We figured we should do it before she starts to show," Cuff called out among the sound of rattling cutlery. Flam's mouth popped open.

"You mean, you're . . .."

"That's right, dear, I'm pregnant," Mary said. If there was any shame in the words, she didn't show it. Flam's mind lurched, and his first thought was to wonder who the father was—Cuff or Strait. Then it occurred to him Cuff might very well have the same uncertainty, but was willing to marry her nonetheless, and that impressed Flam deeply. Cuff's looks and barbs and gruff manner had initially caused Flam to dislike the cop, but books had taught Flam that the true measure of a man lay in his heart and his deeds. He knew, no matter what else, at least his mother was finally in good hands.

"I think I'll have that glass of wine after all," he said.

CHAPTER 27

On the bus ride in to work the next morning, Flam found it impossible to concentrate on his latest book, and kept reliving the previous evening's revelations. In his reading, he typically disliked clichés, and scoffed at worn melodramatic plot lines, but now pat phrases like "we struggled and the gun went off" took on a whole new significance. Even his own small life, it seemed, was not immune to theatrical twists worthy of pulp fiction.

As he sat there pondering his life, Flam's attention was piqued by a girl, sitting across the aisle from him. He had seen her on the bus the week before, and remembered it was not so much her appearance that had attracted his notice, although she was definitely pretty in a quiet, unadorned way, but the fact she had been reading James Joyce's *Ulysses*—not typical commuter fare. Now the girl was unmistakably casting looks his way, glancing up from her book at regular intervals to study him furtively for a moment or two, before quickly dropping her gaze back to the book on her lap.

At first Flam was titillated, but then he realized that, wrapped up in this morning's post-traumatic musings, he had been staring absentmindedly off into space where the girl was sitting directly across the bus from him. She, not realizing he was lost in his thoughts, probably now suspected him of ogling her. The thought sent blood racing to his cheeks, and he deliberately forced his attention back to the pages of his novel, but concentration continued to elude him. Now that he was conscious of the girl, he couldn't stop himself from sneaking a look to see if she was still watching him.

The girl seemed to have relaxed, and was again engrossed in her book, although Flam couldn't make out what she was reading today, noting only than it was a hardcover, and of a comparable thickness to the Joyce offering of the previous week.

As he stole glances at her, Flam studied her looks. She wore a simple, white cotton blouse, buttoned modestly to the base of the throat, and a conservative, knee-length navy-blue skirt. Her dark brown hair was parted in the middle and pulled back in a small ponytail. Her face was seductively friendly, and hinted at intelligence. Flam guessed she was about his own age, and surmised she probably worked in a downtown office somewhere. Flam was forced to cut his observations short, however, because just then the girl's eyebrows gave a slight quiver, giving Flam enough forewarning to avert his gaze, and avoid again getting caught looking at her, as she stole another glance at him.

The girl got off a half-dozen stops before Flam's own destination, and as she gathered her belongings, Flam chanced a final look and saw the book she was reading was *Don Quixote*. Whether it was a fond remembrance of Cervantes' tale of the knight of La Mancha, which Page Turner had introduced him to a decade earlier, or a subconscious approval of the girl's choice of literature, he smiled. He was convinced, as she rose to exit, revealing a petite and well-proportioned figure, that the girl was also smiling ever so subtly back at him.

The encounter on the bus, however insignificant, managed to brighten Flam's mood a little and get him through the morning, which was again full of endless menial drudgery peppered by rebukes from The Hell Man. Charlie noticed Flam's good spirits when the two found themselves alone in the garage working on a hearse together— Flam wiping down the interior, while Charlie changed a sparkplug and whistled along to a Count Basie song, playing softly from his small radio.

"Hey, Flam, you're a happy cat today," the big Fijian commented. "Careful you don't smile, DaddyO . . . it might break your face."

Flam's face did not in fact break as he smiled at the joke. "I don't know, Charlie . . . it still sucks being me, but some days life almost seems worth sticking around for . . . if only to see how the story ends."

"'*Not with a bang, but a whimper,*' " Charlie quoted in the way of a reply, earning another smile from Flam, "or maybe both, if you can find the right girl." The big man obviously found his own joke hilarious, and let out a huge reverberating laugh, so loud, low, and rumbling Flam could feel it in his chest cavity. Charlie choked off his laugh, and looked around nervously before sticking his head back under the hood of the hearse, but a deep chuckle persisted, making it seem like the car's engine itself had sprung to life.

"Hey, Charlie," Flam asked after a second, "how come you called your jazz band The Cannibals?"

"'Cause we all come from Fiji, of course. Don't you know anything about our history? They used to call us The Cannibal Isles on account of how our warriors would sometimes eat their enemies when they killed them in battle."

Flam did actually vaguely recollect having read something about the practice somewhere in his thanatological wanderings, but had not equated it with Charlie's homeland.

"Hmmm . . . so that's why you chose to work in a funeral home," Flam joked. "Makes it easier to grab the occasional snack, no doubt. No one ever looks below the waist in those coffins, after all. Mind you, you'd have to get to the body while it's fresh, and before Leetch injects it with that embalming cocktail of hers. Well, I promise I won't tell anyone, if you promise to keep me off the menu."

Charlie thought that comical, and exploded in another huge laugh. "Okay, DaddyO, it's a deal. No leg of Flam for me. You're too scrawny anyway . . . wouldn't be good for much more than a midnight snack anyway."

Flam reflexively reddened when Charlie made a pun of his name, but let it pass, knowing by now the handyman meant no malice.

"I wouldn't do it to you anyway, Flam," Charlie continued, looking very serious all of a sudden, "on account of you're my friend. It was a big disgrace to get eaten, you know. In Fiji, you call someone *bokola*—that means 'cannibal meat'—it's a very, very big insult. I should know . . . I got called that a lot when I was a little boy."

"You? How come?"

"On account of my name—Charlie. My grandfather served with the Fiji Defense Force during World War II, and got turned on to jazz by the American GIs. He practically force-fed it to my Tata after he came back home, and it was like a religion in our house . . . that's why I'm hip to the jive, DaddyO. Tata named me after Charlie Parker, his favourite sax man. But a couple of the other kids in my village, Waisale and Naiogabui, thought Charlie was a weird name, and used to bully me and insult me all the time, even though we're practically all Methodists on the islands, and there's a lot of kids with English names . . . just not a lot of Charlies. That is, I got picked on until middle school, when I grew four inches, and put on thirty pounds in one summer. Then I never heard *bokola* again. But I never forgot it. Maybe that's why I'm the only one in the family who ended up leaving Fiji."

This suddenly all-too-familiar story of being tormented because of a name inevitably dragged out painful, suppressed memories from Flam's own school days. Although there should have been some silver lining of solace in knowing his own suffering had not been unique, a dark cloud nevertheless eclipsed Flam's previously upbeat mood.

"Speaking of jazz," Charlie went on, "you ever get a chance to work on some lyrics for us? We may be getting a gig soon, and we're trying to put together some original material. We got some instrumentals happening, but a couple of us are pretty good crooners, and we're looking for something with vocals we can get down with."

"Well . . . kind of," Flam hesitated, then went over to where he had taken off and neatly folded up his suit jacket (just the way Joe had shown him), and pulled out his dog-eared notebook from the inside pocket. Flipping past the assorted jottings and snatches of verse he still compulsively wrote down whenever poetic inspiration struck him, Flam located the pages he'd devoted to a handful of attempts at composing jazz lyrics. Only one song was in a form any way complete, and seeing it now in its raw, draft form, Flam had second thoughts about showing the material at all. It was too late. Charlie had followed him over, and was already bending down and trying to make out the words.

"Here. My handwriting's pretty bad . . . I'd better read this to you," Flam offered. He straightened up and struck a recitalist's pose, picturing himself standing spotlit on a stage in a smoky jazz club. Trying purposely to pour a maudlin mood into his voice, he read out the bluesy stanzas to Charlie. The way he was feeling of late, it wasn't much of a stretch.

The song was about being alone in the middle of a crowded city, and had been largely penned in one night when an emotionally numbed and browbeaten Flam had dragged himself home from work, feeling lower than a worm in Hades. As he recited, Flam suddenly had to fight back tears, as the original emotions that had fueled the composition flooded back to him.

When he was finished, Flam looked up at Charlie who was just standing there, silent, his mouth slightly agape. For a second, Flam thought the big man was trying to find a diplomatic way to avoid telling him just how much he had hated the verse, but then, to the poet's surprise, Charlie stepped over and gave him a huge hug, so tight it squeezed the wind out of him.

"Crazy, man . . . that's supermurgatroid!" the Fijian exclaimed, allowing breath to rush back into a stunned Flam. "You sure you never wrote anything like that before? Oh, man, I dig it! We can definitely work with that. The boys'll blow their tops when they hear it. Yeah, I see my sax, and maybe one trumpet with a mute, kinda wailing back and forth during the chorus like there's a boy and a girl crying in apartments across from each other, dying of loneliness when love is right under their noses."

"You really like it? You're not just saying that?"

"Listen DaddyO, when it comes to my music I don't screw around. I mean, the cats and me have been writing songs . . . mostly rip-offs of other guys, and some aren't even half bad . . . but this, man, this is eighteen karat. You've got the gift, and that's coming from a guy who was raised on both Browning *and* Cole Porter."

"Well, I'm not very musical," Flam said, almost apologetically. "The rhyming wasn't especially hard, but it was tough to know what kind of beat to give it . . . I mean, without knowing the tune."

"Well, I'll try to come up with a melody that will do it justice, but I ain't gonna change a single word of this honey, I promise you that."

"Oh, it wouldn't bother me if you did . . . I'm just glad you liked it," Flam said, Charlie's gushing praise now embarrassing him a little. "Here, let me copy it out for you . . . got any paper?"

Charlie went off to his handyman's cubicle, returning with a sheet of Morton's stationery. Flam began copying out his creation, using the hood of the hearse as a writing surface, with his Fijian friend watching and grinning the entire time. The pair was so raptly engrossed in their transcription, they didn't hear the door to the garage open behind them.

"Well, well, well . . . there they are in black and white!" came a voice, making them jump out of their skins. The Hell Man was standing there, hands on his hips, with a look of utter triumph on his face, as if he'd just stumbled across the pot of gold at the end of the rainbow. Behind him loomed Pugsley and Steptoe, malicious smirks of anticipation painted on their faces as well.

"What are you two up to?" Bruno asked, sauntering over to turn off Charlie's radio. Caught red-handed, Flam's face turned colour to match.

"It's . . . it's nothing really," he said, "I was just writing something out for Charlie." He tried nonchalantly to collect his handiwork, but this only served to attract Bruno's attention, and he snatched the paper and the notebook from Flam's hands.

"What have we got here?" Bruno demanded triumphantly. He studied the sheet of paper, but seemed to be having difficulty making sense of its content, so he opened the notebook instead and began flipping through its pages. Flam was aghast at the thought of The Hell Man being privy to these most intimate of thoughts and emotions,

and made to grab the notebook back. Bruno was too fast for him and
jerked it out of reach, while Pugsley and Steptoe moved in and each
grabbed one of Flam's arms.

"Give that back, it's my private property," Flam protested as he
squirmed under his captors' grip.

"Private, my ass. *This* is written on the firm's stationery, and
whatever you're trying to pull, you're doing it on company time.
I'm just going to keep this and show it to Mr. Morton." Bruno was
clearly excited by the prospect, as if after weeks of fabricating petty
excuses to chastise Flam, he was thrilled to finally have some concrete
misdemeanour to hang on him. Flam tried again to break free of
Pugsley and Steptoe so he could retrieve his precious notebook, but
lacked the strength to outwrestle them.

"Whoa, take it easy, Bug Boy, or you'll need an ambulance,"
Pugsley growled as he wrenched Flam's arm backward, causing Flam
to wince and cry out in pain. The agony and humiliation instantly
transported Flam back to the schoolyard beatings of his boyhood. *This
is my lot in life*, he thought, *I'll only be able to escape it when I'm dead.*

Unexpectedly, the hands gripping him loosened, then relented
altogether, and now the grunts and whimpers were coming from behind
him. He turned around to see his tormenters practically dangling in
space. Charlie had clamped a giant hand on the back of each of their
necks, and was holding them as helpless as a pair of kittens.

"Give it back to him," Charlie demanded, sounding more weary
than angry. Bruno hesitated and then, sizing up the situation, handed
everything over, his eyes burning holes in Flam. Charlie promptly
released Pugsley and Steptoe, who immediately scurried out of reach.

"You'll be sorry you did that," Bruno hissed at Charlie, "we'll
get you for assault and battery, and have your big black ass thrown
into jail."

As soon as these words were uttered, the mental haze of self-pity
and resignation clouding Flam's thoughts vanished, and were replaced
with a deep concern for his friend. No one had ever stood up for him
before, and he'd be damned if he'd let The Hell Man hurt Charlie.

"I don't think so," Flam spoke up, having analyzed the verbal threat. "Technically, I was the one who was accosted first, and I could press assault charges." The legalese dialled Flam back to his college days studying Funerary Law, when, in his typical, overzealous fashion, he'd checked out and pored over additional stacks of legal texts. The specific topics of his assigned study had been covered quickly, but Flam had greedily plunged onwards, for the law had often figured prominently in the plots of many of his favourite books, and he wanted to know more. He soon saw that legal statutes ultimately consisted of nothing more than words and phrases that could be read and weighed, and Flam had digested these law books with the same intensity and zeal that marked all his prolific reading. Although he had found the subject dull and had soon moved on to other more satisfying reading, the sharp-minded Flam probably retained the letter of the law better than most lawyers.

"At worst, we were guilty of the theft of a single sheet of paper, although I would submit that, as employees of this company, we have a certain intrinsic right to its resources while on the job . . . but you certainly had no authority to take my personal notebook, and those two ruffians absolutely had no right to physically lay a hand on me." Flam wasn't as confident as he sounded. He knew there were no independent corroborating witnesses in this case, so it would be his and Charlie's word against the other three—and the law would be, as always, on the side with the most convincing or well-connected lawyers. Moreover, Bruno had Mr. Morton's ear, so there would inevitably be fallout of some sort.

Nonetheless, the words seemed to have an impact, or perhaps Bruno was simply amazed the gangly, passive Flam had actually stood up to him, for he was clearly wavering. Finally, The Hell Man simply smiled and patted his pompadour back into place. "We'll just see who comes out on top of this one, you Grub," he said, no trace of anger evident in his voice. "Now get back to work before I fire the both of you, because when it comes to dealing with goldbricking goof-offs, I'm the law around here." He turned and left the garage, and Pugsley and

Steptoe scampered after him, as if their lives were at peril if they were left behind.

"I'm really sorry, Flam," Charlie said when they were alone again. "I got you into trouble."

"No apology necessary, Charlie. Thanks for looking out for me."

"Anytime, DaddyO. But watch it. That Bruno's shifty . . . and those other two, they're just plain nasty. Don't turn your back on them."

"Here," Flam said, handing over the transcribed lyrics. "I hope it was worth all the fuss."

Charlie smoothed out the crumpled paper on the hood of the hearse before folding the page neatly and tucking it into the breast pocket of his coveralls. "You'd better believe it. Hey, I'll let you know when it's going to get its debut . . . maybe you can come check us out."

"I'd love to . . . I've never been to a jazz club before."

Charlie's booming laugh again echoed through the garage. "Well, we don't get to play the upscale clubs, but it might be an education for you." He winked. "Maybe I'll introduce you to my cousin Minibalitaku . . . we call her Mini, but don't let that fool you. She's got the Duvuduvukulu family build. That girl would crush you if she rolled on top of you, but you'd die a happy man."

Flam was pretty sure Charlie was joking, but even if he wasn't and meant well, the idea of grappling with a female version of his Fijian friend held little appeal for Flam, despite his lonely, virginal state. "Um, thanks anyway, Charlie, but I've been seeing someone," he said. The deception tweaked his conscience, and he hastened to rationalize it to himself. It wasn't really a complete lie. Flam *had* seen the cute Girl on the Bus . . . twice now. And when he lay down in his bed each night and sought temporary relief from the frustration and loneliness of his miserable life, the wild, weird, wonderful Angel still vividly visited his erotic fantasies.

CHAPTER 28

Flam spent the next day on tenterhooks, anticipating The Hell Man's reprisal for the incident in the garage, but Bruno had apparently dismissed it. Or else he was secretly plotting some more elaborate retribution, for he never mentioned the confrontation again. If anything, the frequency and acuteness of Bruno's rebukes seemed to lessen somewhat, although Flam continued to be relegated to menial, behind-the-scenes grunt work, much to his mounting frustration.

Pugsley and Steptoe, however, had clearly not let the matter drop. Knowing they could not easily exact their revenge on Charlie the Man Mountain, they decided, in the finest tradition of bullies everywhere, to pick on a more helpless victim instead.

On Tuesday afternoon, the pair cornered Flam in the top floor room, where an extra stock of the more popular coffins was stored. Flam tried to fight back, but he was no match for the pair, each of whom easily outweighed him by forty pounds or so.

"Not such a big man now that you don't have your darkie pal to back you up, are you, Bug Boy?" Pugsley snarled, as he twisted Flam's arm.

"Let go, you're hurting me," Flam protested with a whimper of desperation in his voice. His plea, however, only earned a laugh from his tormentors.

"Shut up, Grubby, you're going to get what's coming to you," Steptoe hissed, tugging hard on the other arm. They dragged the squirming Flam towards one of the caskets, opened it up, and despite Flam's best attempts at resistance, managed to shove him in, and slam the top shut. As the darkness swallowed him, Flam tried to push the lid open again, but realized immediately its outside latch had been locked. Coffin construction, he knew, focussed on preventing the lid from flipping open unexpectedly, rather than providing escape mechanisms for the occupants. He was trapped inside a thickly padded, solidly built coffin, and the outside world, including Pugsley and Steptoe's snickers and taunts, was now barely audible.

Flam, however, did not panic. He knew, without six feet of soil entombing it, that this model of casket was not airtight, and enough oxygen would come through the seams to eliminate any danger of suffocating. Realizing the pair of bullies on the outside wanted him to scream in terror and beg for mercy, he grew determined not to give them that satisfaction.

He worked himself into the proper position and folded his hands onto his chest. The lining of the coffin was exquisitely soft and satiny. *Funny how the living go out of their way to pamper unfeeling corpses*, he thought, and in fact, he was far more cozy and comfortable than if he had been at home lying on the lumpy mattress of his old, second-hand bed.

An unusual calm engulfed Flam. He felt like he was back in his boyhood apartment, lying behind his wall of books, safe from the acrimony of his parents and the cruelty of his schoolmates. Where only minutes earlier he had been terrified and distraught, now he felt safe and content.

He closed his eyes and took a deep breath, and let himself drift away. Lately, he seemed to be perpetually tired. Indeed, he had barely had the energy to do anything when he got home since he'd started working at the funeral home—the double shifts followed by the long bus ride home so completely drained him. It seemed like he barely had enough time to feed himself, then read a chapter or pen a few lines of poetry, when it was time to get to bed, so he could grab a few hours' sleep before getting up early and doing it all again.

What a life. But at least tomorrow I finally have a day off, he thought. His previous request to be excused for the evening so he could take his night class, had de facto made Wednesday his official (and, lately, only) day off. To boot, he would also have his first paycheque, to supplement Grammy Sexton's cash gift, and could now perhaps start digging his way out of the black hole of his dead-end life.

All these thoughts swirled through his head as he lay, relaxed, in the satiny comfort of the coffin. So comfortable was he that he eventually drifted off, thinking about his pending day of parole, and all the things he would now be able to afford to buy.

Outside, the triumphant, taunting noises had stopped, replaced by an urgent whispering back and forth between Pugsley and Steptoe. If Flam heard them, it did not initially register. Some half-awareness of a change to the world around him did, however, finally wake Flam, although he kept his eyes closed, reluctant to let go of the warm fuzziness of his nap.

"Is he okay?" he heard Steptoe whisper, and it dawned on Flam the duo had become concerned by his silence, and had opened the lid of the coffin. Subtly, he held his breath and remained rigid.

"Oh my God, he's suffocated," Pugsley whimpered.

"No way, there's plenty of air in there," Steptoe insisted, sounding like he was trying to convince himself as much as his partner.

"Maybe he died of shock," Pugsley countered. "Shit, we're in big trouble." Flam felt a hand reaching for his neck in search of a pulse and opened his eyes.

"Good evening," he joked, imitating a vampiric Bela Lugosi. "Is it time to feed?" He fully expected the duo to slam the lid shut again, and wouldn't have minded one bit if they had, but either out of relief that he was unharmed, or disappointment that their prank had failed to have its full effect, the two just stood there, unmoving. Flam took advantage of their temporary paralysis to locate the latch on the bottom lid, and swung it open so he could extricate himself from his prison.

As soon as Flam had crawled out of the coffin, Pugsley seemed to recover, and he grabbed his victim by the lapels.

"Next time you won't get off so lucky," he growled, his face so close Flam could smell the residue of a tuna sandwich lunch. "Don't fuck with us or we'll put you into one of those boxes for good." Despite the ominous nature of the threat, it was clear he had lost his interest in pursuing the matter, and Flam just stared him down.

"C'mon, Josh," Pugsley said to his accomplice, "let's go, before someone comes looking for us. We'll get Bug Boy here later."

Flam allowed the duo a safe headstart before exiting the storage room himself. He headed downstairs to seek out Bruno, and discover what latest occupational banality his boss had come up with. The Hell Man was in his office, plodding through paperwork, and Flam stood meekly by, waiting to be noticed and directed to a new chore. Eventually, Bruno looked up from his administrative ministrations, and saw Flam standing there. A look of supreme annoyance crossed The Hell Man's face, and he dropped his pen onto the desk with a pronounced clatter to emphasize his irritation.

"Yeah, yeah, you Grub," Bruno muttered, "I see you there. I don't know how I'm expected to get my work done when I have to keep on your back every minute to make sure you don't make a mess of everything you touch. If you ask me, Morton's would be better off without you, and to hell with the threats from your crooked cop friend."

Flam swallowed hard, wondering if the shoe was about to drop, and he was going to get dismissed from his job. He had ultimately come to terms with Sergeant Cuff's heavy-handed intervention on his behalf. Despite the long hours, low wages, and constant abuse that came with the new position, Flam wanted to stay on the job. He was determined to prove his worth, and wanted a chance to provide the kind of support and bereavement counselling he still believed was the kind heart of his profession.

Bruno continued to stare for another minute, seemingly out of insults, and evidently disappointed he was getting no reaction to his abuse. Finally, with a heavy sigh, he just waved at Flam dismissively.

"Well, don't just stand there picking your ass, go vacuum the hall then clean the client bathroom . . . and I mean it when I say *clean*. Now beat it."

Flam turned to leave, relieved, when a shout from Bruno halted him in his tracks.

"Stop!" Bruno commanded angrily. Flam's heartbeat sped up as he turned to see Bruno up from behind his desk and coming at him.

"Jesus Christ, just look at you. Disgraceful, that's what it is," Bruno chided, while Flam followed his gaze and tried to figure out what was amiss now. The Hell Man grabbed Flam's arm and yanked it forward, revealing a tear along the shoulder seams of the suit. Flam realized the damage must have occurred when Pugsley and Steptoe had wrestled him into the coffin upstairs, and debated whether to tell Bruno what had happened.

"What the hell's wrong with you?" Bruno continued to rant, warming up to his tirade. "What if a customer saw you? What kind of impression do you think that would create? Our image . . . our decorum is *everything!*" Flam murmured apologies, and pleaded ignorance as to how the unseemly coming apart at the seams might have happened, reckoning there would be no advantage in blowing the whistle on the bullies who had perpetrated the deed.

"I want you to get to the front office right away, and see if Mrs. Clarke has a safety pin or something to fix the damage . . . and, for heaven's sake, make sure no visitor sees you. Shit, you're some piece of work."

Flam obediently did as he was told. The private knowledge that, in this case, he was completely blameless, helped him to preserve his calm. When he stuck his head in the door, the abrasive Mrs. Clarke was at her computer, slapping the top of the monitor and cursing with a fervour and repertoire of expletives worthy of a street thug. Flam shyly explained his dilemma, waiting for the inevitable acerbic response, but to his surprise Mrs. Clarke was helpful and almost polite, seemingly relieved to have an excuse to abandon the battle with her computer.

"When I started here, I had a nice reliable typewriter," Mrs. Clarke groused after she had ordered Flam out of his jacket, and was inspecting the damage. "These damned computers are a royal pain in the ass if you ask me. You spend more time trying to get them to work then you do actually working on them. That blasted thing's been freezing up on me all day . . . seems I can't go two minutes before it stops."

"Would it be alright if I had a look?" Flam asked, walking over to examine her antiquated PC. He took his own longstanding mastery of the devices for granted, and never understood why so many others, such as Mrs. Clarke, disliked them. Unlike the people who caused him so much anguish in life, computers were safe, predictable, and reliable.

"Be my guest," Mrs. Clarke said, as she began rummaging through her desk drawer for her emergency stash of needle and thread. It didn't take Flam long to understand why Mrs. Clarke was having so much trouble. The machine had no space left on its hard drive, plus it appeared to have become infected with a virus.

After deleting as many extraneous files as possible, including several unused temporary files that appeared to have been left behind by previous crashes of software, Flam used the computer's Internet connection to download some free anti-virus software, and removed no less than a half dozen pieces of malware from the system. During this time, Mrs. Clarke had turned the arm of Flam's jacket inside out, and was sewing the seam of the shoulder back together again. She glanced up occasionally, and watched Flam's deft digital machinations, but said nothing.

In the process of troubleshooting the system, Flam noticed someone had been regularly using the computer's web browser to access pornography—which accounted for the proliferation of viruses. The culprit had also left gigabytes of images and videos cached in the computer's memory.

After first turning off the computer's sound and making sure Mrs. Clarke's line of sight did not allow her to see what was on the screen, Flam did a quick scan of the illicit material. He soon saw the perpetrator had a fetish for the most brutal and violent kind of pornographic material, including bondage and rape. Quite recently, according to the dates, the pornophile had developed a taste for snuff films, where the victim was, be it real or simulated, killed in front of the camera.

The time stamps on the pornographic files showed they'd all been accessed in the evenings, after Mrs. Clarke had gone home for the day. Flam instantly suspected one or both of the terrible twosome—Pugsley and Steptoe—were the culprits. Whoever was doing it was not savvy enough, however, to clean up after himself, and eventually Flam was able to track down a cached user name for a web site called GoDropDeadGorgeous.com. The name, Curious George, pointed the finger squarely at Pugsley.

By now Mrs. Clarke was finishing up her sewing job, having displayed remarkable dexterity, despite the fatness of her fingers. Flam quickly closed down all evidence of his prying, and rebooted the now-healed system.

"There you go," Flam said. "You really should get Mr. Morton to spring for some extra memory and a larger hard drive, but I think you'll find it works a lot better now." He made no mention of the porn sites or viruses he had discovered, keeping this knowledge to himself for now. From the look on Mrs. Clarke's face, you would have thought Flam had just conjured up a rabbit out of a hat.

"You know a lot about these things, eh?" she asked, clearly delighted. Flam shrugged and gave a modest grin.

"I guess. I've been working with them since I was a kid," he replied.

"Listen," she said, handing back his repaired jacket, and turning to the computer screen to start up one of her office applications, "this confounded thing is supposed to be able to print out formatted mailing labels. Do you think you could show me how to do that?" Flam obliged, and also unravelled several other mysteries that had evidently been haunting Mrs. Clarke. When he showed her how to get the accounting software to print out a consolidated report of the overdue accounts, she actually let out a squeal of delight and gave him a big hug.

"Oh, baby, where have you been all my life?" she cooed. Flam couldn't help but smile as he put on his jacket and inspected her handiwork. There was just the slightest hint of an irregularity along the seam, but otherwise it appeared presentable.

"I'd better get back before Bruno tears a strip off of me," he said, heading for the door.

But just as he was exiting, Mrs. Clarke called after him, "Oh, Flam." He turned and saw softness in her eyes instead of the usual flinty displeasure. "Thank you," she said sweetly.

"Thank *you*," Flam answered, pointing at his shoulder. "Let me know if you have any other problems . . . I'd be glad to help."

"Oh, don't worry," she laughed, suddenly looking like a loveable auntie instead of the old witch Flam had always thought her, "I will."

CHAPTER 29

Flam woke early on his day off, despite an enormous desire to sleep in (made all that much more tempting by a delicious erotic dream he had been having about Angel). He was at the front of the line when his bank branch opened. His first order of business was to get an international money order to repay Page Turner for the advance he'd lent Flam before departing for Thailand. Despite remonstrations from his old mentor that there was no urgency in settling the debt, it had been weighing heavily on Flam's sense of obligation. With the leftover cash from his paycheque and Granny Sexton's windfall now lining the pocket of his jeans, his next order of business was to buy a new suit—all that much more crucial given the original was already starting to show its wear.

The business card Joe had given him simply said Fine Tailors, and listed an address in the west end of the city. Flam turned over the card and examined the note Joe had added on the back in Hebrew, puzzling over the lines of unfamiliar characters written there in a precise yet pleasing hand.

The neighbourhood of the shop was unfamiliar to Flam. After circling the block twice to find a parking spot, he ended up walking by the doorway twice before spotting the small, tarnished brass sign that indicated the tailor shop was not on street level, but at the top of a long, narrow flight of stairs, much like the walk-up to his boyhood flat. A small bell tinkled as he walked through the door, and he found himself standing in a room crammed full with stacked bolts of cloth. A large cutting table dominated the middle, and on it lay the beginnings of a navy blue pinstripe suit.

A slight, bearded, fifty-something man came out of an inner room in response to the shop's bell. He was wearing a grey, old-fashioned, vested suit, and had a tape measure draped around his neck. He peered at Flam quizzically from over the top of bifocals, clearly disapproving of the sloppily dressed young man before him, and stiffly asked if he could be of service. Flam handed over the card, and watched an instant change in the man's demeanour when he read the note from Joe on its back.

"*Very* pleased to be of service, sir," the tailor said, giving a little bow. "My name is Izhak Szabo, and I am the proprietor of the shop. Now, if you would please be so kind as to raise your arms so I may take your measurements."

Flam obliged, and marvelled at the efficiency with which Szabo went about his work. Flam had expected questions to be asked about style, colour and fabric, but the tailor moved in silence, and in a matter of minutes handed Flam back the card and said, "Please come back after Saturday . . . I will have a lovely suit ready for you then."

"But . . . what . . ." Flam stuttered, caught totally by surprise, "I mean, how much?"

"Oh no, sir. No charge. My compliments," the tailor replied, bowing again. Flam just stood there, incredulous, and his pale, black-eyed astonishment was so pronounced Szabo just had to laugh. "I am deeply indebted to Joash Schneider, and it gives me profound pleasure to be able to make any small measure of repayment. Not to worry, leave everything in my hands. I'm sure you will be quite satisfied with my product. Now, if you please, I have much work to do."

Flam was then practically pushed out the door. He stumbled down to street level, still somewhat in a daze, unsure whether to laugh from delight or cry from the generosity being bestowed upon him. As he walked along the avenue, dazzled by the morning's bright sun, which felt strange after the weeks of windowless gloom he had endured inside Morton's Funeral Home lately, an idea began to form as to how he might be able to repay little old Joe Schneider for his kindness.

Flam put more mileage on his old Fairlane in that one day than he had in weeks. One by one, items were crossed off his list of things to do and buy, including a fresh supply of groceries, toiletries from the drugstore (including his first-ever bottle of men's cologne), and an oil change from Lightning Lube. Basking in self-satisfaction, he returned home, and parked himself in front of his computer.

Ever since Joe had mentioned losing contact with his granddaughter, Ester, Flam had felt that somehow he might be able to help track her down. He had made a point of remembering the name of Ester's husband, and now did a Google search for any references. Not surprisingly, given the man worked in the software industry, there were several hits, and Flam eventually found the work address and email for Colby Sharp, Director of Sales for the London office of Semprix Systems, and was quite certain this was the right person. He printed out the information, and resolved he would persuade Joe to try re-establishing contact with his estranged granddaughter.

Finally, to accompany the money order he'd acquired earlier in the day, Flam wrote Page Turner a short letter. In it, he heartily thanked his mentor again for the money he had given Flam to acquire the first suit, no matter how inexpensive it had been. Flam was already thinking of it as his *old* suit, but purposely omitted any details of the damage the clothes had suffered, or his complaints about the co-workers at the funeral home. Despite the unhappy conditions Flam had experienced on the job thus far, he still felt profoundly grateful to Page for having helped him secure the position. Flam ended the letter with a jovial entreaty for his old friend to email details of life in Shangri La once the newlyweds had settled in at the university.

There were several conflicting emotions tussling within Flam as he sealed the envelope and carried it down to the post box. It felt wonderfully satisfying to discharge his financial obligation to Page—Flam experienced an immediate spiritual lift from having done so—but he also knew he could never truly repay Page for all he had done for him over the years. At the same time, he missed his friend so terribly. As much as he hated to admit it to himself, and as much as he sincerely wished Page nothing but happiness, Flam was bitterly jealous of the old bookmonger's new life and fresh chance at love.

Flam returned to his apartment. He planned to read a few chapters of his latest book before walking over to Prentice College for his night class, but ended up falling asleep before he had finished the first page. He awoke with a start an hour later to discover he was running quite late, and sent several stacks of books, surrounding his sleeping area, tumbling down as he leapt out of bed in a disoriented panic. Although the school was extremely close by, and he doubted if the moribund Professor Abbott would be bothered to interrupt his monotonic pedantry if anyone came strolling in even two hours late, Flam was still at heart incurably punctual. Feeling frivolously affluent, he opted to drive the few short blocks to school, and pay for parking in order to save time.

His intimate knowledge of the local alleyways that fed into the hinterlands of the campus paid dividends. With a little bit of uncharacteristically aggressive driving, Flam made it to class just as Professor Abbott was writing down the numbers of the day's relevant chapters on the blackboard, before shuffling to the podium to drone on about the rise of Islam.

Joe was sitting closer to the front, and turned to give a small wave and a friendly wink. Although Flam responded with a smile and a nod, he actually had someone else on his mind, and his spirits nosedived when, after looking around twice in search of her white, spiked head, he concluded Angél was again absent. He didn't even bother trying to convince himself she might still arrive late. He sadly resigned himself to the obvious fact she had quit the course, and was gone from his life for good.

As always, Flam had to fight to stay awake in the class, as the robotic Professor Abbott seemed to be blandly regurgitating the textbook, which Flam had already read cover to cover twice. Rather than succumb to the professor's pedantic anesthesia, Flam opened his notebook and worked on a short, sarcastic poem titled "Where Angels

Fear to Tread." The piece started out as a lament on love's elusive nature, but in the second hour, something of the lecturer's monologue sunk in, and Flam had a minor epiphany as he glimpsed a grander metaphysical mosaic among all these religions that Professor Abbott, like Moses, was leading them to, although apparently he was not able to partake in any of them himself.

With minor changes, Flam's poem went from bewailing, "Why can't I find love?" to "Why can't I find God?" The creative exercise preoccupied him so thoroughly he was completely surprised when class ended with the professor's perfunctory, "That's all for tonight," and the other students, groaning and yawning, hauled themselves to their feet.

Flam joined up with Joe, and offered to treat for their usual coffee and snacks at Java Gardner's. The walk over, as short as it was, seemed to be more of an effort than usual for Joe. Flam did most of the talking as they shuffled slowly along, fighting a temptation the whole way to simply hoist Joe onto his back and carry him piggyback.

Once they were seated at the café, Flam brought the conversation around to that morning's trip to the tailor shop, and confessed his consternation he was not being charged for the new suit. Joe listened patiently to Flam's complaint, a little smile working its way onto his face as his young friend vented.

"Oi vey, Flam, you continue to surprise me," Joe chuckled. "Most people would not think twice about accepting a gift while you . . . you make it sound like I have just placed some terrible curse upon you. But you are missing the point entirely, because you are thinking only about yourself. First of all, consider Izhak Szabo who, like you, feels kindness is a tremendous burden. Poor Izhak has been in constant despair, because I was generous to him, worrying I will soon die without allowing him a chance to settle his perceived debt to me . . . not understanding that I care not one iota whether I am ever repaid. So, tonight, Izhak is a happier man because his burden is a little lighter.

"And also think of me . . . an old man who has cheated death, and is waiting for that debt to be settled, as it inevitably must be. I am not afraid of dying, but I despise not living . . . being helpless, or a burden. Tonight *I* will sleep a little better knowing that, even at my age, I am still able to make a slight difference in this world, and to pierce the omnipresent shadows with a small beam of light. I consider your independence admirable, but it is a bit misguided. If you find kindness such an aberration, then find some way to pass the light on, but do not extinguish it."

Feeling somewhat chastened, Flam simply replied, "Amen." He then used that moment to pull the printout of Colby Sharp's address out of his pocket, and slid it across the table to Joe.

"What is this?" the old man asked as he unfolded the paper and stared at it blankly. A bewildered look seemed to grow over him, and to Flam it appeared as if the old man might break out into tears. Flam waited politely for a response, but after a minute or so Joe still had said nothing, nor even taken his eyes off the paper. The silence was weighing so heavily on Flam he was starting to wonder if he had unwittingly committed some colossal *faux pas*.

"I'm 90 per cent sure that's your grandson-in-law," Flam finally said, desperately wanting to shatter the spell Joe was under. "You'd probably be able to chase him down through the company switchboard, but that's his direct email address there, and I'm guessing he checks it pretty regularly, even when he's away from the office."

Still Joe said nothing, and a visibly worried Flam reached across the tiny table, and rested a hand on the old man's shoulder.

"Joe . . . are you okay? Please tell me I didn't do something stupid."

Whether it was the physical contact, or the childlike concern in Flam's voice, Joe finally looked up and managed a weak smile. "No, no, my dear Flam, this was . . . is . . . wonderful. Forgive my reaction. I suddenly had this overwhelming feeling, as if a recurring premonition had come to pass. It was . . . disconcerting, like I had left my body, and was floating above the room and looking down as my past, present, and future collided. Ach, no doubt you think me a dotty old man, and *mein doktor*, she would probably say I have just had a seizure of some kind, and would order me into the bowels of some infernal machine to be subjected to more tests. Rest assured, however, I am well, and very, very grateful to you . . . more than you can possibly imagine. But also, I must confess, somewhat frightened. What if Ester has grown to despise me? What if she still refuses to talk to me?"

"Do you remember telling me last week about the quarrel you had with your own parents?" Flam asked, and Joe nodded glumly.

"Well," Flam continued, "I remember you saying that eventually you relented and wanted to find them . . . to reunite with them, and that you're sorry you didn't get a chance to do so."

"I shall regret it to all eternity," Joe agreed.

"You did say Ester was a lot like you. Don't let her end up feeling the same emotional pain. My guess would be she's probably not still as angry as when you two had your big fight. And what's the worst that can happen . . . you'd basically be no worse off than you are now. Sure, it would hurt terribly if she were to slam the door on you a second time, but what if she didn't? What if deep down inside she really still loves the grandfather who raised her, and longs for a chance to reconcile, but is just too proud—or scared—to take the first step? Isn't that possibility worth the risk?"

Joe suddenly laughed out loud—a surprisingly deep, completely uninhibited laugh, which sounded as if it should have come from someone much larger than the tiny gnome of a man. "Listen to this!" he guffawed, "me, the ancient elder, practically a rabbi, receiving such wise counsel from someone who has barely entered adulthood. *Mazel tov!*" Joe grabbed Flam's hand and kissed it, catching Flam off guard, and causing his face to redden.

"Blessings upon you, Flam, my friend. You are completely right, of course. Suddenly I have an urge for something a little stronger. Will you join me in a brandy? Excellent. Excellent." Joe stopped and moved his head a little closer. He looked embarrassed. "But if you could do me one more favour—I have heard it mentioned many, many times, but . . . perhaps you could explain this thing you call *email* to me."

Flam cheerily obliged, taking Joe to the back of Java Gardner's where the Internet café was set up, and showed the old man how to work a mouse and use email. With Flam's help, Joe, who was a remarkably quick study, signed up for a free email account. Aided and encouraged by his young friend, and bolstered by more brandies,

Joe composed a brief and somewhat cautious note, and fired it off into cyberspace.

Afterwards, Flam ushered Joe safely onto the bus homeward, and then headed back to the parking lot to retrieve his Fairlane. In addition to the effects of the alcohol, he was feeling an almost giddy sense of satisfaction over all that had been accomplished that day, and especially over the kindness he had managed to perform for Joe. Flam wasn't quite ready to admit belief in some greater force at play, be it God or some ebb and flow of cosmic currency among people, but tonight he felt more optimistic and alive than he had in weeks.

So engrossed was Flam in his sense of goodness and near-godliness, the sound of rapidly clicking heels behind him didn't sink in until it was too late. Suddenly someone leapt up onto Flam's back, throwing him off balance, and causing him to slam heavily into the side of his car. Flam's heart began to pulse madly, and panic began to race up his throat, and threatened to spill down his pant leg.

This is it, he thought. *I'm going to die.* The actual idea of death was not in itself the most terrifying, but rather the realization that, after the obligatory autopsies had been concluded, his remains likely would be turned over to Morton's Home. It was, in fact, the last place on earth he wanted to end up, and he chided himself for not leaving behind firm instructions on how and where he wanted his last rites performed.

It was the sweet, familiar smell that registered first, followed shortly afterwards by a giggle of pure, childish delight. The weight left his back, and Flam found himself being spun around to stare down in Angel's pretty, supremely amused face.

"Hey, Tiger. Did you miss me?" she asked, and before Flam could give an answer, crushed her mouth against his, and sent her tongue enthusiastically in search of the fillings in Flam's dental work. After what seemed a blissful eternity to Flam, she pulled back to beam serenely into his face. She looked different—her hair was not white, for starters, but more of a darker, streaked blonde, and far less spiky. She was also not dressed all in white, as she had been every time Flam had seen her previously, but wore a simple denim miniskirt and a brown tank top through which her nipples were clearly visible

"Wow, you look different," Flam offered.

"Still sexy, I hope," she giggled, and came beside him to slip her arm into his, and rest her head on his arm.

"'If eyes were made for seeing/Then Beauty is its own excuse for being,'" Flam said, at a loss for words of his own.

"Did you write that?" Angel asked.

Flam shook his head. "Sorry, no, it was Emerson."

She nodded at that, as if she should have known it all along, and stared quietly off into the night, still clinging tightly to his arm. After a few seconds, she looked up at him, and reached up to tuck back an errant lock of hair. "You cut your hair," she said. "I like it. You look more mature. But is everything okay with you? Your aura's looking kind of, well, limp." The comment made Flam blush, unmistakable even in the parking lot's anemic light, and Angel laughed.

"Listen," she said, "I know it's late, but you said once you live close to here. Mind if we go back to your place?"

Flam blushed again. "Um, sure, if you want . . . and if you don't mind the mess."

"Great," she said, and rewarded him with a kiss on the mouth. "My stuff's just over there . . . I have to grab it first." Flam walked her over to where she'd cached a small knapsack and an odd-looking plastic box with a handle on top. It wasn't until they started driving back to Flam's apartment that he heard a scuffling sound from the box, and realized it was a carrying case for some kind of animal.

"It's my cat," Angel explained, noting his surprise, "I didn't want to leave him alone. That's okay, isn't it?" She leaned over to kiss him on the cheek, and Flam just smiled like an idiot. At this point, he was so captivated, he would have allowed her to bring along a rattlesnake.

The closer they got to his apartment, the more Flam now started to worry about what Angel's reaction might be to his living place. Not that it was filthy, for Flam found quiet meditative solace in the rituals of washing dishes and doing regular housecleaning, but what little second-hand furniture he possessed had been acquired cheaply—

and showed it. Moreover, every room of the apartment, tiny to begin with, was crammed with stack upon stack of books. *Still, there's nothing I can do about it now*, he reasoned, *I am who I am*. Besides, more than anything he wanted to be alone with his gorgeous, intoxicating Angel, and he just hoped she wouldn't laugh in his face outright . . . or go screaming out of the apartment.

He needn't have worried. She did giggle when she first walked through the door, and saw the amazing floor-to-ceiling cascades of books, but then immediately dropped her things and came over to wrap Flam in a hug. "It's just like I thought it would be," she said. "Somehow I figured a smart guy like you would be rolling in books."

"Can I offer you something?" Flam asked hospitably, not wanting her to see just how much he lapped up her attention. "You're in luck . . . I went shopping this afternoon."

"How about some coffee . . . instant will be fine. That is, unless you and Joe haven't overdosed on caffeine already tonight. How is my dear, sweet, little old Joey anyway?"

"He's alright," Flam said, going into the kitchen to boil some water. "We've been having some nice chats the last couple of weeks."

"I just knew you two would hit it off," she said, her voice disappearing around the corner as she snooped around the rest of the apartment. A few minutes later, she returned to the kitchen, and slipped up behind Flam to watch him fiddle with the coffee fixings. Her body pushed up hard against his back, and Flam could distinctly feel her ample breasts pressing into his back. A hand slipped under his T-shirt and began to playfully massage his belly, having an instant aphrodisiacal effect on him. She stood up on tiptoes and nibbled on the base of his neck, giggling as he made a mess trying to pour out the hot water with a nervous trembling hand.

"I'll take mine black," she instructed, "but aren't you having any?"

"Whew, if I had a coffee now, it would keep me up all night," Flam explained, and Angel let loose a hearty laugh at that, and then reached down and caressed the bulge in his jeans.

"Silly boy," she cooed, "that was the whole idea." And then her mouth was on his again, and there was no denying her interest and attentions. Everything after that took on a heart-pounding, head-spinning surreal quality, as heat and shivers, hard and soft, fast and slow, all blurred into one delicious, unbelievable fuzzy dream come true.

She led him to the bedroom, and undressed him as he stood mesmerized, then pushed him down onto the mattress. Standing above him, she slowly, expertly, erotically removed her own clothes, floating gracefully above him, and gyrating to some secret music only she could hear, her ripeness and firmness and roundness more beautiful and breathtaking than anything he could have imagined. And just when he thought he was going to cry from the want and the anticipation, she lowered herself down and slid beside him to kiss him, and caress him, and then they made love, again, and again. He had been worried he might not remember all he had prodigiously read about the mysterious universe of sex and sexuality, and how to please a woman, but in the end it didn't matter. Without uttering a word, she took charge and guided him to her preferred spots and positions, and her moans and sighs instructed him. The rest all came naturally.

Afterwards, as he desperately held onto her, feeling her breathing, and revelling in her contact, and taste, and smell, he searched for something to say, but couldn't find it. It was as if the top of his head and all the brains in it had been blown off into the heavens. It was her giggle that broke the silence.

"I just realized I don't even know your name." Her statement was casual and matter of fact, as if this was some piddling detail that had not been germane to their actions, and she had just thought of it now. Flam, though, had been keenly aware of the omission of his name from the moment they had met, and every minute thereafter.

He swallowed hard, figuring it could not be avoided now, and not even contemplating a fabrication. "It's Flam," he answered, then reached over to take the hand that was resting on his chest, and gave it a little shake. "Pleased to meet you, Angel," he said, and they both giggled at the humour of being introduced after they had just made love.

"Actually, please call me Angela, or Ang. Angel is . . . *was* . . . my stage name."

"Stage name? Are you an actress?"

"You might say that, but not the kind you're thinking of. I was a stripper."

"A stripper!" Flam couldn't keep the surprise out of his voice.

"Yeah, you know . . . a peeler . . . exotic dancer . . . bump-and-grinder . . . burlesque queen . . . pole dancer . . . stripteaser . . . fox on a box . . . .." Her voice took on an angry tone. "Why? You got a problem with that? Most guys would give their eye teeth to screw a stripper."

"Whoa . . . I'm not judging you. I think you're absolutely fantastic. I've just never met a stripper before, Ang," Flam countered, giving her a kiss on her forehead. "Are they all as wonderful as you?"

She giggled, and snuggled back into his chest with a sigh. "Sorry, it's just that I met a lot of jerks when I was dancing." She lapsed back into silence until, a short while later, she reached down and took hold of his flaccid penis, which immediately started to come to life.

"And what's *his* name?"

"Name? He doesn't really have a name."

Angela propped herself up on an elbow so she could look him in the face. "Oh, c'mon . . . are you trying to tell me no chick ever gave him a nickname." Flam blushed, and it took a few seconds for her to clue in. "Oh . . . you mean . . . you never . . . I'm the first? Oh my God, you're a *virgin*."

Now Flam was beet red, and it was his turn to take offense. "What's the matter, you have something against virgins?"

"No, no . . . it's just I've never done one before." She tried to suppress her giggles, but it only caused her to end up laughing out loud. Thinking he was being ridiculed, Flam rolled over and turned his back on her, not wanting her to see the hurt in his eyes. Knowing she had given offence, Angela followed him to his side of the bed and kissed him hard, and instantly knew from his response she was being forgiven.

"Seeing as this is a first for both of us," she whispered, sliding slowly downward, "we'd better make sure it's a night we—you, me, and the Cock With No Name—never forget." And with her hot breath and some deft movements of her tongue, she managed to wake the dead.

Later, as he lay exhausted and numb, and completely amazed at what had transpired, Angela suddenly took on a worried look. She pulled herself up onto him so she could look him directly in the eye. "Listen, I need to ask you a big favour."

"What's that?" Flam asked.

"I want you to take care of my cat."

"Cat? Me? For how long?"

"I . . . I don't know. I'm going away, and it may be for a long time . . . and I want to leave him with somebody I trust and know will take good care of him. Will you do that for me?"

"Going away? Where? When? I mean, I just found you," Flam stammered, his world suddenly cold and lonely all over again.

"Oh, crap . . . you're not falling for me, are you, Flam, just because we hopped in the sack together? Listen, don't get me wrong, you're a really great kid. Lord knows it would be tempting to put a ring through your nose and ride you until you drop, or my nickel runs out, and to know you're the kind of guy that'd really take care of me . . . who wouldn't screw around on me. But I'm not looking for a man right now . . . well, other than for that itch you just scratched nicely, thanks."

Flam remained silent, not knowing precisely what he did feel for this eccentric and wonderful Wiccan woman, other than lust, but he did know he didn't want her to now just walk out of his life. Wanting to cry, but not wanting to be seen, he curled up into a ball and rocked back and forth, stifling his sniffling.

"Aw, sweetie, you're not about to cry, are you?" Angela asked, clearly moved by Flam's reaction. "Wow, you're really a sensitive guy . . . but I guess I should have known that after the poem you wrote for me . . . although I'll be honest, I hardly understood a word . . . no, no, don't get me wrong, I totally loved it, it was so freakin' wonderful that you wrote it for me . . . . no one's ever been that sweet to me before. You know, in a way, it's your fault I have to go away."

"What do you mean?" Flam asked, using his palm to wipe away a rogue tear.

"Well, that night, when you told me you thought this coven I was in was pure bullshit . . . oh, I know you put it a lot more gently than that, but I could tell it's what you thought . . . well, I'd already been thinking the same way. And the way you explained how you were searching for . . . well, searching for God in a way, I guess, you made me realize it's what I needed to do.

"I'd already started the journey with the sisters . . . they saved me, you know. I was a mess, partying in the strip clubs when I wasn't dancing, and snorting coke, and screwing whatever guy I ended up with at the end of the night, sometimes taking money for it. Then I met this other dancer, Crystal, and she introduced me to the others, and they helped get me straight and turn my life around. That was good, and it was exactly what I needed, but I didn't really believe in it the same way they did . . . I mean, I *wanted* to believe, wanted to more than you could imagine, but in my heart . . . in my soul, I guess . . . I didn't believe.

"After I talked to you that night, I knew I had to follow my heart, even if it meant leaving behind something safe and good for me. Man, I wanted to make love to you so badly that night . . . I hadn't had a man in a year. Me and some of the other girls, we'd crawl into bed together some nights, and we'd take care of business, and it seemed to be okay for them, but I needed something more in that department too."

"So, what are you going to do now?" Flam asked, more than a little surprised at how he had managed to have such a profound influence on this maddeningly mercurial woman, whom he had never been able to fully understand or, he'd thought, truly connect with.

"First of all," Angela answered, looking up from his solar plexus where she had buried her nose and was revelling in his scent, "I'm going out west to visit my mum and dad, and tell them I love them and forgive them, which will come as a real shock, because they figure *I'm* the one that needs forgiving, the tight-assed hypocrites . . . God bless them. After that, I'm going to travel. Who knows, maybe to Africa or someplace, and spend some time at a retreat or mission or something, helping people who really need it and don't care who I am or where I've been. I'm going to see if I can find some answers. I'll be honest, I'm not 100 per cent sure about my path yet—I think you can appreciate that—but I'm going to see if my heart will lead me to God."

"Do you really have to go?" Flam pleaded, hating the whiny tone he heard in his own voice. "I mean, God's everywhere, right, which means he's right here too. You don't have to go all the way to Africa to find him."

"Oh, don't be such a baby," Angela castigated him. "I'm not the right girl for you, whether I stay or not, and I think you know that. You need someone younger, and a helluva lot smarter; someone who's into books and poetry too . . . who's got an aura to match yours. Trust me, she's out there, and you're going to find her."

Despite his relative inexperience with women and the optimism obviously intended by the words, Flam nevertheless couldn't help being saddened by the rejection implicit in Angela's words. He fell silent, already feeling the cold emptiness in his life her departure would leave.

"You never answered my question," Angela prompted him then, when Flam looked confused, added, "I mean, about taking care of Mr. Whiskers."

"Mr. Whiskers? Is that what you call him?"

"You can call him anything you want . . . he doesn't really answer to his name, but he's really, really sweet, and he won't be any trouble at all. Please? Pretty, pretty please? Didn't I just make you feel really good?"

"Oh, alright," Flam sighed, knowing it would be pointless to try to resist. He was starting to feel exhausted and wondered what time it was, knowing he had to be up for work soon. He closed his eyes, figuring it was better not to know how late it really was, but was jolted awake by the feel of a rough tongue against his chin, followed by Angela's unmistakable giggle. She had gone to retrieve the cat, and brought it up to Flam's face. Everything has its price, Flam pondered, and just as the thought occurred to him, he decided he was going to call the cat Mephistopheles. He smiled to himself, and promptly fell asleep, as the cat purred and nestled up to him.

He didn't know how long he had been unconscious, but later some unfamiliar sound woke him. He groggily looked up to see Angela, fully dressed, standing in the doorway with her knapsack. She waved and blew him a kiss.

"Wham! Bam! Thank you Flam," she giggled, and then was gone.

CHAPTER 30

The first serious heat wave of the summer had arrived, and The Girl on the Bus was dressed accordingly. She had on a sleeveless white blouse, just transparent enough that the frills of the brassiere beneath were discernible, and she was not wearing panty hose beneath her typical, navy blue institutional skirt. Seated slightly behind her and out of view, Flam was able to study The Girl attentively without fear of being caught in the act.

She was reading yet another new book, and although Flam was unable to make out its title, he was fairly certain it was a book of verse, judging from the general appearance of the printed lines of text arranged on the pages.

That morning, The Girl had pulled her hair up atop her head, and Flam couldn't help but admire the enticing nape of her naked neck, before following the path down and across to take in the contours of her bare arms. He found himself fantasizing about what it would be like to have this enticing creature in his bed, and to make love to her the way he had grappled so blissfully with Angela mere hours ago.

Despite the meagre amount of sleep he'd had, Flam was still riding the emotional crest of last night's lovemaking, even if the experience was somewhat tainted with the bitter reality that his amorous liaison with Angela had been a one-time proposition. But there was something else, now that the molten passion of the night had congealed in the cool reality of day—an emotional hangover from the excesses of pure animal lust that felt surprisingly like remorse, almost as if he was guilty of infidelity.

The Girl closed her book and slid it across her knee. She turned to stare vacantly out at the bright morning, either having found something in the verse to make her contemplate life, or having remembered something in life to make her lose interest in the verse.

Flam leaned forward and made out the title of the book—*The Poetry of Sappho*. His heart revved up at the revelation, and the temperature of his longing for The Girl on the Bus suddenly rose dramatically. He wondered how many other people on the bus had even heard of that exotic Greek poet who (Page Turner had related to him at an early age) was often proclaimed as The Tenth Muse, never mind would actually choose to read an entire volume of her verse as commuter fare.

Something outside caught The Girl's attention, and she swivelled around, ostensibly to track whatever the object of interest was as it retreated behind the bus. Flam was caught off guard and suddenly found himself staring directly into The Girl's soulful and highly inquisitive brown eyes. He tried to take advantage of this magical opportunity, to hold the eye contact and parlay it into some sort of non-verbal communion, but his shyness triumphed, causing him instead to look down at the neglected book in his own lap. *She's probably gay anyway*, Flam rationalized, now remembering Page's comment that Sappho, born on the island of Lesbos, and arguably its most famous citizen, had been taken to the breast of the lesbian community, who claimed same-sex leanings in her lyrics.

When Flam again chanced another glance at The Girl a few minutes later, she had returned to her book, and he deemed it safe to ogle her again. *If she is a lesbian*, he told himself, *it's a damned shame*. A newfound first-hand intimacy with the female form exerted its influence, and he found himself lost in delicious contemplation of erotic gymnastics with this exquisite stranger. He pictured the two of them lubricated by sweet summer sweat with limbs wrapped akimbo around one another like wild grape vines. The fantasy sustained Flam until The Girl's usual stop arrived. As she got up to leave, he could have sworn (or was it wishful thinking) she offered him a sly little half-smile over her shoulder before sliding nimbly past the other passengers in the aisle and stepping off.

Something was unmistakably amiss at Morton's Funeral Home when Flam arrived. The side entryway was locked, and after banging fruitlessly for several minutes on the old wooden garage door, Flam went around to try the main entrance. There, he found a police cruiser parked outside, half on the sidewalk, with no sign of its occupants. The home's front door proved to be locked as well, leaving Flam to wonder how he was supposed to report to work.

After his emphatic tapping on the large, stained-glass windows that dominated the front of the building failed to stir any notice or movement inside, Flam walked half a block to the nearest pay phone, and dialled Morton's main number. On the fourth ring, Mrs. Clarke answered, out of breath and clearly agitated.

"It's me, Mrs. Clarke . . . Flam. I can't get in. All the doors are locked," he complained.

"Yes, yes . . . it's alright now, they're just taking him out now," she answered.

"What? Taking who out?" he asked, bewildered. Then, down the street, he spotted Charlie being led out of the building in handcuffs by two police officers. Flam dropped the phone to sprint over and find out what was happening.

"Charlie, what's wrong?" he exclaimed, but the big Fijian had his eyes screwed tight and tears were streaming down his face. He seemed not to be hearing anything. Flam turned his attention to the policeman nearest him, a stout, thick-necked man with a shaved head.

"Officer . . . what's going on here? Why are you arresting him? What's he done?"

"Mind your own business," the cop growled out of the side of his mouth, more concerned with how the two of them were going to wrestle the giant into the back seat of the cruiser.

"Look, I work here . . . and I know this man, I can vouch for him. I'm sure there must be some mistake."

"Ain't no mistake, mister," the other cop, a swarthy older man with a military moustache, interjected, "this gorilla went berserk in there . . . busted up an office pretty good, plus he threatened to kill a couple of guys. Someone locked him up in a room, but he tore the door right off its hinges . . . that's when they called us. We had to pepper-spray the bastard . . . it was either that or shoot him."

Flam had difficulty accepting the reality of the situation, believing someone else had to be responsible for whatever had happened. Somewhere in the back of his mind a suspicion was starting to grow, and it had Pugsley and Steptoe written all over it. He turned to see if he could get some sense out of Charlie, who was still standing like some large, stunned animal, although he was now shaking his head and blinking his eyes rapidly, evidently to try to wash out the residue of the chemical used against him.

"Charlie . . . it's Flam. Can you hear me? Are you okay? What happened in there?" Charlie seemed to recognize the voice, and turned his head in Flam's direction.

"Flam, is that you? Can you believe what those two bastards did to me?"

"Who? Was it Pugsley and Steptoe? What did they do?"

The young cop interrupted, wanting to take advantage of Charlie's relative calm to load him into the cruiser. "C'mon buddy, into the car . . . you can tell them your story down at the station."

As the policeman tried to force Charlie's head down through the rear door of the vehicle, the Fijian let loose a bellow of rage, and pushed away violently. Flam saw one cop place his hand on the butt of his pistol, and realized Charlie was in serious trouble if he continued to resist.

"Listen, Charlie," Flam said softly, "you have to stop fighting . . . you'll only make it worse. Go with the officers, and I promise I'll get to the bottom of this . . . I'll find a way to help you out. You trust me, don't you?"

Charlie smiled his gargantuan smile, and for the first time a bit of his old self seemed to have returned. "Hey, I trust you, Flam . . . you're my friend. But look out for those two lying barracudas, or they'll get you too. Okay, Flam . . . I'll calm down if you say so, but please, you've got to swear you'll help me."

"I swear, Charlie . . . I'm going to help you. Just don't make it any worse on yourself."

Charlie complied and was wedged into the cramped confines of the cruiser's back seat, the arms handcuffed behind him, forcing his body to contort into a clearly uncomfortable position. Flam was going to try to convince the cops to let him ride along, but just then Bruno appeared in the doorway of the funeral home, and gestured urgently to Flam.

"Quick, you Grub . . . get in there and help clean up the mess before the customers start showing up," Bruno demanded angrily, almost as if he blamed Flam for the situation.

"What happened in there, Bruno? Why is Charlie being arrested?"

"That black bastard killed Hannah's dog . . . then went berserk when Mr. Morton fired him."

"There must be some mistake. Charlie would never do something like that . . . he doesn't have a mean bone in his body," Flam protested.

"Josh Steptoe and George Pugsley were witnesses . . . they caught him in the act. And for someone who doesn't have a mean bone in his body, he sure did a number on Mr. Morton's office. If I were you, I wouldn't be so quick to stand up for him . . . you're already on shaky ground yourself."

Flam shut up, instantly understanding the nature of the conspiracy he was facing. He realized stealth and patience were required here, not bravado. He obediently followed Bruno into the building, and was led into Mr. Morton's inner office, where all of the staff members of the home seemed to be congregated, and were flitting around in frantic activity. In the midst of it, Mr. Morton was sitting limply, evidently stunned by the events that had just transpired. Bruno gestured at the broken coffee table, whose glass top had been shattered, and its legs wrenched completely off.

"Pick up that broken glass and carry the whole lot out back to the garbage," Bruno commanded.

"No, I need him," a voice interrupted, causing Bruno to spin around angrily and face off against the speaker. It was Mrs. Clarke, standing with plump aplomb, hands folded across her mammoth breasts, and a look of bulldog determination on her face.

"Mr. Morton's computer is broken, and I need to be able to connect to the files on it to do the office work. So I need Flam to help me get everything figured out," Mrs. Clarke insisted.

Bruno blinked, looked at Flam, then Mr. Morton, then back at Mrs. Clarke, trying to digest this latest information, and wondering how to handle the apparent affront to his authority.

"Grub knows computers?" was all he could manage in the end.

"He's a little wiz," Mrs. Clarke answered, a grin betraying her delight at being able to seize control of the situation, "so get one of those other bozos to do your dirty work, while Flam and I try to keep this business on its feet. No computer means no contracts, no bills, no mail-outs . . . .."

At this, Mr. Morton finally stirred and looked up. "Oh that won't do . . . that won't do at all," he complained.

"Alright, alright," Bruno conceded impatiently, waving Flam off. He turned to Pugsley and Steptoe, who had been standing around idly watching the interchange. "You two, get this place cleaned up right away," Bruno instructed them. "Come on. Make it snappy. Mr. Morton needs to be able to get back to work."

When Flam found himself alone later with Mrs. Clarke, he was able to get the full details on what had happened with Charlie. The previous evening, Hannah Leetch had helped preside over a vigil. Afterwards, she had returned downstairs to the embalming room to discover her dog Sarah missing. A search had ensued, and Sarah's lifeless body had been discovered in the garage under a hearse. Charlie had long ago left for the day, but Pugsley and Steptoe were quick to testify they had earlier witnessed Charlie slipping poison to the dog.

This had been enough evidence for Bruno to phone Mr. Morton at home and insist Charlie be fired with cause the moment he showed up to work the following day. Mr. Morton, with Bruno standing beside him for support, had reluctantly initiated the dismissal earlier that morning. Charlie, upon learning the charges and hearing who the accusers were, had reportedly gone berserk, yelling and threatening violence against the duo. Bruno and Mr. Morton had managed to slip out of the office and lock Charlie inside, whereupon the big man had proceeded to smash up the furniture, before ultimately ripping the door right off its hinges, and setting out in search of Pugsley and Steptoe. The police had then been called, but when Charlie had refused to leave the premises before confronting his accusers (who were showing rare intelligence, if not courage, by hiding in a storeroom), he had been pepper-sprayed and taken into custody.

"Why on earth would Charlie poison Sarah?" Flam asked, but Mrs. Clarke just shrugged. Flam's instincts screamed that his friend—despite the imposing physical presence and occasional banter about the ferocity of Fijian warriors—was by nature really a very gentle man. He would not have killed the dog, even if by chance there had been some bad blood between him and Leetch's pet.

The whole sordid situation continued to buzz about Flam's mind like a swarm of angry bees, as he went about troubleshooting the problems with Mr. Morton's computer. The only thing that made sense to Flam was that Pugsley and Steptoe had deliberately set up Charlie just to get rid of him—possibly for manhandling the pair earlier in the week.

As far as the computer went, only the monitor and keyboard that sat on the desk had actually been damaged in Charlie's fit of destruction. The system unit itself, which had sat safely shielded under Morton's large oak desk, was unharmed, except for having its power cord wrenched out of the wall socket. However, the antiquated system was now refusing to start up without a keyboard, and this was the reason Mrs. Clarke was unable to establish a connection.

Flam was anxious to get out and try to help Charlie, so he volunteered to personally go down to the computer store where Morton's had an account, and to buy all the replacement components needed. He sweetened the deal with an offer to acquire some extra memory and disk storage for Mrs. Clarke's own machine. Once out on the street, he headed straight to a phone, and called Sergeant Cuff's precinct.

Whoever answered the phone was curt and discourteous at first, instantly raising Flam's anxiety level. "Look, this is his . . .." Flam faltered for a moment, the plunged right in. "This is his future stepson, and it's extremely urgent I talk to him."

"Hang on," the voice relented, and a few minutes later returned with a direct number for Cuff's cellphone, saying the sergeant had approved passing it on. Flam dialled again, and this time was greeted by Cuff's characteristically gruff voice, although the detective actually seemed amused to have Flam calling him.

"Flam, my man, what kind of trouble are you in now? What did you do—steal some books?" In the past, Flam would probably have been angered by the flippant tone and personal jabs but now he had come to accept Cuff's jokes.

Flam wanted to address Cuff intimately, but wasn't sure what to call him. "Dad" didn't quite seem appropriate, and "Sergeant Cuff" was somehow too formal given their newfound relationship.

"It's Lee, right? Look, Lee, I have a friend at work who's just been arrested, and I'm positive he's being framed." He proceeded to tell Cuff the whole story. There was a silence at the other end before the cop responded.

"I'm not sure what to tell you, Flam. Even if, like you figure, your pal didn't kill the dog, he did do everything else, and as long as Morton presses charges, it's going to end up in court. I can find out the bottom line on the charges for you, and help you get him bailed out, but if you can't get those two guys at the home to recant, he's going to need a good lawyer. Sorry."

Flam had been hoping for something more positive, and his heart sank at the news. "Okay, Lee, thanks anyway. Let me know about the bail."

"Hey, kid," Cuff interjected. "Did your mom talk to you about Sunday yet?"

"Sunday? No, why?"

"We finally gave up trying to find a time and place to get married here in town. Apparently it's high season for weddings—you know, June brides and all that—so we're just going to get hitched down in the Bahamas next week. My buddies are throwing us a little send-off, and Mary and I want you to be there. It's at Bootleg Bill's down on River Street, any time after four in the afternoon."

"Um, thanks. I'm actually working Sunday but I'm off early. I'll drop by afterwards."

"Do that. It would break your mama's heart if you weren't there. Sorry again about your friend. I'll see what I can find out."

Flam hung up the phone, his face contorted in rapt thought. Mere mention of his mother's remarriage had again touched a nerve, but Flam shoved those depressing thoughts aside. He concentrated instead on devising a plan to help his friend. Cuff had only confirmed what Flam had already suspected—Charlie was in trouble as long as Morton believed Pugsley and Steptoe's lies. If only there were some way to turn the tables on the pair and expose them for the conniving, malignant twosome they really were.

Flam hastened off to the computer store, and purchased all the replacement equipment for the office, charging it to Morton's account as instructed by Mrs. Clarke. Returning by taxi, he lugged everything into the office, and inside an hour had Mr. Morton's computer working again, as well as having upgraded Mrs. Clarke's own system, to purrs of appreciation, and pats on the back from the rotund secretary.

In Flam's absence, Mr. Morton's office had been more or less restored to order. It did look somewhat barer, though, as the removal of the smashed furniture had left a noticeable gap in the room's decor. The only remaining indication of the earlier altercation was a missing door, and splinters in the jamb where the hinges had been forcefully yanked out of the wooden frame.

Once the repair work with the office computers had concluded, Bruno reappeared almost immediately to press Flam back into service. Now that Charlie had been dismissed, it seemed Flam was expected to take up some of the custodial slack, at least until a replacement could be hired.

When Flam tried to protest that he was not a janitor, The Hell Man reeled and snarled at him impatiently. "You'll do whatever I tell you . . . or you'll find yourself out on the streets with that oversized friend of yours."

So on top of the regular menial duties that had already come to be Flam's exclusive responsibility, he now had a new host of janitorial chores to perform—at least inasmuch as he *could* do them, for many of Charlie's mechanical labours, such as the maintenance of the home's vehicles, were quite simply beyond Flam's abilities.

Pugsley and Steptoe soon caught wind of Flam's new misfortune. They tracked him down as he was washing out garbage cans in the rear, so they could witness his latest humiliation firsthand and hurl some additional taunts and insults his way.

"Hey, check it out," Steptoe chortled in a fit of poetic inspiration. "It's the Flim Flam Man, making his garbage can spic and span."

"Rub a dub dub, Grub," Pugsley chimed in. "Make sure none of your grubby relatives are crawling around in the bottom of those cans."

Flam's face reddened in anger, and he desperately wanted to lash out at the duo—to blurt out how he knew they'd fabricated their testimony against Charlie, and that he'd find a way to get even. Even in Flam's state of rage, though, common sense prevailed, and he realized it would not be tactically prudent to reveal his intentions or suspicions. Instead, Flam just fumed and ground his teeth as he continued his cleaning chore, until finally the two bullies grew bored and returned to their own duties.

As the hours went by with no word from Cuff, the promise made to Charlie to find a way to help was starting to weigh heavily on Flam'. He was beginning to feel despondent over his powerlessness—not just in Charlie's case, but in life in general. The euphoria with which he'd started this day was long gone, and the memories of his delicious lovemaking with Angela now seemed like some vague dream. The lack of sleep was also catching up to him as he toiled into the evening and a second shift, and soon he couldn't remember when he had felt more miserable. Everyone close to him was deserting him, it seemed—Page, his mother, Angela, Charlie—and leaving him alone to flounder in his dreary, pointless life.

At the end of his overtime, instead of heading straight for the bus stop, Flam wandered upstairs to the storeroom where Pugsley and Steptoe had previously stuffed him into the coffin. Physically and emotionally spent, Flam shuffled aimlessly around the room, admiring the craftsmanship of the caskets arranged there, and rubbing his hand lovingly over the exquisitely finished wood of the various models. He seemed to find a sort of numbing comfort from being among these containers for the dead.

One magnificent, highly-varnished, cherry-wood coffin in the corner drew him to it. He found himself going over, opening the lid, and crawling inside, revelling again in the feel of the cream-coloured, crepe interior. Flam reached up and pulled the lid down, leaving it open just a fraction. He instantly felt a serenity as the darkness swallowed him, shutting out the pitiful failure that was his life.

"*'Tis a consummation devoutly to be wished, to die, to sleep,*" Flam quoted Hamlet, and he suddenly felt an overwhelming desire to heroically end his troubles so he would not have to face another soul-sucking day of meaningless, joyless existence. *How will I do it? If I snuck downstairs, what could I find to kill myself?* He thought about hanging himself, but did not recall having seen rope anywhere in Charlie's maintenance room. He knew there were ample poisonous substances on the premises, but was unsure whether any of them would act swiftly or effectively enough to kill him instead of simply leaving him retching and writhing in pain.

It seemed to Flam the most efficient way to dispatch himself would be to lie on top of Hannah's stainless steel embalming table and cut his wrists with a scalpel, allowing the table's built in channels and gutters to neatly drain off his blood. Then it occurred to him that Pugsley and Steptoe might be the ones to discover his corpse, and he imagined the sort of abuse they might inflict upon it. Although he would, by then, be just so much dead flesh and long past the point of caring, he refused to give his hated co-workers a final victory of this sort.

No, he thought, *better to commit the deed at home, and leave a note full of detailed instructions on how to dispose of my remains.* But thoughts of home reminded him of his mother, and it dawned on Flam that committing suicide now would ruin her impending wedding. The current of thought then continued south to the Caribbean, and from there across the globe to Fiji, and now he remembered his pledge to help Charlie. The burden of that unfulfilled promise was what ultimately spurred Flam out of his self-pity.

Reluctantly, he left his snug, varnished refuge, and headed back downstairs. Noting Bruno was preoccupied with an evening vigil in the main chapel, Flam snuck into the office, and used Mrs. Clarke's phone to call Lee Cuff.

"Flam, there you are," Cuff exclaimed. "What kept you? I left you a message hours ago."

"Message? I didn't get a message."

"Really? Hmmm . . . some guy with a low, buttery voice, had a hint of an accent, said he'd pass it on. Must have been around three or so."

Bruno! Flam was infuriated and vowed to finally have it out with The Hell Man, but at the moment was more interested in learning how Charlie was doing.

"So what were you able to find out?" Flam asked.

"Your friend went in front of a judge this afternoon. He's been granted bail pending trial, but the last time I phoned, around suppertime, they told me he was still in his holding cell. They say he hasn't even made a phone call . . . he's just sitting there like he's in some kind of trance." Cuff went on to give Flam the details of how he could arrange to post bond for Charlie's release. "I gotta be straight with you, Flam, your buddy's in a heap of trouble. If he's convicted on all counts, there's a good chance he's looking at jail time."

Flam mumbled his thanks, and hung up the phone. As he was getting up to slip back out into the hallway, he heard noises outside the door. Heart pounding, he looked around desperately for someplace to conceal himself. Seeing the door to Mr. Morton's office was still missing, Flam scurried into the next room, and dove beneath the desk. From his hiding place, he had a clear view of the outer office, and was somehow not surprised to see Pugsley and Steptoe slink in and hustle over to Mrs. Clarke's computer.

"Look, George, I'm not so sure about this," Steptoe was protesting. "What if The Hell Man comes in and catches us."

"Are you kidding?" Pugsley replied. "Did you see the hottie he was chatting up in there? Besides, this'll only take a minute." Flam watched from his hiding place as Pugsley logged on to one of his illicit websites, then produced a digital camera from his pocket, and plugged it into the computer. Evidently, Pugsley and Steptoe were not only fans of the sick pornography Flam had stumbled upon earlier, they were contributors as well.

"Oh, man, you were really into it," Steptoe chortled, suddenly more concerned with the images on the screen than fear of discovery. "And *you* said she was too old."

"Yeah, she wasn't half bad once we put some makeup on her," Pugsley agreed, starting to stroke himself as the photos began to arouse him. "Look, here's the one where we both screw her at the same time . . . see, I told you the self-timer would do the trick."

"Yeah, until that damned dog stuck its nose up my ass."

"Well, we don't have to worry about the fucking mutt anymore . . . and tagging that nigger with it was pure genius, if I do say so myself."

"Yeah, well, just as long as Hannah doesn't find out . . . she's liable to come after you with one of her knives," Steptoe countered, clearly the chronic worrier of the duo.

"Don't sweat it. As long as the two of us stick together, everything will be cool."

"So how much do you figure they'll pay us?"

Pugsley mulled it over. "Enough for us to afford a video camera, I think . . . and then they'll pay even more for full-motion movies next time."

"Yeah, well, who knows how long it'll be before we get another chance . . . might only be old men coming in again for a while."

"Well, we'll just have to be patient, won't we? Unless you're ready to take the next step, and, you know, drum up our own business."

Even from a room away, Flam could see Steptoe swallow hard. "Oh, man, you know I'd love to, George . . . I'd just want to be totally sure we didn't get caught. Maybe. Maybe."

Pugsley finished his transfer of images, unplugged the cable, and shut down the computer.

"You sure you got everything? Bug Boy was in here working on the computers today, you know," Steptoe cautioned.

"You worry too much, Josh. I've moved it all onto the Internet now, right? They don't have the password. That fucking Grubby won't be able to screw things up here. Man, I'm still pissed off he spoiled things with that Sexton chick. She was really prime."

"Yeah, well, it's your own fault for fingering her right in front of the guy. He practically puked."

"Yeah, yeah, my mistake, but I thought he might be, you know, into it . . . he has that kind of sick, pale look, like he's half-dead himself."

Steptoe laughed out loud before catching himself. "Well don't worry about Bug Boy. If he gets in the way, we'll take care of him the same way we took care of Charlie."

That warranted a congratulatory high-five slap from Pugsley. "Okay, let's get out of here. C'mon, I'll buy you a drink to celebrate."

After the pair had left, Flam waited a bit longer to make sure they didn't return unexpectedly, then came out of hiding and went over to Mrs. Clarke's computer and turned it on. Once the system had booted up, Flam promptly checked the cache on the computer's web browser. As he had suspected, Pugsley had previewed some of the images after transferring them to the pornographic website. As a consequence, a copy of some of the sordid photos had been kept on the computer itself. Flam quickly duplicated these images and emailed them to himself. His heart was pounding from fear of discovery and he badly wanted to get out of the room as quickly as possible, but he now had a flash of inspiration, and decided to hang in and perform one more task.

Flam searched around the Internet until he found a website that offered free spyware, and selected a program advertised for keeping tabs on cheating spouses. He downloaded the software, which would allow him to secretly track and record any programs opened and keystrokes entered from Mrs. Clarke's computer, and configured the covert software to only activate itself in the off hours. Finally, his fingers increasingly clumsy from mounting panic, he turned off computer and lights, and left the room . . . only to walk smack dab into Bruno, standing out in the hallway.

"What the hell," Bruno growled. "You Grub . . . I thought you'd gone home. What were you doing in the office? You've got no business in there!"

Flam deliberately forced himself to remain calm, although he felt like he was visibly shaking and his knees would collapse under him at any second. He contrived a casual half-smile, then reached into his breast pocket and pulled out his dog-eared notebook.

"I went looking for this," Flam said as indifferently as his fear-stricken nerves would allow. "I lost it under the desk when I was fixing Mr. Morton's computer this morning."

Bruno's eyes narrowed as he contemplated Flam's story. "Next time come and ask me for permission to go in there first. And if I find anything's missing, you'll be sharing a cell with that crazy black friend of yours."

Flam raised his arms to the side, allowing his jacket to fall open. "You have my permission to search me. Please, I don't want any undue suspicion lingering over me."

At first Bruno looked as if he were going to take Flam up on the offer, but then his expression was supplanted by one of disgust, as if he were loathe to touch the underling. "That won't be necessary, but don't let it happen again. And for God's sake, go buy yourself a new suit, will you? This one looks like it belongs to someone at a homeless shelter."

Flam grew livid, wanting to scream out that his suit was so wrinkled and worn because of the physical labours he was constantly required to perform in it, and that he might as well wear a pair of coveralls to work. Prudently, he held his tongue. He had one more urgent task to perform that night, and wanted to get away as quickly as he could.

"Yes, sir. Good night, Mr. Helman," Flam said in as even a tone as he could muster and walked nonchalantly away.

The sleepy-eyed young policeman behind the duty counter seemed almost relieved when Flam approached him for Charlie's release, with requisite paperwork and adequate bond all duly secured and processed. "The guy was starting to drive me batty," the cop complained as he presented the final documents for Flam to sign. "Wouldn't eat, wouldn't do nothing except sit there like he was on drugs or something, and mumble some weird-ass voodoo shit."

Flam was tempted to correct the policeman, and point out that voodoo originated on the opposite side of the planet from Fiji, but diplomatically stayed mum.

"Hey, what gives?" the cop exclaimed after reading what Flam had written. "Is this some kind of joke? 'Flam Grub' . . . yeah, that's real funny. Do you want to end up inside the cell with your pal?"

Flam reddened, embarrassed yet again by his accursed name, although somewhat mystified by the cop's vehement reaction to it. He stood there dumbly, unsure how to react.

"Come on, Smart Alec, put your real name down. Take my word for it, you don't want to get me pissed off."

Flam blinked, now more than a little confused. "But that *is* my real name," he protested. "Believe me, I wish it wasn't."

The policeman continued to look skeptical and increasingly angry, even going so far as to rest a hand on his pistol grip, so Flam pulled out his wallet, and showed his driver's license.

"Far out," the cop said, then laughed out loud. "Ha! Ain't that something . . . just like the movie. Well now I can say I've met Flam Grub."

Flam began to wonder if the cop wasn't himself high on something, but the policeman offered no further objections, and picked up the phone to call down for Charlie's release. Ten minutes later, Charlie shuffled through the door with a vacant expression on his face, looking as if his mind had been sucked up into the jet stream and whisked across the globe. Two sour-looking cops were practically pushing the prisoner in front of them.

"Charlie!" Flam shouted out, teary-eyed at seeing his friend again. The big man stirred at the sound of the voice, and the patented smile ripped his face.

"Flam!" he shouted out in a deep voice that rattled the cinder-block waiting room. "I knew you'd come for me. I've been praying to the old gods, especially to the demon goddess Lilavatu. I had a vision you were surrounded by great shifting currents of flame, and had a small magic animal in your hand that helped you lay waste your enemies. Hallelujah!"

"Charlie! And here I thought you were a devout Methodist. Make up your mind," Flam chastised him jokingly.

Charlie grinned. "I *am* a Methodist, but they made it quite clear in Sunday school you cannot petition God with prayer. For my reward in the next life I place my soul squarely in the merciful hands of the Lord, amen. But when it comes to dealing with evil in everyday life, faith alone is not enough. I figure you have to fight fire with fire, and no one's better for that than the old gods. And, see, Lilavatu, she came through for me."

Flam was too elated to debate the metaphysics of cause and effect. He stepped up and gave Charlie a hug, almost feeling like a child again as he was swallowed up by the Fijian's gigantic frame.

"Come on, let's get you signed out and on your way home," Flam instructed, "then I can fill you in on the whole story."

CHAPTER 31

The Girl on the Bus was reading a Coleridge collection, seemingly unaware that Flam, seated facing her and slightly down the row of benches, was unabashedly staring at her, mesmerized by this alluring woman who intrigued and aroused him more each time he saw her.

By now, Flam knew The Girl got on the bus three stops after his own and almost always precisely at 7:50 a.m. So, this morning, he had deliberately chosen when to start his own commute—letting two earlier buses go by in the process—in a successful attempt to end up on the same vehicle as The Girl.

He had never seen her reading the same book twice, and was beginning to wonder whether she really was poring through entire books at such a rapid pace or was perhaps only selectively sampling the volumes. Her choice of poetry and weighty literary classics fascinated Flam, although he found it almost too good to be true. He theorized she might just be an English major at the university, and was absorbing the books under some degree of academic duress while she travelled to a summer job downtown.

Regardless of her likely motivation, Flam fantasized about being able to meet her, and pictured them sharing their intimate feelings about the works of the literary greats she was reading. True, now that Angela had initiated him into the universe of corporeal pleasure (allowing Flam to fondle first-hand her stately pleasure domes), his bedtime fancies surrounding The Girl had taken on a more physical timbre. Still, he could feel that his yearning for her transcended mere lust. It was as if some invisible, yet irresistible, cosmic bond had formed between them, its force threatening to yank him out of his seat, and drag him down the aisle towards her.

He heard his name called from the rear of the bus, and spun to see who was addressing him, but failed to recognize anybody there—in fact, no one was even looking in his direction. Almost all the seats were occupied by commuters either napping outright or sitting in zombie-like states of early morning stupor. The exception were two teenaged boys who were sitting together and apparently discussing in earnest the latest summer blockbuster action film.

Flam was positive he had heard his name, and began wondering whether the lack of sleep was starting to catch up with him. It had been well after 1 a.m. that morning when he had returned home from bailing out Charlie, and Flam had immediately gone to his computer to make sure he'd successfully received the illicit photos purloined from Pugsley and Steptoe.

Flam had vacillated over those pictures, worried they might not be enough to incriminate the dastardly duo and exonerate Charlie. As he had stared at the images, his stomach turned with a disgust and anger that cut through his fatigue. He recalled the indignity he had seen firsthand being performed on Cindy Sexton's body, and how he'd been too much of a coward then to stand up against the pair of perverts. Perhaps, now, Cindy too would have some final justice. Or would she? Flam noted that Pugsley and Steptoe had been careful never to allow their own faces to appear in the photographs. And, although the scene appeared generally recognizable as the embalming room at Morton's, Flam surmised that many such rooms around the world might be configured in a similar way. The only clear-cut evidence appeared to be the identification of the corpse itself, but the cadaver had been heavily made up and adorned with a garish red wig. In the shots Flam had managed to obtain, the face was always partially obscured to some extent.

Flam had originally hoped to start the day by revealing the photos to Mr. Morton, but the way in which Bruno was always so quick to believe Pugsley and Steptoe now made Flam wary. He doubted his evidence would, in fact, be deemed irrefutable. With Charlie out of jail, however, Flam felt that now he had some time. It was better to make sure his final thrust was a lethal one, than to go off half-cocked and destroy his own reputation as well. Resigned to the fact this drama still had a scene or two to play out, Flam returned to earth from his musings. He glanced back in the direction of The Girl on the Bus and found her staring appraisingly at him.

The Girl instantly returned her gaze to the poetry text on her lap, allowing Flam to study her pretty face. He wondered whether she had indeed been checking him out or whether he was misinterpreting a casual glance he'd intercepted midway. How badly he wanted to believe this intriguing girl might have some interest in him, and part of him started to assert he should simply slide across the aisle and introduce himself. But Flam's introversion was so deeply ingrained in his being by now, he could not make himself do something so audacious. So a spat broke out between the two voices in his head— one calling for action and boldness, the other counselling caution for fear of inevitable rejection and subsequent dejection.

The Girl's stop arrived, and with a final furtive glance his way (of that Flam was now almost certain), she slid a bookmark into place, eased her book shut, and stood up to disembark. As she stepped gracefully off the bus, she tossed her hair slightly in a way that made Flam's heart beat faster with longing. He had an impulse to ring the bell and dash after her, but predictably he found himself lacking the character necessary to act so boldly. The habitual chorus of self-loathing soon began to wail from deep within Flam's being, and as an antidote against the familiar sadness, Flam pulled out his notebook and began rendering his feelings and thoughts into verse.

The therapeutic exercise worked so well he ended up missing his usual stop, and had to backtrack a couple of blocks towards work. Walking briskly to avoid being late, Flam hurried past a variety store that opened early in an attempt to wring some business out of morning commuters. He stopped dead in his tracks as something astonishing caught his eye.

There, lying on the sidewalk, printed in the top banner of a newspaper still waiting to be freed from its bundle, was a teaser stating, "Flam Grub An Instant Hero." Bending over to make out the details, he saw an accompanying photo of a vaguely familiar looking actor, holding an enormous pistol, and looking properly menacing. There was a cutline underneath the photo that read "Brock rocks as *The Graveyard Poet* breaks opening weekend records. See Entertainment." None of this in any way explained to Flam why his name was featured on the newspaper, and he made to flip to the indicated inside page, but the polyethylene strap that securely tied the stack of newspapers together made it impossible.

"Hey mister, you want paper, you wait," a voice called from the doorway, and Flam turned to see the variety store's Korean proprietor approaching with a precarious grasp on four plastic pails full of cut flowers. Flam waited impatiently while the man placed the flowers on the wooden racks at the front of the store and trundled over to snap the band with a rusty old pocketknife.

Flam fumbled with his change as he bought the newspaper, and quickly flipped to its Entertainment section, his curiosity burgeoning almost beyond containment. The story in question was a review of a new blockbuster movie, called *The Graveyard Poet*, which had opened the previous weekend, and starred Hollywood heavyweight Brock Harrow, current king of the action genre. Still confused, Flam read on, and his mouth popped open when he discovered the character Harrow played in the movie—and "destined to be an instant classic figure in cinema," according to the reviewer—was named none other than . . . *Flam Grub*.

Standing bemused on the sidewalk, as the morning commuters milled past him, Flam was having trouble accepting the reality of the moment. As far as he knew, his despised name had always been completely unique, a grotesque freak of nomenclature that had been his curse, and his alone to bear. How had it now ended up being shared by a fictitious character in a major motion picture?

Flam returned to the article, and searched for more citations of the name. He discovered the fictitious Flam Grub was a mysterious wandering stranger, loosely based on a samurai character created by legendary Japanese filmmaker Fukazawa Sosoomi. In *The Graveyard Poet*, the poetry-spouting ex-Marine has forsworn violence for solitude, but is predictably sucked into the affairs of a family in trouble—and the inevitable climaxing bloodbath, as he deals the bad guys their well-deserved comeuppance.

After a couple more minutes of pondering did nothing to shed any light on the unreal turn of events, Flam let the original urgency of his own little reality reassert itself, and hastily resumed his trip to work. The closer he got to Morton's, the more the stresses and challenges facing him there began to loom large and weigh heavily upon Flam's thoughts. Soon, the anomaly of possessing a cinematic counterpart was all tucked and folded away in Flam's thoughts as neatly as the newspaper under his arm.

Uncharacteristically, Bruno was not laying in ambush to chastise Flam for being late (by four minutes), and to press him into gruntwork. Flam wandered the oddly deserted building for five minutes in an unsuccessful search for his supervisor, before trying the front office to see whether Mrs. Clarke knew of The Hell Man's whereabouts.

In between pants and wheezes, for Mrs. Clarke seemed especially unwell that morning, she told Flam that Bruno had rushed out to deal with some urgent problem. Apparently, it involved an early-morning removal of a body by Pugsley and Steptoe, who usually arrived at 6 a.m. and started their day by retrieving corpses of people who had passed away in the night.

"Seems nobody told them the guy weighed 350 pounds," Mrs. Clarke explained with a chortle, or perhaps it was just some bad air escaping, "and he'd croaked in his room up in a converted attic, with a very narrow staircase. They couldn't use the gurney, and when they tried to carry him down the stairs, they dropped the guy and smashed the railing. The wife is freaking out and threatening to sue. Bruno went rushing out to give them a hand and hopefully calm down the Missus."

"So . . . everything working okay with the computers?" Flam asked, capitalizing on the absence of any relayed orders from the boss, and preferring to hang around the office than voluntarily deliver himself into the cruel clutches of the vacuum cleaner or wet mop.

Mrs. Clarke spotted an opportunity. "Well, yes and no. The machine runs like a charm now, but I'm still having trouble with this new accounting program." Soon, she had Flam unresistingly keying receipts into the computer while she got on the phone to complain in exquisite detail to some crony about her latest medical misfortunes.

With Mrs. Clarke's attention diverted, Flam was able to check on the spyware program he'd installed earlier, to see what activity it had logged. As he'd hoped, Pugsley and Steptoe had gone straight to the computer when they'd arrived at the crack of dawn, apparently to verify their perverse submissions had been received during the night, and perhaps to see how much payment was forthcoming. Flam's surreptitious software had logged every location visited and captured every keystroke entered by the dirty duo. He now had complete information about their secret Internet accounts, including their passwords.

Flam's heart was throbbing with the suspense as he kept one eye on the jabbering Mrs. Clarke. She, however, had just started reciting her litany of health complaints, and thus remained completely disinterested in Flam's online activities.

Flam signed into the private members-only areas of the fetish websites Pugsley and Steptoe frequented most often, including *Stiffs That Make Us Stiff* and *Sex To Die For*, and browsed all the photos he could find. To his delight, not only were there additional shots that clearly showed the face of the female corpse they'd molested, but there were pictures of Sarah, Hannah Leetch's dog, entering into the scene. These were followed by a shot of the dog, evidently in distress, with a pair of hands wrapped around its neck while something was shoved down its gullet.

The face in that photo was still mostly out of the frame, but enough of the visage remained for Flam to discern it belonged to Steptoe, judging from the cruel snarl of its mustachioed mouth and the pronounced double chin. Most importantly, the perpetrator was clearly white, thereby exonerating the dark-skinned Charlie.

The enthusiasm in Mrs. Clarke's phone conversation started to wane, so Flam hastened his pace. The previous evening at the police station, he'd picked up a Crime Tips email address. Selecting the most damning of the photos, he hacked into Pugsley's web email account, and used it to send the images to the authorities, attached to a full confession (sprinkled with deliberate spelling mistakes) that named Steptoe as the instigator.

Finally, just as Mrs. Clarke was saying her goodbyes on the telephone, Flam shut down the extra programs, and cleared all history and traces of his activities. By the time the secretary had rolled back to her desk, Flam was again innocently entering receipts into the accounting program.

"How's it going?" Mrs. Clarke asked.

"Almost done," Flam answered brightly, although there was a basketball-sized knot in his stomach, and he prayed his blushing face wasn't too obvious. He badly wanted to get away from the computer and flee the room, but reined in his panic and forced himself to act indifferent. "Say, Mrs. Clarke . . .."

"Fanny. You can call me Fanny."

"Fanny, then. I was curious about this receipt I was keying in . . . five cigar humidors at $18.50 each. I haven't seen a trace of cigars anywhere around the home, unless they're Mr. Morton's private stash."

Mrs. Clarke burst out laughing, although the ill-advised outburst soon turned into a fit of coughing. When she recovered, she pulled out the Morton product price list and indicated a line item. "See these special imported mahogany funeral urns, $900 a pop?" She winked. "Not a bad markup, eh?" Flam's mouth popped open. This was not something they had taught at Prentice College.

"I tell you, son," Mrs. Clarke continued, "don't let that old bier baron ever plead poverty to you. He knows how to filch the coins off a corpse's eyes. Still, I feel kinda sorry for him."

"How so?"

"Well, he's the fourth generation Morton to run this home . . . had his only child, Don Jr., all lined up to keep the tradition going. Poor kid drowned while canoeing up on Lake Ochiwawa a few years back, and it looks like the line's going to end at Donald Q. Morton IV. That's why Bruno's always hustling around from sun to sun."

"Bruno?"

"Yeah, he figures he's a cinch to take over the business from Morton once the old man retires . . . or croaks. Bruno's the one always pinching pennies and cutting corners. He's the guy you've got to watch out for."

"Speaking of Bruno, I'd better get to my chores or he'll have my head. If he comes looking for me, tell him I'm up cleaning the consultation rooms."

"I will . . . and thanks for your help again, Flam. It's good to know you're around to cover for me."

"Anytime, Fanny," Flam said, and slid out the door. In the hallway, he had to stop and regain his composure, relieved his covert operation was over. He hoped desperately the salvo against his dastardly co-workers had found its target . . . and wanted to be far away from the scene when it did.

When Bruno returned and tracked down Flam, busily at work polishing the furniture, The Hell Man was visibly in a foul mood. By now, Flam could read Bruno like a dime store novel. The underling knew what sort of brutal day was forthcoming, especially given that a number of Charlie's former custodial chores were again being added to Flam's workload. Still, he tried not to let his boss's cruel caprices affect his mood, and even managed to steal the time to write a hokey little ode to himself while he worked. It sang the praises of Flam as *Ubermensch*, the unlikely but ultimately triumphant hero. By the time the evening descended, however, with still no sign of Pugsley and Steptoe's reckoning having arrived, Flam was again feeling ragged and despondent. His mental poetic composition had by now degenerated into a lament of despair. On several occasions, he found himself having to fight back rising tears of self-pity.

Why haven't they been arrested? Flam wondered when, somewhere around 8 p.m., he clearly heard Pugsley and Steptoe guffawing merrily along the lower corridors. *Did I get the email address wrong? Perhaps the police won't act. Maybe it's out of their jurisdiction, or there isn't enough evidence for an arrest. Or maybe it's not even against the law. Perhaps I should have sent the photos to Mr. Morton . . . or to Hannah.*

Flam's shift finally ended, and left him wondering what to do next. Although the prospect sent instant tremors through his stomach, and made his face feel like it had been shoved under a heat lamp, he resolved to sneak back onto Mrs. Clarke's computer, and risk another attempt to incriminate the perverse pair. But when Flam neared the office, Bruno was seated right outside in one of the faux Louis XIV lobby chairs. The Hell Man was smiling neutrally, as beside him a sniffling, white-haired, black-clad old woman guided him through the pages of a thick, ancient photo album. Bruno glanced up with an inquiring look, forcing a panicked Flam to abandon his scheme and walk right by and out the front door.

Outside the weather was hot and muggy, and twilight was still holding out over the darkness. Flam realized it was Friday night, for the sidewalks were busy with manic young revellers hurrying by in search of sensory stimulation, or eager lovers intertwined around each other like runaway honeysuckle vines.

The sight of all the happy people only highlighted the isolation and ennui Flam felt. Whatever heroism he'd felt earlier now drained like water down a gutter, leaving him feeling worthless and defeated. As if to punctuate his wretchedness, he glanced up and saw his bus pulling away from the stop down the street, meaning at least a twenty minute wait at this time of the night.

Sitting alone in the bus shelter, he pulled out his notebook and started rereading the "Ode to The Girl on the Bus" he had been composing earlier that day. Although typically his own worst critic, and seldom one to admire his own handiwork, he found himself smiling appreciatively at the phrases he'd penned. Inspired anew, he bent over to finish the stanza.

Later, on the way home, and working on his poem, Flam happened to glance up as his bus passed a Cineplex where *The Graveyard Poet* was playing. The lineup for the next showing of the movie ran for a full city block, and Flam recalled the bizarre coincidence that had surfaced concerning a cinematic doppelganger. He wondered if that cosmic quirk of nomenclature would lead to even more humiliation in the future.

He sighed and returned to his writing, wishing he was already home and hidden safely in his bed—the same bed where, a hundred years ago it almost seemed now, he had held a beautiful, voluptuous, sensuous woman in his arms, and felt the ecstasy of lovemaking. The memory sparked a new train of thought concerning The Girl who was subject of his poem-in-progress. Inspired anew, Flam rode it all the way home.

CHAPTER 32

The ringing of his phone woke Flam from a bottomless sleep shortly after 5 a.m. Groggy and disoriented, he had to fumble for a few seconds to locate the offending instrument, and it took a supreme effort just to croak a "hello" into the handset.

"Grub? Bruno Helman here. We have an emergency. We need you to come in to work right away."

Flam forced his eyes open into a squint, and looked around in search of his clock radio's red display. "What . . . now? It's only five o'clock."

"I said it was an *emergency*. Come in right now or don't bother coming in ever again."

"Okay, okay, hold your hearses. I'm on my way."

"Can you be here inside an hour?"

The cobwebs were clearing, and it was beginning to dawn on Flam just what might be at the core of this early morning flurry. His mood suddenly brightened.

"No problem . . . I'll take my car. Traffic should be pretty light at this hour on a Saturday. I'm going to hop into the shower now, and I'll be there by six. "

On the drive in, Flam grasped for the first time what a serious impact the removal of Pugsley and Steptoe might have on the operation of the funeral home. His motive had simply been to exonerate Charlie. However, if in the process Flam had managed to orchestrate the evildoers' dismissal, then it seriously reduced the operation's staffing, at least until the pair could be replaced. That potentially offered an opportunity for Flam to move up in the Morton Funeral Home's hierarchy. Finally, he might have a chance to perform the kind of work—ushering the dead out of this world with dignity and respect, and ministering to the bereaved—he had hoped for when joining the funerary profession.

The Hell Man was out front, leaning on the hood of the hearse, and looking visibly upset, when Flam arrived. There were no apologies or explanations given. Instead, Flam was instantly scolded, as was now Bruno's habit. At one point, he reached towards Flam, causing him to reflexively recoil as if he were about to be attacked. It turned out the annoyed Hell Man was simply trying to straighten out Flam's appearance, including picking some cat hairs off his shoulders and lapels.

"You barely look presentable," Bruno grumbled, "but if we're lucky the family will be too distraught to care. Just keep your mouth shut, and follow my lead." Flam realized he was going to help retrieve the body of someone who had passed away during the night.

"Where are George and Josh?" he asked, feigning naïveté and hoping to get all the gruesome details of how the dastardly duo's downfall had played out. Bruno, however, remained grumpily tightlipped.

"They quit," was all he would say, and lapsed into silence for the duration of the trip.

Flam frankly didn't mind. He preferred this reticence to the constant castigations Bruno normally unleashed. Besides, Flam was too busy trying to conceal his delight at the successful way his secret stratagem had played out.

As they approached the address where they were to pick up the deceased, the neighbourhood began to look familiar. When they stopped, he realized they were barely half a block from the tailor shop he had visited that week. A feeling of unease overtook Flam as they hauled out the gurney from their hearse, and approached the front door of a venerable brick apartment building with an impressive, white granite façade.

A man was waiting to let them into the building, and Flam was disturbed to see it was Izhak Szabo. The tailor gave him a nod of recognition, and without a word, led them towards the door of a ground floor apartment. Even before entering, Flam knew whose body they would find. There, lying in his bed and looking peaceful, almost happy in death, was old Joe Schneider.

"Here is the death certificate," Szabo said. "The doctor says he died in his sleep of heart failure. He was advised many times not to overexert himself . . . he was even prescribed a wheelchair . . . but he was a very proud and stubborn man, and insisted on fighting as long as he could before the disease took him. I think he would be extremely grateful to have ended this way."

"Disease?" Flam asked, puzzled, for Joe had not mentioned any illness.

Szabo nodded. "Cancer, initially of the liver, but it had started to spread. The pain was, I imagine, extreme, but he somehow managed to tolerate it with the help of his medicine, and to go about his business nevertheless. Why, just this past week, he suddenly developed a new passion for computers—he began spending hours every day down at the local Internet café. Can you believe it . . . at his age? A most remarkable man."

Bruno had been reading over the death certificate to make sure all was in order to allow them to legally begin their duty, and had only been paying cursory attention to the conversation. Szabo went over to the bedside table, and picked up an envelope.

"And these are instructions for his funeral. He prepared them quite recently . . . as if he knew he was about to die."

Bruno reached for the envelope, but Szabo shook his head, and handed off the envelope to Flam instead. "No, they are for *him*. Joash was most specific. He wanted Mr. Grub to be in charge of the arrangements."

Bruno's mouth constricted into a tight line of disapproval while he pondered the unexpected development.

"But of course," Bruno finally replied. "Whatever he wished. May we take Mr. Schneider now?"

Szabo waved them to their work, and Flam followed Bruno's lead as they carefully removed and bundled up the bed sheets for disposal, slid Joe's remains into the body bag, and placed it on the gurney. The whole time, Flam was consciously fighting to stop the trembling in his hands. When the zipper of the black vinyl bag closed over Joe's face, Flam had to squeeze back tears. Only the thought that he had been entrusted with the responsibility of supervising Joe's final journey provided the resolve to perform the necessary steps.

The tiny old man's corpse weighed practically nothing, and the two had little trouble wheeling him out to the street and into the hearse. As they drove back to Morton's, Flam opened the envelope and solemnly read Joe's last request for his funeral rites. In his past thanatological research, Flam had naturally studied the funeral practices followed by the various religions, and noted that Joe's instructions were for a traditional Jewish burial. The body was to be washed in the ritual of the *taharah haMetim*, and in his precise, tight hand, Joe had included the name of a presiding rabbi and the contact information for the leader of the *Chevra Kadisha*—the special volunteer group of individuals who would perform the ceremonial preparation of the body.

The letter also included instructions about where to place funeral notices, a budget range for the coffin, suggestions about choice of music, a specified charity where donations could be sent in lieu of flowers, plus a half-dozen telephone numbers of individuals Joe had particularly wanted to be present at the final ceremony. It was all very neat, thorough, and pragmatic, but ended with a personal postscript specifically just for Flam:

My dear young friend,

It is clear to me you are (as some of my more metaphysically inclined peers would say) an "old soul" who appreciates the place death has in the universe. After all, you have chosen to work in death's constant presence.

Nonetheless, I suspect you may be troubled, and perhaps puzzled, by the circumstances of my departure from the world. Surely you know that, for many who are dying, it is only the will to live—a sort of spiritual stubbornness—that keeps our hearts beating. I believe this was the case with me, for I should have been dead many times before and long, long ago. But, finally, and with your help, I have managed to resolve the last outstanding items of business in this physical life, and so, with no reservations, speed happily towards the next, for I am so very, very tired of living, and will be blessed if I can indeed depart on my own terms.

It also gives me supreme pleasure to have you conduct the final arrangements for my corporeal remains, for I know you will carry the responsibility with professionalism, dedication, and aplomb. I always believed in doing business, whenever possible, with people I knew personally. Getting to know you, no matter how brief our friendship may have been, allows me to follow this practice to the end. And, towards that end, in addition to your conventional duties, I am also requesting you write the final epitaph for my headstone. Izhak Szabo is the executor of my estate, and a separate fee for the performance of that creative duty has been included in the financial details, for I fully trust you to fulfill the commission. I offer no suggestions, for not only do I have the utmost confidence in your talent and poetic sensitivity, and know you will craft something I will be very proud of, but I also wish it to be a surprise for me.

May our mutual God, and any others who care to do so, bless you, and grant you health, a long life, and the happiness you deserve.

Your good friend and sincere admirer,
Joash Jacob Schneider.

By the time he had finished reading the note, a fine mourning mist had enveloped Flam's eyes. He turned to look out the hearse's passenger window, not wanting Bruno to see him in that state. The tears, however, were less for Joe, and more for Flam himself. Despite Joe's flattering words and the trust the dying old man had just placed in him, Flam felt betrayed and abandoned yet again. He did not share the same weighty confidence others were expressing in him. How was he expected to continue to find the strength and courage to face his miserable life all alone, especially when the people he truly cared about did not themselves seem to care in the least about deserting him?

As they neared Morton's, Bruno let loose a long sigh, and Flam's attention returned to inside the hearse, and to thoughts of the goings-on at the funeral home. He suddenly was reminded he had at least managed to salvage one friendship by clearing Charlie's name—not to mention having artfully delved out some well-deserved retribution to the perpetrators of the injustice. This brightened Flam's mood a little.

As if on cue, Charlie himself was there waiting when they backed the hearse into the funeral home's garage. Flam's heart leapt at the sight, and he bolted from the hearse as soon as it stopped. He wrapped Charlie in a big hug, although his arms proved unable to complete their circumnavigation of the Fijian's giant bulk.

"Good to see you, man," Charlie said through a wide toothy grin worthy of a shark. "You did it."

"Oh, wow, Charlie . . . it's so good to have you back."

The bright look on Charlie's face dampened, and he pointed down to a cardboard box lying at his feet. "Um . . . I just came back to pick up my things, and to write Mr. Morton a cheque for the damage I did."

"What? They're not going to give you your job back?"

Charlie shrugged. "Don't want it back. I'm going home, Flam."

"Home? You mean to Fiji? But why?"

"Remember when I told you I'd promised the demon goddess Lilavatu a sacrifice? Well, she held up her end of the bargain, now I have to hold up mine."

"I don't understand. What sacrifice? Why do you have to leave?"

"I promised I'd sacrifice my life in this new world and go home to my own people. When I get there, I have to build a new boat—a dugout canoe—and burn it. Only then will my debt to Lilavatu be settled."

"That's crazy," Flam protested, vaguely aware he sounded like some whining child but not caring. "You can't really believe in all that pagan mumbo jumbo."

"'*There are more things in heaven and on earth. . .*'" Charlie retorted. "I'll tell you what I *do* believe, and that's a promise must be kept, even if maybe it turns out it's just a promise I made to myself."

"'*And this, above all, to thine own self be true,*'" Flam offered, since *Hamlet* had been brought up.

That earned a smile from Charlie, and he wrapped a tree-limb-sized arm around Flam's shoulders.

"I knew you'd be hep to it, DaddyO. Besides, this ain't totally new . . . me and the boys been talking about going back for a while now. Here, we'll always be second-class citizens. The white folks call us niggers, and the black cats call us pakis. Shit, just look at how quickly everyone here believed I'd done in that dog. Man, back home we'll be cool cats. The band will have a new lease on life too, instead of the sorry-ass gigs we get around here. We've all been saving up our scratch, and first thing back home we're going to wax a disc and make a big splash."

"I . . . I don't want you to go," Flam said, his voice barely above a whisper.

"Hey, man, I'll miss you too, but time for ol' Charlie to split this train wreck and get a new scene." Charlie stuck out his oversized hand for Flam to shake. "Glad I met you, Flam Grub. You're jake with me, kiddo, and I know you're going to be okay. I'll write when I get home and I'll send you our CD. Maybe you can write us some more lyrics."

Bruno had been standing by, impatiently watching the exchange, and now he pounded on the back of the hearse. "Hey, you Grub, we don't have all day. In case you've forgotten, we've got a body back here to tend to."

Charlie chuckled and delivered a final slap on the back, which sent Flam staggering. "Your albatross is calling," the big man said, then without another word picked up his box of possessions and walked away, merrily whistling eight beats to the bar.

Flam returned to his duties, now dejected to his core by the morning's events. He wheeled Joe's corpse to the embalming room and unzipped the body bag, again fighting back tears as he looked down at the old man's passive face.

"Oh, Joe," he whispered. "Why are you all doing this to me? What am I supposed to do? How can I go on all alone?" Joe's serene expression gave no hint of an answer. Flam gazed down at the peaceful countenance, and felt an overpowering urge to take Joe's place on the table—to permanently leave behind the oppressing weight of his lonely, miserable life.

Flam's maudlin introspection was interrupted by the sound of the door opening. He turned and watched Hannah come into the room, absentmindedly holding the door open for an instant until she realized there was no dog trailing behind her.

She came over towards Flam, and for a minute he thought she was going to challenge him for trespassing on her turf, but she surprised him by enveloping him in a hug. Her small frame shuddered in his embrace, and when she pushed back to look at him, she seemed older, sadder, and more human than he'd seen her before.

"Thank you," Hannah said, smiling slightly. Flam supposed she was talking about the Pugsley and Steptoe affair, but wondered how on earth she had discovered Flam's role in dealing justice to the duo. More from caution than modesty, he opted to deny any involvement.

"What for?" he asked.

She smiled benignly and patted his cheek. "That's okay, dear, your secret's safe with me. But the police dropped by last night with photographs and this email confession from George Pugsley saying he and Josh were the ones who killed my Sarah." At this, she paused to spit at the ground before continuing. "Plus lots of other twisted, nasty business. Anyway, even though the sick perverts were falling over themselves to blame each other, the police still wanted to ask me a whole bunch of questions.

"Funny thing, though. There was a time printed on the email they showed me. The one thing the detectives never *did* ask me is how Pugsley was supposed to have sent that note when he and his sicko crony were off on a call with Bruno, busily hauling in that overweight corpse . . . right around the time my gal pal Fanny happens to have mentioned *you* were in the office working on her computer."

Flam shrugged and tried to maintain his neutral expression, although he suspected he might be blushing. "I'm so glad justice was done, for Charlie's sake, but, really, this had nothing to do with me. I'm sure there are a hundred other possible explanations."

Some of the friendliness drained out of Hannah's expression, and she appeared more her hardnosed old self as she snorted and turned towards the bagged body lying on the gurney. "Okay, have it your way. So what's the story with this stiff? The usual drain out and Draino in?"

Flam bristled a bit at Hannah's crude occupational humour. "No . . . no embalming or anything. He's an Orthodox Jew. Some of his people will be in to wash and prepare him, but not before tomorrow. Today's Saturday, and they won't work on the Sabbath . . . and besides, I haven't even phoned them yet."

Hannah absorbed the information and shrugged. "Well, I suppose we better get him stowed away into a meat locker then. Hmmm . . . can't remember the last time we had a Jew here. They usually go to the Kirsch Home on Wexler Street. So how come you're calling the shots on this one?"

"I knew him . . . he was a friend of mine. It was his specific request," Flam answered as they extracted Joe from his Naugahyde cocoon, and moved him into one of the drawers in the morgue cabinet.

Hannah chuckled. "Oh, I bet Bruno loved that one. You sure have an odd bunch of friends, Flam. Still, you watch out for them, and that's something."

Sure, I watch out for my friends, thought Flam as the stainless steel door shut on Joe's carefree face, *but my friends don't give a shit about me . . . don't care one bit about taking off to the four corners of the planet, or to the next world, and leaving me all alone.*

Making the arrangements for Joe's funeral service and burial were a welcome change from Flam's usual menial duties, although his shyness made it extremely difficult at first to telephone perfect strangers and initiate the conversations. However, once the subject of Joe's demise had been broached, Flam proved to have a polite, empathetic, and well-spoken telephone manner that universally comforted and impressed the people to whom he spoke.

Unfortunately, Joe's thoroughness in specifying the requirements of his own funeral, and Flam's efficiency in executing them, meant most of the required details were disposed of in a matter of hours. With the ranks of Morton's staff so heavily decimated by recent events, Flam inevitably found himself back down on his knees, cleaning and scouring again.

He was wiping down and disinfecting the staff toilet bowls when Bruno tracked him down in the early afternoon to inquire about the status of Joe's arrangements. Flam used the opportunity to press his boss about prospects of promotion in the coming new order. While Flam half-expected some coy, noncommittal, let's-wait-and-see put-off, he was shocked by the maliciousness of Bruno's response.

"Listen here, you Grub . . . just because you conned some old Hebe friend of yours into letting you run his burial, it doesn't make you a funeral director. Christ, you're just a kid who's barely been here a month. Can I ask you a question? Have you even gotten a down payment or a signed contract for that guy? No, I didn't think so. Well, if we get stiffed, it's coming out of *your* salary.

"Then there's your appearance. Frankly, I'm embarrassed for Morton's every time a customer sees you. You look like you're one of the living dead yourself, all the way down to that stupid name of yours. 'Hello . . . I'm Flam, Lord of the Grubs, come to feed on your dearly departed loved one.' They'd run screaming out of here! Yes, clearly we're going to have to hire some new staff . . . but that doesn't mean you're moving up into my turf. Count yourself lucky just to have a job."

Bruno stormed out, and left behind a tongue-tied Flam fumbling flaccidly for some sort of cutting retort. He angrily tossed the toilet brush aside, and hauled himself to his feet, feeling like he could barely stand up under the weight of the hostile universe crushing him.

A white, pitiable face stared back at Flam from the bathroom mirror, and he studied it critically, Bruno's scathing insults still stinging in his memory. He perceived only flaws—a weak chin, sunken and dark-ringed eyes, pale and pasty skin. It was a face utterly devoid of the heroism and strength they wrote about in his books. He couldn't bear to look at it any more. He closed his eyes and pressed his forehead against the cold surface of the mirror. It reminded him of how Joe's dead flesh had felt when Flam had touched it, and he again experienced a powerful urge for the cool finality of the grave. He wondered how it was Joe had seemingly managed to simply will himself to death, without any external force or agent.

Almost as if they had a mind of their own, Flam's feet carried him out into the hall and up the back stairs to the top-floor storeroom. The familiar gleaming coffin lay in its cradle, again beckoning him towards it. He opened its lid and slipped into the lustrous crepe womb. As he closed the cover, he was enveloped in a comforting darkness. Inhaling deeply, he tried to command his heart to simply stop beating, but the tension had the opposite effect, and he could distinctly feel the amplified rhythm of his pounding pulse. Impatient with his uncooperative organ, Flam held his breath instead, determined to bring about self-asphyxiation by resisting the urge to inhale. After a minute or so, however, the pained longing for air was so impossible to ignore he had no choice but to let in his breath with a huge gasp, followed by a sob of disappointment.

He lay in the darkness, contemplating his next move, wallowing in the sheltering darkness, and wishing it would last forever. He knew, however, death would not come (promptly, at any rate) simply by lying there. Any magical means lucky old Joe might have used to manifest his own death were not within Flam's power. No, some external tool would clearly be necessary for Flam's self-destruction. Whatever that as-yet-undetermined instrument of death might be, it lay outside the lacquered box.

Flam was in no hurry to leave his quiet, comfortable casket, though. He was drained and so very tired—not just from the week's sleep deprivation, but also from the painful events and constant erosion of hope in his miserable life. The darkness wrapped itself around him like a lover, and he felt protected by the fragrant wood surrounding him. He took a deep breath and relaxed.

A sardonic snatch of verse snuck into Flam's thoughts, and he found himself weighing it, then refining it, and tweaking it some more. It summed up everything he was feeling at that moment, and the entire laughable, lamentable human condition as well. So pithy and trenchant was the couplet, Flam wracked his memory to recall from whom he might be plagiarizing that particular bit of poetry, before conceding proudly he had conceived it himself. It struck him that the verse would be ideal for the epitaph Joe Schneider had requested—an appropriate closing punctuation mark for the old man's life, worthy of being carved in stone and lodged above his earthly remains for posterity.

As much as a childish part of him both resented and envied Joe for dying, Flam finally acknowledged that the old man was, at the core of things, blameless. Furthermore, Joe had entrusted him with a sacred responsibility. No matter how abandoned Flam might feel, it amounted to little more than selfish, petty petulance, and he realized he had a solemn duty to perform. Death would just have to wait. Right now, Flam needed to find a pen.

CHAPTER 33

On Sunday morning, the Jewish contingent converged zealously on Joe Schneider's remains, having first piously waited out the Sabbath. Flam watched in fascination as the group of volunteer men, who comprised the *Chevra Kadisha* at Joe's synagogue, performed the ritual cleansing of the corpse. An ancient, slightly hunchbacked rabbi, wavering uncertainly on his feet, but possessed of a fine, deep singing voice, delivered the appropriate accompanying prayers.

Afterwards, Joe's body was wrapped in a traditional white linen burial cloth, ready to be transported to its coffin, an exquisite oak-beech composite that had been imported a few years previously from Germany but never sold. Flam had reasoned that Joe, although he would be buried in the New World and had not set foot on his native soil in seven decades, would have appreciated the piece of his past provided by the imported casket. Flam also knew the price had been deeply discounted to move the merchandise and was a bargain, and so felt proud of the win-win situation the coffin's sale represented for both business and body.

In the early afternoon, Izhak Szabo showed up carrying a nylon suit bag, and a confused Flam wondered if he had misunderstood the Hebrew ritual of the burial cloth. It was certainly customary for relatives of Morton's non-Jewish customers to select the attire worn for viewings and internment. Flam had on a few occasions even helped Hannah wrestle clothes onto corpses, so he assumed Szabo had brought special garments to be put onto Joe, despite the prevailing custom.

The tailor, however, broke into a laugh when questioned, and held the bag up for Flam instead.

"No, no, my friend," Szabo said, looking extremely pleased. "This is *your* suit . . . the one I measured you for earlier this week. Have you forgotten so soon?"

Flam had certainly not forgotten, for each time Bruno had castigated him lately for being shabbily dressed, Flam was reminded that sartorial reinforcements were forthcoming. He had, however, avoided nagging Szabo about the matter, not only because the work was being done *gratis*, but also now because of the likely impact of Joe Schneider's death on the old man's protégé.

"Well, I guess we've both been a little busy," Flam said, opening the suit bag to inspect its contents.

"I made it according to Joash's specifications, may God take his soul. It is meant for daily wear, but is as fine a suit as I've ever made, if you'll forgive the immodesty." As he said this, Szabo was running his fingers across the shoulder seam of the jacket Flam was currently wearing, at the spot where Mrs. Clarke had previously sewn up the tear.

The suit was an appropriately sombre funereal black, much to Flam's relief. "It looks lovely," he said.

Szabo smiled. "Feel the material," he insisted.

Flam did as instructed, and when he stroked the cloth an appreciative smile came over his face to match Szabo's own grin. The fabric was seductively smooth and soft, reminding Flam of the lining of a top-of-the-line coffin.

"It's made from the finest Italian silk," Szabo cooed, clearly proud of his creation.

Flam blanched. Although this was beyond the experience of a poor kid from the inner city, he had nonetheless read enough to know the kind of opulence—and cost—Szabo was talking about. "Oh my gosh," Flam exclaimed, "I . . . I can't accept this. It's too much."

"Nonsense. It's a *fait accompli*," Szabo insisted. "Wear it in good health, and with my and Joash's blessing. Now, if you will do me a kindness, please put it on so that I, vain man that I am, may admire my handiwork."

Flam excused himself and adjourned to the washroom to change. Upon re-emerging, it was apparent even he could feel an immediate difference in the quality of the tailoring, just by the way the suit fit and felt. The garment followed his contours immaculately and accented the strong features, such as his long legs, while compensating for certain anatomical shortcomings, like hiding his habitually slumped shoulders with a touch of extra padding.

"Ah, much better," Szabo purred. But then he studied his product for a moment, shook his head, and suddenly pounced forward. Before Flam could resist, he had been stripped of his tie, and Szabo was knotting his own around Flam's neck. The tailor sighed as he expertly worked a Full Windsor, and slid it up into position. "I'm afraid this will have to do for now," he lamented. "Next week I shall bring you some proper shirts."

Flam protested. "Please, you've done so much already. I can't begin to repay you for all your kindness and generosity, especially since, I presume, you won't accept any payment."

"Oy, will you stop it! I've already told you, this I did for Joash, and I am glad to do so."

Szabo thought about it, however, and reached into his inside pocket to extract a small stack of business cards. "Tell you what. Should anyone ask about the suit, please give them my card. That will be payment enough."

Flam accepted the cards and pocketed them. "With pleasure. I must say, Izhak—and I don't pretend to know anything about it—this suit is fantastic. It just feels so . . . so right."

Szabo gave a formal bow of his head in acknowledgement of the compliment. "Then you have discovered a secret that is as old as civilization. Clothes make the man, and the tailor makes the clothes. Ergo, the tailor makes the man."

Szabo gave Flam one more critical look, and reached into his inside pocket to extract a small tube. He squeezed out a clear lotion, and rubbed it between his hands. "If you will permit me one last alteration," he asked, and when Flam nodded his consent, Szabo quickly rubbed the lotion onto Flam's head, then extracted a comb and smoothed back the hair.

"*Voilà*," Szabo pronounced. "And now that we have put an end to this bit of business, perhaps you can tell me how the arrangements are progressing for dear Joash's farewell from the physical world."

Flam filled him in on what had been accomplished to date, and told him that the service and burial had been scheduled for the next day.

"That's within the three days dictated by Jewish custom," Flam pointed out. "Since the remains are not embalmed, we'll keep him refrigerated until just prior to the ceremony, especially since he was quite old and was being treated for cancer. He looks quite peaceful though. I don't think there will be any problem with an open casket service."

"Good. I see Joash was wise to choose you for the arrangements."

Flam shrugged off the compliment. "Joe pretty much made his own arrangements, but I'm very glad to be of service. Mind you, my boss is somewhat unhappy about one thing . . .."

"About the lack of a down payment or a contract, no?" Szabo prompted.

"Yeah. How did you know?"

"You forget, Flam, I too am a business man. So let's dispense with this outstanding irritant right away. If you will be so kind as to prepare the invoice, I would be only too glad to pay it in full."

"There's one other thing, too," Flam added, "the inscription for Joe's tombstone."

"Ah, yes, he intimated you were a poet as well as an undertaker, and that he was entrusting you with the creative assignment. Have you finished?"

Flam nodded, and after a brief moment of panic when he thought he'd lost his notebook, before realizing it was still in the old suit, he flipped to the appropriate page, and read out loud to Szabo the proposed epitaph for Joash Schneider. The tailor seemed genuinely moved by the poetry, and placed his hand on Flam's shoulder.

"I am not schooled in such matters, but I think it's beautiful, if perhaps a little cryptic and dark . . . but somehow I think Joash would have approved."

"Do you think so?" Flam asked. "I don't mention God directly, and I know Joe was a religious man."

Szabo chuckled. "Joash was a pious man in his devotions—mostly out of guilt, I think, for having forsaken his religion in his youth, and having not died with his family as a consequence—but I always got the impression that, as he grew older, his mind grew more open, and he sought a grander design."

"Grander than God? Is that possible?"

"Joash used to say that a God is only as great as His followers . . . go around the corner and He may cease to exist."

Szabo retrieved a chequebook from his inside pocket. "You know that Joash allocated a separate stipend for this poetic commission. As his executor, I deem it fulfilled."

It was Flam's turn now to turn down payment. He shook his head. "That's okay. You and Joe have been so very kind to me. It's the least I could do. I don't want the money. It was only one verse anyway, so please consider it a gift. Morton's Funeral Home, on the other hand, will not be so generous with their expenses. I'll go get an invoice made up . . . why don't you make yourself comfortable here in the foyer, and I'll be back in a bit."

Although he had worked with the home's accounting software and was fully capable of generating an invoice, Flam knew it was not something he was allowed to do on his own. Being a Sunday, Mrs. Clarke was not in, so Flam had little choice but to seek out Bruno for assistance. Before doing so, however, he used the master price catalogue to prepare an itemized, handwritten list of the costs so far, plus those that would be incurred the next day for the service and trip to the cemetery for the final internment.

Flam then tracked down Bruno, finding him brooding in his office, evidently contemplating the misfortunes of the past forty-eight hours. He barely acknowledged it as Flam slid the paper across the desk and explained the listing, until the words "payment in full" were spoken, and then The Hell Man stirred to life.

"Damn, you Grub," Bruno groused. "You should have done this yesterday when Mrs. Clarke was in . . .." But then he stopped in mid-sentence, and stared at Flam with a peculiar expression.

"Er . . . I know how to generate an invoice," Flam offered, puzzled by the odd look on Bruno's face. "I could print one off if you let me." Bruno still said nothing, even as he slid out from behind his desk and came closer. Flam resisted an urge to step backward as his boss approached. "So? Can I go ahead and do the invoice?" Flam asked. Bruno still gave no indication he had heard Flam's words but then, as The Hell Man reached out and fingered the lapel, the focus of his trance was revealed.

"That . . . suit."

"Do you like it?" Flam asked, giving a half-turn to afford a better view. "I just got it today."

"It's . . . it's absolutely magnificent. Where on earth did someone like you get a suit like *that*?"

Flam smiled. He was tempted to throw the previous day's "Hebe friend" comment back into Bruno's face, but opted to exploit the opportunity instead. Flam reached into his pocket and handed Bruno one of Szabo's business cards. "In the small-world department, my tailor is the one waiting for the bill for Mr. Schneider's funeral. You remember Mr. Szabo. He's down in the foyer. Why don't you go talk to him while I pop onto Mrs. Clarke's computer and print off an invoice?"

When Flam returned to the foyer, he was amused to see Bruno standing poised like a statue while Szabo, who apparently never travelled without the tools of his trade, recorded The Hell Man's specifics.

"Flam," Bruno called out merrily, as if addressing an old chum. "Did you know Mr. Szabo here learned his trade on Savile Row in London?"

Flam attended patiently while the tailor finished his measurements, and wrote them down on a swatch of paper that magically materialized from an inner pocket. Szabo then shook hands with Bruno, who gave Flam a friendly pat on his back before returning to the office.

Flam whistled. "Wow. I've never seen him in such a good mood before," he told Szabo. "He almost seemed human."

The tailor chuckled. "He told me he's been looking for a decent tailor for two years. I think perhaps he will become a good customer, albeit a demanding one." Szabo noticed the printout in Flam's hand. "Ah, you've brought the bill. Good . . . one more final detail we can dispense with."

CHAPTER 34

It was almost 9 p.m. before an uncharacteristically merry Flam was able to make it to the prenuptial-cum-farewell reception being held for his mother and Lee Cuff. Whether it was due to a mellowing of Bruno's mood, or just circumstances brought about by a dire shortage of staff, Flam had not spent the remains of the workday mired in his usual menial chores.

In addition to managing the flower orders for an evening service, he had been allowed to drive by himself to the morgue at a local hospital to fetch a newly released body. Bruno, happy to be able to strike while the iron was hot (and corpse was cold), had also exploited Flam's newly revealed skills with the office's software to obtain a contract and invoice during the course of the evening.

The celebrants at Bootleg Bill's were well lubricated by the time Flam arrived. He pushed his way through packs of tipsy policemen, who were clearly enjoying themselves, judging from the animated conversations and uninhibited laughter as they wavered on liquefied legs. He found the guests of honour at the bar, surrounded by a retinue of hard-looking, hard-drinking men who seemed cut from the same cloth as Cuff.

"Hey, look who's here!" the groom-to-be exclaimed happily upon catching sight of Flam. In his haste to leave his bar stool and embrace the new arrival, Cuff spilled part of his drink, but his tottering movements testified that a good portion of alcohol had otherwise safely found its way into the bloodstream.

"Wow, man. What kept you?" Cuff asked, seeming genuinely happy to see Flam. "The slave drivers had you working late again, eh?"

"Yeah, I'm dead-tired," Flam acknowledged, not intending the pun, but nonetheless pleased when it earned a gargantuan guffaw from the cop.

"Good one," Cuff laughed. "Hey, speaking of which, I gotta introduce you to the guys." He guided Flam to the edge of the circle of men, and raised his voice to garner attention.

"Gentlemen, your attention please. I want to introduce you to Mary's son, and my future stepson, the one, the only . . . *Flam Grub!*"

There was a brief moment of silence, then the group exploded into a loud roar of laughter, with one of the cops actually falling off his barstool in the process. Flam was infuriated that he had been brought over just to be purposely and publicly embarrassed. He could feel the blood racing to his face, as the familiar humiliation from his cursed name struck home yet again.

Then the realization overtook him that the men were not laughing out of derision, but out of delight. Appreciative cries of "No way" and "Are you kidding me?" emanated from the gathering, and a grinning Cuff was clearly revelling in the revelation. The cops practically fell over one another to shake Flam's hand and slap him on the back, one of them exclaiming, "I *loved* that movie," and another, "Oh, wow, you're freaking famous." Cuff, spotting an opportunity, ordered a round of shots, including one for Flam, and solemnly pronounced a toast: "To our very own Flam Grub."

Through all this, Mary had been beaming quietly on the periphery of the clique with a proud, happy look on her face. As the emptied shot glasses came clattering down loudly on the bar, she rose and came over to give Flam a wet kiss on the cheek and a long hug.

"Hello, dear," she said after finally releasing him. "You look very nice this evening."

"And right back at you, beautiful," Flam retorted, the infectious mood of the celebration, and the double shot of rye, going straight to his head. But he meant what he said. His mother was dressed in a pair of shape-hugging designer blue jeans, and wore a tight-fitting, low-cut white cotton top that testified to the fact that, even after three decades and one child, Mary's breasts still piously faced upward towards Heaven. Her hair was pulled back in an unprecedented ponytail, making her appear almost girlish, despite the fact that she had a grown son and was pregnant with another child. Flam could not recall ever having seen her look more beautiful. She seemed happy too—as animated, in fact, as any soused soul in the place, though Flam was pleased to see that, out of deference to the fetus within her, she was drinking only ginger ale.

"You know why they were toasting you, don't you?" she asked.

Flam nodded. "I haven't seen the movie yet, but I read all about it," he explained, almost apologetically. "I guess I should go see what all the fuss is about."

"Lee took me to see it this afternoon," she said. "It was much too violent for my taste, but, sweet Lord, I just couldn't believe my ears when I heard that actor say your name. The theatre was quite crowded, you know, even though it was the afternoon matinee, and at the end, when the hero gets back on his feet to . . . well, I won't spoil it for you, but all the young people around us started chanting 'Flam Grub, Flam Grub' out loud. Good heavens, what an experience."

Cuff joined them carrying a pair of replenished shot glasses, and forced one into Flam's hand. "What are you two going on about?" he asked before finding that Mary's neckline required a kiss and nuzzle.

Mary giggled. "Lee, stop it, you're positively brazen," she chided, but made no move to push him away.

"My mother tells me you guys saw *The Graveyard Poet* today," Flam said, annoyed with himself at the jealousy he was feeling from the couple's intimacy.

"Damned right," Cuff laughed, then started chanting, "Flam Grub. Flam Grub." Behind him a number of the revellers took up the intonation for a few iterations before terminating in a whoop and another round of downed shots.

"So, how does it feel to suddenly be famous?" Cuff asked.

"Well, I'm not exactly the one who's famous. Through some bizarre twist of fate, I've suddenly found myself sharing the same dumb name as some popular fictional character, that's all. I mean, how the hell did they come up with that same name for a movie?"

"Search me, but you should be thrilled . . . the flick's setting box office records, and you could become your own minor celebrity in the process."

"Ha! My name's never caused me anything but grief . . . and I don't see how this is going to help in any way."

Cuff shrugged. "You never know. Flam Grub's got cachet now . . . it's kind of like your own personal brand recognition."

"You have no idea what it's like to be ashamed of your name."

"Are you kidding me? Do you know what Lee stands for? It's short for Hanley—it was some great uncle's name. I hated it, and always went by Lee. Then, in Grade 3, one of our teachers insisted on addressing each of us by our full names, and the kids found out, so they started calling me Han . . . and it stuck with me all the way through high school."

Flam thought about it for a second, then smiled. "Oh, I get it, Han Cuff."

Cuff frowned, clearly still sensitive to the matter. "Yeah, it's always funny when it's someone else."

"So I take it then the kid's not going to be called Hanley Cuff II," Flam suggested.

"Not on your life. If it's a boy, it's going to be Tom, and Jane, if it's a girl."

"Tom Cuff . . . that's okay," Flam said.

Cuff grinned. "Your mother hasn't told you?"

Flam's eyes went from the cop to his mother, searching for some clarification. "Told me what?"

"It's Flam, dear," Mary told him, then when Flam's vacant expression showed that he still didn't understand, added, "not Cuff . . . the child's surname will be Flam."

Flam looked at Cuff to see if this decision displeased him in any way, but the cop grinned benignly and draped an arm lovingly around his betrothed.

"And you're okay with that?" Flam had to ask.

"Sure . . . it means the world to your mother, and that's good enough for me. Hell, I'll call the kid Attila the Hun if it makes her happy."

"Oh, Lee, stop it!" Mary chided, feigning anger, but rewarding her man with a kiss on the cheek anyway.

"That's amazing," Flam sighed, again biting back a flash of jealousy at the romance that had blossomed in his mother's life. "So, is everything set for the honeymoon?"

"It's not a honeymoon . . ." Flam's mother started to say, then caught herself. "Oh! I guess it will be, once we're married." The idea clearly had appeal, and a goofy smile pasted itself on her face.

"It's all taken care of," Cuff confirmed. "Turns out, it's a stock service at the resort we're staying at. They've arranged for the license, the minister, flowers, photographs, the whole kit and caboodle."

"I hope you don't mind too much that we're not taking you along," his mother asked, "but we just want it to be the two of us, with no fuss. Maybe you can come visit us at Christmas."

"Christmas? How long is this honeymoon going to be?"

Cuff gave Mary a stern look. "You haven't told him?"

"I haven't had a chance," Mary snapped back. "I hardly see him anymore, do I? And I've been so damned busy getting ready to leave."

"*Hello* . . . I'm right here," Flam interrupted. "What's going on? What haven't you told me?"

"I've got my thirty years," Cuff explained. "Hell, I was just a kid when I joined up really, so I'm taking early retirement. An old buddy of mine works for one of the big casinos in Freeport, and he's gotten us both jobs—security consultant for me, administrative assistant for my beautiful bride."

"Wow, not exactly church work, is it, Mother?" Flam commented sarcastically, fighting hard to combat the anger unexpectedly coming to a boil inside of him. He had already felt alienated by his mother's impending remarriage, and now the betrayal was complete—outright abandonment as she and her lover jetted off to live in the Bahamas, and left him to wallow in the cesspool of his empty, meaningless life.

"The hell with them," Mary retorted angrily, a nerve apparently having been touched. "I've worked my ass off for those hypocrites for almost twenty years, and when have they ever shown me an ounce of gratitude?" She seemed to catch herself, and blushed with the realization. "I don't owe them anything. I haven't taken any vows."

"What about me?" Flam asked weakly, not having meant for it to be out loud, and certainly not intending to sound as petty and pitiable as he did. His mother looked startled.

"Oh, Flam, what are you saying?" she asked, coming over to press against him. "You're an adult now, living on your own." She reached up and stroked his cheek. "Even as a child, you were always off in another world—someplace where I didn't belong. I never thought you needed me . . . you never seemed to need anyone."

Behind them, the celebrants at the bar exploded in laughter over some shared joke, and Flam remembered where he was, and what the occasion was being celebrated. He forced a smile, and gave his mother a hug.

"It's nothing, Mother . . . forget about it. I'm just going to miss you, that's all. But I'm happy for you, really, I am." He glanced at Cuff, who had been looking sheepishly down at his feet during the whole exchange. "I'm so happy for you both," Flam told him, offering the cop his hand. "No matter what, I know she's in good hands. Hey, how about a toast to the bride and groom?"

Afterwards, when the happy couple excused themselves to say goodbye to some departing guests, Flam headed off to the picked-over buffet table in search of whatever leftovers might remain to help soak up some of the booze in his belly, which was starting to have its effect. As he was assembling some rye bread and corned beef, a stranger strode directly over and curtly introduced himself as Art Barker. The man had a big plastic smile, which stood out from a well-tanned face, attire that was noticeably smarter than the other guests, and a poised, confident manner about him.

"Did I hear right?" Barker asked pointedly. "Your name is Flam Grub?" Flam nodded, and uneasily bit off some of his sandwich, wondering where this was headed. "I mean, that's your real name," Barker pursued, "not a stage name or something like that?"

"Yeah, that's right," Flam admitted, wishing for the umpteenth time in his life it wasn't so.

"And you didn't go to court and have it changed to Flam Grub?"

Flam shook his head. "Hell, no, it's my birth name."

"So, what's your full name?"

"That's all there is. It's just Flam Grub. No middle name."

"And Flam . . . is that short for something?"

Flam was starting to get annoyed. "No . . . listen, what's this all about?"

Barker softened his tone. "C'mon, just humour me. It's nothing bad . . . might even be a big deal for you. Can you prove it? Do you have some ID or something with you?"

Flam grudgingly put down his sandwich, fished out the driver's license from his wallet, and held it up for Barker to study, generating a big, satisfied smile from the stranger.

"Well, I'll be damned. Listen, do you have a card or something?"

In fact, Morton's Funeral Home had not considered its junior member to deserve his own business cards, causing Flam to frown as he shook his head no.

"Well then, how about giving me your phone number or email address?" Barker persisted. When Flam's reluctance became apparent, the man added, "Listen, there might even be some money in it for you."

There was something intangible in the man's expression that won over Flam's reticence. "Okay, fine . . . I'll give you my work number," he consented, so Barker produced a BlackBerry, into which he keyed the number Flam dictated to him.

As he studied the entry, Barker seemed as delighted as a kid who'd scored a big-time autograph, and then he extended his hand.

"A pleasure meeting you, Flam Grub . . . I hope to be talking to you very soon," he said, somewhat formally. His eyes flitted admiringly over the fabric of Flam's suit, before turning and plunging back into the crowd, without any further explanation of the reason for his interest or the nature of the potential moneymaking opportunity.

The party appeared to be waning now, although the clique of hardcore merrymakers at the bar was still celebrating with Bacchanalian abandon. Their drunken din managed to compete successfully with the room's stereo system, which continued to throb vintage rock-and-roll, even though there were no couples out on the dance floor. Flam looked around, feeling a little lost, and decided that he needed another drink too. He grabbed a few wilted carrot sticks, and headed for the bar.

CHAPTER 35

The Girl on the Bus had never looked lovelier. Despite being hung over and sleep deprived, Flam had taken an earlier bus than usual, reasoning he needed to get a jump on his busy Monday at the home, and was surprised and delighted to see The Girl come on board. She was wearing a black, hip-hugging skirt, and today's version of her habitual white blouse was sleeveless and unbuttoned just far enough to reveal the top of a peach-coloured camisole.

As much as he found her physically attractive, it was The Girl's little mannerisms that provided an endless source of fascination for the admiring Flam. Her upper lip would curl with appreciation when she read a particularly engaging passage, and she would then habitually tuck a forelock of hair behind her ear and stare up at the roof of the bus, evidently memorizing the stanza. The way she held her book was almost reverent, and she turned the pages slowly, with a clear sense of anticipation.

When an opportunity presented itself, Flam changed seats. He slipped into an available spot immediately behind The Girl, and instantly lost himself in her tantalizing closeness. He had to fight an urge to lean forward and stroke the exquisite nape of her slender neck. Today's book, he discovered after some discreet craning of his own neck, was the *Rubaiyat of Omar Khayyam*, large slices of which he knew by heart. The very thought of this amazing woman also sharing a passion for such poetry sent tremors of emotion through Flam.

Is it possible to fall in love with someone you don't even know . . . with whom you've never exchanged even a single word? Flam wondered, even though his pounding heart and sweating palms were already bearing testimony to the truth. With his subject so near that the inspiration practically hung like a vapour, Flam pulled out his notebook and continued crafting his poem about The Girl, his own unopened copy of W.H. Auden's *Look, Stranger!* serving as a writing surface.

Engrossed in his composition, he didn't see The Girl's stop arrive. As she rose, she half turned and glanced at him, taking in the book and the open notepad, before her gaze moved upwards, and for the most fleeting of moments locked on his. As Flam watched her exit the bus, taking a playful little jump as she stepped onto the sidewalk, whole new paroxysms of feeling swept through him like a runaway bushfire. Admittedly, his experience was limited, but this growing powerful attraction to The Girl on the Bus was unlike anything he had ever felt for a woman before, as different as a volume of poetry was to a technical textbook.

Lucy, he recognized now, had been an infatuation, sparked by close proximity to her beauty—and, no doubt, constant exposure to her pheromones—and fueled by his personal desperation, plus a misinterpretation of her friendliness. Angel, on the other hand, had been nothing more than an interpersonal romp in the park—a physical attraction that had reached its wet, sweaty zenith, but would have been foredoomed to disaster in terms of any sustained relationship, so disparate were his and her respective mindsets and personalities.

In both cases, as devastating as the departure of the woman had been for Flam in the short term, he now realized he was better off in the long run. If either woman had chosen to stay—to use and abuse him, and purposely exploit his naïve sensitivity for her own selfish purpose—the scope of the inevitable final betrayal and abandonment would have been far greater, and the post-apocalyptic emotional fallout significantly more poisonous and far reaching.

So why did he think The Girl on the Bus would be different? Was it simply because Nature had randomly arranged her features and limbs in a pleasingly symmetrical way that approximated some societal ideal? Although Flam felt The Girl's face was one he could stand to look into every day for the rest of his life and would retain its appeal well into old age, he also knew his attraction was far more than mere physical yearning. Nor was it because The Girl evidently possessed a degree of intelligence, and seemed to share his love of literature. Flam realized she could easily be some academic hostage forced to absorb the books under pressure, and might not even appreciate their essence.

The powerful force behind Flam's attraction to The Girl, he was forced to admit to himself, was something else—some ineffable quality. It was as intangible as the auras Angel claimed to see, pulling him as inexorably towards The Girl as a plant is drawn up through the soil in springtime in search of the sun.

Flam sighed. It was probably just as well he didn't have the nerve to approach her. He was only sparing himself the inevitable heartache of rejection and ridicule. What was he going to do—sit down uninvited next to her some morning and introduce himself? "Hi, I'm Flam Grub?" The name had been humiliating enough before, and now she would probably think he was some weirdo wannabe, pretending he was a character from a movie.

Flam flipped to the back of his notebook, where he'd previously written out dozens of possible new names for himself. *Maybe now's the time*, he thought, *everyone's gone and I'm left all alone. Maybe it's time for a new name and a new start*. He tried a few on for size, picturing himself seated next to The Girl on the Bus.

Hi, I'm Penn Wilde. Hi, I'm Gawain Melville. Hi, I'm Eliot Frost. Any one would be a blessed salvation from the accused Flam Grub, and yet, as always, none of the prospective names sang out with that primal perfection on which he sought to stake his whole identity, his very being. After a while he gave up his onomastic gymnastics, and returned to writing his poem.

An unfamiliar vehicle was parked directly in front of Morton's garage doors when Flam arrived for work. The lettering on the side of the battered white Astro van read simply *Salvador and Sons, Service*, but did not elaborate on what the exact nature of their service might be. Wondering if some new calamity had befallen his workplace, Flam hastened inside, and almost stumbled over a short, stocky man kneeling near the door. The stranger was dressed in matching green work pants and shirt, and was patching a crack in the concrete floor using a glob of mortar from a white plastic pail.

The man muttered something indiscernible, but after sizing Flam up, gave a deferential nod and held his tongue. Somewhere further inside the building, the drone of an electric motor could be heard. Flam followed the sound to find another, younger man in an identical green uniform pushing a venerable industrial-grade Eureka over the hallway carpet. The cleaner looked up briefly, and in his critical, hard-eyed stare, Flam could immediately see the family resemblance to the older man he'd bumped into back in the garage.

Another Salvador son was in the process of restoring the inner office door when Flam stuck his head in, looking for the orders of the day. A smiling Mr. Morton, supervising the carpentry operation and clearly pleased to see order being restored in his dominion, waved affably at Flam, and directed him down to the morgue, where Joe Schneider's body was being groomed for its final journey.

"He's almost ready," Hannah Leetch said, putting aside the scissors with which she had been trimming Joe's beard before dabbing a final touch of blush on the cadaver's cheeks, gently using a Kleenex to rub the make-up over the pale skin. "Get the coffin, will you, dear?"

Flam fetched the casket he had selected for Joe, noting with amusement as he wheeled it down the hall how the cleaner working the rug hastened to make room for the coffin's passage. The worker was unaware the casket was empty, but seemed excited to finally see evidence of death here in what would otherwise be just another mundane venue to vacuum.

After Flam and Hannah had transferred Joe's remains, Hannah pulled out an atomizer, and sprayed something around the casket's interior. She smiled at Flam.

"My own special concoction," she explained. "The odour probably wouldn't have been noticeable, but we don't want to take a chance people will start turning their noses up during a long ceremony." Flam nodded, fighting to maintain his professional detachment. He tried to remember this was no longer Joe, but just a slab of dead meat ready for disposal, and yet, in the sleeping face, he could still see his friend, whose life had touched his profoundly even in such a short period of time.

Hannah read Flam's mood and placed a hand on his shoulder before reaching over to close the casket. She turned and took Flam's face in her fingers.

"When Sarah died," she told him softly, "I brought her home, and laid her down in her doggie bed. I sat there the whole night, just staring, waiting . . . like she was going to wake up any minute and start wagging her tail. Funny, huh? Someone who deals with dead people every day, and I'm sitting there, unable to accept the reality of death when it touches me directly, like I figure I'm immune, or entitled to some special treatment just because it's my job. Finally, around four in the morning, Sarah's body begins to smell, and that's when it hits me she's gone, and that I'm just staring at one more corpse. I took her down to an old church cemetery a few blocks away, and buried her off in a quiet corner, under a maple tree. I guess it wasn't exactly legal what I did . . . sort of a grave robbing in reverse."

"How did you come to have Sarah here with you in the first place? I would never have imagined a funeral home allowing it."

"About seven years ago, I went with Bruno and Morton on a pickup at a rooming house . . . it was an all-women's place, so they figured it would be a good idea to have me along. Well, this dog— Sarah—was there, guarding the body, and didn't want to let anyone near it. She was still just a puppy, really, but was barking and snapping at anyone that came close. But she calmed down when I talked to her, and she let me pick her up. The landlady didn't want her . . . said the dog shouldn't have been there in the first place, so I took Sarah back to work. I guess we grew on one another. When Morton told me to get rid of her, I threatened to quit."

Hannah smiled at the memory, but there was a hint of tears in her eyes. "I miss her terribly . . . my husband died years ago, and we never had kids. Sarah was all the family I had. I'm glad you nailed those two bastards." She seemed to remember something else then, and her lips closed into a hard line. "I'm ashamed to say now I called Charlie some pretty nasty things when I thought he'd done it. I'm sorry I didn't get a chance to apologize . . . he kind of left in a hurry."

Flam hugged Hannah, wanting to reassure her all was forgiven, although knowing Charlie had left bearing bitter resentment towards those who had been so quick to condemn him. Some day, Flam hoped he'd get a chance to pass on the apology.

The door gave a squeak, and Bruno came into the embalming room, hoisting an eyebrow at the intimacy of the scene before him. He opened his lips, and Flam could almost see a cutting remark taking shape, but the mouth suddenly shut. When The Hell Man spoke, it was simply to ask, "All set?"

They wheeled Joe to the main chapel in silence. Flam was still too intimidated by Bruno to inquire whether the new cleaning crew was a permanent arrangement, and if his own duties were to change as a result. But other than explaining the arrangements for driving to the cemetery—Bruno would take the hearse, Flam the lead limousine, and Hannah a second limo, while Morton stayed behind to mind the home—Bruno left Flam alone to run the service, not rebuking or criticizing him even once. At one point, Bruno reached his hand towards Flam, and he had to fight the reflex to recoil. Bruno, however, simply wanted to brush away a piece of lint from the lapel on Flam's new suit, doing so with all the care and tenderness of a parent adjusting a runaway lock of hair on a favourite child.

Joe's funeral ceremony was far better attended than Flam had possibly imagined. The guests who had come to pay their last respects were soon standing at the rear of the main chapel, then spilling out its doors into the hallway. Joe had mentioned he was an elder of his synagogue, but his popularity clearly spread beyond his own Jewish circle, and the congregation included an eclectic mix of faiths, ethnicities, and age groups.

As the people were filing in, Flam was approached by a petite, dark-haired, attractive woman who appeared to be in her late thirties. She was in the company of a tall, well-groomed, blond man a few years her senior.

"Are you Flam?" the woman asked. When Flam said yes, she introduced herself as Ester Sharp, Joe's estranged granddaughter.

"This is my husband, Colby," Ester told him, although Flam had guessed as much. "I just wanted to say thank you," Ester continued evenly, radiating the confidence and willfulness Joe had described. "Grandpapa told me you were the one who helped him get in touch with us ... he said you even tracked down Colby's email address for him."

"I was glad to help . . . I liked your grandfather a lot. He loved you so much, and deeply regretted the falling out."

"That was my doing ... I can be pretty headstrong," Ester said, emotion entering her voice for the first time. "If it hadn't been for you, he might have died without me saying sorry, and telling him how much he meant to me . . . how much I owed to him."

"I get the feeling he wouldn't have let that happen," Flam replied, "that the need to make up with you was the one thing that kept him going."

Ester smiled sadly. "I think you're so right. In his last note—after we'd made up and taken turns apologizing and forgiving and assuming the blame—he told me he felt like a great oppression had been lifted from his flesh, and he felt eternal peace was entering him. I didn't think much of it at the time, but it's like he knew he was about to die. When he didn't email me the next day, I just knew something had happened. Then Izhak phoned, saying Grandpapa had passed on the number I'd sent him, and I found out what had happened. I agreed Colby and I would come and sit *Shiva*, seeing as we're the only living relatives left, although there was no shortage of volunteers to fill in."

Ester smiled and lifted a foot to show Flam her shoe. "See, no leather . . . and no perfume or make-up either. Mind you, Colby here was somewhat aghast at wearing canvas shoes with a black suit, not to mention going unshaven, and not showering after a trans-Atlantic flight." She added in an undertone, "He's none too crazy about the no-hanky-panky rule either . . . oh, Colby, are you blushing? That's so sweet. I may be a card-carrying goy now, but Grandpapa raised a good little Jewess."

Flam was pleased, for Joe's sake, that Ester had agreed to attend, and was choosing to observe the traditional Jewish funeral customs. He gave her a conspiratorial wink. "I hope that's not his good shirt," he said with a sly grin, remembering it was also customary for the seven primary mourners to have their shirts ripped—known as tearing the *kria*.

"What does he mean?" Colby asked. Ester and Flam laughed.

"Come on, love," Ester said, taking her husband by the arm, "I'll explain it to you as we find our low stools."

Colby seemed resigned to yet more indignities. "Low stools?" he muttered weakly as he was led away.

In the doorway, the same ancient rabbi appeared who had been present the previous day for the ritual preparation of Joe's body. The rabbi stared in consternation at the crowd before him, as if the Red Sea itself were impeding him, until Flam hurried over to usher him in. Following a brief consultation, the service began.

After the traditional and religious rites had been completed, a series of speakers came to the front to elegize Joe. With the exception of Izhak, who told the touching story of how, as an orphan, he had been taken under Joe's wing and taught the tailor's trade, none of the orators was familiar to Flam. Through their narratives, a fuller picture of the remarkable old man began to unfold. They were all identical in the generosity, tolerance, wisdom, and humour they portrayed, but each added a new chapter to the life of Joash Schneider beyond the snippets already known to Flam.

He learned that Joe had once strong-armed a local politician to approve the building of a neighbourhood mosque. On another occasion, Joe had beaten off a mugging attempt by a juvenile thug, then stood before the judge to plead leniency for the troubled youth. One speaker related how, to keep his mind sharp in old age, Joe had memorized something new every day, from a complete inventory of world capitals, to entire scenes from the plays of Goethe, his favourite author.

During the war years in London, spent safely sewing in quiet obscurity the way Joe had told it, he had saved a trio of tots from the collapse of a flaming building during an attack by the infamous V-1 rockets, also known as buzz-bombs or doodlebugs. He had eschewed acknowledgement of that deed, and his heroism had only been recognized when he ended up at the same hospital as the children for treatment of the severe burns he had sustained during the rescue.

Afterwards, during the trip to the cemetery, the rabbi, who rode in the back with the Sharps and Izhak Szabo, related some of the heated debates he'd had with Joe. The cleric told how he had once become so enraged by Joe's insistence that the Jews had become like abused children who themselves grew up to become abusers, and needed to be more tolerant of their enemies—"to turn the other cheek, as the prophet Jesus once instructed us"—that the rabbi had threatened to excommunicate his heretical friend.

"'Go ahead!' Joash taunted me," the rabbi recounted with a fond smile as Flam watched through the rear-view mirror. "'You may have the keys to the temple, but do not believe for a minute you hold the keys to Heaven.' I like to think I have become a more tolerant and open-minded man, and this I owe to Joash Schneider."

During the solitude of the drive back to Morton's—after the graveside ceremony had been concluded, the passengers dropped off, and goodbyes rendered—Flam began to feel his mood steadily darken. The distraction that the activity of the past few days had offered was now gone, and he felt alone and powerless. It was as if all the profound grief from the mourners at Joe's funeral had been compressed into a single malignant cloud, and was being channelled into Flam's psyche, like air rushing into a breached vacuum. He considered his miserable, isolated state, and could not imagine further enduring a lifetime of lonely, wretched days—abandoned by even the few he had cared for, and destined to serve as the butt of fate's cruel whimsies.

He marvelled at how Joe had managed to keep his faith as a fortress against life's adversities, while still having the courage to examine and even question that faith. Flam's own beliefs—although what precisely those might be he was at a loss to define—could supply him no such sustenance. Nary a single deity offered so much as a glimpse of its possible existence. His soul, if he had one, did not choose to commune with him, and all the words he had greedily devoured like a glutton over the course of a lifetime provided no spiritual sustenance.

If Joe had been privy to some fundamental life-altering wisdom, he had failed to pass it on, and now he lay dead and buried—mouldering beneath the ground in an imported coffin, discounted 20 per cent to move the merchandise.

Whatever honour Flam had initially felt at being anointed to direct Joe's funeral seemed meaningless now. It had all just been a business transaction with an astute old acquaintance, Flam told himself. He could not possibly have held any special distinction in Joe's life, especially in the face of the testimony of so many others who had known him much longer, and far better.

The sign for an upcoming on-ramp came into view, and Flam opted to take the freeway to expedite his trip across town. As he sped along the expressway, he passed under the very same bridge where he had stood as a teenager, and had contemplated hurling himself to his death. The sun was high in the sky, and as the concrete sliding overhead spilled its shadow across Flam's windshield, he vividly recalled that past moment of anguish and despair. In memory, it felt no less painful than this one, and he looked up, half-hoping to see, in the shining corona of the structure's eclipse, some dazzling holy apparition come to save him.

Flam recalled having read somewhere a theory that suicide statistics failed to take into account those people who ended their lives by purposely crashing their cars—any potential social stigma for the

surviving family, not to mention insurance disputes, neatly resolved
in the process. He glanced down at the steering wheel to see if the
limousine possessed air bags, and seeing none were installed, was filled
with a sudden impulse to finally perform the self-destructive deed he
had contemplated so often.

Flam jammed down on the accelerator pedal, and was thrust
backwards into the plush leather seat as the vehicle's powerful engine
roared and its speed increased rapidly. His heart was pounding like a
jackhammer as the limousine hurled along on the edge of control, and
Flam stared at the geography that rushed towards him, trying to select
the perfect location for his crash. He did not want to take a chance he
might botch the job and be left a helpless, drooling cripple—an added
ignominy to the spiritual paralysis that already handicapped his life.

Up ahead, an overpass and its massive supports rose into view.
Flam observed that the giant concrete pillars sat on a paved strip that
was barely a dozen yards from the road, and miraculously were not
segregated from the highway by any guardrail, nor surrounded by any
crash protection. Instinctively, he knew this was the right spot. With
the speedometer showing a speed of 200 kilometres per hour, his
vehicle was sure to be totally obliterated by a head-on collision, even
with the protection of a large front hood and heavy metal body. In
that fiery union of cement and steel, Flam's lifetime of suffering would
cease at last.

The moment of self-annihilation was just a few ticks away. Flam,
who had been fighting hard just to keep the speeding car centred in
its lane, tensed in preparation for swerving directly into the abutment
at the appropriate instant. He felt no fear, nor anticipation. Instead,
he only felt mildly disoriented, as if he'd already jumped off a high
structure, and was freefalling into oblivion.

Suddenly, he heard music, the clearly unmistakable chorus of
Beethoven's *Ode To Joy*, coming from inside the vehicle. Flam knew
the limousine had no radio—Charlie had told him once that Old Man
Morton considered it an unnecessary frill for a funeral conveyance—
and this music was certainly not being played by some otherworldly
orchestra, nor sung by a heavenly choir. It was a tinny, synthetic,

monophonic sound, and it was definitely coming from directly behind him.

Flam whipped his head around to look in the back seat, a lump in his throat as he imagined what mysterious unearthly entity might be seated there, but he saw nothing. In the few seconds his attention had been distracted by the mysterious music, the concrete pillar he had intended to crash into whooshed past him and retreated rapidly in the rear window, and with it the chosen moment of self-destruction dissipated.

The music had ceased but Flam, breathing heavily, with heart pounding, hands sweating on the wheel, and feeling strangely light-headed, as if he had just woken from some nightmare, took his foot off the gas pedal, and guided the car across the highway's lanes and onto the shoulder. Trembling, he put the vehicle into park, and just sat there, mesmerized by everything that had just occurred. He tried to make sense of it all, and to deal with the kaleidoscope of emotions that had just enveloped him.

Once again the digitized snippet of Beethoven chimed out. Now Flam spotted the source of the sound—a cellphone lying at the foot of the rear seat—and climbed into the back to grab the device. When he picked up the phone, he noted with wide-eyed shock that further blanched his already pale face the incoming-call display read "JOASH."

"Hello?" he answered, his hand trembling as he held the phone to his ear.

There was a brief silence, and then a woman responded. "Uh . . . hello. Who's this?" The voice sounded vaguely familiar.

"It's Flam Grub."

There was a self-deprecating giggle. "Oh, hi, Flam, it's Ester Sharp. I misplaced my cell, and was just calling myself to see if I could hear the ring. Thought maybe I'd accidentally packed it in my suitcase or something, but I guess I must have dropped it."

"Yeah, it was on the floor in the back of the limo."

"Crap, I'm always losing the damned thing. I'm going to have to get myself a holster or something. Well, thank goodness I found it. Just hang on to it for me, will you? We'll swing by the funeral home on the way to the airport to grab it."

"Say, Ester. The call display said 'JOASH.'"

"Yeah, I'm at my grandfather's place, just picking up some keepsakes."

"I like the ring tone."

She had to think about it for a second. "Yes, my dear old *zayde* loved Beethoven too."

CHAPTER 36

Hurricane Byron descended on the Bahamas with screaming, powerful winds that cut a deadly swath from Mayaguana to Bimini. The storm then bounced over towards south Florida in a bid to cause enough destruction to join Beulah, Betsy, and Bob on the list of permanently retired hurricane names.

Flam's mother had called once to announce the couple's safe arrival, but that was well before the storm's onset. When Flam tried to reach them later, he discovered the power lines were down and all telephone communications with the archipelago had been cut off.

The last news report to make it out of the islands before the blackout, which was now being replayed over and over by virtually every TV network, was from a gonzo BBC journalist trying to make a name for himself by standing in the teeth of the raging hurricane. The reporter had been killed on camera when a piece of corrugated tin roofing spun into frame at 200 kilometres per hour and struck him on the head.

Worrying about the fate of Mary and Lee did little to improve Flam's already melancholy state of mind. Not even the news that the presence of the custodial Salvador clan was going to be a long-term arrangement, thereby spelling Flam from cleaning duties, could brighten his murky mood.

It was Old Man Morton himself who let Flam know of his elevated status in the home's hierarchy, although the owner was quick to mention that it was not a formal promotion, and there would be no corresponding increase in salary. Morton had apparently been heavily lobbied in the matter by both Hannah Leetch and Mrs. Clarke, the latter urging that Flam be allowed to take over some of the computer-related office duties, especially since she was contemplating some elective surgery in the near future. Even The Hell Man had allegedly put in a grudging good word on Flam's behalf, albeit with the caveat that at least one additional hireling—someone larger and stronger— would be necessary for body removal detail, since Flam was not deemed physically suitable for the task.

Flam could not really complain about his vocational step forward, and was truly gratified that other employees had spoken up for him. Still, he was left with the distinct impression that both Morton and Bruno wanted to keep Flam behind the scenes, performing administrative support roles, and therefore away from the grieving customers he so longed to help. He recalled Bruno's earlier, scathing remark about the inappropriateness of the Flam Grub name for a would-be funeral director, and couldn't help wondering how serious The Hell Man had been when delivering that admonition.

Days went by and still Flam received no word from his mother. By now, Hurricane Byron had moved on and was drowning Dade County in a record-setting deluge of wind-whipped rains. Despite the media's new morbid preoccupation with the devastation in Florida, pictures of death and destruction were also surfacing from the Bahamas, and these vivid scenes only served to raise Flam's anxiety levels.

Although he felt guilty for placing it in the same league as the life-and-death worries over Mary and Lee's welfare, there was a further dampener on Flam's mood. The Girl on the Bus was missing from the morning commutes. Flam had even taken to rising an hour earlier, and getting on successive buses to try to find The Girl. He would get on each bus, wait to see if she got aboard, then disembark at the next stop and rush back to try the following vehicle.

After performing this futile on-again, off-again bus waltz each morning, Flam would finally give up and ride in to work defeated and crestfallen. *She's probably taking vacation or maybe she's gone on a business trip,* he rationalized, and then he would try to tell himself to be realistic. *Why should I care anyway? She doesn't know me . . . we've never even exchanged a single word.* Still, no matter how much he tried to soften the psychological blow, it felt like more rejection and abandonment.

The Girl's unexpected disappearance from his life became just one more sad disappointment sapping his already sagging spirits. With each new day of frustration, the poem Flam had been writing to The Girl, which was already rife with heart-rending themes of unrequited love, took an even more plaintive tone.

Mrs. Clarke's absences from the home were becoming more frequent and prolonged, and Flam was glumly growing resigned to his new role as a designated backroom paper pusher. Still, the job had its advantages. For starters, he had a new schedule, and was no longer expected to work late into the evenings. On the night of his Wednesday class, he was able to leave in plenty of time to make it home, change out of his suit, grab a quick snack, and walk to the campus.

Flam realized he was now attending the Comparative Religion class more out of habit than any hope he would learn anything new or might experience the divine epiphany he had longed for when he first enrolled. Without the presence of Angela or Joe, the class that night felt especially pointless and empty. Professor Abbott droned on about the history and tenets of Buddhism, preferring, as usual, to catalogue its myriad facets rather than examine any spiritual profundity.

The credos of the popular Eastern religion seemed to lend themselves in particular to the teacher's dry approach. Flam soon felt like he should be entering the content into a spreadsheet as Professor Abbott tediously inventoried Buddhism's dogmatic keystones—The Three Jewels, The Four Noble Truths, The Noble Eightfold Path, The

Five Precepts, The Three Marks of Conditioned Existence—as if he was reciting an accountant's ledger. At the break, Flam collected his books and simply left, deciding on the spot to drop out of the course, and not caring about the black mark it would leave on an otherwise exemplary academic record at Prentice College.

During the walk home, he found himself pondering a passing comment Professor Abbott had made that Buddhism was sometimes considered more a philosophy than a religion, primarily due to its absence of a Supreme Deity. In his own Catholicism, a single moment of sincere repentance would guarantee a place in Heaven despite a sinner's past deeds—"*the grace of God is found between the saddle and the ground*" the old proverb went. Buddhism, on the other hand, required a lifetime of stringent devotion for a practitioner to accumulate enough karmic points to have a shot at nirvana.

It was much easier, he conceded, to look for salvation outside than within, and perhaps that was his problem. Whenever he pondered the vastness of the universe in all its entropic perfection, he instinctively felt the presence of some greater force—call it God—but it was beyond comprehension, too large to be able to get his arms around. All he truly had—all he'd *ever* had—was himself, and in the end wasn't that the crucible where true spirituality was forged? There was a commonality among all religions that preached the need to purify oneself—to strive for perfection through morality and meditation. Perhaps God lay hidden inside every one of us all along, obscured by the walls of want and delusions of the flesh. At Joash Schneider's funeral, one of the elegists had described how the old man was fond of Goethe, and a snippet of that poet's verse returned to Flam: "*We are our own devils; we drive ourselves out of our Eden.*"

It's true, Flam pondered. *I sure know how to bedevil myself, don't I? That's the irony. Everyone is looking for the meaning of life, like it's some great hidden secret, but all the answers we need sit in plain sight all along. I've read thousands of books, but if I treat the knowledge they contain as abstraction and don't put it into practice in my own life then I'll end up . . . well, I'll end up right* here.

The next morning, Flam was quietly keying some new items into the product inventory program, marvelling as always at the hefty markups, when the telephone rang. He practically dove across the desk to grab the receiver before Old Man Morton, who was napping in his inner office, could take the call. Moments like these were Flam's only opportunity to directly interface with the public. He knew there was a good chance the caller might be someone who had just suffered a loss, and might be in need of consoling.

"Flam Grub, please," a male voice said, the transmission somewhat faint and stippled with static. A lump rose in Flam's throat, as he had the sudden trepidation some distant official was calling to notify him of his mother's death.

"Speaking," he replied, and held his breath.

"Flam, baby!" the man exclaimed enthusiastically. "It's Art Barker." When the silence at Flam's end betrayed a lack of recognition, he added, "We met the other night at Bootleg Bill's. You gave me your number."

"Oh, yeah," Flam replied, remembering the brief encounter with the tanned, pushy stranger who had quizzed Flam about his name. "What can I do for you?"

"Flam, I know it's really, really short notice, but how'd you like to be on *The Billy Reno Show* tonight? They'll pay for the trip, and will toss in four thousand bucks to boot."

It took a second for Flam to digest what he had heard. Although he preferred books to the boob tube, his ancillary reading and web surfing excursions nevertheless roamed far enough afield for him to be fully aware of who Billy Reno was—a silver-haired television icon, and for decades the undisputed master of the late night television talk-show . . . which begged an obvious question.

"Why on earth would Billy Reno want me on his show?"

"You're gonna love this," Barker answered, his enthusiasm practically gushing over the phone line. "Brock Harrow's going to be on the show tonight plugging *The Graveyard Poet*. So, when I told the producers I could get them a *real* Flam Grub, they loved the idea . . . you know, kind of a fantasy-meets-reality sort of thing."

"So, what would I have to do?" Flam asked, still skeptical.

"Nothing, really, other than maybe pose with Brock and Billy for some publicity shots. Hey, it's a talk show . . . you just come on and talk. That is, unless you got some talent you want to show off. Do you, like, sing, or juggle, or do stand-up or anything like that?"

"Well, I do write poetry . . . ."

"Poetry? Well, whatever. Listen, kid, they really only want you for your name, but it's still a fantastic gig."

Flam hesitated. Somehow it just seemed to him like yet another potential instance of being ridiculed because of his name, and this time the joke would be shared by millions of viewers. He expressed these doubts to Barker.

"Are you kidding me?" Barker retorted. "You've got it all wrong. Being on TV automatically makes you special, even if you just spend your whole career taking pies in the face. And this ain't some local amateur hour we're talking about here . . . it's *The Billy Reno Show* for chrissake! Guys wait their whole lives for a shot like this. I'm telling you, you'll be fighting the chicks off with a stick. And let's not forget the money . . . four K's not bad for one night's work, wouldn't you say?"

"Well, I don't know about fame, but I admit I could certainly use the money. It's awfully short notice, though. I mean, what are the logistics? When would I have to leave? When would I get back? I'm not sure I can get any time off work."

Barker explained the details. If Flam consented, a first-class ticket would be booked for him on a late afternoon flight to New York. Barker, who was already in the city, would be waiting at LaGuardia Airport with a limousine to bring Flam into Manhattan for the show's broadcast. After that, the network would have its corporate jet on standby for Flam, and he would be able to return home that very night.

"Tell your bosses this is their chance for some great publicity," Barker persisted. "If they give you a hard time, *I'll* have a talk with them."

There had, in fact, been no resistance whatsoever from either Old Man Morton or Bruno. It turned out that Morton had been plagued with insomnia ever since his son's drowning, and habitually prowled the late night TV channels as a consequence. He was a devoted fan of Billy Reno, and almost never missed a show.

"This is a fantastic opportunity, my boy," Morton proclaimed, pounding Flam enthusiastically on the back. "Why, just think, our very own Flam on TV. *The Billy Reno Show!* Imagine that. Well, I couldn't be more excited."

Bruno, on the other hand, was a little more pragmatic. Taking Flam aside afterwards, Bruno put his arm around his underling's shoulder and muttered conspiratorially, "Try to sneak in a plug for Morton's when you're on the air. Be subtle, though . . . act like it just slipped out naturally. It'll be great for business."

Then he looked Flam over and asked, "What are you going to wear on the show?"

Flam shrugged. "I hadn't thought about it and nobody's said anything. Something casual and contemporary I guess . . . maybe my jeans and a pullover."

Bruno rolled his eyes and shook his head. "No, no, no. Trust me. That look only works for rock stars. Billy Reno's legendary for the clothes he wears—although admittedly he doesn't have to pay for them. You should dress to impress. If you really want to look trendy, then ruffle your hair and forget the tie . . . but wear a white shirt and definitely that black suit. Black always looks great on camera."

Bruno chuckled, and a smile materialized—the first Flam had ever seen on that face. "I'm normally in bed by eleven," Bruno told him, "but I'm definitely going to stay up late tonight." He offered his hand and Flam, tottering on the verge of shock from the change in The Hell Man's manner, took it. "Good luck, Mr. Grub," said Bruno.

CHAPTER 37

Flam had never been on an airplane before. Since the dark inner passenger within him was almost hoping for a plane crash, there was no fear of flying to distract him, and with all the services and privileges of a first-class seat, he thoroughly enjoyed his flight to New York. He had gotten mildly tipsy en route, mainly due to the unwavering attention of an efficient and flirtatious flight attendant, and had happily passed his time completing and polishing his "Ode to The Girl on the Bus."

As promised, Art Barker was waiting at the airport with a limousine, and played tour guide during the drive into Manhattan. Barker pointed out the requisite landmarks to an ogling Flam, who felt like he had fallen headfirst into some neo-classical American novel, so familiar to him already were all the place names.

At the television studio, Flam continued to be treated royally, and was so busy being pampered and fussed over he had no time to become nervous about his impending live appearance. The hair-and-makeup artist, one Millie Barber, was a highly skilled veteran who, while appreciating the steady, well-paying work *The Billy Reno Show* afforded, seldom got to show off her true abilities. She gleefully seized upon Flam's passing comment that he wished his hair looked more fashionable. He emerged out of Millie's chair with the sort of casual and stylishly unkempt look that can only come from an hour of meticulous cutting and blow drying.

As show time approached, Flam was ushered to the Green Room, where guests were typically sequestered before being announced and led out onto the set. Billy Reno had a legendary *modus operandi* of not welcoming guests beforehand, wanting their meeting in front of the audience to be spontaneous and sincere. Flam ended up having the luxurious waiting room, which included a bar, several widescreen TVs, and a mini-arcade of video games, entirely to himself.

The other guests on that night's show, as Flam learned, would be cutting it close, arriving in tightly orchestrated intervals just in time for their on-air appearance. Brock Harrow, the *ersatz* Flam Grub, was dropping in on his way back from emceeing a roast. The other A-list guest, reclusive rock-and-roll legend Christmas McZeal, was down the hall in a recording studio laying down a guest soundtrack contribution for an episode of one of the network's smash prime time dramas.

One of the things that made *The Billy Reno Show* notable, aside from the celebrated status of its longstanding host, was the fact it was broadcast live, not prerecorded—an obligatory two-minute delay as required by the network's censors notwithstanding. While the seconds ticked down to the start of the show, a palpable electricity filled the air as the frenzied production team wrangled near-chaos into the slick, on-air presentation that still clung to the number one position in its time slot after twenty-five years, albeit precariously of late.

Flam watched, utterly mesmerized, contrasting what he saw on the television set with the behind-the-scenes view of the proceedings as seen through the Green Room's huge window, which took up almost an entire wall. The show started routinely enough, with its famous theme song and introduction, followed by Billy's legendary monologue. It was after this segment that the show's viewership would wane each night, as millions of viewers across North America turned off their sets and went to sleep, while others channel-hopped to see what guests were on the competing talk shows.

Flam instantly saw the tension that overtook the broadcast as they readied for the crucial final hour of the show, and it soon became apparent Billy Reno was not the mild-mannered and affable host he appeared to be on camera. This night in particular felt like a disaster in progress, and Reno was soon nervously smoking cigarettes, barking orders, and swearing at the production staff during every commercial break or cutaway.

First of all, Christmas McZeal was late walking down the hall from the recording studio, forcing the production team to launch into a back-up skit featuring Reno's co-host and perennial second banana, Amos Bush, known more for his booming, patronizing laugh than his acting skills. While the comedic interlude seemed passable on camera, Reno was nonetheless visibly fuming as staffers were sent out to drag McZeal onto the set.

When the musician, dressed in tattered jeans and a faded T-shirt, did finally walk out from behind the curtain to riotous applause from the audience, there was something odd about his behaviour. It made Flam wonder if McZeal had been drinking, or partaking in some sort of recreational pharmaceutical.

McZeal had brought along his famous guitar, Lulu, but seemed more interested in silently fingering some phantom composition on her strings than engaging Reno in meaningful conversation. The rocker seldom even raised his head, and his replies were either monosyllabic near-grunts, or barely audible disjointed ramblings. Reno made the most of it, regurgitating all the latest news that had been provided by McZeal's publicists, and mugging incredulity for the camera during the bizarre replies. At one point, he subtly mimed a drinking gesture coupled with a jerk of his head towards his guest, breaking up the partisan audience in the process.

When the prearranged moment came for Reno to ask McZeal to join the show's house band to play something off his latest CD, the musician shocked everyone by declining the invitation.

"Aw, man, not right now . . . maybe later," McZeal told his wide-eyed host, "Lulu's been at it all day. She's, like, totally played out." As a groan went up from the audience, Reno tossed his pencil up in the air in a gesture of mock resignation, and rolled his eyes as he looked in the camera.

"We'll be right back . . . I think," he laughed. But as soon the director cut to commercial, Reno's smile evaporated, and he was out of his chair, looking like he was about to pummel the recalcitrant musician. The host had to be physically restrained by the assistant producer, who grabbed Reno by the arm and led him off to the side for a conference.

Flam could not make out the substance of their conversation, although the pair's heads repeatedly swivelled in McZeal's direction, and the assistant producer kept looking anxiously at her watch. Suddenly, she brightened and gesticulated to the wings, where, larger than life as always, stood Brock Harrow, resplendent in an Armani tuxedo.

The look of relief on Reno's face was obvious as he climbed back into place behind his desk and waited for the break to conclude. Flam assumed the host would cut his losses with the uncooperative McZeal and immediately introduce his next guest, but Reno apparently had other ideas.

"We're back live with rock-and-roll legend Christmas McZeal," Reno said as soon as the band had finished its short musical introduction and the red light had reappeared on the principal camera. He turned towards McZeal and leaned a little closer.

"So, Chris, I know you've been out promoting your new solo album, *Dr. Jekyll in Naugahyde*, but what's all this I hear about an Ipso Fatso reunion tour?"

Through his window, Flam saw some of the house band members exchange looks, and a noticeable buzz rippled through the audience as well. Even Flam knew McZeal had been the lead guitarist for the Ipso Fatso group when it had reigned over the pop charts for several years, before breaking apart amongst bitter infighting following the death of one of the band members from a heroin overdose. Although Flam was not enough of a contemporary music fan to know all the fine details, he saw McZeal immediately stiffen, as if he had been jabbed with a cattle prod.

"What the fuck? Who told you that?" he exclaimed. Up in the control booth, the network censor jerked to attention and began bleeping out the expletives.

Reno played dumb. "Oh, I thought I read it somewhere," he said nonchalantly, although he was lying and no such article had appeared anywhere. "Something about a six-month world tour starting next January. Don't tell me Lulu wasn't invited."

"If that (bleep) bastard thinks he can steal Ipso Fatso out from under me he's got another (bleep) thing coming," McZeal raged, his face reddening. "That (bleep) pretty boy's got as much musical talent as a (bleep) organ grinder's (bleep) monkey . . . he did sweet (bleep) all on those songs he's got his name on . . . I did all the (bleep) work, and now he thinks he owns the (bleep) band! Well my lawyer's going to have something to (bleep) say about that."

Flam had no idea who McZeal was raging against, but Reno clearly did. "Are you saying you'd take your former bandmate Justin Thyme to court to prevent any Ipso Fatso reunion tour?"

"I'd personally rip that (bleep) (bleep's) heart out, is what I'd do!" McZeal retorted, then slumped back into his chair, stamped his foot like a huffy child and began to fret while fingering Lulu's frets.

Reno faced the camera, feigning surprise. "Wow, folks . . . there you go, you heard it here first. Sounds intense . . . and, hey, speaking of intense, it's time to bring out my next guest. His new movie is breaking box office records, solidifying his place as one of the biggest action heroes the big screen has ever seen. Ladies and gentlemen, please welcome Mr. Brock Harrow!"

Harrow made his entrance, staging a brief mock fight with an uncooperative curtain as he did so. He stood on stage eating up the audience's fervid applause for a few seconds before strutting over to shake Billy Reno's hand and take a seat. There was a comical moment of confusion as McZeal stood up to greet the arriving Harrow, then practically ended up in his lap when the two went to sit down in the same chair. Amos Bush, the co-host, had to guide the disoriented rock star to a new place on the adjoining couch.

After an exchange of pleasantries, Harrow got right down to shamelessly promoting *The Graveyard Poet*, to the point where even the normally patronizing Reno seemed uncomfortable with the unfettered self-aggrandizement. Once the obligatory clip from the film had been screened, affording Flam a first view of his cinematic alter ego, Reno tried to guide the conversation into other territory. Harrow, who earned a percentage of its gross revenue, kept stubbornly returning the conversation back to the movie.

Reno's annoyance became obvious. At the next commercial break, as Millie Barber, the make-up artist, was hastily summoned onto set to touch up Harrow's face, the host stormed off backstage for another quick cigarette. The assistant producer hurried over to him for a quick conference, and shortly afterwards she popped into the Green Room to fetch Flam.

"Alright, Mr. Grub. It's time," she instructed him. "You're going on in a couple of minutes. Billy's going to finish up with that blowhard Brock, then improvise a segue, so just stand behind the curtain and wait for your cue." She looked him over, and seemed satisfied with what she saw. "You look great, so just relax, follow Billy's lead, and have yourself a pleasant chat, okay?" She guided him into position and gave him a reassuring pat on the shoulder.

For the first time since arriving in New York, Flam felt nervous as the proverbial butterflies rose to dance around his stomach. A host of other assorted worries also took flight and began to flutter around his thoughts, finally focussing on suppressed concern for his missing mother and her paramour, and this managed to take his mind off the impending public appearance.

"We're back with Brock Harrow," Reno's voice announced from the other side of the curtain. "Say, Brock, did you happen to catch the President's comment the other day?"

"Why, no, Billy. What was he doing . . . promoting my movie?" Harrow joked.

"Well, you could almost say that. He was reacting to the latest threats on U.S. citizens, and he said, 'They keep pushing us, figuring we won't fight back, but if they keep it up they're liable to find out they're dealing with Flam Grub.' What do you think about that?"

"I think I should send the president an autographed copy of *The Graveyard Poet*, saying Flam Grub is behind him 100 per cent," Harrow crowed, giving the cheering audience a big thumbs-up sign.

It was just the opportunity Billy Reno was looking for. "Well, as a matter of fact Brock, Flam Grub is behind *you!*" he said, clearly relishing the element of surprise. Harrow stared at the host vacuously, brow furrowed as he tried to understand what was going on, although the practised, glimmering, camera-ready grin never left the movie star's face.

"I've got a real surprise for you, Brock. My enterprising producers have been busy little beavers, scouring the continent, and they've managed to track down, and bring here for a very special exclusive guest appearance . . . his first time ever on television . . . none other than *Mr. Flam Grub!*"

The band broke out into the theme from *The Graveyard Poet*, and the audience, prompted by flashing *Applause* signs, starting clapping, sight unseen. The assistant producer gave Flam a little shove, and out he stepped onto the brightly lit set. The audience's enthusiasm spontaneously picked up when they set sights on the black-clad, black-haired young man. Flam acknowledged them with a wave, and headed over to dispense with the handshakes and game of musical chairs as the other guests shifted seats to make room for him.

"You two have never met, have you?" Billy Reno asked Flam once the applause had died down, gesturing towards a speechless Brock Harrow.

"No, sir," Flam conceded, then turned towards Harrow, "but I just want to say what an honour and privilege it is to share the stage, and my name, with such a talented and storied cinematic personality." It was said so sincerely and politely, the audience again broke out into applause, this time without any prompting from studio signs.

Reno quickly covered the basic biographical background of age and place of birth, and then asked Flam how he had come by his unusual name.

"Well, Mr. Reno, my parents had a fight . . . and I lost," he answered, earning a big laugh from the spectators.

Reno smiled wryly and returned to his note cards. "It says here you used to be teased a lot because of your name, and once even considered changing it. So how does it feel to have such a famous name now?" Flam was surprised by the depth of the personal information. He realized it must have come from Art Barker, who had engaged Flam in seemingly casual conversation about his past during the drive into Manhattan.

He was suddenly tempted to launch into a rant about how much he had always despised the name, and how its legacy of pain and humiliation still cast a debilitating shadow over him, but the significance of the setting predominated. He remembered a comment Page Turner had once made during stage directions to the boy Flam reciting on the bookstore counter. Theatre was not about being true to yourself, Turner had told him, but about being true to what the audience wanted you to be.

He grinned, and gestured ostentatiously about the stage, as if to say, "Just look at all this," catching and acknowledging a supportive look from Christmas McZeal in the process.

"Well, you could say it's growing on me by the minute." That garnered another round of spontaneous applause, and to Flam it felt as if the audience somehow understood his life had not been easy, and this moment of tribute, although not deliberately sought, was nevertheless deserved.

The sly look on Billy Reno's face let everyone know something juicy was coming. "Now, Flam, I understand that you're an *undertaker* in real life. Wow! What's that like?"

"I've really only just started," Flam explained. "Mostly I do odd jobs, some administrative stuff on the computer, and occasionally they let me help with the body pickups." He leaned towards Reno as if he were taking him in his confidence. "But, Billy, what I really want some day is to *direct*."

The take-off on the classic Hollywood gag caught Reno by surprise, and he laughed so hard he almost snorted coffee out his nose, and all the spectators unabashedly followed suit. Flam grinned sheepishly, relishing the inimitable sensation of having connected with an audience, but nevertheless feeling like he had to explain himself.

"No, but seriously, Billy, I know my profession gets a bad rap sometimes, but I consider it a grave responsibility . . . no pun intended. Death is perhaps the single most feared and awe-inspiring aspect of our lives, and it's been that way since we were first able to ponder the universe. Many anthropologists consider the advent of formal funeral rites to be one of the earliest signs of intelligent behaviour, helping to denote our graduation from *homo erectus* to *homo sapiens*, so I consider myself the trustee of a solemn, sacred trust as old as humankind."

After an evening spent trying to drag intelligent conversation out of an erratic, spaced-out rock star, and a self-promoting Tinseltown popinjay, Billy Reno was finding this talk pleasantly stimulating. There was something about the young man that fascinated him—a rare combination of innocent eagerness and arcane wisdom, with a hint of soulfulness forged by suffering. Knowing full well his body language alone would influence how the viewers accepted the guest, Reno leaned forward on one arm and let them know he was truly listening.

"And as varied as humankind," Reno suggested.

"That's so true. Different cultures, both today and in the past, have had an amazingly wide variety of practices governing the dead and dying. What can I say? I find death absolutely fascinating."

And so, Reno knew, would his audience. "Tell me about some of the more unusual funeral practices you've heard about," he prompted.

So Flam did, describing how mummies in Egypt had their brains pulled out through their nostrils with special tongs, then how a ritual slitter cut the body for removal of organs—but because this was paradoxically deemed to be defiling the body, the perpetrator was then ceremonially chased after by others, who hurled insults and pretended to try to stone him.

He talked about the Eastern practice of dressing the deceased in multiple layers of clothes, always odd-numbered, and of the steps taken in some Balkan villages to prevent the deceased from returning as a vampire. He explained about wakes, coins for the ferryman, Viking funeral ships, and several other traditions designed to help properly equip the dead for the afterlife. His eloquence, eagerness, and depth of knowledge were impressive and infectious, so that when the time came for the next commercial break Billy Reno hated having to interrupt him.

They came back on the air, and Reno asked Flam, "So, what about today, here in North America . . . if I came to you what kind of funeral would you recommend?"

Flam appeared surprised by the question. "Oh, no, Billy . . . it's not what *I* think, it's what's right for you and your family, whatever that may be. Which is why everyone should plan ahead. Hey . . . you only die once! If you wanted to be taken to the cemetery on a Harley Davidson, or have your head cryogenically preserved, or have your ashes blasted off into space, I'd be only too glad to oblige, because a funeral is partially a celebration of a life—a tribute to the person who has moved on to the next world. But, perhaps most importantly, my job is also to take care of the living, to make sure they're consoled, and comforted, and treated with fairness and respect." Out in the audience someone broke into singular applause, and his fellows enthusiastically followed suit. Flam turned and smiled at them in appreciation.

"So, what about you, Flam? What kind of funeral would you choose for yourself?"

"Hmmm, good question. I'd have to say of all the traditions I've encountered, I'm generally partial to the Parsi approach. After a lifetime at the top of the food chain, I think it's only fair that I return the favour by going to the back of the line, so to speak. So, after having a death mask made, I'd let the carrion eaters and insects have my body, and when they've stripped it bare to the skeleton, then dump my bones in an ossuary—that is if some medical school or prop-house doesn't want them. I've always found it funny how so many religions preach that the flesh is just a vessel for the soul, and yet they have all these hypocritical rituals for obsessing over a dead body."

Reno chuckled over that one. "So, tell me, what does Flam Grub do for relaxation when he's not ushering mortals into the underworld? Is there a special someone in your life right now?"

Flam blushed so deeply you could see it in the fifth row. "Not really, Billy, although there *is* this one girl I'm very, very fond of and I'm hoping to get to know better. As for my spare time, well, I guess I'm kind of a compulsive reader, and I love poetry."

"Poetry?" Reno exclaimed, this unusual and contagiously likeable guest having put him in an introspective mood. "Wow, can't remember the last time someone admitted to reading poetry. Did you know I majored in poetry back in my college days?" That admission generated happy hoots and clapping from the spectators, and Billy grinned sheepishly. "So, who's your favourite poet?" he asked.

"Oh, gosh, there's so many of them, Billy!" And Flam launched into a wildly enthusiastic praise of all poets, citing Blake, Dickinson, Shelly, Eliot, Yeats, Thomas, and Frost, explaining how they were all part of an ongoing ancient poetic tradition, like an eternal torch being passed from hand to hand. "Still, I'd have to say, overall, the ultimate poet is Shakespeare. Even his prose was poetic."

"Ah, The Bard, of course," Reno sighed, then quoted, "*Unthrifty loveliness why dost thou spend / Upon thy self thy beauty's legacy?*"

"*Nature's bequest gives nothing but doth lend / And being frank she lends to those are free,*" Flam responded.

Reno mugged an "I'm impressed" look at the audience. "So, do you do any poetry writing of your own by any chance?" he asked.

Flam hesitated, tempted to deny it, but he had found Billy Reno an empathetic and agreeable person to converse with so far, and saw no reason not to be forthcoming.

"Well, truth be told, I do write some poetry," Flam admitted. "In fact, I just finished a poem this afternoon on the flight here. It's dedicated to that girl I mentioned."

Reno smelled an opportunity and seized on it. "Well, hell then, let's hear it!" he exclaimed. He turned to the congregation. "What do you say, folks? Do you want to hear Flam Grub read his new poem?"

The spectators broke out into wild applause and started stamping their feet. Flam sat there stunned for a moment, trying to figure out how to escape this unforeseen predicament. In fact, he had not really expected the poem to ever be read by anyone else, truthfully not even The Girl to whom it was dedicated. But the audience sensed his reticence, and increased its insistence, now chanting his name, and it was obvious he could not decline.

"Okay," he assented, "I will." As the gallery thundered its approval, Reno guided the young performer to the centre of the stage where a microphone had been brought in, and the house lights dimmed.

Flam pulled out his notebook and flipped to the appropriate page. "I call this 'Ode to The Girl on the Bus,'" he told the listeners with a shy smile, and then he began to recite. In his mind the years melted away, and he was again the boy on the bookstore counter, performing to Page Turner and his inner circle.

So, Flam Grub proceeded to slowly and dramatically pour out his emotions in verse, painting a poignant image of his tragic life, using the smell of diesel fumes and the ugliness of the streets and the hollow expressions of the commuters as metaphors for his inner pain and disappointment and loneliness.

Behind him, the band stirred. They were all highly skilled and experienced musicians who, while they appreciated the steady employment *The Billy Reno Show* offered, seldom got to demonstrate their true virtuosity. One by one, they joined in, starting with the drummer, who had instinctually felt the rhythm in Flam's words, and together they raised a sad, soft, impromptu musical accompaniment.

To everyone's surprise, Christmas McZeal rose from his place on the couch. McZeal had been born in a speakeasy on Christmas Day, hence his name, and had literally been raised on the blues. Now he felt those blues calling him again. He strolled unbidden across the set, plugged in his guitar, and joined the ensemble, adding a sad, understated, virtuosic counterpoint to the haunting refrain.

Flam continued to recite, occasionally closing his eyes against the remembrances of pain the poem was conjuring. Then, like a soft evening breeze stirring the trees, the words picked up. He began to speak of The Girl, and how beautiful she was to behold, and how she represented hope, and love, and deliverance against the cruelties and caprices and despair that poisoned everyday existence. He spoke of how fulfilled and happy beyond words he would be, if only he could, somehow, bring The Girl into his life.

When he finished, there was an ever-so-brief moment of silence, seemingly hanging suspended in the haze of studio lights. For a second, Flam thought he had disappointed everyone—that his poem had been a complete failure—but then the audience started whooping and clapped louder than before. McZeal came over to give Flam a hug, then Brock Harrow joined them, and demonstrated his great strength by hoisting Flam up onto his shoulder like some victorious hero, and carried him back to Billy Reno's interview chair.

Reno stood up, and turned Flam around to face the audience. "Flam Grub, the undertaker poet, ladies and gentlemen," he announced, which was the cue for yet another raucous ovation.

The band started playing the show's theme song and Reno glanced at his watch. "Well, what do you know, we're out of time. I'd like to thank my guests . . . rock-and-roll legend Christmas McZeal . . . Chris, you're going to be on the coast next week, right?"

"Yeah, Billy, I do two shows in L.A. on Monday and Tuesday, then Seattle on Wednesday and Vancouver on Thursday."

Reno gestured to Brock Harrow. "And, of course, *The Graveyard Poet* is in theatres across the country. Go see it folks if you haven't already . . . .."

"Or go see it again, even if you have!" Harrow urged.

"And, finally, I want to thank my very special guest, Flam Grub. Flam, we loved having you here. Will you come back sometime?" Flam nodded dreamily, still in a daze over everything that had just occurred. Had he been a regular viewer of the show, he would have known he'd just received Billy Reno's trademark personal endorsement—a way of telling his producers, and the world, here was an up-and-comer worth a return engagement.

"And, of course, you'll be appearing at the body shop next week, as usual," Reno concluded with a grin.

"That's right, Billy . . . Morton's Funeral Home on Station Street. Bring us your dead!" *There, that ought to make The Hell Man happy,* he thought, joining the others as they waved goodbye to the camera while the theme song picked up and credits began to roll across the television monitors.

CHAPTER 38

Dozens of messages flashed their presence on Flam's voicemail when he got home, exceeding the capacity of his answering machine's memory. First he tended to the demands of Mephistopheles, né Mr. Whiskers, and had the placated pet purring at his feet. Afterwards, Flam sat in amazement at the strange syrupy voices that had materialized in a matter of hours, all pleading to meet with him, and proposing once-in-a-lifetime opportunities for public performances or lucrative appearances on other talk shows.

There was also now a business card from Art Barker in Flam's pocket, passed along just before the network's Lear jet had whisked their guest back home. Barker had predicted the avalanche of publicity the appearance on *The Billy Reno Show* would garner, and had formally offered to serve as the newfound celebrity's agent. Flam was now beginning to see the innate wisdom of retaining a professional representative . . . not to mention having his telephone number delisted.

Exhausted, he fell asleep reliving the surreal events of the past twelve hours. He had barely entered the first stage of sleep when he was ripped back to consciousness by a phone call. He had forgotten to close his blinds before collapsing into bed, and through the window he could see the magenta haze of coming sunrise on the horizon.

Assuming the call was from another intrusive show business type phoning with the mother of all offers, Flam rolled over and let the answering machine intercept the call. When he heard his mother's voice, he tumbled out of bed to pick up the telephone.

"Mother . . . is that you? Where are you? Are you alright?" Flam quizzed the receiver.

"Oh, Flam, darling, thank goodness. It's so good to hear your voice. I'm sorry for calling you so early, but I wanted to reach you before you left for work. I tried leaving a message last night, but your confounded machine wouldn't let me."

"Sorry about that. It's a long story . . . but I'm so glad you called. Are you guys okay?"

"Yes dear, we're fine . . . well, physically, at any rate, although we've just been through a horrible ordeal."

"Yeah, I saw the news reports. It said there was a lot of damage and quite a few people killed. I was starting to worry about you."

"You needn't have, dear. Between my Lee and my Lord, I was in good hands, although I must confess I've had the fright of my life."

"I'm so sorry, Mother. What a way to start life in your new home."

"Not *my* new home . . . I have no intention of living here. It was bad enough with that awful sun burning my poor, fair skin, and the constant humidity growing mould everywhere, not to mention sand getting into everything, but I'll be damned if I'm going to live in a place where the howling winds can come down and carry your house away. You should see the ruination it's caused, like Judgment Day itself. Besides, dear, the casino's badly damaged, and it may be a year before it reopens, so they've reneged on those jobs we'd been promised."

"So what are you two going to do now?" asked Flam.

"Well, Lee says we could squeeze by on his pension, and just do nothing, but I think we're a little young for the sedentary life, don't you? So he's contemplating doing some independent investigation or security consulting back home, and I'm thinking of returning to the church . . . well, at least until the baby is born. But this time I'm going to stick to helping those that truly need it. Heaven knows there are enough of those. I believe it's what the Good Lord wants me to do, and why He sent the storm."

"You're truly blessed if you believe God speaks to you directly," Flam told her. He regretted the words the instant they left his lips, and fully expected an angry rebuke.

Mary's reply was calm, almost condescending. "I think God speaks to all of us, dear, even to a know-it-all like you. The secret is to listen. You know, Flam, I feel sorry for you sometimes."

"Oh yeah? How come?"

"It's those damned books of yours. You've crammed your head with so many conflicting ideas you're afraid to trust any one of them, like you're worried you'll offend all the others. You need to find faith, dear."

"You mean *your* faith, don't you?"

"Nonsense, that's not it at all. I don't believe the Catholic Church is the one exclusive way to God, any more than I think the drunkards, and bombasts, and buggers you may find there cancel out the whole institution. God is not about the religion, the religion is about God . . . provided you let Him in."

"I feel like *I'm* the one that's been shut out," Flam complained.

"Listen, Flam. I realize I wasn't much of a mother to you sometimes when you were growing up. I punished you when I really wanted to get back at your father. That's why I know I'm blessed to be given a second chance for motherhood at my age, and I've promised God I'll do better this time." There was a deep sigh and a long pause before her voice came back on the line.

"Flam?"

"Yes, mother."

"You do forgive me, don't you?"

"Yes, mother . . . I forgive you."

"God bless you, Flam Grub."

"I hope so, mother . . . I hope so. If He can find me."

Again that morning, despite running back to his stop to board the same bus four times in a row, Flam saw no sign of The Girl on the Bus. Somewhere in his subconscious, he realized, he had been harbouring a tenuous hope that by reciting his poem on TV—publicly laying bare his innermost feelings for this elusive woman—it might have served as some preternatural incantation to draw The Girl to him and deliver her into his lonely life.

But what were the odds she would be watching that particular show, especially so late at night? She was, after all, an early-rising working girl. And even if she had been watching, would she recognize him, or know that he was talking about *her*? And, suppose all that was true. Why should she even care in the slightest for a gangly, pasty-faced ghost spotted on the morning bus?

Flam faced up to the unflinching, bitter reality of his folly, and made a pact with himself. *From this moment forward*, he told himself, *I'm going to stop making a fool of myself. No more hopping on and off the same stupid bus in a futile, quixotic search for fairytale romance. No more wasting my time on silly love poems to oblivious strangers.*

As he finally took a seat and rode resignedly downtown to work, Flam was positive he saw the occasional person peering quizzically at him. He wondered if one late night television appearance had been enough to shatter his anonymity, or if those people studying him were even sure why he looked so familiar to them. Just to be safe, he buried his nose in his current book, a hard-covered copy of *The Pilgrim's Progress*, and tried to look inconspicuous for the remainder of the commute.

He was later than normal getting in to work, and Mrs. Clarke was already at her desk. "Well, well, here's our very own celebrity at last," she called out merrily when he entered. Where Flam might once have coloured from the attention, now he simply smiled pleasantly and gave a little bow.

"Mr. Morton wanted to see you when you got in," she informed him. Flam nodded and headed towards Morton's office.

"No, hon, not in there," Mrs. Clarke corrected. "He's in the first consulting room." Flam spun to go in the opposite direction. "He's in with clients," she called after him. The information surprised Flam, for it was unprecedented for him to be included in such meetings.

When he reached the designated room, he wavered outside the door, nervous at the prospect of interrupting the conference within. *Come on, Flam,* he urged himself, *you just appeared in front of millions of people. This is a piece of cake in comparison.* The mental stratagem worked so well he had to be careful not to start grinning when he stepped into the room.

"Ah, here he is now," Morton called out upon Flam's entrance, as if they had all just been sitting around waiting for his arrival, although the paperwork in process on the table indicated otherwise. "Flam, I want you to meet Mr. and Miss Adams. They're making final arrangements for their grandmother. She passed last night."

"I'm so sorry for your loss," Flam told the couple, evidently brother and sister, who were sitting at the table, but they looked anything but bereaved as they rose to shake Flam's hand.

"Caught you on Reno last night," the man beamed.

"So pleased to meet you. I'm a huge fan," the woman added, as if she had been following Flam for years.

Flam mumbled his thanks and was invited by Morton to sit down and join the meeting, although it quickly became apparent to Flam that his presence was superfluous as Morton expertly walked the Adams through the catalogue of funeral services. Flam did notice, however, that the two clients would turn to him, almost subconsciously it seemed, for some gesture of approval before actually agreeing to any suggested purchase.

After they had concluded their business with the Adams, Morton was exuberant. "This is wonderful, Flam, just wonderful. The phones have been ringing off the hooks all morning, and they're all talking about you and *The Billy Reno Show.*"

Morton spotted The Hell Man in the corridor and called him over.

"Well, what do you think of my new rainmaker, Bruno? Too bad we couldn't have gotten *you* on TV years earlier, eh?"

"Yes, it's certainly good for the home," Bruno agreed, although his tone was less than enthusiastic.

"Good? Why it's fantastic. It's the best advertising we've ever had. I may have to hire some extra staff just for young Flam here . . . and we'd better get some business cards printed up for him pronto. Take care of that, will you Bruno?"

"Certainly, Don. I'll drop everything and get right on it." The sarcasm was practically dripping off The Hell Man's tongue, but Morton seemed oblivious to it as he walked off.

"Hey, maybe they should say 'Flam Grub, Undertaker to the Stars,'" he joked over his shoulder.

As soon as Morton was out of earshot, The Hell Man turned on Flam. "Well, Grub, you're not running the place quite yet. As long as you're still working under me you're going to earn your salary. Go and bring down a Number 12 Beech to Hannah. When you're done that, you can polish up all the caskets in the show room and clean the windows in the chapel. You've also got to make up the time you missed yesterday, so I hope you don't have any plans for tonight."

"I thought we had cleaners now, and I wasn't going to have to do that kind of work anymore."

"Do what I tell you!" Bruno snapped, and stomped away to prove the matter was ended.

Flam was left standing there with his mouth hanging open in shock. All the progress he had made recently raising his vocational lot in life seemed to have disintegrated. He felt the old familiar despair begin to wrap itself around him, like a thick, black mantle threatening to suffocate him and drag him down into the ground. Inevitably, the first notion of death-as-relief soon crept into his thoughts.

No, he told himself, *never again*. He considered for a moment going to Morton and complaining about Bruno's unfair treatment, but instead headed in the opposite direction, after The Hell Man.

He walked into Bruno's office without knocking. The Hell Man was sitting at his desk, holding his forehead, and glared up at Flam when he entered.

"Listen, Bruno, I'm not going to lie to you. I like the new order of things around here . . .."

"I'll bet you do," Bruno snorted back. "I've been working here for fifteen years, and you think, with your fifteen minutes of fame, that you're just going to suddenly take over."

"Please, hear me out, Bruno. I like it, because I finally may get a chance to do what I came into this business to do—to help the bereaved in their hour of grief, and to do it with compassion and respect. But there's so much I still have to learn, and I know you're the one that can teach me. I'm not trying to compete with you. Rumour has it you may take over the home some day. I hope so. You've certainly earned it. If I help bring in some business, then I'm glad—for all of us—but it doesn't mean I'm trying to take over, okay? On that you have my word. I work for you."

The Hell Man's brow had scrunched down, but he said nothing in reply, so Flam turned to leave the office. "I'm going to go do all those things you asked me to do now, Bruno. Thanks for letting me speak my mind."

Half an hour later, Bruno approached Flam in the showroom. The Hell Man watched his underling buffing a casket for a little while, and then stepped forward.

"Did you really mean what you said, Flam . . . you know, about wanting to work with people in mourning?"

"Every word of it."

"Well, then, forget the polishing. There's this woman coming in shortly . . . she was in yesterday afternoon to make the arrangements for her husband. She's bringing in a suit for the deceased to wear at tonight's viewing. The contract . . . well, all that's done already, but, Christ, the woman's a real basket case. Maybe you can talk to her."

"I will. Thank you, Bruno."

The Hell Man gave a dismissive wave of his hand. "Don't mention it. Not my favourite part of the job anyway. I'd sooner deal with the stiffs than the snifflers."

CHAPTER 39

As Flam left Morton's late that night, he was again caught off guard by the frenetic activity he encountered on the streets, as the city's denizens celebrated another sweet summer Friday night.

So much had happened in just one week: the Dastardly Duo exposed and Charlie exonerated, only to go home to Fiji; Joe Schneider dead and buried; Flam's mother remarried, then lost and found in the eye of a hurricane; a trip to New York and sudden celebrity thrust upon him; and finally, redemption and elevated status at work.

Still, there was a giant black hole at the centre of his thoughts, so dense and powerful it sucked in all his cheerfulness and allowed no light to escape. As Flam trundled towards his bus stop to begin the long ride home, he was painfully aware of the laughing couples passing by. The atmosphere of love practically permeated the humid air around him. Meanwhile, he was all alone, seemingly condemned by fate to an interminable solitude. His situation was made all the more pathetic and depressing by the knowledge he had stumbled upon a potential soul mate in the midst of a crowded, uncaring world. Against all rhyme and reason, he had given up his heart to her, only to have the potential of a resurrecting joy grounded and crushed before it could take flight.

Predictably there was no bus in sight, and faced with the prospect of a protracted wait, Flam seated himself on the bench and pulled out the book he was currently reading. He allowed himself to become submerged in the story, and did not look up when another prospective rider entered the bus shelter.

"You work late," a soft female voice said, somewhat matter-of-factly, but with just a hint of questioning inflective. Flam glanced up and felt his heart momentarily lose its footing. The Girl on the Bus was hovering in the entrance of the shelter, looking at him uncertainly.

"Crazy day," Flam replied. "Suddenly, I'm popular."

The Girl smiled and held up her own book. "That's okay, I didn't mind waiting."

Her liquid brown eyes locked on his, and Flam could feel his pulse quicken. There was a conspicuous quiet as they studied one another. Finally The Girl spoke again, as if she felt an explanation was necessary, "I temp out for the summer and I changed offices this week. I don't take our route anymore. The last morning I saw you, on the bus, I . . . I didn't know they were going to move me. If I had, maybe I would have said something to you." She shrugged. "I don't know. Probably I wouldn't have. I'm pretty shy."

"I wanted to say something too," Flam replied. "I thought about jumping off the bus and running after you, but I was afraid. I mean, well, you know . . ."

"You were afraid I'd reject you."

"Yeah, something like that. I cursed myself for being such a coward."

"Well, that was pretty brave what you ended up doing . . . going on *The Billy Reno Show*, I mean, and reading your poem. It was really beautiful."

"I didn't plan any of that. It all just kind of happened."

"Well, I'm glad it did. If it hadn't, then you and I would never . . .." She stopped herself and dropped her eyes. Flam could read her uncertainty for the future, and realized then what courage it must have taken for her to come looking for him—to sit waiting outside a funeral home all evening for a chance at romance with a perfect stranger.

He stood up, and took a cautious step forward. "It's okay now. We . . . we found each other, didn't we?"

The Girl nodded and smiled. Flam suddenly wanted nothing more than to wrap her up in his arms and squeeze tightly and never let go. Instead, he gestured with his head out towards the street.

"Want to go grab a cup of coffee or something?"

"Yeah, I'd really like that."

Side by side, and in silence, they started out down the sidewalk, but after a few steps Flam stopped abruptly and turned to face her.

"Hey, I don't even know your name."

"Nothing as cool as yours, I'm afraid. It's just plain Jane . . . Jane Williams."

"Well, hi, Jane. I'm Flam." He tentatively slipped his hand in hers, and was relieved to feel her grip tighten in return.

"I can't believe this is happening," she whispered. Her eyes were closed, as if too much happiness was making her dizzy. "It's like something out of a book, except that I never thought anything like that would ever happen to me. I figured I was doomed to just read about life, and not really live it."

"From now on, Jane, we write our own story."

CREDITS

Thanks, as always, to Elsa Franklin for her faith and support. My sincere appreciation to all those at Blue Butterfly Books who believed in and fostered this book, including my editor Dominic Farrell, Cheryl Cooper, Sonia Holiad, David Leadbitter, and of course, the big caterpillar himself, Patrick Boyer. Special thanks to Jim Miller, Laura DiCesare, and Peter Jagla for their invaluable seminal insight, and to my other early readers, Brian Bell, Barry Sutherland, and Caroline Opoka for their feedback and encouragement. And, finally, a tip of the hat for the commentary from Cordelia Strube and her Rye High class – Randal Heide, Ed Lee, James Papoutsis, Brian Jantzi, Scott Mathison, Kim Murray, Valentina Gal, Trisha Causley, and Heidi Sundwall.

ABOUT THE AUTHOR

A writer and digital media producer, Dan Dowhal was born and raised in Toronto's culturally feisty Queen West neighbourhood and lives and works there to this day. Endowed with a pathologically self-expressive nature, his precocious childhood included writing plays, performing on stage, and being paraded around public speaking competitions.

His writing deftly balances left- and right-brain characteristics, a quality partly explained by his schooling as an engineer, work as a computer programmer, and a later return to academia to earn a journalism degree from Ryerson University. While at Ryerson his penchant for writing bloomed. He received the A.O. Tate Award for reporting, and was elected editor-in-chief of The Eyeopener student newspaper.

Re-entering the working world, Dan Dowhal's rare blend of talents was recognized by IBM and the company snapped him up, leading to a prolonged stint with Big Blue as a writer, manager, and research scientist. Then, in the Nineties, Dan and his two brothers founded The Learning Edge Corp., a producer of interactive digital content, where he continues today as the company's chief writer, editor, and creative director.

Away from the keyboard, Dan shifts gears to chase balls, pucks, and flying discs. The author is also currently learning to fly airplanes and lay stones. For a complete change of pace, however, he retreats to his northern cabin beside Algonquin Park where he walks in the woods and talks to trees.

INTERVIEW WITH THE AUTHOR

 Readers of your previous novel, skyfisher, *will find* Flam Grub *a very different book, both thematically and stylistically. What accounts for that?*

DAN DOWHAL: I'm not tied to any particular genre of fiction, and don't tend to think in terms of sequels, so stylistically I go where each individual story takes me. In the case of *skyfisher* it was much more of a speculative social commentary, and I thought it worked best told in the first person by an insider who was also a somewhat morally suspect narrator. *Flam Grub*, on the other hand, is primarily an intense psychological study of the central character, and because of its atypical nature—it is in many ways a modern fable, despite being full of some very unsettling themes—I adopted a more stylized third-person narrative and tone.

As a reader I seek variety, and I guess that carries through in my writing too. But I think readers will find an overall consistency in voice.

Names, and the impact they can have on our lives, are a major theme throughout Flam Grub. *Do you really believe names have such a powerful influence over us?*

DOWHAL: Well, we all have one, don't we? And, after all, we are social creatures by nature, and names are our connection with the rest of humanity—our identity. What do we call it when someone becomes successful? We say they've "made a name for themselves"—although, in today's world, we might just as easily say they've established a brand.

But, especially for young people who are still seeking their place in the world, the names they're given by their parents can have a profound ability to influence them, for better or for worse. Just look at how the need to fit in has created this long-standing practice in North America where immigrants Anglicize their names, or adopt pseudonyms. Throw in pet names, nicknames, pen names, name calling, legal name changes, and so forth, and there's plenty of grist for the literary mill.

 Poetry also plays an important role in Flam Grub. *Are you poetically inclined yourself?*

DOWHAL: I'm certainly a fan of poetry, but so far I've only dabbled in it as far as writing any full-blown verse goes. I have too much respect for the craft to trivialize it. Or maybe I'm just too lazy—good poetry takes a lot of hard work.

There's a reason none of *Flam Grub's* verse actually appears in the book. He is, after all, meant to be an exceptional poet, and I didn't think any verse I could offer the reader would do justice to his fictional poetic prowess.

Mind you, as a writer I find poetry can often influence my own style. Depending on the specific nature of a narrative, I sometimes do purposely strive for a lyrical quality in the prose I write.

Flam Grub again touches on the subject of comparative religion and the quest for human spiritual understanding, which are at the core of your previous novel, skyfisher. Is this then a universal theme in your books?

DOWHAL: No, it's not meant to be, and other than some cavorting wiccans that will appear briefly, I can say that my next book does not deal with religion at all.

But, I should point out that the manuscript for *Flam Grub* came first, and it was the religious ideas that I explored briefly in that book that got me thinking about a novel that focussed entirely on the subject, and led to the invention of the Phasmatian Church for *skyfisher*. It just turned out that the latter was published first.

Flam Grub, the protagonist of the book, is a very unusual character. Are there perhaps some autobiographical elements there?

DOWHAL: We draw on first-hand experiences wherever we can, but unless a writer has led a truly extraordinary life, she or he had better learn to invent and extrapolate in a hurry. I have a lot of empathy for Flam, and will admit to generally being an introvert by nature, but other than being surrounded by books at an early age, I did not lead his life.

Unlike poor Flam, I had brothers, a loving, albeit tough, mother, and a street full of friends. I played sports and participated in extracurricular activities, suffered minimal abuse because of my name, and generally fit in with my peers. Still, despite those fundamental differences, I somehow had no difficulty getting into Flam's head, and feeling his suffering . . . even if I was maybe losing patience with him a little in the end.

There are a lot of disturbing themes in Flam Grub, *such as suicide and abuse, but it's ultimately an uplifting book, isn't it? Just how would you categorize this novel?*

DOWHAL: Good question. Because we live in a world that loves its labels, I've been wrestling with that one. Unfortunately, *Flam Grub* turns out not to be an easy book to pigeon-hole . . . and, by the way, I give Blue Butterfly Books full marks for having the conviction to publish something that does not easily fit the commercial mould.

In the end, when pressed, I would have to categorize it as literary fiction, although it's really up to others to decide its literary merits. Let's see, I could also say *Flam Grub* is a dark, neo-Dickensian coming-of-age story, or a modern homage to the Orpheus myth, or just the story of a screwed-up kid learning to overcome his handicaps.

More great reading from Blue Butterfly Books

If you enjoyed *Flam Grub*, you might also like the following novels from Blue Butterfly Books. Your local bookseller can order any of them for you if they are not in stock, or you can order direct by going to the Blue Butterfly Books website:

www.bluebutterflybooks.ca

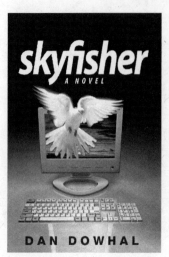

Three New York ad men conspire to create the Phasmatian Church, the world's first major online religion, as a get-rich-quick scheme. When the Church goes viral, power lust and greed turn Sky Fisher, Phasmatia's leader, into a ruthless megalomaniac. Fearing for his life, one of the co-conspirators flees to the countryside, and writes a tell-all exposé of the unholy messiah.

skyfisher: A Novel, by Dan Dowhal
Soft cover / 6 x 9 in. / 259 pages
ISBN 978-1-926577-06-7 / $19.95 US/CAN
Features: author interview

International investment broker Paris Smith is the star of his firm until the loss of his wife shatters his soul and affects his money game. A high-stakes gamble to save his career is threatened when treachery from unexpected quarters seems to collapse the financial arrangements in his complex $100-million bond deal like a house of cards.

Coming for Money, by F.W. vom Scheidt
Soft cover / 6 x 9 in. / 263 pages
ISBN 978-0-9784982-8-3 / $24.95 US/CAN
Features: author interview

ABOUT THIS BOOK

What's in a name? More than you might wish for, if your name is "Flam Grub."

Flam Grub is a contemporary fable–the familiar yet strange story of a lonely heart who despises his own name. Familiar, because most of us experience a stage where we'd rather be called almost anything other than the name we have. Strange, in Flam's case, because just about everybody else dislikes his name too. From his parents' battlefield at home to the hostile frontlines of the schoolyard, most find it easy to mock, bully, and ostracize the boy cursed with the unusual name.

The more the hypersensitive Flam finds himself alone against the world, the more he retreats into the safety of mediocre performance, into the seductive contemplation of death, and into his private fortress of books. As adulthood arrives, the angst-ridden and lonely Flam struggles to escape the netherworld of his own life.

Full of humour and sadness, edgy wit and quiet moments of insightful reflection, Flam Grub recounts the coming of age of a downtrodden, poetry-writing young man pursuing his chosen career as an undertaker, who longs for love and acceptance, and searches for spiritual truth—until fame unexpectedly calls his name.

Both an endearing tale and a shrewd send-up of contemporary life, Flam Grub is the second book from the rich imagination and skilful pen of new Canadian author Dan Dowhal.

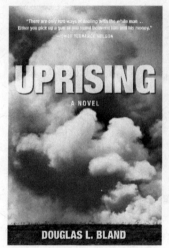

When impoverished, disheartened, poorly educated, but well-armed aboriginal young people find a modern revolutionary leader in the tradition of 1880s rebellion leader Louis Riel, they rally with a battle cry "Take Back the Land!" Coordinated attacks on Canada's strategic energy supply facilities soon have the armed forces scrambling and the country's leaders reeling.

Uprising: A Novel, by Douglas L. Bland
Hardcover / 6 x 9 in. / 507 pages
ISBN 978-1-926577-00-5 / $39.95 US/CAN
Features: author interview, maps

When Yaroslaw leaves his Canadian home to spend a short holiday in Ukraine searching for family heirlooms his grandparents buried during the Second World War, he has no inkling his personal explorations will draw him into a dangerous quest for Europe's greatest treasure, or that he will be caught up in the swirling intrigues of Ukraine's "Orange Revolution."

Yaroslaw's Treasure: A Novel
by Myroslav Petriw
Soft cover / 6 x 9 in. / 293 pages
ISBN 978-0-9784982-7-6 / $24.95 US/CAN
Features: author interview, maps

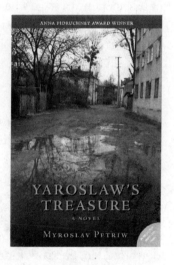

Blue Butterfly Books
THINK FREE, BE FREE
bluebutterflybooks.ca